Dᴀᴠɪᴅ

C000131153

David Gee has worked in London and the Persian Gulf. His previous novels include *Shaikh-Down* and *The Bexhill Missile Crisis* (a prequel to *Lillian and the Italians*). He lives on the South Downs near Brighton.

His website and blog are at www.davidgeebooks.com

LILLIAN AND THE ITALIANS

DAVID GEE

For Katherine
and Carmine
with love from the author
— saluti ed auguri —
David

Lillian and the Italians

Published by The Conrad Press in the United Kingdom 2021

Tel: +44(0)1227 472 874
www.theconradpress.com
info@theconradpress.com

ISBN 978-1-913567-65-1

Copyright © David Gee, 2021

Typesetting and Cover Design by: Charlotte Mouncey, www.bookstyle.co.uk

The Conrad Press logo was designed by Maria Priestley.

Printed and bound in Great Britain by Clays Ltd, Elcograf S.p.A.

in memoriam
Jean McKenzie and
my parents, Raymond and Lydia Helsdon

PART ONE

VENICE: August, 1966

It is extraordinarily difficult to establish Venetian facts.
JAN MORRIS

As the train rattled onto the causeway with a klaxon roar, Lillian caught her first glimpse in thirty-one years of the spires and domes of Venice shimmering in the midsummer haze above the electric blue lagoon. Most of the buildings on the landward side were utilitarian – warehouses and multi-storey car-parks – but this was still unmistakably a city that floated on the sea, the mere notion of which was exotic to someone whose feet had always been firmly planted on the ground. Lillian felt the return of something she had forgotten from her honeymoon all those years ago: the spell that Italy could cast over a foreigner – a spell which had called like a summons to Andrew, the 'Prodigal Son' she was here to track down.

With another klaxon belch from its diesel engine the train began to slow, no longer overtaking cars and buses on the adjacent road bridge. When Lillian and George came here on their honeymoon in 1935 the train had been drawn by a steam engine which whooped and whistled. Its elegant *wagons-lits* were very nearly as romantic as the Orient Express ('We can't afford that,' said George, lumberjack turned builder. Lillian, the property developer's widow, could now afford the Orient Express but it had stopped running in 1962). Today's train had ordinary carriages and modern sleeping cars that were about as romantic as a camper van. And Lillian was alone in her stiflingly hot First-Class sleeper – a widow since last year, her children and grandchildren scattered to the winds.

Shuddering to a stop inside the terminus station, the train was greeted by a cacophony of over-amplified announcements on the public-address system and the shouts of porters and people waiting to meet the new arrivals. The last of the horde that had boarded in Milan with much noise and huge quantities of baggage now poured onto the platform. Lillian and her fellow First-Class travellers disembarked more soberly.

A porter, guessing that she was English, addressed her as 'Lady' in the voice of a taxi-driver in a New York movie. Lillian gave him the name of her hotel which she had been told was only a short walk from the station.

'Listen, lady,' the porter began in a confidential but worldly tone, leaning on his barrow, 'I make you da proposition. Porter not s'posed to go after da front of da *stazione*, but for one t'ousand lire I take you and dis cases to your 'otel. Okay?'

A currency that dealt in thousands was intimidating. Mistaking Lillian's hesitation for haggling, he gave a shrug born of long experience. 'Okay, lady. Seven 'undred fifty. Is 'alf of one pound in your money. Okay?'

'Thank you very much,' Lillian said. 'That will be fine.' She hoped there wouldn't be an embarrassing scene when they arrived at her hotel and he tripled his fee. Members of her golf club who'd travelled in Italy had cautioned her against the natives – rogues, they claimed, to the last man and even child.

She followed him into the main hall of the station and out to the steps leading down to the canal-side. Across the canal was a church of stained white marble with a green dome topped by a cupola with a statue above it. Fifty yards away a slim balustraded bridge, crowded with pedestrians, spanned the canal. The sunlit water was a dull shade of green, visibly dirty and more than a bit smelly. Nevertheless, with motor-launches and vaporettos and gondolas plying busily up and down, it was breathtaking. This was Venice's High Street: the Grand Canal.

The porter bumped his trolley down the steps and off to the left, into a narrow street flanked by bars and glassware shops and crammed with idling tourists. Shouting a way through the throng, the porter pushed his trolley on to the entrance to a hotel. Lillian gave him 1,000 lire out of the money Bob Sadler had provided her with and made it plain that she expected no change. The porter bowed low. 'You are a fine lady,' he said. Lillian smiled.

A hotel porter came out to fetch her bags and, once the formalities of registration were completed, escorted her to her room on the second floor. It was agreeably cool but gloomy with the shutters drawn. She'd booked a double room – single rooms tended to be tiny and cramped. The décor was Empire style: flock wallpaper, velvet curtains and bedspread, huge mahogany wardrobes and chests-of-drawers. Lillian hoped that a 500-lire tip was sufficient for this porter's labours. As soon as he left, she opened the shutters. One window gave onto a small piazza, the other directly onto the canal.

This stretch of the Grand Canal, from the railway station

bridge up to the first bend, boasted no notable palaces, but Lillian was nonetheless delighted. The buildings were old and faded and in varying stages of decay; some had terraces and roof gardens; two almost directly opposite had blue-and-white mooring poles beside their landing stages; all bore marks from the ravages of water at their base. Vaporettos threshed the water as they pulled into and out of the station stop. Gondoliers exchanged shouted conversation as they passed one another.

It was noisy, it was decidedly smelly: it was *Venice!*

And her son was here. Maybe less than a mile away.

Her heart raced at the thought of seeing him. Tomorrow.

By the time she had unpacked and showered and changed into a skirt and blouse, it was early evening. Looking out of the window at intervals Lillian savoured the colour of deepening twilight on the faded walls of the houses and the murky waters of the canal.

Hungry from missing lunch (the dining car had been removed from the train at Brig, the last station before the Simplon tunnel), she dined on minestrone soup and a veal cutlet, served with a salad but no potatoes. Where was Andrew dining, she wondered, and who was he with? She thought of trying his telephone number again; Continental Directory Enquiries had found it for her last month; then it had taken the operator more than three hours to discover that the number was 'out of service': this, he'd informed her, could mean that the phone was unpaid or not working or even disconnected.

It would be best to just go to his address tomorrow, as planned. Back in her room she took out the piece of paper Bob Sadler had given her on the day she'd announced her decision to go to Italy and find her son. She didn't need to look at it – it was burned into her memory – but it provided a link between the day of her decision and today, the eve of its realisation.

'Well, I think you'd be mad to go gallivanting off to Italy,' said Amy, never one to mince her words. Lillian had to resist the urge to throw one of the new cushions. Having said her piece Amy, who was strong on flouncing, flounced to the kitchen. Water was soon heard to flow, although Lillian had said to leave the tea things for her cleaning lady tomorrow.

Bob moved round the settee and seated himself at its other end, vigilant of the creases his wife had remorselessly pressed into his charcoal-grey suit.

'Lillian,' he began and her spirits sank at the solemnity of his tone, 'you know the disappointments Amy and I have had from our – how shall I describe them? – our *feckless* children. She wouldn't like to hear me say it, but I've come to regard them as *lost* to us.' He paused before adding bluntly, crushingly: 'Isn't Andrew *lost* to you?'

Lillian had spent years defending her son against criticism from his father and, latterly, his sister. She was not going to be crushed by Robert Sadler. She shook her head. 'I can't accept that,' she said. 'I know he's a – "rolling stone", he's been drifting further and further from Hastings since he left school, but I won't think of him as lost. I've lost *George*. Sylvia's as good as lost, she's so far away. Andrew's all I've got left, now.'

'Have you still got him?' Bob persisted callously. 'He's never invited you to Italy.'

Lillian twisted a white handkerchief in the lap of the black linen dress she'd worn to two other funerals since her husband's last year: an 80-year-old woman from her bridge club and a 68-year-old former mayor whose widow took her grief on a Caribbean cruise and came back engaged to a fellow passenger. Today they had cremated the previous manager of Bob Sadler's bank.

'All the more reason for me to go and look for him,' Lillian said.

He sighed, conceding the point. 'Have you given any thought to how you'll go about it?'

'His letter last year came from Milan. There must be a British consulate, where he'd have to register as an alien. That's probably the best place to start.'

'Go to Venice,' Bob told her.

Lillian shook her head. 'I don't think he's still in Venice. That's where his first card came from, but the other cards and the letter all came from different places.'

'He's in Venice,' Bob said. He fished inside his jacket for his wallet and took out a slip of paper which he unfolded and passed to her. Squinting to decipher the three short handwritten lines without her reading glasses, Lillian read:

> *Andrew Rutherford Interiors*
> *San Marco 253*
> *Venezia*

Somewhere, Lillian thought, in the loft perhaps, she might

still have Robert Sadler's earnest declarations of love in that small cramped bank clerk's script which had not changed in thirty-three years. Her hand shook.

'How long have you had this?'

'Since October. American Express in Venice telexed it to us after I put your solicitor in touch with our overseas branch in London when he was probating George's will.'

'But you didn't think to give me his address before today?' She no longer wanted to throw things, she wanted to lay into him with her fists. She could not recall ever feeling so angry or so betrayed.

He met her gaze levelly. 'I discussed it with the solicitor and we both felt that it should be left to Andrew to contact you. Which he did. Lillian, if he'd wanted you to be able to stay in touch with him he'd have given you his address himself.'

Lillian felt that if she didn't move she *would* strike him. She rose and walked to the window. The garden was dry. It hadn't rained since a shower at the weekend. A clatter from the kitchen indicated that Amy was hard at work.

Lillian looked across at Bob on the sofa – thinning grey hair over a pale narrow face that always reminded her of Leslie Howard: handsome but – weak. 'I shall never forgive you for this,' she said and had the satisfaction of seeing a hurt expression on his face. She crossed to the sofa, slipped her feet back into her black court shoes and walked through the conservatory to find the watering can.

Andrew was not lost. And if he was, she would find him.

With a feeling of nervous anticipation Lillian walked onto the landing stage and joined the queue for tickets. At nine-fifteen the sun was already high; it was going to be another searing hot day although the canal lent a sense of coolness. The vaporetto was packed with tourists who jabbered in many languages. As they rounded the first bend and some of the finer palaces came into view, Lillian felt a pang of nostalgia for George. Except for the fact of being in a boat on the Grand Canal, nothing struck a chord in her memory. Perhaps thirty-one years was long enough to forget anything. And yet she could still recall the excitement of exploring this beautiful city with her new husband; and she remembered trivial details, like his awful flannelette pyjamas which she had insisted on replacing with a pair in silk paisley from a street market stall. George had floundered at first, a builder out of his depth in this city built on water, but he'd soon taken charge, waving his arms and raising his voice as if ebullience alone would make these bloody foreigners understand him. If only he was with her now. She was here to find Andrew but without George it was she who was lost.

The loud voice of an American behind her interrupted her thoughts. He was reading to his wife the guidebook description of the Ca' d'Oro as the vaporetto pulled in at another landing stage; this palace with its three elaborate loggias was clearly exceptional. People took pictures of each other against the marble-pillared backdrop. She would be in some of these photographs: what would they make of her, a middle-aged Englishwoman (would they guess that she was British?) in a pleated brown skirt, yellow blouse, beige cardigan, low-heeled shoes, holding firmly on to a leatherette handbag (Bob Sadler had warned her not to carry luxury accessories or wear jewellery other than her wedding ring)? Did she look like them, another tourist? Did she look like a mother on a vital quest?

The Rialto bridge, as the boat rounded the next bend, was familiar as much from films and paintings as from Lillian's honeymoon; she didn't recognise the plain wooden bridge beside the Accademia. After another stop on the left close by the Gritti Palace Hotel, the vaporetto crossed the canal, now much wider, and stopped below the octagonal white marble church of (the American was still reading to his wife) Santa Maria della Salute. Ahead of the boat the golden sphere on top of the customs house glowed in the sunlight. Now, as they re-crossed to the San Marco stop in front of Harry's Bar, the great vista of St Mark's Basin opened up: the Giudecca, the island of San Giorgio, the broad glistening waters of the lagoon.

As she rose to join the other disembarking passengers Lillian's gardener's eye noted boxes of geraniums and hanging creepers on the trellis above a mooring station for gondolas. The gondolas danced on the turbulence of the sunlit green water. She followed a gaggle of tourists along the tree-lined promenade to the square beside the Doge's Palace and on into the Piazza San Marco itself. There was a faded photograph in one of Lillian's albums of George and herself sitting in at an outdoor café where, she remembered, a small orchestra had played music in the Palm Court style.

Ignoring the architectural splendours, the babble of the sightseers, the whirr of pigeons' wings and surging memories of her honeymoon, Lillian applied herself to finding number 253. She shivered at the thought that she must now be within a hundred yards of Andrew, her handsome, talented and – what was the word Bob Sadler had used to describe his children? – *feckless* son.

The corner shop under the colonnade nearest the base of the bell-tower was No. 40, the first of many glassware dealers. Lillian crossed the piazza, walking along the shadow of the bell-tower to be out of the sun. The last shop on this side was No. 145. Facing it, across the narrow street that began under the clock-tower of the two bronze Moors, was a bar: Nos. 301 and 302. Beyond the bar was an alleyway and then Thomas Cook's whose doorway confusingly bore the numbers 289-305. She had thought how well *Andrew Rutherford Interiors* must be doing to operate from premises in St Mark's Square; now it looked as if his business was hidden down a side street.

She investigated the street of shops behind the clock-tower. On her left the numbers rose towards 200; on her right they descended promisingly in the direction of 250. No. 258 sold umbrellas and leather goods. 257 was another glassware shop. 256, on a corner, was a menswear boutique. Beyond an alleyway – still more glassware: No. 231.

Although the sun was not directly overhead and the street was pleasantly cool, the narrow thoroughfare induced a feeling of claustrophobia, of suffocation. She turned into the alley beside the menswear boutique. A similar but less smart-looking shop next door was No. 255. Lillian's pulse quickened: nearly there! Beyond the second menswear shop a tunnel-like passage led to a small courtyard where a patch of sunshine highlighted the shabbiness of the buildings. Beyond this passage – a camera shop: No. 236.

Another dozen steps brought her into a tiny misshapen

square dominated by the grimy black side-wall of a church. A souvenir shop on Lillian's left as she entered the square was No. 234. On the far side of the square a pharmacy bore the disheartening number 606.

The whole system was beginning to appear a huge conspiracy to keep Lillian from finding her son. Retracing her steps, she ventured into the short tunnel between the camera shop and the men's outfitters. As she came into the scruffy lozenge-shaped courtyard she found instantly on her right a badly varnished door in a featureless five-storey wall that bore the number 253 and, below two other nameplates, a small black square with white Gothic script which read:

Andrew Rutherford
Interior Designer

This ugly building in a squalid courtyard was far below the expectations generated by the piece of paper Bob Sadler had given Lillian. Was this Andrew's office or his home? Whichever, it was the place she had set out to find.

Forty-eight hours ago she had left Hastings in the Sadlers' Austin Princess, heading for Dover and the start of her quest to be reunited with her son. On the ferry to Calais and on the long train journey to Paris, through the Alps and on to Milan and, finally, Venice, she had endlessly rehearsed this moment:

'Hello, Andrew. Long time no see!'

'I just happened to be passing…'

'Can you advise me about redecorating my lounge?'

As well as these and other bantering openings she had also imagined simply falling into his arms. She had not rehearsed

– hadn't dared to – his response. Now that she was actually outside his front door, she felt tense and apprehensive. She took a deep breath and pressed the bell beside his nameplate. It rang on what sounded like the second floor, but after several minutes and two more pressings no one came.

A red-and-green plaque next to the top bell advertised the *Touring Club Italiano*. Lillian tried this but again obtained no response. The middle plaque, brass, was engraved with two names, one an '*Avv.*', the other a '*Dott. Proc.*' Whatever they meant, ringing their bells also yielded nothing.

An open doorway adjacent, No. 252A, proved to be the rear entrance to the umbrella and leatherware shop in the main thoroughfare. A young woman caught Lillian's eye and beckoned her into the shop.

'Do you speak English?' Lillian began hesitantly.

'Yes, signora, but only when you are speaking slowly.'

'I am looking for Mr Rutherford.'

'Excuse, please?'

'Ruth-er-ford. In the house next to your shop.'

'Ah, *sì*, Signor *Rutterfort!* He is not here since many weeks. His working make him often to go away. You are wanting him to work for you, in the house?'

'I'm his mother,' Lillian said. 'From England.'

'His mother,' the girl repeated solemnly. 'You did go to his house?'

Lillian gestured at the ceiling. 'He doesn't live here?'

Struggling for words and with much gesticulating of her chubby hands, the girl launched into an explanation. Another assistant, an older woman, dealt with the customers who came into the shop.

The building next door was Andrew's office. His partner or employee ('the man which work with him'), a Signor Marini, came to the office once or twice a week. There was a part-time secretary but, August being the holiday month, she too was away.

The girl was not sure where Andrew was living. He'd lived in Venice when he first came to the city but had subsequently moved to Murano where Mr Marini had a house. Murano, Lillian knew, was where Venice's famous glass was produced. Since Mr Marini had married earlier this year, the girl was sure that 'Signor Rutterfort' must be living somewhere else, but she didn't know where. Plainly she found it odd that Lillian did not know her own son's address.

'You have look in telephone book?' she suggested and when Lillian said that she'd only been given the number for 253 San Marco which had been out-of-order for the last four weeks, the girl made another gesture with her hands dismissing the Italian telephone system. Leafing through the directory she turned it round with her finger against *Rutherford Andrew, Interior Designer, S. Marco 253* and the number Lillian had tried a dozen times from Hastings. Strange to think that for – how many? – of the last four years, while she worried about where he was and how he was, he'd been a mundane entry in the Venice phone book, had she only known where to look. Next the girl thumbed through the M's and held the book open while Lillian copied out Mr Marini's address and telephone number – it was in a place called *Burano*, not Murano. The girl offered the use of the shop's phone, and Lillian, weighing the advantage of an interpreter against the embarrassment of speaking to Andrew's unknown business associate in front of a witness, said, 'This is all very kind of you.'

The girl dialled the number and greeted whoever answered with a torrent of Italian, still gesticulating with her free hand. Passing the telephone to Lillian, she said, 'Is *la signora* Marini. *Meesees* Marini. She speak English.'

'Mrs Marini?' Lillian said into the telephone.

'Mrs Rutherford?' A female voice of indeterminate age.

'I'm – Andrew's mother,' Lillian explained hesitantly.

'I know that,' the voice said in effortless English, sounding both sharper and younger. 'The girl said you're calling from San Marco, but shouldn't you be in Hastings?'

In spite of her anxiety Lillian laughed. 'Well, wherever I should or shouldn't be, I'm in Venice.'

'Goodness me,' Mrs Marini said, sounding exaggeratedly English. 'Did Andrew know you were coming?'

'I was rather hoping to surprise him,' Lillian said, aware that this must sound preposterous. There was a pause at the other end of the line and then the woman said, 'Oh dear, this is very difficult. I have no idea where Andrew is right now. My husband's not here today, but I doubt if he knows any more than I do.' Except for a slight foreign accent she was sounding more English with every sentence. 'If only you'd written first or sent a telegram–'

'I tried telephoning,' Lillian said, 'but the line's been out of order for a month.'

After another pause Mrs Marini said, 'I think I'd better speak to my husband. He's in Ravenna at the moment.'

'But you said your husband doesn't know where my son is either.'

'No, but – after you've come all this way, the least we can

do is to try and find out.'

'Nothing's wrong, is there?' Lillian asked anxiously. 'Andrew *is* all right?'

The other woman gave a short bitter laugh. 'Oh yes, he's all right. Nothing much has gone wrong for Andrew since the day he set foot in Italy.'

Not knowing how to respond to this acrimonious remark, Lillian said nothing.

'Well, anyway,' Mrs Marini went on, 'I'll try to get hold of my husband and call you back later, if I may. It probably won't be until this evening, since there isn't a telephone in the house they're converting. Will it be convenient if I call you between seven and eight?'

Lillian assured her that it would and gave her the name of the hotel and her room number.

'You have my sympathy, Mrs Rutherford. I know what it's like to feel cut off from your family,' the woman said, unexpectedly, just before she hung up.

Lillian took out her purse to pay for the call, but the girl pushed the money away. Wondering if she ought to make some unnecessary purchase, Lillian settled for thanking her profusely. The girl ushered her to the front entrance, shook her hand and sent greetings to Signor Marini and Signor 'Rutterfort'.

Almost in a daze, Lillian walked back to the clock-tower and into the Piazza San Marco. The sun in the square was now fierce. She decided to take coffee while she collected her thoughts. The outside tables at Quadri's, where she and George had been photographed thirty-one years ago, were unshaded except for those in the arcade which were all taken. Lillian crossed to Florian's on the opposite side, where there was shade over most of the outside tables. A quartet, strongly featuring an accordionist, was playing 'As Time Goes By'.

Sipping a coffee which was too frothy for her taste and came with a bill more appropriate to a three-course dinner, Lillian felt alienated from the noise and bustle of the square, almost disoriented.

Mrs Marini had a rather jaundiced attitude towards her husband's partner or employer or whatever the arrangement was. And where, in God's name, was Andrew? Why would he go away without telling his associate where he was going? It was all very mysterious, very worrying.

The shop assistant knew more of Andrew's life in Venice than his mother. His business attracted customers from Ravenna, wherever that was, and elsewhere. He'd had at least three homes since Lillian last saw him. He had failed to put down roots even in this most majestic of cities. Sussex, London, Venice – Andrew would always be a 'rolling stone'. In the four years since Lillian had last seen him he had not gathered any moss.

There was a whole chapter of his life which she knew nothing about. Her quest was plainly an intrusion. The Sadlers were right: she shouldn't have come.

HASTINGS: 1962

On the last Friday in October 1962, at the height of the Cuban missile crisis, Andrew had arrived by taxi at ten-thirty in the morning. Lillian was pruning blackcurrant bushes. George, recovering from his second stroke in three years, was doing a jigsaw puzzle on the dining-room table with his one good hand.

Tanned from a recent Mediterranean holiday, Andrew looked very continental in a dark green blazer and white slacks. He was staying in Bexhill with Laurence Dickinson, a local hotelier who'd been a friend of Andrew's since his schooldays. He brought Lillian up-to-date on his home (a flat in South Kensington) and his office (a display and artwork agency in Mayfair he'd formed last year in partnership with a colleague from Selfridges). He talked about the latest West End shows and some society scandal which had been eclipsed by the trial of the Admiralty spy Vassall. He said he was thinking of breaking up with his girlfriend, whom he'd introduced to Lillian over tea in Fortnum & Mason's, the Honourable Fiona Something-hyphen-Jones, a glamorous and brittle blonde debutante who was as un-promising daughter-in-law material as any of her predecessors – not that wedding bells had ever, even faintly, sounded in Andrew's life.

'I've been thinking I may go and live abroad,' he announced. Lillian looked up from her pruning. 'Oh?' she said. 'What's brought this on?'

'I just feel I'm about finished with England,' he said casually, as if giving up his country, a flourishing new business, an elegant home he'd decorated himself, his life in London, his friends and interests, was no more difficult than giving up smoking. Perhaps it wasn't: Lillian had never smoked. It was a relief that George was beyond voicing his feelings. He had not forgiven Andrew for declining to join *George Rutherford & Son, Building Contractors*, the firm whose name had anticipated Andrew's birth. George had swallowed his disappointment when Andrew announced in 1956 that his Modern Language course at Bristol University would lead to a career in teaching.

There had been a mighty row when he took a summer job window-dressing for a local department store before he went up to university (where he dropped out after two terms), and a worse one when he came home from national service and announced that he was going to do the same job in London. He told his parents he was 'just about finished' with Hastings. Now he was finished with England.

'Where are you thinking of going?' she asked.

'I'm not sure. Italy maybe. There are some exciting things going on in interior design there.'

'Is that what you want to concentrate on?'

'Well, I'm a bit fed up with shop windows and posters. Will you mind?'

Lillian straightened up and turned to face the twenty-four-year-old son her husband considered to be a wastrel and whom her mother would have called a 'reprobate'. Tall and slim with dark, almost black, hair swept back from his narrow face, he took after neither of his parents; in fact he resembled Lillian's maternal grandfather, a Baptist minister whom she only knew from photographs – a heart attack had felled him in his pulpit long before Lillian was born. Morally, of course, Andrew was at the opposite end of the spectrum. Who would be next in the long line of girlfriends or – Mother would faint at the thought – mistresses: some sultry beauty from Roman high society?

'Will I mind if you go away?' she echoed. 'Of course I'll mind, but if it's what you want to do you must do it.'

'Are you sure you won't mind?' he asked again less than ten minutes later. Lillian minded very much, but she rephrased her previous answer: 'It's your life,' she said; 'you must lead it your own way.'

Later they went in and had tea with George. Lillian interpreted George's strangled attempts at speech. The Italian venture was not mentioned. After tea Lillian drove him down to the hotel Laurence Dickinson owned on the Hastings seafront. She stayed for one round of cocktails with the two men.

Two days later, on Sunday, the day Khrushchev backed down over the Cuban missiles, the day Laurence's house in Bexhill was burned to the ground, Andrew turned up at nearly midnight in Laurence's Bentley. He had a Frenchman with him called Charles; Andrew pronounced it as *'Sharlz'*. A year or two younger than Andrew, Charles had come to Sussex to be Laurence's chauffeur. He spoke English with little accent and few grammatical errors, although with Andrew he talked mainly in French. Lillian found his film-star looks disconcerting. Andrew slept in his old bedroom in the attic, 'Sharlz' in Sylvia's former room, now painted in nursery colours for the grandchildren.

After breakfast the next morning they left for London. Two weeks later, still driving the Bentley, now stuffed with suitcases, they returned, arriving at Sunday teatime. They were leaving the next day for France and Italy. Andrew had resigned his partnership in the Mayfair agency and surrendered the lease on his penthouse flat in Onslow Gardens. He left some of his luggage in the attic and asked his mother to store the rest of his personal effects when they were delivered by Harrods; his furniture was being sold with the lease.

In spite of the warning of this decision two weeks earlier, Lillian was nonetheless panicked by the suddenness of its realization. She'd had no time to prepare George, whose seesaw recovery was going through a bad patch; any emotional outburst might set him back weeks.

In fact George took it calmly, fatalistically. Their son was a lost cause anyway: what really was the difference between South Kensington and Southern Europe? Lillian fed him his dinner before dining with Andrew and 'Sharlz' at the Mermaid Inn in Rye, a favourite for family celebrations. The mood in their corner of the handsome Tudor dining room was far from celebratory. Even Andrew was not on form. Charles struggled to make conversation, talking about Cézanne's Provence where he'd spent most of his boyhood. Racked by anxiety over George and the feeling that she was losing altogether the son she loved, Lillian was relieved when Charles drove them home in the Bentley.

Back at the house, while Charles went to run a bath for Andrew (the way he waited on her son hand and foot was another thing that disconcerted Lillian), George did something Lillian had not seen in the twenty-seven years of their marriage: hunched in his wheelchair, he wept, tears pouring down his face. Whether he was weeping from the frustration of being turned into an invalid or because Andrew was hammering a last nail into the coffin of his father's dreams Lillian was not to know, for she never questioned him about it. Visibly shaken, Andrew went upstairs to take his bath and did not reappear until morning.

And in the morning he left. A hired Mercedes was delivered before breakfast. For a five-pound tip the man from the car-hire firm was only too willing to return the Bentley to Laurence Dickinson at the hotel. Charles seemed to have left Laurence's service, although Andrew could surely not afford a full-time chauffeur, still less a valet.

Lillian wheeled George out to the drive while Charles and

Andrew were loading suitcases into the boot. Charles shook hands with Lillian and George and thanked them for their hospitality in his beautifully modulated English before seating himself behind the wheel of the Mercedes.

Andrew embraced his mother and kissed her on both cheeks, and then – something he had not done since he received a scooter for his seventeenth birthday – he hugged his father. He climbed into the front of the car beside Charles and they drove off. Andrew waved once as they turned into the main road.

Lillian and George watched the car until it disappeared round a bend in the road. Neither spoke. Lillian did not cry; it was as if George had wept for both of them the night before.

VENICE

Signora Marini rang at seven-thirty. After a light lunch in her hotel Lillian had gone out again, feeling restless after the morning's frustrations. Following the signs to the Rialto, she wandered among the stalls where thirty-one years ago she'd bought silk pyjamas for her husband of four days. Now she had no one to buy things for; there was nothing in all of Europe that Sylvia couldn't obtain more cheaply in Hong Kong, and Andrew would not welcome his mother's choice of pyjamas. She drank a cup of weak tea under a quayside awning before retracing her steps to the hotel, where she took a long siesta. She was about to step under the shower when the telephone rang.

The Italian woman's tone was less brittle this time. Her voice conveyed concern, even a measure of warmth. Signor Marini, she said, would cut short his work in Ravenna and return to

Venice tomorrow in order to see Lillian, by which time they hoped to have news of Andrew's whereabouts.

'Is it usual for my son to go off and leave Mr Marini in charge of the business without even saying where he is?' Lillian asked.

The other woman hesitated a moment before replying. 'Not exactly,' she said. 'Although it's quite common for them to be working on projects in different places.'

'I understand that,' Lillian said. 'My late husband was a building contractor, so I'm familiar with some of the work involved. But surely you always know where he is?'

'Well –' Mrs Marini hesitated again – 'we do know who he's with and we have some idea of the area they're in.'

'I don't think I understand.'

'It's not as complicated as all that, really. He's cruising in my father's yacht with my youngest brother.'

'So he's just on holiday?'

'Well, you could call it that, except that they've been away for nearly three months.'

'Three months!' Lillian echoed. 'Surely Andrew can't afford to leave his work for that long?'

The sharpness of her tone during the first call returned as Mrs Marini replied: 'Andrew always manages to afford to please himself, as I'm sure you must know.'

'But I gather your husband is able to run the business without him?'

'No,' the other woman said simply. 'Carlo's very good at chasing up deliveries and organizing workmen, but the creative side has always been Andrew. This house in Ravenna is the last project on the books. If Andrew doesn't come back, then that's the end of the business.'

'But surely he will come back?'

'Who knows? Personally, I don't think he will.'

'Well, I'm appalled at his irresponsibility,' Lillian said.

Mrs Marini sighed. 'I'm afraid Andrew's life here has not been marked by a show of responsibility. Mrs Rutherford, there's so much more to this than I can begin to explain. And there's a lot I'd rather leave to my husband to tell you. May I invite you to tea tomorrow, and then Carlo will take you back to Venice for dinner?'

'That's very kind of you,' Lillian said, 'but couldn't Mr Marini just come to Venice and dine at my hotel?'

'Well, yes, he could, but it would be rather nice to meet you. I would offer to come to Venice myself, but I'm having a rather awkward pregnancy and boat journeys are a bit of a trial.'

'I'm not very keen on them myself normally,' Lillian admitted, 'although I'm beginning to enjoy them here. I'm sorry you're having a difficult pregnancy. My daughter had some bad months with her first child. I was very lucky with Andrew and his sister.' Lillian felt a spasm of grief for her own first pregnancy; it had ended in a miscarriage, something she could not mention in conversation with an expectant mother. She wrote down Mrs Marini's instructions as to which vaporetto she must take to the Fondamenta Nuove to connect with the ferry service to the islands. A neighbour's son would be waiting by the ice-cream stall at the Burano landing stage. Lillian should ask for Marcello.

After another night of fitful sleep – her room was oppressively hot with the window shut against mosquitoes – Lillian returned to St Mark's Square on the vaporetto and pretended to be a tourist. The gold mosaics in the cathedral she remembered from her honeymoon, but had she and George queued to see the *Pala d'Oro*? A golden altar-screen studded with precious stones would have appalled her puritan Baptist mother; even Andrew might be scathing about its garishness. Outside in the square it was, if anything, hotter than yesterday. After viewing the world-renowned Bridge of Sighs Lillian abandoned her plan to tour the Doge's Palace and returned to her hotel on foot in the relative coolness of the lanes.

She had little appetite at lunch and settled for her third meal of soup and an omelette. Doubtless the waiters assumed she was one of those English visitors who instinctively mistrusted foreign cooking.

The ferryboat to Burano, not much bigger than a vaporetto, was crowded with sightseers and local inhabitants. Lillian squeezed herself onto a seat beside two fat Italian women in the saloon at the rear.

The motion out in the lagoon was no greater than in the canals. The longest stretch of the forty-five-minute journey was from Murano, with its red Victorian-looking factories; past a trio of abandoned islands with crumbling walls and derelict buildings; then on into a channel between the two halves of another island, agricultural on one side with a village on the other. The boatman called out '*Mazzorbo*' as they docked below a pink villa with green shutters.

Now the boat made a wide turn before docking again on the village side. The boatman bellowed '*Burano*' and the remaining passengers moved towards the doors.

At the ice-cream stall by the landing stage Lillian asked the buxom woman in charge for Marcello. She gave a shout and a boy of about five or six, with a wide grinning face and curly chestnut hair, came running across from a slab of stone where he'd been sitting. He began chattering away to Lillian in Italian. His hands moved in gestures she could not interpret. The brown eyes pleaded.

Leaning across the counter, the woman intervened: 'He want *gelato*. Ice-cream.'

'Oh well,' said Lillian, 'let him have one.'

Marcello took his time before choosing a chocolate lollipop with an ice-cream centre, shaped like a rocket. Lillian paid the woman.

Taking her hand the boy hurried her past a parade of lace-stalls into an alley between two terraces of houses. Abruptly the path ended and there was a narrow canal running left and right before them, lined with barges and rowing-boats. On both sides of the canal were rows of tiny houses, painted in bright reds and blues and greens.

Slurping his ice-cream, Marcello led her towards a wooden bridge at the junction of this canal and another. A few buildings along on the intersecting canal he stopped at a house that was painted in a faded shade of blue. The glass front door with elaborately wrought brass-work was ajar; the boy pulled Lillian inside.

Two or three rooms had been converted into a single long narrow room. On the white front wall there was one small window with a white venetian blind. The opposite wall, also white, had glass doors opening onto a pocket-sized patio garden with climbing plants and antique statues. To the right of the windows was a narrow modern open-plan kitchen separated from the rest of the room by a slender serving-bar with a chocolate-brown surface. The two longer walls were the same faded blue as the outside of the house and hung with a mixture of modern abstract paintings and old etchings gold-mounted and framed in Regency green.

Lillian recognized her son's hand in this décor and also in the choice of furniture: two pale blue denim settees, a glass-topped coffee table and matching dining table, chocolate-brown moulded plastic dining chairs and a green Tiffany-style lamp, all set off by a deep-piled orange carpet. The room was contemporary, stylish and, for her taste, overdone.

The woman who descended the white wrought-iron spiral staircase beside the front door might similarly have emerged from the pages of a fashion magazine. Mrs Marini, in spite of advanced pregnancy, looked poised and chic, wearing an ankle-length billowing dress with a swirling yellow-and-white pattern. She was younger than Lillian had expected from the voice on the telephone, in her middle twenties, no taller than Lillian, with long fair hair and a slender angular face. She smiled.

'Mrs Rutherford, it's a pleasure to meet you.'

'Thank you for inviting me, Mrs Marini.'

'Please, you must call me Adriana.'

They shook hands. Adriana Marini spoke rapidly to the boy, Marcello, and he shook Lillian's hand before scampering out the door.

'He's an enchanting child,' Lillian said, not knowing how to introduce what she had really come to discuss.

'Isn't he?' She gestured Lillian towards the settees. 'Andrew once said that Marcello wasn't born, he just fell from a

Tintoretto ceiling.'

Andrew had taken Lillian to all of London's major galleries, but she could not with any confidence distinguish one Italian Master from another. She smiled by way of answer as the sofa's soft upholstery engulfed her.

'Marcello's mother is a widow,' Adriana went on. 'Her husband drowned in a freak storm last winter. He was a fisherman. Silvia's had to go back to work. She's a supervisor in one of the lace factories. I keep an eye on Marcello for her until he starts school next month.'

'Sylvia. That's my daughter's name.'

Adriana smiled. 'But I think you spell it with a "y" in English. How is your daughter? And your grandchildren?'

'Very well, thank you. They live in Hong Kong now.'

'Do they? I don't think we knew that.'

That 'we' sounded odd. As if she and her husband thought of themselves as part of the family. 'My son-in-law's firm sent him there two years ago,' Lillian elaborated. 'He's an investment banker.'

'That's the same business as my father,' Adriana said.

'Really? My daughter came back with the children last year when – her father died. They stayed more than a month.'

Another smile. 'That must have been a great comfort. Now, what can I offer you by way of a drink?' She moved to the kitchen. 'People say that lemon tea is more refreshing, but according to Andrew tea with milk is better. Needless to say, I've been taught to make a proper English cup of tea!'

'I prefer milk in my tea,' Lillian said. 'No sugar, please.' She sensed that the younger woman, despite her poise, was as nervous as herself at this meeting. Adriana chattered on, deftly parrying Lillian's efforts to turn the conversation to the more serious topic of her son's absence. And yet there were constant references to 'Andrew always says this' and 'Andrew introduced me to that', as if she were as eager to talk about him as Lillian.

Slowly Lillian was able to piece together some of her son's life. He and Carlo Marini had met Adriana last autumn when they were restoring an apartment in Milan next to the one in which she lived with her aunt. Andrew and Carlo had at that time been living in this house on Burano which Andrew had modernized. At some point – Adriana was vague about dates – Andrew had gone to live in Sottomarina, at the southern end of the Venetian lagoon, and Adriana had married Carlo and come to live in Burano.

In March Andrew went to Siena to design a new interior for one of the city's banks. In the event his plans were rejected, but by then he'd met Adriana's two brothers who were studying in Siena. In the middle of May he and the younger brother took themselves off in the yacht to see the Aeolian Islands off the northern coast of Sicily. No direct news had been received of them since then, although an acquaintance of Carlo's had reported seeing Andrew two weeks ago in Ischia – 'In the Bay of Naples: do you know it?'

After a while Adriana excused herself to go and rest. The whole eight months of her pregnancy had been difficult, she said, because she suffered from a weakness of the blood, a form of anaemia. After showing Lillian the bathroom upstairs Adriana left her to return to the lounge while she retired to her bedroom.

Lillian kicked off her shoes and stretched out full length on the settee. Soon asleep, she awoke briefly when Marcello came in carrying something which he put in the refrigerator. He crept out, grinning impishly at Lillian.

When she next awoke it was to find a familiar face looking down at her. Still drowsy, she registered the broad mouth and dark-brown hair and thought it was Andrew. Then realizing who it was, she swung her legs round and sat up in a single abrupt movement.

'But you're – "Sharlz",' she stammered, feeling instantly foolish.

He laughed, teeth gleaming white in his tanned face. 'It really should be *Carlo*, Mrs Rutherford. I was born here in Venice, but since I was mainly brought up in France I used to favour the French version of my name.'

'I'm sure I thought you were a Frenchman four years ago.'

Carlo Marini smiled. 'Well, there was a bit of confusion over my identity at Mr Dickinson's house where Andrew and I met. Speaking French sort of "set us apart".' He sat down on the other settee. 'You know how he is,' he added with another disarming smile.

'You sound just like him,' Lillian said, pleased with this discovery. 'Your wife does too, but you're even like him in build and colouring. For a second or two just now I thought you *were* Andrew. It's strange that I didn't think of the similarity when you were staying with us.'

Carlo smiled again. 'You're not the first person to see a resemblance. We've often been taken for brothers.'

Lillian remembered her manners. 'Don't let me keep you from your wife. She's upstairs resting.'

'I guessed as much. The poor girl's having a very tiresome

pregnancy, as I expect she told you. I'm sorry she had to leave you on your own.'

'Don't apologize. I appreciated the rest. This heat is rather more than I'm used to.'

'You couldn't have picked a worse month,' he said. 'But I can understand your wanting to find Andrew after – losing your husband last year.'

Was this the reason why she was here? It was part of it, yes, but not the whole of it. She didn't know what to say in reply.

'I told Andrew he should have gone home to see you,' Carlo added.

'He wrote me a very nice letter.' Even to her it sounded inadequate.

'The lack of contact with his family is something I could never accept.'

Lillian sighed at this echo of her daughter and Bob Sadler. 'I learned a long time ago that Andrew wanted to go his own way in life,' she said. 'I never liked it, but – I've come to accept it. Really it's wrong of me to come out here like this, interfering in his life.'

'Nonsense. You're his mother. You have every right. But I'm sorry that he isn't here when you've come all this way.'

'Do you suppose that I am going to find him?' she asked. 'I'd hate to just give up and go home.'

'Oh, we're going to find him all right,' he assured her. 'It's just a matter of locating this yacht he's on. And I've made a start on that.'

At this point there was a noise from upstairs. Carlo got up from the settee. He suggested that Lillian go and sit in the garden while he went up to see Adriana.

Lillian put her shoes on and went out to the patio. The white rattan-cane chairs were padded with vivid orange-and-blue cushions. The little garden was now completely shaded. A reproduction of the Mannekin-pis splashed water into a tiny fishpond, contributing, if a little vulgarly, to the impression of coolness.

After a few minutes Carlo reappeared. He had changed out of his grey business suit into a pair of dark-green slacks and a pale-yellow shirt. Smiling at Lillian, he busied himself behind the breakfast bar with a cocktail-shaker.

'I remember Andrew saying you're a keen golfer,' he said when he came out with the shaker and two sugar-frosted glasses on a tray. 'And I know English golfers are great gin-drinkers, so I've made us a Tom Collins.'

'I don't play as much golf as I used to,' Lillian said. She smiled. 'But you're right. I am partial to a drop of gin. I'm not sure I know what a Tom Collins is, though.'

'It's a sort of glorified gin fizz,' he explained: 'gin and lemon juice. I've gone fairly heavy on the lemon. You don't have the look of a serious drinker.' He turned on a smile that took the edge off this impertinence.

Lillian laughed. 'That's good news at least,' she said. Carlo poured the drinks and seated himself opposite her, resting his moccasined feet on a footstool. Lillian thought again how much he resembled Andrew, not only superficially in appearance but in the same air of casual ease and confidence. She took a sip from her glass. It was not as sharp as she'd expected from his description. 'This is very good.'

'It should be. In the course of my somewhat chequered career, I've had more than one spell as a cocktail barman.' He offered her a cigarette, which she declined.

'Is your wife all right?'

'I'm afraid she's rather poorly. She can't seem to keep anything down. Our friend Silvia –' he smiled – 'your daughter's namesake – sends over dishes for her, made of egg and milk, that sort of stuff, but the poor girl can't always hold down even those.'

'That reminds me. While I was having a nap the little boy brought something in and put it in the fridge.'

'That's Adriana's dinner for tonight, I expect.'

'I hope my visit hasn't made things worse for her. I know how a difficult pregnancy can affect one's nerves.'

He held up his hands in a typical Italian gesture that seemed at odds with his English accent. 'Please don't distress yourself on that account, Mrs Rutherford. Adriana's nerves have been in a bad state for some time now. Your coming here can't possibly have made any difference.'

He paused. 'Well now, there's obviously a lot you're dying to hear. To begin with, I've rung Fausto Monfalcone – his brother Fabrizio is the boy Andrew is sailing with – Adriana told you about them?'

Lillian nodded. 'Your wife's brothers,' she said. 'And the yacht belongs to your father-in-law.'

'It's not quite as straightforward as that, but that's part of a very long story which I'll tell you over dinner. I thought I'd take you to Cipriani's on Torcello. Have you been there before?'

'I don't think so. I haven't been in Venice since my honeymoon in 1935. I can't remember what I have seen before until I see it again.'

'Cipriani's is owned by the same people as Harry's Bar, and like Harry's was a big hang-out of Hemingway and his crowd in the Fifties.

'Anyway, as I was about to tell you, I've spoken to Fausto in Siena. Their father is in the States at the moment, but he's the head of a formidable business organization which his son can use to get the yacht traced in no time. It has a radio, of course, but Fabrizio's likely to keep it switched off in case his father's trying to reach him to nag him about his schoolwork.'

Lillian suddenly realized that Andrew was on board a rather more substantial vessel than the kind of glorified dinghy George and Bob Sadler had hired for fishing trips in the Channel. 'I hope Andrew hasn't made him neglect his studies,' she said.

'According to Adriana he's a lazy student at the best of times. In fact he's an utterly irresponsible boy. He has this absurd notion of himself as a sort of junior playboy. We did hear purely by chance a couple of weeks ago that they'd been seen in Ischia, so they may well still be somewhere around the Amalfi Riviera. Fausto promised to make some enquiries and get back to me as soon as possible. The Prince has a villa at Amalfi and hotels on Capri and Ischia.'

'The Prince?'

'Didn't Adriana tell you? Her father is Prince Massimo Monfalcone.'

'No, she didn't,' Lillian said, a little breathlessly.

At Carlo's suggestion Lillian went up to the bathroom to freshen up before dinner. Marcello had arrived with his mother while Carlo was still elaborating on the Monfalcone 'empire', which consisted of hotels and villas throughout the Italian mainland and islands.

When she turned off the water she could faintly hear Silvia's gentle voice talking to Adriana Marini in the adjoining bedroom. The Italian Silvia was a striking young woman of Adriana's age, her alabaster face framed by auburn hair drawn severely back in a style that complemented the starkly simple black dress of a widow. She had greeted Lillian in broken English.

So Andrew was cruising the Mediterranean with the son of a prince-cum-hotel-tycoon. Laurence Dickinson owned hotels along the coast of Sussex and Hampshire, but he was just a businessman, like George, a member of Lillian's golf club.

She heard Carlo join the conversation in the next room. He called her into the bedroom to say goodbye to his wife. The rest seemed to have done Adriana no good at all. Beneath a white counterpane she too was almost colourless; the angularity of her fine features now appeared more a morbid symptom of her illness than an aspect of good bone structure. Lillian stammered an apology for the intrusion of her visit.

Speaking in a weak tone, Adriana assured Lillian that it had been a pleasure to meet her, that she hoped to see her again. Silvia shook Lillian's hand and murmured a few words.

Outside the front door Marcello jumped into a smart motor-boat the size of a Venetian taxi-launch. He was coming with them to Torcello, Carlo said, to stay with his grandmother. They helped Lillian aboard. There was a small curtained cabin, but she elected to sit on a folding padded seat in the cockpit. Marcello stood inside Carlo's arms, holding the wheel as they puttered past the berthed barges and skiffs, under another wooden bridge and out into the lagoon.

The boy whooped with delight as Carlo increased speed and they skimmed between fishing nets slung from low poles and on into the channel the ferry had used. Now there were marshes on both sides, the reeds thick with a plant the colour of heather. Carlo gunned the motor down and they turned into a narrower canal; branches overhanging a low wall drooped almost into the water. A long S-bend brought them to a low slender stone bridge. Fifty yards further the canal ended in a sharp curve under a second bridge. Other launches were moored along the final stretch, taxis from the city and a few smaller motorboats. Carlo deftly slipped between two of these craft, cutting the motor, and looped a rope over a wobbly pole in the water.

Marcello was ashore in seconds. Carlo gave Lillian his hand as she stepped onto the bank. They walked up to the bridge. Beyond the canal stood a two-storey pale-yellow building with a single gable in its red shingle roof. A sign on a wooden frame with climbing plants and an awning proclaimed it to be the *Locanda Cipriani*.

The boy took the lead as they walked along a tree-lined path toward a church of pale brick and stone without the ornamentation that characterized Venice's churches. It had a separate bell-tower, similarly plain, and a red brick baptistery with a colonnade of worn slim pillars. This was the oldest cathedral in the lagoon, Carlo told her, with mosaics dating back to the eleventh century.

Marcello led them through the wrought-iron gate of a private house opposite the church and ran to a sinister-looking statue of a large figure with a face like a gargoyle, hunched in a half-sitting position under vines laden with tiny white grapes. To Lillian's surprise the boy climbed into the lap of this monstrosity, wrapped his arms round its thick neck and kissed the fearsome face, giggling as he did so.

Carlo laughed. This was the home of Silvia's parents-in-law, he explained; the old man was one of the custodians of the buildings. They pretended that this statue was the boy's great-grandmother who had been turned to stone as a punishment for gossiping. Marcello continued to giggle and hug the great head.

After a few words from Carlo the boy shook Lillian's hand robustly before running into his grandparents' house. Carlo ushered Lillian out of the garden and back along the path in the direction of the Cipriani.

'If you want to go in and see the family, please don't hold back on my account,' said Lillian. 'I'm in no hurry to eat.'

'I'm afraid there's what you might call bad blood between us,' Carlo said. 'Silvia's husband and I were cousins and boyhood friends, but later we had a – a falling-out.'

'Silvia's a very good friend to your wife,' Lillian said when he showed no sign of elaborating on this feud.

'She is indeed,' he agreed.

'It broke my heart to lose my husband last year –' was it his resemblance to Andrew that made this easier to say? – 'but at Silvia's age it's a much greater tragedy. Will she always wear black?'

'Until she marries again. That's the custom here.'

'I hope she does. It's a terrible waste of such a beautiful and gentle person. And the boy will need a father, especially when he's growing up.'

Carlo hesitated. Then he gave a bitter laugh that bore echoes of his wife's. '*I'm* Marcello's father,' he said.

Carlo was clearly a familiar and favoured patron of the Cipriani: he was greeted warmly and with much joshing by the waiters.

The maître d' seated Lillian ceremoniously at an outside table under a lattice of vines with bunches of black grapes. Hanging oil-lamps converted to hold electric light bulbs glowed in the deepening twilight.

'I've been coming here for years,' Carlo said as he sat down opposite her. 'I used to bring ladies here in the days when I made my living as a gigolo.' He laughed cheerfully. 'They're probably thinking I'm back in business.'

'I certainly hope not,' Lillian said primly, almost snatching the menu proffered by the maître d' as camouflage for her embarrassment.

She declined a further aperitif. Carlo ordered another Tom Collins for himself. He insisted that she try two of the house specialities, their own cannelloni and calf's liver in an onion sauce.

When their order had been taken and Carlo's drink arrived, he tipped his chair back and lit a cigarette. He smiled at Lillian.

'It's a long story.'

'Which one?' she enquired coldly: 'Andrew's or yours?' The revelations that he was Marcello's father and had been a gigolo had blunted her open-mindedness towards this handsome young man whose life had been so closely linked with her son's.

Carlo laughed again, an easy natural laugh. 'Both,' he said. 'They're inextricably tied together. Even now, though it's months since I last saw or even spoke to him.'

'I'm not sure I understand.'

'I don't expect you to. In fact I doubt that you ever could. There's so much you don't know. And I'm not sure how much I should tell you.'

'I'd honestly rather you didn't hold anything back. Andrew

and I were always very close, although I guessed he was – keeping things from me even before he came here.'

'Well, as an Italian I'm used to male secretiveness. But I'm only half-Italian. My mother was English, or at least Scottish. She was a "free thinker", one of those unconventional women who reacted against a Victorian upbringing. She died in France when I was sixteen, but long before then we had a complete rapport. There was nothing I couldn't tell her, discuss with her.'

'And your father?' In spite of her reservations Lillian's curiosity had been roused.

'Oh, he was just a simple fisherman who captured the heart of an eccentric Scotswoman who came to paint Burano. He loved her, although he probably never even began to understand her. He died when I was only a child, so I didn't really know him. Theirs is a fascinating story in itself.' He took another gulp at his drink. 'But that's by the by. I only mentioned my mother because there were things I felt able to confide in her which most sons wouldn't be able to discuss with their mothers.' He made a vague gesture with his hands.

'I wish I had some inkling of what you're talking about,' Lillian said.

'I'm sorry, Mrs Rutherford. I suppose the problem is with the things I'm trying *not* to talk about.'

'Frankly you frighten me. Your wife seemed to imply that Andrew has left Venice for good. Did he leave under some kind of cloud? Has he committed some sort of crime?'

Carlo smiled. 'No, nothing like that. Although –' he laughed briefly – 'Andrew would have loved to leave Venice under a cloud, as you put it. He does have a flair for the melodramatic. Actually there was a bit of a scandal here a couple of years ago, when a few people did leave very much under a cloud. No, it's just that – there are some things it's not easy to talk about with somebody else's mother.' He tailed off with another expressive gesture.

His parents' brief history, with its aura of romance and adventure, had helped to dispel Lillian's fleeting hostility. Now, as she saw where his story seemed to be leading, she felt her embarrassment return. Affecting a casualness that was far from real, she said, 'Don't feel you have to spare my feelings. I know that before he left London Andrew had a whole string of girlfriends. I'm afraid I was very strictly brought up myself, but I think I came to accept that Andrew lived by a – different standard.'

She paused, and then, since Carlo still seemed reluctant to continue, she added: 'You've already told me that Silvia's son is your child, so if Andrew has some similar dark secret, then for God's sake tell me. I can appreciate your – your respect for my age and the fact that I'm his mother, and I don't expect you to spell it out in chapter and verse, but please, you must tell me *something*.'

Carlo sighed. 'Oh dear,' he said. 'It's not going to be easy.'

The cannelloni arrived at that moment, along with a carafe of white wine. As they ate, Carlo began to fill in the missing three and a half years of her son's life.

Their first year had been a struggle, he said. UK Exchange Control penalties, two extravagant months in Paris and the South of France on the way to Venice, and the down-payment on the lease of an attic flat in a decaying palace on the Cannaregio virtually exhausted Andrew's capital.

'Why didn't you live in your house in Burano?' Lillian asked.

'Burano wasn't chic enough for Andrew.'

'But an attic was?'

'An attic in a *palazzo* was,' he said with a smile.

While Andrew modernized the apartment to advertise his potential in the interior design field, Carlo took a job as barman at the Europa Hotel where he'd worked once before. Thanks to some old contacts of Carlo's Andrew began to receive the odd commission: posters and exhibition catalogues; window-displays; the redecoration – at marginal rates – of a few small apartments.

As his reputation increased, the commissions became bigger and more frequent: house conversions in the hills to the north of Venice; a penthouse flat for a university professor in Padua; a ski lodge in Cortina for a film producer from Rome (Lillian and George had received a New Year card from Cortina in 1964); two villas on the Aga Khan's Costa Smeralda in Sardinia; eventually, a small palace off the Giudecca for a nephew of Countess Volpi, the doyenne of Venetian society.

Carlo quit his job at the Europa so that he could supervise the 'works-in-hand', leaving Andrew free to move on to the design side of new projects. They rented the office in San Marco and engaged a secretary. Andrew now decided that it might after all be amusingly '*déclassé*' to live on Burano and commute to the office by motor-launch. They used the profits from the sale of their lease to damp-proof and modernize Carlo's house, which had only been intermittently occupied since his father's death in 1946. The installation of a shower and a fold-up bed converted Andrew's studio at 253 San Marco into a pied-à-terre for those nights – 'there were many of them,' said Carlo - when his social life kept him in Venice.

Lillian leaned back as the waiter placed her main course in front of her. The calf's liver was served in a sauce of onion and pungent herbs. Carlo sent Lillian's compliments to the chef. The maître d' returned with a single long-stemmed yellow rose, the colour of the outside of the restaurant, with the chef's compliments.

They watched through the lattice of vines the last minutes of a spectacular sunset. Carlo broke the silence:

'I suppose you know he's a terrible social-climber?'

Lillian laughed. He grinned.

'And a name-dropper! Is it true he knows Princess Margaret?'

'One of his girlfriends was her god-daughter,' Lillian said. 'He spoke to her at some first nights and a couple of parties.'

'And – excuse me asking this – is he really a second cousin of the Duke of Devonshire?'

Lillian laughed again with genuine delight. '"Second cousin" is a bit strong! My mother-in-law used to say her father's family was distantly related to the Devonshires, but my husband and his brother always took it with a pinch of salt. We decided Andrew must get his snobbishness from his grandmother.'

Lillian felt another great surge of grief for George. How he would have laughed to hear this latest instance of their son's name-dropping his dubious ancestry! Would she ever again have someone to share these moments of droll humour with, she wondered; or would she now only laugh with strangers, like this grinning partner of Andrew's who knew nothing of the aching sorrow behind her smile?

'I was sure he was making it up,' he confessed and went on to talk about Venetian high society while Lillian struggled to finish her meal. There was a constant round of parties, he told her: luncheons and dinners, receptions and cocktails, variously given by local notables and wealthy foreigners. Through his work and his ingenuity Andrew contrived to be on every guest list, cultivating the acquaintance of counts and countesses, princes and princesses, a French duke and duchess, even the former queen of one of the satellite Communist states.

'One way or another he found a way to charm them all,' Carlo said. 'Andrew is a real chameleon, changing his colour to suit every set, every ambience.'

The apex of Andrew's social career came in September 1964 when he was invited to the Volpi Ball, the most glittering event in Venice's calendar which took place annually at the end of the film festival.

Although the Hemingway crowd had dispersed even before the author's death in 1961 and the Jet Set had largely deserted mainland Italy in favour of Sardinia, anybody who was *somebody* – 'and quite a few who were nobody,' Carlo added – descended on Venice for at least part of 'the Season' which began in mid-August and culminated in Countess Volpi's ball in the second week of September. Among the guests at the 1964 Volpi Ball were Jacqueline Kennedy, Mick Jagger, Richard Burton and Elizabeth Taylor, and Aristotle Onassis.

'Andrew revelled in it,' said Carlo. 'He went to Milan to order a new dress suit especially for the occasion.'

'Did you go?' Lillian asked.

'Oh no, I wasn't included in the invitation. He took an American sculptress and from what I heard, left her to fend for herself while he got himself introduced to as many of the bigger celebrities as he could corner. He talked about it for weeks.'

Lillian declined a dessert or a liqueur. She drank a cup of

black coffee while Carlo ate a chunk of stale-looking local cheese and served himself from a bottle of grappa which the wine-steward left on the table.

She was sure there was more – much more – to be told. 'You said something earlier about a scandal two years ago,' she reminded him; 'and some people leaving under a cloud. Was Andrew involved with these people?'

'Well, yes, he was,' Carlo admitted. 'Except that he didn't really get into that set until the year they left. For our first year we were busy just trying to make ends meet, although right from the start Andrew was sniffing out the local scene to see who was worth getting to know.'

'But why did these people leave?' Lillian persisted.

Carlo paused for a moment, sipping his grappa, before embarking on a description of what he called 'the moral climate of Venice'. In spite of all the nobility and the artists and the Jet Set visitors it remained, he said, a small and gossipy community, very provincial: 'a lot like Hastings, according to Andrew!' Lillian laughed at this improbable comparison. Every season produced its crop of scenes and scandals, he went on, and certain families were known to have outrageous skeletons in their closets; but for the most part the residents led circumspect lives in a town where it was impossible to keep anything secret for long.

In recent years a number of very rich new immigrants had settled in the city, buying and restoring apartments and palaces, entertaining and befriending the local nobility and expatriate artists. During the summer of 1964, one of these newcomers had exceeded the relatively elastic bounds of propriety by insulting the wife of the chief-of-police on the beach at Lido.

The incident triggered a strong reaction from the normally easy-going *questura*.

The first victim of the ensuing 'purge' was not the man who had offended the *questore*'s wife but an art dealer from London who, despite the intercessions of influential friends, was expelled from the country. He was put on a train to Paris where, within days, he committed suicide. Others were similarly ejected or had their residency permits revoked. A few more chose flight as the wisest course, resulting in a minor exodus in the autumn of 1964.

'And was Andrew involved in this "exodus"?' Lillian asked.

'It was about then that we moved to Burano,' said Carlo. 'Although this really had nothing to do with it.'

'But why did they leave?' she enquired again. 'This poor man who killed himself, what was he guilty of?'

Carlo poured himself another grappa. 'Well, the *questore* – chief-of-police – was a strange and vindictive man, a Sicilian. He had a few bees in his bonnet: Communists –' he shrugged – 'and one or two other things.'

She gave a derisive laugh. 'Come now, Sharlz – I'm sorry – Carlo – I know I'm just a country bumpkin, but you can't expect me to believe that people who could afford to restore palaces were Communist sympathizers.'

Carlo drained his glass at a single draught. He looked straight at her.

'They were homosexuals,' he said.

A waiter refilled Lillian's coffee-cup. She picked it up with fingers that suddenly trembled. 'Are you trying to tell me that my son is a homosexual?' She pronounced the word in the popular English manner, with a long first 'o': *Homer-sexual*.

'I'm sorry, Mrs Rutherford,' Carlo said.

Lillian sat in the small cabin of the launch as it surged across the black waters of the lagoon under a deep violet sky in which only the moon and Venus were visible.

Grateful for the privacy, she wept. Bob Sadler had been right: Andrew was lost to her, further away than his sister and the grandchildren, as lost – almost – as George. The closeness she thought she'd shared with her son, the closeness she'd boasted about to Carlo, had been founded on an illusion. She had never really known him, who he was – what he was.

Preoccupied with this revelation of a different Andrew from the one she'd come to find, she was unaware of the route the launch was taking until, just as they emerged under a canal bridge into St Mark's Basin, ahead of them a cruise liner escorted by two tugs steamed majestically out of the Giudecca, blotting out the church of San Giorgio.

Awed in spite of herself, Lillian dried her eyes and went forward to stand beside Carlo, keeping her balance with her hands on the windshield. The launch rocked as they crossed the liner's wake. Finally appreciating the cardigan she had carried for two days, she sat down on the padded seat in the cockpit and drank in the view of the floodlit Doge's palace, the *campanile* and the Salute. Carlo smiled at her. Reducing speed as they entered the broad mouth of the Grand Canal, he pointed out some of the palaces, telling her who lived or had lived in them.

Another memory surfaced from her honeymoon: the jolly gondolier who'd ferried them from the Rialto to St Mark's, naming the palaces and their owners – counts and dukes and princes. She even recalled, faintly, the scandalous tales he'd told them of the lives of the nobility. George had been sceptical; Lillian believed every word because she wanted to believe that aristocrats still, in 1935, despite wars and revolutions, lived a life removed from the morals and conventions of ordinary people.

Now, repeating the experience thirty-one years later, these were the homes of people Andrew knew or had known. Here was the converted monastery that Barbara Hutton had bought early in her matrimonial career. Here, an exquisite Renaissance palazzo whose owner's homosexual lover had sparked off the 1964 'purge' by insulting the *questore*'s wife. Here, a low white building with a beautifully terraced garden that housed Peggy Guggenheim and her collection of modern art; she sometimes paraded drunk and nude on the terrace to attract passing gondoliers. Lillian was shocked at how easily she accepted this titbit of outrageous gossip (she knew that Peggy Guggenheim's father had gone down with the *Titanic*; *Titanic* lore had been a hobby of George's). Here was a stately sombre palace that had formerly belonged to Winston Churchill's mistress (the notion of a rival for 'Winnie's' darling Clementine was one that Lillian would not believe). Here was the British consulate; and so on – churches, galleries, showrooms, the homes of rich nobles and exiles.

As she must have done on her honeymoon, Lillian was content to sit back in the gently rocking boat and surrender herself to the spell of the moonlit canal. She twirled the stem of the yellow rose in her fingers. Glimpses of dim alleys and backwaters contributed as much to the aura of enchantment as the blatant splendours of the Rialto Bridge or the floodlit Ca' d'Oro. And yet, within the elegant drawing room of a building just before her hotel a family was watching television only feet above the water, as indifferent to the magic and mystery of the Grand Canal as the residents of a semi-detached house in Hastings to the road outside their front door.

'I'm sure it hasn't all been easy for you,' she said, surprising herself with the calmness of her remark, as they glided to a standstill at the landing-stage of her hotel, 'but how lucky you've been, you and Andrew, to have lived with all this.'

ISLAND OF GIGLIO

Fabrizio yawned. Too much local wine, too much dope. Also he was bored. For the second day running they had sailed the fifty kilometres to the volcanic outcrop of Montecristo only to find the sea too choppy for snorkelling. *Il frocio* (he always thought of him as 'the queer') lacked the nerve to try scuba-diving and Fabrizio was wary of going down unaccompanied.

The Corsican girl had joined them for dinner again. Her mother had another headache. The girl was sure her mother was screwing one – or possibly all three – of her absent father's crew. The liver in the purportedly best of Porto Giglio's few restaurants had been indigestible, the red wine as heady as Marsala. The girl ate and drank with relish, prattling away to *il frocio* in French, a language in which Fabrizio was far from proficient.

Back on board his father's yacht (half the length and a quarter of the draught of the Corsicans') they drank more wine – and smoked. A moonlight swim failed to clear Fabrizio's head. And the girl kneed him in the groin when he tried to fondle her breasts underwater, although he was certain she had been groping *il frocio*.

The lighthouse beam swept over the small harbour, briefly illuminating the girl sprawled on the padded banquette facing the cockpit. She was wearing Fabrizio's robe. She wore it carelessly, exposing most of her over-large untanned breasts which were already beginning to sag. Her face was unmemorably pretty; the dyed blond hair, still wet, clung to her skull. Her eyes were closed but she was not asleep. A smile played at the corners of her mouth.

Reclining on a lounger inside the cockpit, *il frocio* was watching Fabrizio watch the girl, also with an amused expression. He too wore a towelling robe, drawn tightly across his chest with only his calves and feet exposed. Unlike the girl, who'd merely discarded her swimming costume in the aft cabin and put on the robe, *il frocio* had lingered in the forward cabin to dry and groom his hair. After the first joint and their swim he reverted to his usual mentholated English cigarettes, while Fabrizio and the Corsican girl rolled and smoked two more joints.

Sitting cross-legged on a cushion on the deck with his back against the gunwale, Fabrizio still wore his bathing trunks, a brief slip which barely contained a swelling erection. A few drops of water ran out of his hair and he shook his head. He felt a flare of anger that the girl seemed less interested in what he was putting on show than in that which *il frocio* modestly kept hidden.

Fabrizio rose unsteadily to his feet, crossed to the girl and tugged open the robe. Her eyes opened, she started to laugh and pushed him away with both hands. He clung to the robe and she rolled off the bench with the cushions still beneath her. Her head banged onto the deck and she shouted a curse as tears streamed from her eyes. The robe had fallen completely open. A thin neat scar crossed her belly: an appendectomy? A surgical abortion? The triangle of dark brown hair below the scar resembled damp moss.

Fabrizio fell on her and pawed at her breasts. She cursed him again and struggled. He put one hand over her mouth and with the other started to pull off his trunks, trapping the girl with his weight. He glanced up as the lighthouse beam passed over again. *Il frocio* still wore an amused expression. The sound of cats hissing and growling carried clearly across the water from the rocky hillside beyond the harbour.

The body beneath Fabrizio squirmed. After a last triumphant glare in the direction of the Englishman, he concentrated his attention on freeing himself from his trunks. His mouth slavered at the Corsican girl's wobbling breasts with their wide flat nipples.

From his chair above the writhing pair Andrew Rutherford looked down and laughed.

VENICE

After breakfast Lillian took the vaporetto all the way to Lido, thinking that a quiet day in the shade beside a beach would give her time to reflect on what she'd learned last night; it simmered in her mind like a pot on the stove. But Lido was not a quiet place in which to lift the lid and inspect the 'stew' that was her son's duplicitous life. The avenue to the beach was jammed with buses and taxis, cars and motor-scooters and dawdling people with shopping baskets and picnic hampers and loud unruly children. Halfway to the beach her patience gave out; she turned and jostled her way back to the vaporetto. Venice didn't seem to have any quiet corners. It might be better to go back to the hotel.

Then, as the boat approached the first of its stops on the return journey, she saw that it was about to dock beside a park at the far end of the promenade that led eventually to the Doge's Palace and Piazza San Marco. Quickly disembarking she explored the park; it was far from tranquil but not as busy as Lido. She found an isolated metal chair beneath a straggly pine. Had Andrew walked in this park, sat beneath this tree?

But it was not the last three-and-a-half years of Andrew's life that her mind immediately focused on, but the years preceding them, the years when she had imagined that his life still belonged, at least partly, to her.

Day or weekend trips to see Andrew had been the high spots of Lillian's life after he moved to London at the end of 1959. Sylvia's wedding and the birth of the twins were highlights that Lillian was able to share with George, who doted on his daughter, but a similar bond tied Lillian irrevocably to her son. On her own with Andrew she was able to 'let her hair down' in ways her mother would have considered indecent and George a waste of money. Mornings spent shopping in Harrods or Liberty's. Lunches in fashionable restaurants in Knightsbridge or Mayfair. Afternoons visiting art galleries where Andrew knew the exhibitors or inspecting displays he had designed. Dinners in cosy haunts of his in Soho or Chelsea. A slightly risqué comedy or revue. Some trashy film she wouldn't dare suggest to George. A new soprano at Covent Garden; Eartha

Kitt at the Talk of the Town; Marlene Dietrich in Golder's Green. Sunday boat-trips on the Thames or a ride to a country inn in a chauffeur-driven hired car.

Being with Andrew was, to Lillian, the height of what in her own youth would have been called 'fast living'.

And now, sitting under a salt-ravaged tree in the city he'd adopted, she forced herself to confront what Carlo had told her last night: this other life of her son's which he had so carefully kept from her. Lillian's strait-laced upbringing hadn't prepared her for such a revelation. After George's second stroke they'd given up having the *Daily Telegraph* delivered: George could no longer concentrate on reading and Lillian preferred library books to newspapers. But she occasionally bought the *Daily Mail* and through this and the television news she was aware that there was a campaign (and a bill coming before Parliament) to decriminalise homosexual acts between adult males. Lillian did not know – did not wish to know – what a 'homosexual act' was. It was not something that affected anyone in her golf and bridge circle in Hastings.

But now it affected her son. His personal life was not only wayward and dissolute, it was also criminal. He could be sent to prison, like Oscar Wilde in Queen Victoria's time and – what was his name, ten or eleven years ago? – Lord Montagu.

When had it started? And with whom? At University, when he first broke free of the narrow confines of family life and provincial Sussex? During his National Service, where middle-class grammar-school boys were thrown into God knows what sort of low company?

It was hard to see Hastings as a breeding ground for homosexuals, but then she was clearly not skilled in recognizing them. The only one she could recall meeting was Andrew's partner in the Mayfair agency, Algie, whose voice and mannerisms were obviously effeminate, although they'd never discussed it, it hadn't seemed to matter – until now. Surely Algie, who was close to sixty and closer to being an alcoholic, wasn't Andrew's 'partner' in any other, more disgusting, sense?

Apart from Algie the only male friend of his she'd met between the schoolboy son of the family doctor when Andrew was in his teens and 'Sharlz'/Carlo in 1962 was Laurence Dickinson in Bexhill, who'd provided Andrew with 'sanctuary' after the rows with George in the summer of 1959. Laurence was a client of George's, divorced from his much remarried wife and with a teenage daughter who later came to live with him. Surely Laurence could not have been Andrew's whatever-the-word-was? Because if Laurence was, then what about Carlo or even Doctor Yates's son, both of them married men and fathers?

There were aspects to this which she could not, never would be able to, even contemplate – but then she'd never much cared for the series of young women he was obviously sleeping with. Perhaps no mother could come to terms with the notion that her precious son was a 'lothario', still less that he was a pervert.

Exactly what role had those girls played in his life, she wondered: Fiona, Jocelyn, Sandra and Thelma, all of whom she'd been introduced to in theatre bars and restaurants. Had they connived with him to provide a smokescreen, or had he deceived them as he had deceived her?

Wondering what more might lie beneath this stone that Carlo had forced her to turn over, Lillian sighed. Opening her handbag, she took out the letter and cards which on an impulse she'd removed from her dressing-table drawer just as the Sadlers tooted their presence outside the house on Monday. Two postcards, one greetings card and a letter that together comprised all she had known – until last night – of her son's life since November 1962. Three years and eight months, during which her daughter and grandchildren had moved to the edge of China and her husband had sickened and died. She knew their contents by heart, but now she would be able to place them in some sort of context to what Carlo had told her of Andrew's life in Italy.

April 1963

From Venice, a postcard: the head of a girlish-looking boy described as a 'Detail from Titian's *Virgin of the Pesaro Family*' in the church of Santa Maria Gloriosa dei Frari.

> *This young man is an 'island' of Pre-Raphaelite purity in this city which is one enormous over-stuffed monument to the Renaissance. Like him, I seem to be out of time and out of place. But, Venice is all things to all men. Here at least no one can be a fish out of water!*
>
> *Love,*
>
> *A.*

This must have been while they were still settling into Venice. Carlo would have been working in the bar of the Europa Hotel and Andrew was doing up their attic flat in a palace on the Cannelloni canal or whatever its name was.

'What's a "Pre-Raphaelite" when it's at home?' George had demanded, stumbling over the unfamiliar word but much more articulate than when Andrew had left in November.

'They're one of those groups of painters,' Lillian told him. 'You know, like the Impressionists.' Luckily George didn't ask her to name anyone from this School.

'Artsy-fartsy nonsense,' he jeered.

She'd been worrying herself sick for five months – for this? A cocktail-party observation about Venice and art, and – nothing else. No return address: nothing. He didn't want them to be able to contact him. She would not know if he was ill or well, happy or miserable – would she even know if he was alive or dead?

George, stronger now in health and spirits, re-adopted a dismissive attitude towards the son who'd spurned his birthright, but Lillian remained in a morbid mood for weeks. She had experienced a period of the same black depression when she miscarried her first child – a boy it would have been, two years older than Andrew, perhaps the son George might have taken into the business.

January 1964

From Cortina, a greetings card reproducing a nineteenth-century lithograph of an alpine village; inside, '*Happy New Year*' was printed in Italian, French, English and German. All but the English greeting had been lightly scored through with a fine red pen such as Lillian had seen him use on posters. Also in red he'd written:

> *As ever,*
> *Andrew*

This must have been when he was decorating the ski lodge for a film producer from Rome. Carlo was now helping him. They'd opened their office at 253 San Marco. And Andrew was social-climbing among contessas and princes and Peggy Guggenheim whose father went down with the *Titanic*.

'Is this all we get?' George had asked.

'Apparently,' she said.

'Well, there's your precious son for you,' he scoffed.

'Same old Andrew,' Lillian said bitterly; '*"As ever".*' Her despair redoubled.

JULY 1965

Another postcard, from the island of Elba, a view of Napoleon's villa and the Museum at San Martino.

> *My 27th birthday, but at least I'm here from*
> *choice! Like Napoleon's, my exile is a mixture*
> *of reflecting on past glories and expectations*
> *of a glorious future which Time will no doubt*
> *frustrate!*

Thinking of you both,

With love,

A.

It was the third year in which she had no address to send him a birthday card. He had not remembered any of her birthdays – or his father's.

Eighteen months had gone by. They had modernized Carlo's house in Burano and given up the attic in Venice. Andrew had been to that countess's celebrity ball. There had been scandal at Lido, deportations and hasty departures, a suicide in Paris.

What was he doing in Elba? Carlo hadn't mentioned any work in Elba.

Unlike the others, this card was addressed to George as well as to Lillian, and this at least had pleased her. She told him about it but was unable to gauge his reaction, for its arrival followed what proved to be his final stroke from which, in the six weeks that he outlived it, he never recovered the power of speech, no matter how frenziedly he tried, eyes blazing with frustration.

Lillian visited the hospital every afternoon, sitting by his bed, holding his hand and telling him the news of her day, the garden, their friends and neighbours, who had won this or that tournament at bridge or golf. His useless limbs twitched spasmodically as he applied the force of his will to them like a charge of electricity. Loathing the sickness which he had fought so manfully for so long, Lillian loved him more fiercely than at any time since their courtship.

At the end, the nurses told her, he died quietly, in his sleep. His heart gave out; perhaps, like hers only more so, it was simply broken. This was in the first week of September, five months after their thirtieth wedding anniversary and a few days before Lillian's fiftieth birthday. George was sixty-one. Lillian dined with the Sadlers at Rye's Mermaid Inn on her birthday; two days later she cremated George.

7 November 1965

Milan

Dearest Mother,

I've only just learned, from my bank, that you have lost Dad. It's a penalty of cutting oneself off like this that you don't hear about these things until it's too late to do anything to help. Sylvia's always strong on "rallying round" in a crisis; I hope she's been a comfort to you over these past weeks. I wish I liked her more.

And I wish, too late, that Dad and I had made more allowances for each other. I remember holidays we had when Sylvia and I were kids – Cornwall, the Lakes, the Norfolk Broads, Scotland. I'm trying to concentrate on those times and forget what came after. I hope you are not missing Dad unduly and that your memories are only of the good things.

I seem to be getting restless again. Really it's unreasonable, for my life here is full of variety and a fair amount of "glamour", if you can call it that.

I may come home for Christmas. No promises, of course. I would come now, but I still have irons in the fire. There's more magic here than anywhere else I know. If only I could find some way of binding myself to it.

(Sorry, that sounds very mystical and precious. I don't change, do I!)

Love, always,

Andrew

Milan. He and Carlo had now met Adriana who would shortly become pregnant. It occurred to Lillian that the reason Adriana had seemed vague about dates might be because she had married Carlo after he made her pregnant.

Presumably Andrew had by now gone to live at the other end of the lagoon so that Adriana and Carlo could have the Burano house to themselves. But why so far from his office in Venice? Or was this connected to the 'purge' of the city's homosexuals? Had those that remained all retreated to towns and villages on the furthest edges of the lagoon?

This piecing together of his 'restless' history was even more difficult than she'd expected.

Tidying her mother's bedroom (like Amy Sadler's, Sylvia's presence made the cleaning woman largely redundant), Sylvia found the little pile of correspondence in Lillian's dressing table. She came downstairs in a fury.

'You didn't tell me about this letter,' she blazed.

'Yes I did, dear. I told you about it when it came last year.'

'You didn't tell me he said horrible things about me.'

'Well, you'd hardly expect me to. Anyway, he doesn't. He says you're "strong on rallying round in a crisis". Which you are,' she added tactfully. 'Look how you came flying home when Daddy died.' Richard's mother had minded the girls until after the funeral, and then Sylvia and the children stayed on with Lillian for another month. Richard came back with them for Christmas and the New Year, divided (in Lillian's favour) between Hastings and Guildford.

Sylvia was in no mood for compliments. She waved the offending letter. 'He says he doesn't like me.'

'He does not. He says he wishes he liked you more. That's not the same thing.' She suspected it was the same thing. She sometimes wished, guiltily, that *she* liked her daughter more. 'Anyway, you shouldn't read other people's letters.'

'You never told me he promised to come home for Christmas.'

'No he didn't.' Lillian suppressed a sigh of impatience. 'He said: "No promises".'

'Well, he should have. He should have come as soon as he heard about Daddy. He should have let us know his address, so we could have told him Daddy was in a bad way. Running off to Italy at nearly forty, it's ridiculous.' Sylvia also shared

Amy Sadler's penchant for exaggeration; Andrew wasn't even thirty. 'And it's not right. With all you've had to put up with, you really need him. He should be here.'

Lillian released the pent-up sigh. No, she said sadly, but unlike her daughter she spoke only to herself. He must be where he wants to be.

If only he had included his address. But what would she write?

> *Dear Andrew, I don't want you to come home if it isn't what you want to do, but you are all I've got left and I need to be sure that I have still got you.*

Two days after this exchange of spoken and unspoken views of Andrew, Sylvia took Wendy and Jane back to Hong Kong; Richard had left on January 2nd. Just like when they'd flown away in October, the house changed from a children's playground into a mausoleum. After the excitement of sharing, in part, Andrew's years in London, George's illness had provided Lillian with three years of drama, culminating in his death. Now there was only hollow routine.

She shopped, cooked, gardened; she went for long walks; she played bridge and an occasional round of golf on fine days; she and Amy and Alice Pemberton (whose husband had invested in some of George's building projects) raised funds for several charities; she lunched with them and with other friends. She saw some concerts and plays with the Sadlers; she went to the cinema alone or with Amy.

Most of her golf and bridge partners both before and after

George died were female (widows, divorcees, a few of Hastings' many old maids, widowed by war before they could marry), but from time to time she partnered a widower or bachelor from the town's ageing middle class. All were lonely enough to welcome a morning of golf, a bridge dinner; some clearly longed for company on a more permanent basis. In ten months of widowhood Lillian had refused all invitations for a 'date', had gone only to group functions: card evenings, lunch or dinner parties, one reception at the Town Hall.

Was this to be the template for the rest of her life? Golf, bridge, entertaining, good works; they filled her days but they did not fulfil her life in the way that marriage and motherhood had. Her friends, she knew, saw her as grieving but they didn't know how much she seethed with dissatisfaction. She was fifty, a widow, her children scattered far and wide: what was she to do with the rest of her life?

Among her friends only Alice Pemberton had so far suggested that, after an appropriate interval, Lillian should consider remarriage. She was among the most eligible of Hastings' many widows and younger than the majority of her rivals along that elephants'-graveyard coast. If anything happened to Amy, Bob would be on his knees in front of Lillian within days of the funeral. But Amy could drop dead in her kitchen tomorrow and Lillian live for another fifty years – and not marry Robert Sadler. She'd thought she loved him thirty-two years ago but she'd only been marking time, waiting for the real thing to come along. For George. Once you'd known that kind of love, nothing less would do. She could not imagine replacing George. What had held them together was thirty-one years of shared experiences: bringing up the children, struggling to make a success of the business, enjoying success when it came, all their holidays and fishing trips and drives and walks and George just talking to her while she gardened. That shared history was Lillian's life. At fifty she did not expect – or want – to start again, from 'scratch', with a stranger; did she?

When Lillian looked in the mirror, a not-quite-plump woman with a not-quite-plump face stared back at her, permed brown hair that (with some help from Harmony) didn't show any grey; a woman who rarely wore make-up other than lipstick in a temperate shade of red. The word that best described her was 'matronly'. This matron was a far-from-merry widow whose closest living relative could not tear himself away from his chic Venetian life to come home and comfort a grieving mother.

She still had Sylvia, but it wasn't enough. Telephone calls to Hong Kong came through quite quickly, although the hollow echoes on a line that went under the world's oceans for thousands of miles made her daughter and the grandchildren sound as if they really were half a world away. She had promised to go to Hong Kong next Christmas.

But first, she suddenly decided in the middle of July, she would go to Italy and find Andrew.

Even in the shade of the pine tree it was becoming insufferably hot with the sun now directly overhead. There was not the faintest whisper of a breeze. Lillian rose and headed back towards the landing stage.

Bitterness overwhelmed her as she walked through the park. All she had to show for thirty years of marriage, fifty years of living, was a daughter and grandchildren from whom she was separated by more than mere distance, and a son who hadn't trusted her with the truth about his life and who was in any case too busy with his own sordid pursuits to make time for her.

She felt not so much bereaved as *bereft*.

On the vaporetto, oblivious once more to the splendours of the Grand Canal, she decided she would eat her lunch at the hotel, have a siesta and then go to the railway station and enquire about tomorrow's trains. She would go back to Calais, to Hastings, to her life of golf and bridge, jumble sales and the Sadlers. There was no point in going on with this pursuit of Andrew.

Her son was indeed – as she'd admitted to Bob Sadler – a 'rolling stone', rolling wherever impulse or his immoral appetites took him, rolling (his grandmother would have been certain of this) down the road to perdition.

Lillian could not bring herself to wish Andrew '*bon voyage*' along this path he'd chosen to take, but she forced herself to accept that there wasn't – and perhaps never had been – anything that she could do to divert him from it.

The telephone woke her from an afternoon nap that had turned into four hours of deep sleep: the enervating heat and yesterday's disclosures were clearly taking a toll.

It was Carlo, calling from Ravenna. He'd had to return there today; the last client was pressing for the work to be finished.

'I've just spoken to Fausto again, the Prince's other son,' he announced. 'We've almost found his brother and Andrew.'

'What do you mean: "almost"?'

'They've been on an island called Giglio since Tuesday, off the coast of Tuscany. They were seen in a restaurant with a French girl last night and the night before, but today they seem to have gone off somewhere. The yacht's still there, but they're not.'

'Then where on earth are they?'

'Fausto's contact says the French girl's yacht left this morning and hasn't come back yet. It's a bigger boat than Prince Massimo's, with a captain and crew. Andrew and Fabrizio must have gone with them. There are some interesting places to see around there: Montecristo, for instance, which inspired the book by Dumas. Or they might have gone to the mainland. I'm sure they'll turn up, maybe even this evening. Fausto's on his way there to meet them.'

Despite a lifetime spent beside the sea Lillian had always felt nervous about boats. Her head swam at the prospect of some calamity taking Andrew from her.

'The other news,' Carlo continued, 'is that Fausto has been in touch with his father in Las Vegas and the Prince has instructed him to invite you to their villa in Amalfi. Fausto's going to bring his brother and Andrew there once he catches up with them. I've got the train times for tomorrow. You'll have to change in Rome, and one of the Prince's men will meet you in Naples.'

'Actually,' Lillian blurted, 'I thought I'd go back to England tomorrow.'

'Oh, but you can't give up now – when you've nearly caught up with him. Besides, I've got no way of contacting Fausto until he calls me again from Giglio or from Amalfi. Andrew will know you're here. He'll be expecting you.'

'Naples now,' Lillian said with no enthusiasm.

'Yes, you're certainly seeing Italy!' Carlo chuckled. 'Fausto tells me his brother and Andrew were at the Amalfi house last weekend. They're working their way northwards. Fabrizio has to go back to school in Siena next month.'

'And will Andrew come back here then, do you suppose?'

'Maybe. But not for long. I think he's had enough of Venice. He turned down a couple of projects that came our way, and he even stopped seeing his posh friends in the city when he moved to Sottomarina at the beginning of the year. But – he didn't find what he was looking for there either.'

'What is he looking for?'

'I'm honestly not sure. I doubt if he knows himself. Lately he's been very unsettled, wanting change all the time: new places, new faces. Fabrizio's a charming boy, quite captivating in his way, but really he's no more than what the Americans call the "flavour of the month". It'll be a toss-up as to who gets bored first, Andrew or Fabrizio.'

Lillian asked the question that had festered in her mind in the park:

'Is there a reason for this, for him being – like this?' She heard the snap of his cigarette lighter before he answered.

'There are all sorts of theories about homosexuality. Perhaps some men are born that way. A lot of boys give it a try during their teens or later. Some seem to grow out of it, some grow into it.'

'I see,' said Lillian, though she didn't. 'So where do you think Andrew will go when this Prince's son goes back to university?'

'I wish I knew. I doubt if Andrew even knows himself. He might go back to Hastings with you!'

She smiled sadly. 'It's sweet of you to say so, but I'm afraid Hastings doesn't have anything to offer a person of Andrew's – tastes.'

He caught her momentary hesitation. 'Mrs Rutherford, I'm not sure that I've done the right thing in telling you all this about him.'

'No,' she said firmly. 'I'm glad you've told me. It makes a lot of things clearer, things I've never been able to understand. Perhaps, in a way, I *have* always known, but I simply didn't have the experience to put a name to it.' She paused. 'I can't think why he didn't tell me himself, years ago. It makes such a mockery of our relationship, him keeping something this important from me.'

'He would have liked to tell you, he said so to me, but he wasn't sure how you would cope with knowing and he was even more afraid of his father's reaction.'

'Oh well –' she laughed grimly – 'I wouldn't have dared tell George! But I'm sure *I* could have accepted it, given a bit of time. I'm sure I will accept it now – in time. He's my son, I'll always love him whatever he does – whatever he is.'

Embarrassed by this unaccustomed articulation of her deepest feelings, she fell silent.

Carlo exhaled audibly. 'Adriana sends you her best wishes and safe journey, et cetera,' he said.

'How is she?'

'A bit better today. By the way, I should probably tell you a bit about her background before you meet her brothers. They're actually her half-brothers. Prince Massimo wasn't married to her mother.'

'Oh?' Lillian braced herself for more scandalous revelations.

'He was a widower when they met but he never offered to marry her, not even when Adriana came along. He kept her on as his mistress after he married his second wife, the boys' mother, but then when she died – when Adriana was seven or eight – he completely stopped seeing them. He sent money for their support, but Adriana didn't set eyes on him for ten years. Then he turned up at her mother's funeral. Now she sees him exactly twice a year: he takes her to dinner on her birthday and to lunch in the week before Christmas. He still supports her financially, but he's more like a guardian than a parent.'

Lillian's first impression of Adriana yesterday had not been altogether favourable. She'd reminded Lillian – ironically, it now appeared – of the type of woman Andrew seemed to seek out: elegant, cool, somewhat remote. But now a wave of compassion washed over Lillian. The daughter of a discarded mistress, spurned by her father for a decade and then taken up as little more than an unwanted ward, Adriana had had a bleak childhood and a bleaker adolescence. This Prince sounded like a mean-spirited man: Lillian hoped she wouldn't be meeting him before she left Italy.

'The Prince did introduce her to his sons,' Carlo went on, 'and they see a bit more of her. Fausto's a cold fish, very wrapped up in his studies, but Fabrizio likes having a big sister, they're quite close – or at least they were until Fabrizio took up with Andrew.

'Anyway, now you know. Have you got a pen and paper to hand? I'll give you the train times.'

Lillian sighed silently. Andrew had disappeared off the face of the earth, and her quest was turning into an odyssey, acquiring a momentum of its own, sweeping her along with it. But it was her own fault, for coming here and setting it in motion.

Sleepless in the stifling night air, she got out of bed and opened the window. She didn't look at her watch, but it must be close to midnight. She'd bought mosquito-repellent cream at a pharmacy and now she rubbed it into her hands and face before getting back under the single sheet.

She still couldn't sleep. It wasn't the heat or the mosquitoes or even the intermittent nocturnal voices and chugging engines from the Grand Canal. It was Andrew. Far from looking forward to the reunion in Amalfi, she was almost dreading it. It would not be her son she was meeting, only a stranger who looked like her son.

ISLAND OF GIGLIO

The lighthouse beam flared briefly at the window of the darkened room in which Fausto Monfalcone sat drumming his fingers on a cluttered desk top. After a breakneck drive from Siena to the coast and the fifty-five-minute crossing to Giglio during which he paced the deck of the ferry, he'd spent the afternoon cross-examining fishermen and other port users who had reported sightings of Fabrizio and Andrew on or off the island. Now, after midnight, he sat impatiently in the small office which the harbourmaster had put at his disposal. Through a thin partition wall came the voice of the ship-to-shore operator, paid to stay on after the end of his shift, calling ports and marinas in Corsica, Sardinia and along the French and Italian mainland in an attempt to find the missing yacht.

Fausto had communicated to his father in Las Vegas, though not to Carlo Marini in Ravenna, the fact that much of what he'd learned was disturbing. The owner of a yacht which had been berthed next to the French boat on Thursday, kept awake by his neighbours' orgiastic sexual activity, had overheard

Fabrizio and his English companion splashing about in some moonlight bathing with the French girl. The proprietress of a shop that hired out snorkelling equipment had opened her bedroom window after midnight to call her cat in and heard young male and female voices shouting on board one of the yachts.

Of the two fishing-boats that had seen the French yacht at sea, the second had made the more alarming report. Through binoculars one crew-member had observed the yacht rendezvous with a fast motorboat out beyond Montecristo; the French girl and her mother had descended a ladder onto the smaller boat, leaving a man and a boy who matched the description of Andrew and Fabrizio on deck with the crew, which was augmented by two men from the second boat before both vessels set off at different speeds on a heading that suggested Corsica as their destination.

Fausto prayed that his brother had not been taken to Corsica. Anything involving Corsica spelled trouble. In Italy and its islands the Monfalcone name caused doors to open; in Corsica it would cause them to shut.

'*Signore, signore –*'

The radio operator burst into the darkened room without knocking. He was more than twice Fausto's age but like the harbourmaster and the restaurant manager who was the Monfalcone contact on the island he addressed the son of Prince Massimo as 'sir'. Fausto pressed the switch on a desk lamp and blinked in the sudden glare.

'A boat is coming – fishermen – Sardinians – they have caught two bodies in their nets – a man and a boy –'

The difficulty of understanding the radio operator's dialect, the dialect of this little archipelago, was compounded by his agitation. No one liked to be the bearer of bad tidings, especially to the son of Massimo Monfalcone.

'Where are they?'

'Half an hour out, signore.'

Fausto picked up his sweater and went outside, the other man following. They walked onto the nearest jetty. Pools of lamplight illuminated stanchions, coils of rope, torn nets, empty lobster pots, a pile of old car tyres. There were lighthouses at the head of both jetties, but only one whose lamp revolved. The black night sea hissed through the narrow opening and slapped against the harbour walls. A light breeze rattled the ropes on the masts of the pleasure craft moored in the small harbour, of which the Monfalcone cabin cruiser was now the largest.

The radio operator, trembling from more than the night chill on his tee-shirted torso, proposed going to wake the harbourmaster and the local police sergeant, but Fausto vetoed this with a gesture. He didn't want a crowd when the fishing boat came in. He would see what he had to see and then he would do what had to be done.

Like any of these functionaries who jumped at the mere mention of the name of Massimo Monfalcone, Fausto was in awe of his father. He knew the power of his father's rage and also the extent of his father's grief. At eighteen Fausto had already earned his father's admiration and respect, but he was aware that his younger brother, because of his extraordinary resemblance to their mother, had the bigger share of their father's love. He dreaded the phone call he would have to make after he saw what was on the fishing boat.

It was nearer an hour, a long hour, before the chug of a

distant engine preceded the first glimpse, in the sweep of the lighthouse beam, of the fishing boat riding on flashes of phosphorescence in the gentle swell. As it surged through the harbour mouth Fausto stood like a soldier at attention, hands at his sides, a short stocky figure in jeans and a cable-knit sweater, his face set, his expression unreadable.

The radio operator ran to catch a line thrown by one of the fishermen as the boat approached the jetty. There were two more men on deck and a fourth in the small wheelhouse. Masses of live fish, mostly sardines and anchovies, threshed in an assortment of vats and trays on the deck. Near the wheel-house two shapes lay under a tarpaulin.

One of the crewmen offered Fausto a hand, but he ignored it and jumped nimbly onto the deck, striding directly to the tarpaulin which he quickly pulled back.

They lay on their backs, arms at their sides, the older man's right hand accidentally overlying the boy's left. Having been only a few hours in the water, the two bodies were not bloated, although they did possess that ghostly pallor that comes from prolonged immersion. The older man had either been beaten or dragged across some rocks: his face was lacerated. The boy might almost have been merely asleep; there was seaweed in his hair but his face was unmarked, save only for the neat round hole, twin to the older man's, in the exact centre of his forehead.

But the boy was not Fabrizio. He was a year or two older than Fabrizio and as swarthy as a Gypsy. And the older man, although the right age and colouring, was not Andrew.

'I kn-kn-know these men, signore,' said the radio operator, impelled despite his terror to follow the son of Massimo Monfalcone onto this ship with its grisly deck cargo and stammering from a mixture of cold and the release of pent-up tension. 'The boy was a deckhand on the yacht of the Frenchwoman, and the other man was her captain.'

Fausto pulled a wad of money from his jeans pocket. He instructed the radio operator to give it to the fishermen and then go and rouse the police sergeant.

'Do not tell the police about my brother and the Englishman. Say only that the fishermen caught these bodies in their net.'

The radio operator nodded. '*Sì, signore.*'

As he walked back to the harbourmaster's office Fausto looked at his watch and calculated the time in Las Vegas. The news he would have to transmit to his father was not as bad as he had feared, but it was bad nonetheless.

'*Quei porci maledetti di Corsi,*' he allowed himself the satisfaction of a muttered imprecation: accursed Corsican swine.

PART TWO

AMALFI

There is nothing in the world sweeter than Italian love.
And nothing fiercer than Italian hate.

JOHN HORNE BURNS

'Signora Ruthairford?' enquired the priest, singling her out of the throng of passengers on the platform at Rome's Termini station.

'Yes.'

'I am Father Angelo. Sent by Massimo Monfalcone.' A tall, elderly, cadaverously thin man in a black soutane, he took her hand and leaned over it in a brief bow.

'How do you do,' she said. Protestant (and lapsed) Lillian was uneasy in the presence of a Catholic priest. Did he expect her to genuflect? She hoped not – and didn't.

Father Angelo, with a porter in tow, led her along the platform and into the main concourse, bustling and noisy even on a Saturday. They stopped at a kiosk whose drink-stained counter rose from a marble floor littered with cigarette ends and paper napkins. The porter left after exchanging a few words with the priest. Lillian declined to eat anything; she drank a frothy *cappuccino*, Father Angelo a small cup of black coffee with a lot of sugar.

He was, he explained, an employee of the Vatican Bank where Prince Massimo served as an investment advisor. The Prince's current visit to the United States was to inspect potential real estate investments. Lillian pictured land being bought to build new churches and perhaps orphanages and convents.

'Soon I shall retire,' Father Angelo announced. His English was good but he spoke almost entirely in short sentences. 'I will go to Cassino. This is south from Rome. It is where I first became a priest. In the monastery on the mountain. There was a battle there in the last war which lasted four months.'

'Montecassino,' Lillian said. 'My bank manager's brother was killed there, on May the 17th 1944, my daughter's third birthday.'

'I think he is buried there,' said the priest. 'There are cemeteries for the American and British and New Zealand soldiers and a very big one for the men of Poland – more than one thousand graves.' Remembering this terrible battle with its heavy casualties, they both fell silent.

'His name was Arthur,' Lillian found herself saying in a confessional spirit. 'He was the first boy I went out with, my first – we didn't call them boyfriends then – my first "beau".'

'Like Scarlett O'Hara,' Father Angelo said, breaking for Lillian the mood of solemnity Arthur's memory had brought. She burst out laughing.

'You know about Scarlett O'Hara?'

He smiled and became instantly less sinister-looking. 'I have read *Gone with the Wind*.'

'I don't like long books,' Lillian said. 'I've seen the film, of course.' She stopped herself from telling him she sometimes fancied she saw Olivia de Havilland reflected in her mirror. 'Fancy you knowing Scarlett O'Hara!' she said and laughed again.

The porter rejoined them and they proceeded to another platform. The train for Naples was packed, but her First-Class ticket secured Lillian a seat in a compartment that was only half full. Father Angelo insisted on paying the porter (Lillian hoped it was with the Prince's money, not the Pope's) and then bowed low over Lillian's hand again. As the train pulled out of the station her fellow passengers stared with frank curiosity at the Englishwoman who had been escorted onboard by an agent of the Holy Father.

Beyond the warehouses and apartment blocks lining the track Lillian briefly caught sight of a distant gleaming dome that might have been St Peter's. The suburbs finally thinned and they were climbing into the Apennines: tunnelled hills and viaducted valleys with wide shallow rivers and dried-up streams; harvested fields and terraced slopes dotted with trees and barren outcrops – everything parched-looking under the brilliant, relentless sun.

The train made stops every half-hour or so. Lillian fell into a light sleep, dreaming – or perhaps day-dreaming – of tossing boats and stormy Channel seas and Andrew and Sylvia trapped by racing tides at Camber Sands; George, in his fishing coat and wellingtons, ordered Lillian to pull herself together; and Arthur Sadler, young and dashing in his Indian Army uniform, begged her forgiveness for a heartbreak she'd almost forgotten.

It was of Arthur that she found herself thinking, for the first time in years, when she came fully awake again. She stared almost unseeingly at the changing, unchanging view of mountains and valleys and cottages with crinkled red-tiled roofs. Perhaps while she dozed they'd passed the cemetery where Arthur had been buried for the last twenty-two years, the 'black sheep' of his generation of the Sadlers, redeemed by heroic death.

Arthur was the handsomest of three handsome brothers, all born in India where their father, a military adviser to maharajahs, had died of unheroic dysentery in 1928. His widow returned to the family home in Rye, taking in lodgers to pay for her sons' schooling. Lillian, thirteen in 1928, was a baker's daughter who wore sober frocks chosen by her mother; her hair was kept in a tight bun and, except for washing, never let down – literally or metaphorically. Mother only allowed her out on walks and bicycle rides with the Sadler boys because Mrs Sadler was 'Chapel' and had raised her sons to be decent and god-fearing. It was Wilfred, the middle brother, to whom Lillian had felt most drawn in childhood games in the street and out on the marshes, but he went off to teacher training college and married a fellow-student.

At eighteen, Lillian (her hair still in a bun but now buying her own clothes) 'walked out' with Arthur when he came home on furlough from his father's regiment in Rajasthan. Everyone expected them to marry, though she somehow knew that they wouldn't. When he jilted her to take up with a local shopgirl, Lillian was courted by bank-teller Robert, the youngest and most earnest of the Sadler boys. It was now taken for granted that she would eventually marry Bob, but Lillian was waiting to be swept off her feet. And in November 1934 her expectations were again, at last, fulfilled when George Rutherford, whom she remembered as a rough-and-tumble boy at primary school, returned from six years' lumberjacking in Canada with some capital to expand his brother's bricklaying and plastering business. The jilted became the jilter.

A blast from the siren at the front of the train brought her abruptly out of her reverie. The railway was entering the slum outskirts of another large city. In the distance the ground rose steeply to a massive shape that blurred into the atmospheric haze.

She looked at her watch. Three minutes past four. They were due in at twelve minutes past. Even without Mussolini, Italian trains seemed to run very much to time. The heat-hazed mountain must be Vesuvius.

How strange that the priest's mention of Cassino had triggered off a chain of reminiscences. Not for the first time she wondered how her life might have turned out if George in his loud boots and dusty lumberjacket had not come clumping into the office where she worked as a solicitor's secretary to enquire about the procedure for changing a company's name.

'Signora Ruthairford?' What description had Carlo Marini given to these people who instantly picked her out from a trainload of passengers? Her accoster this time was fifty if not sixty years younger than the Roman priest and at least six inches shorter, a stocky boy in a black suit.

'Yes,' she said.

'I am Fausto Monfalcone.' He took her hand and, like the priest, bowed over it.

'How do you do,' she said.

'I am very happy to make your acquaintance.' The

reciprocation of her formality made Lillian feel even less at ease. She wasted no further time on courtesies.

'I thought you were on – the island where my son and your brother went missing. Have they come with you? Are they at your house in Amalfi?' She felt a painful pressure in her chest. If Andrew was here, surely he would have come to the station? Something had happened, something dreadful.

'As you can see, I am not in Giglio,' the boy said pedantically. 'And no, they are not at our house in Amalfi. They have not come back with me.' He seemed determined to answer all her questions. 'I will explain, Mrs Ruthairford. I have a car outside. Please to follow me.' Another elderly uniformed porter picked up Lillian's case and the travel-bag, and for the third time today she marched through a railway station concourse.

The heat of Naples struck her like a blow as they emerged from the marble cavern of the station into the forecourt car park. The dusty air shimmered like the air over a bonfire. Lillian felt perspiration begin to flow under her clothes and even on her scalp.

The old man, not a porter but a chauffeur, produced the keys to a large old-fashioned Mercedes estate car and held the rear passenger door open as Lillian seated herself gingerly on the blistering buttoned-leather upholstery. The boy let himself in on the other side while the old man put Lillian's bags in the back before climbing in behind the wheel. Fausto Monfalcone addressed a few words to him, then leaned back and smiled briefly at Lillian as they backed out of their parking space.

'You have been to Naples before, Mrs Ruthairford?'

'No, I haven't. Is it always this hot?'

'The temperatures are very high this year,' he said. 'Our

house is by the sea. It will be cooler there.'

The huge square in front of the station was chock-a-block with traffic. As they turned into a descending avenue of shops and offices, shaded on one side and bathed in dazzling sunlight on the other, Lillian took stock of her latest escort in the quest for her son.

Beneath dark-brown hair he had a round-jawed face with a prominent nose and an almost English complexion, barely touched by the sun: he was not as tanned as Carlo, nor as handsome. Lillian remembered Carlo's description of him as 'a cold fish, very wrapped up in his studies'. Fausto Monfalcone looked to be a studious boy – there was an aura of the monastic about him – but she had no immediate impression of coldness. Notwithstanding the monkish air and the sober black Sunday suit in which he seemed impervious to the heat, he was only a *boy*, which Lillian found most disconcerting of all. If this was the older of the the Prince's sons, just how young was the one Andrew was with?

The Mercedes was fitted with air-conditioning which was steadily lowering the internal temperature. As they turned into another wide street, Fausto yawned and quickly brought his hand to his face. Lillian realized that his pallor was not an English complexion: he was haggard with exhaustion.

'Excuse me, Mrs Ruthairford, that I am so tired. I have only slept two hours since many hours driving.'

'I'm sorry,' Lillian said. 'You've obviously had a very long day. But you must tell me why you've come here without them. Why didn't you go on to wherever they are?'

'Mrs Ruthairford –' he held up his hands as if to fend off her questions – 'I still do not know where they are, only that they are with these – French people. The harbourman in Giglio was calling all the ports until after midnight, but we didn't find these people's yacht.'

Lillian's chest again constricted. She took a deep breath before giving voice to her worst fear:

'Do you think they've had an accident?'

The boy's bloodshot brown eyes met hers levelly. 'No, Mrs Ruthairford. The weather is good. The sea is calm. I know this because I sailed my father's yacht from Giglio to Porto Santo Stefano in the night and I am not good with boats like my brother, I only go on the sea when it is very calm.'

'But they could hit another boat or something in the water could – hole their hull.' She was aware how melodramatic this must sound. 'You read about ships disappearing without trace.'

'They have not disappeared, Mrs Ruthairford,' he said patiently. 'Not in that way. We just didn't find them yet, that's all.'

'Then where can they be?'

'There are places they can come to shore without going to a port or marina. Many private houses have a –' he didn't know the word – 'place to put a boat. My father's house in Amalfi has a place for this, as you will see.'

'But why have you stopped looking for them?' she persisted. 'Why don't we both go and look for them?'

Fausto wearily held up his hands again. 'Please, Mrs Ruthairford. Many people work for my father. Already they are looking for your son and my brother. My father does not wish for us to go. When they are found, they will fly here. Maybe I will fly to fetch them. My father has an aeroplane in Rome.'

It exasperated Lillian that her quest for Andrew was being

delegated to these faceless employees of a jet-set prince, but she finally fell silent, admitting defeat. The boy closed his eyes. His breath whispered between parted lips. This dark-haired serious youth and his driver, these Monfalcones, were taking her steadily southwards while Andrew and the Prince's other son were almost certainly heading north or at least to the west. She sighed helplessly and went back to looking out of the window.

The houses lining the road through the suburbs were five and six storeys high, many with classical facades but grimy and run-down and festooned with washing-lines. Lillian imagined dingy high-ceilinged rooms behind the drawn shutters: stone floors and large inhospitable pieces of furniture. There were glimpses of the sea, the Bay of Naples, vivid blue, dotted with boats and sparkling in the afternoon sunshine.

The road narrowed and twisted and climbed tortuously up into the Sorrento Peninsula. Progress was slow: cars and buses and trucks queued at bends or squeezed past each other on the brief straight stretches in a barrage of tooting. On the other side of the peninsula they descended to 200 feet above sea level, the road now bordered by a low wall which had crumbled and fallen away in places leaving them inches from the edge of a vertical cliff. More than once Lillian closed her eyes against the dizzying prospect. But it was the most beautiful landscape she had seen outside the Scottish Highlands.

Above the road the coastal mountains rose in green slopes and grey bluffs and brown terraces to dark craggy summits against a sky that mirrored the limpid blue of the sea. There were vineyards everywhere, small orchards and olive groves, scatterings of pine trees, isolated villas and farmhouses; fishing villages clung to the walls of ravines where the sea had cut inlets from the shoreline; ruined towers perched on headlands; here and there a cluster of tourist bars and hotels fringed the road.

They arrived at Positano, which Lillian had seen in Alice Pemberton's holiday photos: hotels, shops and pink and white villas in a chaotic sprawl on both sides of a steep valley behind a beach that was dense with umbrellas and sun-loungers – and people. Even up on the main road above the town, holiday-makers ambled beside the crawling cars: bare-chested men, women in sun-tops, barefoot children in swimming costumes.

Half-an-hour and a few miles later, with a sustained blast on the horn the chauffeur made an abrupt right turn into a narrow parking area in front of a pair of iron gates. Fausto woke, rubbed his eyes and smiled at Lillian before getting out to open and then close the gates behind them. He climbed back into the car and they cautiously descended a steep concrete ramp only inches wider than the Mercedes. The rugged cliff face sprouted clumps of thistles and wild flowers; on the outer side a low rendered wall held the metal supports for a chain-link fence topped with razor-wire.

In front of them a craggy promontory rose to a height of about 200 feet, level with the road they had just left and crowned by a squat stone tower. Three storeys high, it had a parapeted roof and narrowed in the middle like the waist of a Scarlett O'Hara gown. Access was by way of a steep Z-shaped flight of steps. A grilled door opened onto a narrow terrace on the landward side; the only windows were deep niches in the thick walls, also barred.

The boy had spoken of a 'house'. Carlo had led Lillian to expect a villa. Venetian princes, like most royalty, lived in palaces. This prince lived in a castle.

'It's like a fortress,' she remarked. The car slowed to a crawl as they negotiated a tight bend in the driveway.

'It *is* a fortress,' Fausto said. 'In the days of the Amalfi Republic,' he went on, sounding like a tour guide, 'in the tenth and eleventh centuries, this was a signalling tower. Messages were passed with mirrors and flags up and down the coast, and they had to defend themselves against enemies and pirates from Sicily and North Africa.'

Lillian wondered but did not ask why the Prince chose to live in a fortress. A final curve brought them to another set of gates, raw new-looking steel topped with sharp spikes. Behind them stood two men who, in answer to the chauffeur's tooting, had emerged from a large flat-roofed stone-walled building that served as garage and guardhouse. One man had a rifle slung across his shoulders. Lillian decided against remaining silent.

'Why does that man have a gun?'

The men saluted as the chauffeur drove between them and parked in front of the closed garage doors. One of the men shut the metal gates.

'For shooting rabbits,' the boy said. 'There are many rabbits. Maybe Maria – our cook – will make a rabbit stew while you are here. This is one of the specialities of Sicily. Maria is the husband of Alfredo, our driver. They are from Sicily.'

Lillian was not sure she believed the rifleman was merely some sort of gamekeeper, although he was dressed for the part in a rustic-looking dark green shirt and moleskin trousers. He remained at the gate while the other man, more convention-ally dressed in jeans and a grubby white tee-shirt, held the car door open. He bowed as Lillian got out, bowed again as Fausto followed her out of the car.

Lillian became aware of the sound of the sea. It was all around, the splashing and slapping of gentle waves on rock. Another short flight of steps to the left of the entrance gates led down to a bare platform of rock just above sea-level with what appeared to be a small natural boat jetty to one side of it. As promised, it was cooler: a light breeze off the water.

Above them loomed the tower, bulging over two outcroppings of rock. She followed Fausto up the first stretch of the steps which had a low border and no handrail. The man in jeans followed with her bags, then the chauffeur, Alfredo, climbing more slowly. The rifleman stayed below. When the boy paused on the first bend, Lillian, two steps behind, almost bumped into him.

'I hope this is not too much climbing for you,' he said solicitously.

'I'm up and down stairs all day at home,' she said. 'And steps in my garden. Don't worry about me.' Fausto walked into a cobweb suspended from an overhanging gorse bush and brushed a spider out of his hair as he resumed climbing. From the next bend Lillian was able to view the seaward side of the tower, which had bigger windows, arched but still grilled. There was a large drystone-walled terrace with steps down to an expanse of patchy lawn that ended in a low parapet where the cliff began its fall to the sea. A few limp plants struggled across rocks at either end of the parched grass.

Puffing a little now, Lillian was glad to stop. Behind them the two men had paused to light cigarettes. 'Those flowers need some water,' she panted.

'The caretaker must have forgotten,' said Fausto who was also out of breath. 'Alfredo will have to do it. My father enjoys the garden when he is here.'

'Does he spend much time here?'

'Before this year we came every summer for the holidays, but this year my father is very busy and I am doing research for my degree and my brother is on the yacht with your Andrew.'

The sun was beginning its leisurely slide towards the hazy horizon, turning the sea a powdery shade of blue. 'Do you –' she hesitated before choosing her next word –'*despise* my son for taking your brother away from his studies?'

Fausto made a dismissive gesture that reminded her of Carlo. 'My brother stops to study very easily. I don't think Andrew has made this decision for him.'

Lillian sensed that the boy was uncomfortable with this line of questioning. He was not going to be as open to discussing Andrew's activities as Carlo. Surprising her pleasantly, he took her arm and they tackled the last flight of steps side-by-side. The grille at the base of the tower had been left open; the heavy oak door opened as they reached the last few steps and a middle-aged woman in a white smock curtsied them into a small gloomy vestibule with thick stone walls.

The area beyond the vestibule was anything but gloomy. Some thirty feet long and almost as wide through a series of arches on both sides, this bottom storey was a single enormous room. It ended in a wall of French windows, also arched and with decorative wrought-iron beyond them, overlooking the terrace which contained garden furniture and a profusion of plants in urns and tubs.

No stonework was visible inside. The arched walls, plastered or rendered, were painted a pale lemon yellow and hung with Impressionist oils and watercolours highlighted by recessed spotlights. The panelled ceiling was the colour of honey, the carpet a deep shade of orange similar to the one in Carlo's living room in Burano. A refectory table with pew-like benches occupied the centre of the room. Through the arches on the left was a modern kitchen, on the right a cosy living area with leather furniture and a huge marble fireplace containing a large vase of dried flowers in the centre of its outer wall. Only the thickness of the arches reminded that this was an ancient castle; there was no feeling of being inside a fortress.

'Did Andrew decorate this house?' Lillian asked.

'No, my mother did it herself with a decorator from Naples in 1946. It was a wedding present from my father.'

Another woman, older and plumper, dressed in black, emerged from the kitchen to be presented. This was Maria, the cook, the chauffeur's wife. She too curtsied to Lillian but she ruffled Fausto's hair affectionately before returning to her kitchen.

'Maria was my nanny when I was born,' the boy said, as if to justify the woman's familiarity. 'And to Fabrizio. And before me to the children of my father's first wife.'

'You have more brothers and sisters?'

He shook his head. 'No, they died with their mother.'

'How awful. Was it an accident?'

'Yes,' he said but did not elaborate.

'How old were you when you lost your own mother?'

'You know about this? From Carlo Marini?' Lillian nodded. He faced her across the table, standing like a soldier at attention, hands by his side. 'Two years,' he said. 'I do not remember her, only from pictures. My brother was only some months old.'

'It's very sad that the two of you had to grow up without a mother.'

'Yes,' he said. 'Very sad.' Lillian would have liked to move round the table and hug him, but his sober appearance and perhaps the memory of Carlo's words discouraged such a spontaneous gesture.

'How old are you now?' she asked.

'I am eighteen. Soon nineteen.'

'So – I've forgotten your brother's name –'

'Fabrizio. My father calls him Fabio. He is seventeen.'

'Andrew is twenty-eight.' Eleven years older than the prince's younger son. George had been eleven years older than Lillian.

Fausto frowned. Then, gesturing at the maid still standing in the entrance as Alfredo belatedly staggered through the doorway, he said:

'Rosella will take you to your room. She will bring you tea. Please rest if you like. We will have dinner at eight-thirty or nine.'

Lillian realized that he had no intention of talking to her about his brother and Andrew.

The middle-aged maid ushered Lillian up a carpeted staircase to a large bedroom on the next floor, decorated in shades of pink. Two windows, arched and grilled, overlooked the terrace and lawn and the rocky descent to the powder-blue sea. Rosella, who was all smiles and spoke no word of English, fetched Lillian's bags, brought tea on a silver tray, helped her unpack and ran her a bath.

After a ten-minute soak Lillian lay on the pink bedspread and slept for two hours, waking just before nine. She rose and went to a window. On the now floodlit terrace Rosella was laying a table. Someone was dragging a hose across the unlit lawn on the lower level. Beyond the dark figure the sea merged with the night sky into a curtain of blackness. A brightly-lit ferryboat steamed into view, sailing on an invisible sea. Leaning into the embrasure to follow the ship's progress, she glimpsed lights twinkling beyond the next headland, the lights of Amalfi perhaps. She found herself wishing that her friends at the golf club could see her in this unlikely setting. She hoped that George, somehow, could see her.

What did one wear for dinner in a castle? She opted for a high-necked silk dress striped in two shades of burgundy, the most formal she'd brought with her, bought for Alice Pemberton's garden party which was one of her quarter of East Sussex's social highlights. Sitting on a fluffy pink stool in front of a pink-lacquered dressing-table, Lillian painted her nails for the first time since leaving England and put on eye-shadow and a light foundation as well as lipstick.

Tomorrow she would have to insist on going to a hairdresser's. After six days of train journeys and boat trips and walking in hot dusty streets her hair felt grimy, although mid-brown was not a colour that showed the dirt like Amy Sadler's ash-blonde rinse which, in Lillian's opinion, on a woman of fifty-one came close to dressing mutton as lamb.

Recalling the priest's mention of Scarlett O'Hara, Lillian smiled. She had impulsively changed her hairstyle in her mid-twenties. In January 1940, (Andrew was one and a half, Sylvia not yet conceived), she went to the best salon in Hastings and had her hair cut and waved. Friends complimented her fashionable new look; Mother grumbled that she now looked the same as every other woman; George, waiting to go to war, said, 'Very nice, dear.'

She didn't tell George (or anyone) the reason for the change. *Gone with the Wind* the year before had given Lillian a vision of herself as Melanie Hamilton – not 'mealy-mouthed' but, yes, frumpish. (Robert Sadler was dependable dull Ashley Wilkes, although by no stretch of the imagination could Amy be Scarlett, and George made an unlikely Rhett Butler.) Permed hair was, she hoped, less frumpy than the bun she had sported since her teens – Mother's choice.

The years – and pregnancies – had fleshed out the angular features and gawky frame which Lillian had inherited from her Baptist minister grandfather and passed on to her son. Somehow liberated by the perm, she bought evening dresses for the first time in her life and forced George to take her to dinners at the Town Hall and dances on the pier. George did not enjoy himself and was relieved when his call-up, in the summer of 1940, brought an end to frippery. During the post-war years of austerity they went to fewer functions: Lillian got two or three years' wear out of each new dress – until Andrew grew up and moved away and she began a new round of shows and dinners and dances and clothes-buying with her son, the son who had now, improbably and almost unbelievably, led her to a castle on the Amalfi Riviera.

At least the burgundy silk dress looked nice. She ought to wear mascara more often, she decided: highlighting her eyes made her face seem less chubby. All the same, she sighed as she crossed to the door, it was hardly a face – nor, probably, a frock – fit for a prince or even for a prince's scholarly son. Closing the bedroom door behind her, she turned round just as a thickset man in a dove-grey suit reached the top of the stairs.

'Ah, Mrs Rutherford,' he greeted her with a small bow. 'I am Massimo Monfalcone.'

'How do you do,' Lillian said, quickly deciding not to call him 'Your Highness'. She held out her hand, which the Prince lifted to his mouth and gently kissed. Releasing her hand, he smiled at her.

Aware that this was absurdly schoolgirlish of her, Lillian almost went weak at the knees. Prince Massimo was better looking than even the Sadler brothers with their film-star looks. He was not young but he was the handsomest man she'd ever seen.

It was immediately clear (comparisons again) that Fausto took after his father, but he was completely overshadowed – literally so at this moment: the boy had followed the Prince up the stairs and was standing behind him, smiling broadly.

Prince Massimo was an inch or two taller than his son, though not above Lillian's five feet seven. Amplifying the boy's stockiness, the Prince was powerfully built, broad-shouldered with a thick torso. And Fausto's round-jawed face was stronger in the 'original', the nose reminiscent of those in statues of Roman senators and Caesars, the complexion much darker than the boy's, the eyes almost black, the grey hair streaked with black but still very thick.

His age was a surprise; disregarding the previous marriage and Adriana's mother, she had anticipated (not knowing that she would meet him) a man of her own age, the parent of two teenage sons. The Prince was at least sixty years old.

'I thought you were in America,' she said, barely managing not to stammer.

'Well, I decided I'd better come and meet the mother of this young man who's turned my son into a Flying Dutchman,' he said. Lillian was unable to suppress a groan of dismay.

'Please. I feel guilty enough about him already.'

'My dear Mrs Rutherford, there's nothing to be guilty about.' His English, in a mesmerizingly deep voice, was impeccable, as good as Carlo's, but Lillian detected an accent that was more American than Continental. 'In general,' he went on, 'I think we must welcome our children's ability to surprise us.'

Lillian laughed grimly. 'I've had more surprises than I bargained for since coming to Italy.'

He smiled. 'Shall we go downstairs? I'm sure you'd like a drink before dinner.'

'That would be nice,' she agreed. 'But perhaps you need to rest after your long journey.'

'Not at all,' he said. 'I slept through most of the flight from Las Vegas.' Father and son stood back so that she could descend the stairs. A half-dozen matching leather suitcases stood just inside the door from the vestibule. There were now five or six men in the kitchen with Maria and Rosella; the men were all seated at another wooden table with bottles of wine, talking in low voices.

The Prince ushered Lillian through one of the arches into the lounge area. Above the marble fireplace hung a huge antique mirror, but what dominated the room, on the windowless section of wall adjoining the vestibule, was a near-life-size portrait of a fair-haired young woman. Lit by a recessed spot-light, the painting was modern in style although the subject wore a white beaded dress and headband from the 'flapper' era. She possessed an Audrey Hepburn beauty, almost painfully thin with delicate, elfin features, in no way resembling Fausto who, Lillian noticed, had not accompanied them downstairs.

'Your first wife?' she guessed.

'You know about her?' The Prince gestured Lillian towards an armchair.

'Only that you lost her in an accident,' Lillian said as she sat down.

'Her name was Liliana,' he said after a moment. 'The same as yours, Mrs Rutherford.' He smiled again; he had dazzlingly perfect teeth. 'But this is not Liliana. This is my second wife, Lidia, the mother of Fabrizio and Fausto. She also died.'

'Yes', said Lillian solemnly. She hesitated, then added: 'Lydia was my grandmother's name.'

'It's a lovely name. If she had given me a daughter, I would have called her Lidia too. But –' He spread his hands in a gesture that reminded Lillian of Carlo. Alfredo appeared in an archway behind his master, who was still standing. 'What would you like to drink?' the Prince asked.

'Can Alfredo make a Tom Collins?'

'Alfredo can mix cocktails you never heard of, Mrs Rutherford. I often bring recipes back from America.' He gave Alfredo his instructions and the chauffeur who was now a butler withdrew as silently as he had appeared. The voices from the kitchen were no longer audible.

'I'd never heard of a Tom Collins until last week,' Lillian admitted. 'Carlo made my first one in Burano.'

'Of course, you've been to Burano. And you've met my wayward Adriana.' His use of 'wayward' seemed to confirm Lillian's guess that Adriana had been pregnant when Carlo married her.

'Who's going to make you a grandfather very soon,' she reminded him, feeling oddly defensive towards the daughter he'd neglected.

The Prince accepted this with another smile. 'You must forgive me that I waited till now to offer my condolences on the loss of your husband.'

It was odd to be receiving condolences ten months after the event. 'We have both lost spouses,' Lillian said. The Prince, poor man, had lost two.

'And perhaps we also have in common sons who have disappointed us.'

'But you have two sons,' she said, not denying that Andrew was a disappointment to her. 'You may be disappointed in –' she'd forgotten his name again – 'the one who's with Andrew, but you must be proud of Fausto.'

'But of course,' he acknowledged. He sighed. 'It's a paradox, but I am a disappointment to Fausto. Did he tell you about his studies?' Lillian shook her head. 'He is studying law, but although we pretend his legal studies will be of benefit to my companies, his real passion is for canon law and what he really wants to be is a priest.'

'Surely you don't intend to hold him back from his vocation?' Lillian said. It was a surprise that their conversation had so quickly taken such a personal turn. The Prince seated himself in the middle of the settee facing her across a marble coffee table.

'He has a duty to his family, to me, to everything I have built, to the Monfalcone heritage. Fausto knows he cannot turn his back on his inheritance.'

'But you have two sons,' she repeated.

Prince Massimo held up his hands again. 'The other one is

more useless to me than the daughter whose child will not bear my name. Mrs Rutherford, I adore my youngest son. Fabrizio is the image of his mother, whom I literally worshipped. It's wrong of me, but I love him more than Fausto who is the better character. I know Fabio will never be more than a playboy, a – prodigal. If only *he* wanted to go into the Church!'

Lillian smiled. 'He doesn't sound like ecclesiastical material.'

A spark of reflected light danced in the prince's dark eyes as he laughed. 'Oh, the Church has always had its libertines. It might amaze you to know that I originally intended to be a priest.'

'Then why didn't you?' she asked, not admitting that this was, indeed, hard to credit.

'I nearly did, but then my older brother died, and then my next oldest brother, so it became necessary for me to take over as head of the family.'

'Your father wasn't alive?'

'No, he died before my brothers.'

'So many deaths,' said Lillian, giving voice to a thought she had entertained all too often since last September.

The Prince sighed. 'Yes, too many. But –' spread hands again – 'I had to put my duty to the family ahead of my ambitions.'

'Even ahead of your duty to *God*?'

'Are you religious, Mrs Rutherford?'

She blushed. 'Not really. My grandfather was a minister and my mother was very religious, but my husband and I – drifted away.'

The Prince was silent for a moment. 'You have to understand that the Monfalcones are not like other Italians: we are Sicilians. In Sicily, even more than in the mainland, family is everything, even before God.'

'But now you work for the Pope,' said Lillian.

'Did Father Angelo tell you that?' She nodded. He paused for a moment, then said: 'I work *with* the Vatican rather than for it. The Catholic Church and I have overlapping interests in the investment area. Hotels and retail outlets generate a good part of the income that supports the work of the Church.'

'You buy shops and hotels for the Vatican?' Not orphanages and nunneries, it seemed. The idea that the Holy See's collection plates – 'the widows' mites', her mother would have called them – were being ploughed into hotels and department stores offended even Lillian's less puritan sensibility.

Prince Massimo mocked her incredulity with another smile. 'As a matter of fact, I've just bought them a stake in a casino. We live in secular times, Mrs Rutherford.'

Alfredo returned with their drinks on a silver tray. He spoke briefly to the Prince who rose to his feet. 'Dinner will be ready soon. Let's go outside.'

Lillian followed him through the French windows. Candles flickered inside glass tubes on the wrought-iron table which had been laid with a starched white lace cloth and set with silver cutlery and crystal glasses. At each end of the terrace stood a man armed with what Lillian recognized from the cinema and television as a machine-gun.

'These are not rabbit-hunters,' she remarked.

'I'm sorry?'

'Your son said the man down by the gate had a rifle for hunting rabbits.'

'Ah.' The white teeth gleamed. 'Perhaps he didn't want to alarm you. These men are my bodyguards. The man at the gate is guarding the house, guarding my son, guarding *you*, Mrs Rutherford.'

'Do we need armed protection?'

'A man in my position has rivals. In Italy today we do not underestimate the lengths our enemies may go to.'

'I see,' said Lillian, who did not see. George had had rivals in the building trade, but he'd never felt it necessary to protect himself or Lillian with weapons. It was another surprise that she calmly accepted the presence of the two swarthy guards with their guns and their darting vigilant eyes. Moving to the drystone wall she sipped her Tom Collins, which was stronger than Carlo's recipe and sharper in taste. A faint unidentifiable perfume rose from some wild flower on the moonlit slope and there was a background smell of the sea; by straining her ears she could hear a distant splashing as the waves lapped the rocks around the promontory. The night air was warm; there was a hint of breeze off the water, enough to keep mosquitoes at bay.

Prince Massimo had followed her to the wall. Lillian found herself reappraising him in the light of their first, already intimate, conversation. Impossible to think of him as a would-be priest. There was nothing of Fausto's aura of the monk and the scholar: this was the face of a sensual politician or general, a man who needed armed protection from his enemies. Lillian sensed that Adriana's callous father was capable of worse acts than discarding a mistress or ignoring a daughter. Far from intimidating, this sensation was almost intoxicating. Never before had she experienced the exciting frisson of being in the presence of a man who might actually be dangerous.

He was aware of – he was enjoying – her scrutiny. He smiled. 'Sometimes, when I stand here like this, with only the sea and the night sky, I think I am back in Sicily.'

'That is where your heart is,' said Lillian.

'I think a man's heart always belongs to the land of his parents, his past.'

'Yes,' she said. 'I often think of my parents' cosy little house in Rye where I used to look out of my bedroom window and see the marshes criss-crossed with morning mist.'

'Rye is beautiful. I took my wife to Rye, my second wife. We stayed at the Mermaid Hotel.'

'The Mermaid Inn,' she corrected him. 'I had dinner there with Andrew and Carlo the night before they came to Italy.'

A discreet cough from Alfredo announced the serving of dinner. Fausto followed Alfredo onto the terrace and smiled at Lillian as his father pulled back a cushioned wrought-iron chair for her. Rosella served the food – it was a simple meal: tomato soup, chicken with roast potatoes and a salad, followed by an Italian version of 'summer pudding', a dessert Lillian had often prepared for George with fruit from their garden. Alfredo poured glasses of a crisp local white wine.

Conversation was somewhat stilted, the boy's presence forcing them to be more formal. They talked about England, about the Cotswolds and the Lake District, which the Prince had visited, and about London and Brighton, which Fausto knew from school trips. Lillian was relieved when the boy excused himself after the meal, but to her disappointment the Prince suggested an early night for everyone after their day of travelling. One of the guards remained out on the terrace after the Prince closed the French windows; the other guard went to sit in an armchair close to the vestibule, his machine-gun propped against the side of the chair. Maria and Alfredo, alone in the kitchen, were washing up.

Prince Massimo escorted Lillian to the foot of the stairs, said, 'Goodnight, Mrs Rutherford' and kissed her hand before crossing to a side-table where the telephone stood. Only as she mounted the stairs did it occur to Lillian that at no time since meeting her had the Prince offered any news of Andrew and Fausto's brother. And neither had she thought to ask if there was any progress in the search for them. She turned to go back down, but the Prince was already on the telephone, speaking quietly in Italian, and she resumed her way upstairs.

Rosella had laid Lillian's nightgown across the folded-back bedclothes. As she prepared for bed Lillian thought about Prince Massimo, his sturdy physique which was not so different from George's in healthier days, his rich mellifluous voice like a film star's (Laurence Olivier perhaps or James Mason), those deep dark eyes which were like nobody else's she could ever recall. She smiled ruefully at her reflection as she cold-creamed her face. Without his chaperoning son, the Prince would have been the first man she'd dined alone with since George's death last September. She wondered if he shared Father Angelo's familiarity with *Gone with the Wind*. He would know Sophia Loren; did he know Olivia de Havilland?

She went to open a window. The moon shone on the now darkened terrace where the guard rocked back in one of the wrought-iron chairs with his feet on the top of the drystone wall; the tip of his cigarette glowed. Beyond the terrace, beyond the parapeted lawn, the sea, gently shifting in the moonlight, had the black sheen of a beetle's shell.

***

'There is a little progress in the hunt for our sons,' Prince Massimo said, rising to his feet as she came out onto the terrace. For breakfast the table had been shifted closer to the house, to shade it from the sun which was hot even at seven-thirty. A new guard was leaning on the wall at the end that overlooked the steps to the gatehouse.

'Do we know where they are?' Lillian asked.

'No, but we know who are the people they are with.'

'Oh?'

'Their name is Pasquale.' This – he pronounced it 'Pas-kwah-lay' – sounded so Italian that Lillian said: 'So they're not with French people after all.'

'Well, most people would call them French, but they're Corsicans, who don't think of themselves as French any more than we Sicilians think of ourselves as Italians.'

Lillian sat down. The Prince resumed his seat opposite her. He was wearing razor-creased dark-blue slacks and a white short-sleeved shirt exposing masses of hair in its V-neck and on his arms which were tanned and muscular and roped with prominent veins.

'Why has it taken all this time to know their name?' she asked. 'Didn't they sign some sort of register in the port at – the island where they met Andrew and your son?'

'They should have, of course, but a lot of harbourmen are sloppy about these procedures. And it didn't help that the yacht was called *Marie-Christine*, a very common name.'

'So how did you find out about these – Corsicans?'

'Somebody gave us a photo of the captain and finally in Marseille we found someone who recognized him and could tell us who he worked for.'

'Who exactly is "we"?'

He shrugged. 'People who work for me.'

'More bodyguards?'

'A lot of people work for me, Mrs Rutherford,' he said stiffly. 'They don't all walk around with machine-guns.'

Rosella came out with a coffee-pot and a basket with toast under a napkin. She greeted Lillian with a curtsy. Massimo took the pot and poured two cups of coffee. 'I've already had breakfast with Fausto. We're early risers. He's gone into Naples to look at some papers in one of the church archives. I've got some calls I must make, so I shall ask you to excuse me while you eat your breakfast. Would you like Maria to cook you eggs and bacon?'

Lillian added milk to her coffee. 'No, this is plenty, thank you. There is something I would like.'

'Just ask.'

'Could somebody run me into Amalfi to a hairdresser?'

'Is it just for a shampoo, or do you need something like a perm?'

'Just a shampoo and set,' she said. 'Is that a problem?'

'Not at all. It's just that Rosella can give you a shampoo. She used to set my wife's hair – the boys' mother, that is. I wouldn't trust her with a perm or tinting, but for what you need she's more than adequate.'

Lillian would have preferred the anonymity of a salon to being fussed over by Rosella, but not wanting to appear ungracious, she said: 'That's very kind of her – and you.'

'It'll be quicker than going into Amalfi,' he said. 'By the time you're ready I'll have done my calls and can devote the rest of the day to you.'

'Don't stop work on my account,' she said quickly.

He held up his hands. 'Please, I'm glad to have the excuse. I've been to and fro the US so much lately, I feel I've earned a day or two off.'

'What about Andrew and your son and these – people?'

He drank some of his coffee. 'That's already in hand. The Pasquales have businesses in Marseille and in Corsica. I hope my people will quickly find out where they've gone with our two truants. Maria or Rosella can take a message if anyone calls while we're out.'

'I don't mind staying in.'

'Nonsense. You're in one of the most beautiful parts of the world, Mrs Rutherford. You must see some of it.'

'But can't we wait till Andrew and your son get here?'

'We could, but I'd rather show you around while I've got you to myself.' He disarmed her with another dazzling smile. Finishing his coffee, he rose and pushed his chair back. 'Now, eat your toast, Lillian, before it gets cold. Since we shall be in each other's company for a few days, I'm going to call you Lillian. I hope that's all right.'

She nodded and smiled. Anticipating her next problem, he went on: 'We're not real aristocrats, by the way. My title was a gift of the Pope. You must call me Massimo. Or if that's difficult for you, a lot of my American associates call me *Max*.'

'Like Max de Winter.'

'Excuse me?'

'"*Last night I dreamt I went to Manderley again*".'

'Is that a book or a movie?'

'Both. It's the first line of *Rebecca*. Laurence Olivier and Joan Fontaine starred in the film version.' She didn't tell him his voice reminded her of Olivier.

'I expect I've seen it.' Clearly the Prince did not share Father Angelo's taste for modern fiction. He gave a slight bow and went inside. A motor-mower started up on the garden level as Alfredo tackled the neglected lawn. Lillian poured orange-juice from a cut-glass decanter and lifted a piece of toast from the basket. The marmalade, served in the jar, was from Fortnum & Mason. Andrew would have something clever to say about that, she thought.

Despite the Prince's deprecating description of her talents Rosella did as good a job as Lillian's regular hairdresser in Hastings, washing her hair in the pink-tiled bathroom and setting it with the aid of an antique-looking hand-held drier. Rosella had remembered the word 'okay'; by the time they finished Lillian was comfortable in the use of '*si*' and '*no*' and had even progressed to '*bene*' and '*molto bene*'. With difficulty she pressed a 5,000-lire tip on the Italian woman. Picking up the sundress Lillian had shed before the shampooing in favour of a monogrammed towelling robe, Rosella pantomimed washing it; she left with everything Lillian had worn so far, including last night's cocktail dress. For her first excursion with the Prince – *Max!* – Lillian put on a light-blue Marks & Spencer skirt and a long-sleeved man's-styled shirt Andrew had bought her years ago in Fenwick's with vertical light- and dark-blue stripes that had faded to make it one of her favourite tops. She chose a pair of blue flat-heeled lace-up shoes that were comfortable for walking. When she came downstairs he was still on the telephone. He smiled at her and concluded his call.

'Your hair looks nice. She's done a good job.'

'She's a professional. And we got on very well considering we can't speak a word of each other's language!'

He laughed. 'Would you like a coffee before we go?'

'No, I've had enough to drink, thank you.' Aside from the inconvenience of having to request bathroom stops, she had a horror of public toilets, following unsanitary discoveries on touring holidays with George.

The Prince called out a few words to Maria in the kitchen. None of the guards was in evidence, but as soon as they were outside she saw a group of them congregated down by the gatehouse where another, newer-looking car was parked.

It was even hotter than yesterday and more humid with no hint of a breeze. Except for the strain on the knees the steps were not such hard work going down as going up; nevertheless by the time they reached the bottom Lillian felt as if she'd completed the first few holes of a golf round. Massimo led her across to a wooden bench overlooking the steps down to the platform of rock and the barely whispering sea. 'I love this house,' he said as they sat down, 'but these steps make me feel my age.'

She laughed. 'I wouldn't want to do them too many times a day. How does Maria cope with shopping?'

'She doesn't. Once she's here she stays put. Rosella does all the shopping. I've thought of putting a lift in, but it would involve a lot of tunnelling and blasting and cost far more than it would add to the house's value.'

'Surely you're not thinking of selling?'

'Sooner or later I will. I love it here because my Lidia loved it, but this coast doesn't have much to offer the boys compared to Sardinia or some of the other jet-set hang-outs. Positano used to be chic but it's become very touristy.'

'At their age a touristy place ought to be what they'd want: discotheques and bars.'

'Fausto's happier in a crypt full of old ledgers, and Fabio prefers to be seen where it's fashionable to be seen. If he was hanging about in low dives with working-class types and slumming tourists I'd be worried about his security. There's safety in numbers with his rich society friends, but I do worry that he may acquire a taste for dangerous vices.'

Lillian took a deep breath that owed nothing to the steps. She said: 'I hope Andrew won't be a bad influence on him.'

Massimo stared deep into her eyes. He said: 'On the contrary, he may be a better influence than some of the crowd he usually hangs around with. Your son has a certain amount of culture and sophistication. Perhaps some of that will rub off on Fabio.'

'Have you met my son?'

He nodded. 'At Fabio's birthday party in Siena last April. I didn't stay long, I didn't want to spoil his fun with his young friends, but, yes, I met Andrew. He has a lot of charm and although he pretends to be shallow and cynical, I could see that he was a man of sensitivity and deep feelings underneath.' He paused, still looking at her. 'The sensitivity he gets from you, I'm quite sure. The shallowness is, I think, a thing of his own making. His looks come from his father's side, I guess, but there's something that connects you and him just as there is with me and Fabrizio although he's the image of his mother. That something, that connection, is what has brought you to Italy. I would go to the ends of the earth for either of my sons.'

A driver tooted his impatience on the next headland. Lillian's eyes were filmed with tears which she managed not to shed.

'We're keeping them waiting,' she said, gesturing at the group of men at the car.

'They are paid to wait,' he said bluntly. 'This is an important moment for you, for us.' He took her right hand and held it between both of his. 'Lillian, if you need to cry, you should cry. There can be no shame between us, the parents of two difficult sons.'

Freeing her hand, she took another deep breath. 'My son is homosexual,' she said, meeting his penetrating gaze.

'I know this,' he said.

'He's more than twice the age of your – Fabio.' The boy's name was finally fixed in her mind. 'He may – corrupt him.'

Massimo smiled into her eyes. 'My dear Lillian, it's possible that my useless son will "corrupt" Andrew, who has given up the practice of interior design to go sailing with him. My son too seems to be homosexual. Of course at seventeen he may grow out of it, although I think not in his case. It's a disappointment, but there are worse things he could be.'

'I can't think of many,' said Lillian wretchedly.

He mocked her with a gentle laugh and patted her hands. 'By the time I was seventeen I'd made love to every available girl in our village as well as some of their mothers and even some of their brothers.' Lillian, with an effort, managed not to look shocked. 'I was lucky,' he continued. 'Girls were supposed to be virgins until they married, but a surprising number of them were available for the grandson of Don Massimo Monfalcone. For many Sicilian boys to this day homosexual activity is one of the more respectable ways of acquiring a bit of experience before marriage.'

Lillian supposed he was hinting at some form of degeneracy

that was thankfully beyond the reach of her imagination. 'I shouldn't be telling you this,' he apologized. 'I'm trying to make the point that boys do things they mostly grow out of. I did. Andrew apparently hasn't. Maybe Fabio will, maybe he won't, but whatever happens I don't think your son will have much to do with it.'

'Between you and Carlo I seem to be getting a whole new sexual education at the age of fifty,' she said.

He laughed again. 'Is that how old you are? One would never think so. I'm more than ten years older than you. I hope Carlo Marini didn't fill your head with a lot of his French gigolo ideas as he has my daughter's. For all his artistic Scottish mother and his Provençal upbringing he's as Italian as I am – more so, since I'm Sicilian.'

'You sound as if you don't approve of him.'

'I'm grateful that he's taking care of Adriana, but I wonder how much he'd be doing if I wasn't her father.'

How much would you be doing if it wasn't for Carlo? Lillian felt like asking, but however she might feel about it, his treatment of Adriana was *his* business, not hers.

He stood up. 'Let's get going. There will be plenty of chances to talk later.'

Lillian gestured at the guards again. 'Are they coming with us?'

'Two of them.'

'Can a man who works with the Vatican really need all this protection?'

'Yes, Lillian, he can. These are dangerous times.'

As she rose, a sudden thought struck Lillian, and a hot and humid morning was immediately chill. 'Your wife's death was not an accident?' she guessed.

'My first wife, no.'

'And your second wife –?'

'She killed herself,' he said harshly.

'But – this beautiful house, two small sons – why?'

He sighed. 'Later, Lillian, later. There is much to tell you, but this is enough for now.'

The two men who accompanied them were called Federico and Paolo. They could have been, perhaps were, brothers: two dark-haired solidly-built men with long-jawed olive-skinned faces. Despite the heat both wore light windcheaters, presumably to hide their holstered guns. Federico drove, with Paolo beside him. The car, another air-conditioned Mercedes, this one a spacious saloon with smoked-glass windows, inched up the narrow driveway. The supposed rabbit-hunter in moleskin trousers and his jean-clad companion of the day before closed the gates behind them.

They passed through Amalfi which, like Positano, clung to the sides of a steep narrow valley; there was a promenade, a harbour, a scrap of beach packed with sunbathers and splashing children.

Just around the next headland Federico turned onto a steeply rising side-road. The view grew more spectacular with each bend: terraced vineyards, farm cottages on dizzying perches, craggy mountain summits, the great sparkling sheet of the sea.

They parked under a pine tree in the square of a village called Ravello. Federico stayed with the car while Paolo followed a few yards behind as Massimo escorted Lillian on a long meandering walk up shallow steps and down alleyways between houses and garden walls, passing underdressed tourists and overdressed villagers who seemed unbothered by the heat.

Massimo paid for them to enter the grounds of a medium -sized unpretentious villa. It was not the house they'd come to see, he told her, but the view. Paolo again hung back as they passed a small cloister and started down a long promenade lined with lawns and flowerbeds. Hydrangeas and red-hot-pokers predominated. The scent of jasmine and honeysuckle wafted down from a frame over their heads.

The promenade ended in a whitewashed stone belvedere, decorated with a half-dozen white marble busts of the Caesars. At one end a stone-arched gazebo afforded some shade and it was here that Massimo stopped to point out details of a view that took Lillian's breath away. Paolo stood in the shelter of a hedge five yards from them.

To the left, beyond a mountainous peninsula, the Gulf of Salerno faded to a blur in the hazy horizon. To the right, behind a rugged pine-clad crest, the far side of Amalfi could be seen: pink roofs, yellow and white walls. Two more headlands were visible on that side, the Monfalcone castle on one of them. Below the belvedere a sheer drop of several hundred feet ended in more vineyards. Lower down, the slow snake of traffic on the coast road was like a line of children's toys.

'My Lidia loved to come up here and look down on our *castello*,' he said. 'She lived here almost permanently and I came down every weekend from Rome.' He paused before going on: 'You asked why she killed herself. She was very depressed after the birth of both our sons. Some women get like this – you know?' Lillian nodded. 'The doctor was giving her barbiturates to help her sleep and after Fabio was born, when one of her stupid friends chose this time to tell her about me and Clara, she took an overdose.'

'Clara was –?'

'Adriana's mother. She'd been my mistress for seven years when I met Lidia and I only stopped seeing her for the first few months of my marriage.'

Lillian decided to be presumptuous, something she never dreamed of being in England. 'Why did you need a wife and a mistress?' she asked.

He laughed delightedly. 'Come on, Lillian. I don't believe you're that naïve. From the minute I saw her I knew I had to marry Lidia. She was eighteen, so beautiful, so fragile. I was forty-four, I'd been a widower for twenty-two years. I wanted to own her, possess her, make her the mother of my children. I worshipped her, but –' he spread his hands – 'she was only a girl and I was used to women. I thought it was better to go back to Clara than the whores I used to go to before. Men need this, Lillian, they need mistresses – or whores.'

Jack Pemberton was rumoured to have been carrying on with a married woman for many years, a liaison on which his wife, to the infuriation of many at the golf club, had never once passed comment or judgement. Lillian had heard the gossip about Jack Pemberton, but she knew there had never been any about George.

'Not all men need it,' she told Massimo Monfalcone quietly and confidently. 'I'm quite sure my husband never had a mistress or went with – whores.' This last word, which she had seen in print but never used before, sounded strange from her own mouth.

'Perhaps he did and you never found out,' he dared to say.

Lillian resisted the urge to slap him. 'No,' she said firmly.

'Then I wonder where your son gets it from,' Massimo said with a casual laugh.

'Not from me, I assure you,' said Lillian quickly. She laughed at her primness. Massimo smiled and led her out of the gazebo. They descended some steps into what must have been landscaped years ago as a patch of woodland, almost English in appearance. Walking to a bench in the shade of an oak tree that might have graced a Sussex village green, they sat down. Paolo leaned against a pine trunk some twenty feet away and lit a cigarette. The air smelt of pine and, faintly, jasmine against a background aroma that was perhaps simply the smell of summer, of parched soil and dried-up plants. Massimo smiled at her again. He said: 'You have a million questions to ask me.'

She laughed. 'A million-and-one!'

'Start with the one,' he said.

'Adriana was born before you married Lidia?'

'Five years before.'

'Why didn't you marry her mother when she became pregnant or if not then, after your wife died?'

'I don't know why you're so interested in Clara. She's the least important of the women in my life. And although I feel a certain responsibility to her, Adriana is the least important of my children.'

He was even more heartless than Carlo had prepared Lillian to expect. 'She's the mother of your grandchild,' she reminded him.

'Yes, but born on the wrong side of the blanket.'

'Only because you didn't marry her mother.'

He held up his hands as if to fend off the blow she was

mentally launching. 'All right,' he acquiesced. 'I didn't marry Clara because Clara was my mistress. It's only in America – and perhaps sometimes in your country – that men marry their mistresses. When I met Clara, at *La Scala* in Milan, she was what the French call a *poule-de-luxe*, the mistress of one of the city's top industrialists. I became fond of her: by the time Lidia died and I stopped seeing Clara, she'd been my mistress for ten years, but if I'd married her, made her a princess, I'd have been laughed out of every house in Italy. I took care of her, provided for her until she died, I went to her funeral, I continue to provide for Adriana, I shall provide for her child – my grandchild,' he conceded with a smile and added: 'for your sake as much as for my daughter's.'

Lillian gave a small nod to acknowledge this elaborate and rather false-sounding attempt at gallantry. *I could never love a man like you*, she thought to herself, a thought which was, in itself, a surprise. One minute he was turning on the charm at full blast, the next he was showing his callous – perhaps his real – side. Having loved a man who, whatever his faults and failings, she knew to be true, she could never love a man who made a boast of faithlessness.

'It's early,' he now said, 'but shall we go to lunch? This mountain air gives me an appetite.'

They stood up and, as casually as his son on the steps up to the tower yesterday afternoon, he took her arm as, dogged by the watchful Paolo, they followed a winding path through the trees that led them back up to the promenade. Lillian wasn't sure whether she liked him holding her arm or not.

They lunched in a restaurant on the southern edge of the village, with a view of vineyards and the Gulf of Salerno and, looming over everything, the jagged spine of the mountain range.

Federico had moved the car, which was now parked just outside the restaurant. He and Paolo took turns at sitting in the car and eating on the farther side of the dining room with a view of the entrance and the door from the kitchen. The restaurant was a matriarchy: an elegant middle-aged woman greeted them, her daughter took their order and her granddaughters served them. Over lunch – pasta with ham and mushrooms, herb omelettes, a fruity local white wine – he continued to talk about Lidia, the boys' mother, the youngest daughter of a prosperous Neapolitan family with which he'd had unspecified business dealings. He did not seem to think it odd – perhaps in Italy it wasn't odd – that a man in his forties should court a girl of eighteen. Her family had approved the match – no doubt a rich prince was a great catch whatever his age. Lidia had loved him as much as he had loved her, he insisted – after all, she died for love.

It seemed to Lillian that in his mind the tragic ending of this second marriage had given it the status of an operatic love story. Courtesans were also the heroines of grand operas, Lillian was aware, still thinking of Adriana's mother, but Lillian had been raised to despise women who sold themselves whether cheaply or expensively. She couldn't shake off the comparison with Alice's husband and his seedy affair with (the rumour mill had it) a bookmaker's wife.

She would have liked to get the Prince talking about his first marriage which had ended – more Shakespearean than operatic – in the death of his wife and children, but it seemed unreasonable to tax him about this earlier tragedy when he was still caught up in its sequel.

Lunch finished, they returned to the car. Paolo now drove as they descended the winding road to the coast. No messages awaited them after the wearying climb up to the tower. Massimo proposed a siesta.

The great stone walls were an effective thermal barrier: her room remained cool even after she opened the window. Removing her skirt and the striped shirt, she lay on the bed in her underwear and was almost instantly asleep.

When she awoke, the sun was low in the sky. She had slept for four hours again. The worst of the heat had dissipated but it was still humid and the air held the kind of charge that, in Hastings, usually preceded a thunderstorm. She looked out the window. A different man was on guard duty, one of the pair from last night who'd presumably spent the day sleeping. The table was unlaid; perhaps they were to eat indoors. Alfredo had been busy in the garden: the rock plants already looked revived and as well as mowing the grass he'd dug out and re-seeded some of the bare patches.

Rosella again brought tea and ran a bath. Lillian found herself warming to the idea of a life attended by servants. In the wardrobe, after her bath, she found the burgundy dress on a hanger perfectly pressed. In the chest of drawers lay the rest of her clothes, everything washed and ironed, with perfumed sachets.

She decided against wearing her best dress again and settled for another skirt, this one dark-blue, mid-calf and pleated, with a white blouse with a single frill at the neckline and a pair of black low-heeled court shoes. She made up as carefully as she had the previous evening when she'd thought she was only to dine with a prince's son. With make-up the resemblance to Melanie Hamilton faded slightly, she hoped.

When she came downstairs Massimo was again on the phone. Fausto, in tee-shirt and jeans, stood beside him; he bowed at Lillian. The kitchen was in darkness. She went into the lounge and sat beneath the portrait of her grandmother's namesake, the young, inexperienced, betrayed second wife, dead by her own hand. After a few minutes the Prince joined her.

'That was my man in Marseille,' he said. 'It seems these Pasquale people have taken our two boys to Corsica.'

'Do we know where exactly?'

'That's the next stage. I've got Fausto working on it. I like him to do these things. It's good training for when he comes into my business.'

'What will he do – manage one of your hotels?'

'Hotels are only part of my business: restaurants, wholesale liquor, wine of course, soft drinks, real estate. I have an interest in shopping malls in towns in America I'd never heard of before.'

She realized that this rich prince was a very rich prince indeed. He could have bought out George and Laurence Dickinson and Jack Pemberton with his factory. Aware of her presumption, she asked: 'And is the Pope your partner in all of this?'

He smiled. 'The Pope is not my partner in anything. His Holiness does not soil his blessed hands with even Peter's Pence. But the Vatican Bank is a partner in some of my operations.'

'Like the casino you've just bought.

His smile was indulgent, a teacher rewarding an apt pupil. 'Yes.'

'And what else?' She was genuinely interested, not just being nosy. Having been George's bookkeeper in the early years of the business, she'd continued to help with the financial planning of most of his major projects.

Massimo was still smiling. 'My dear Lillian, you go too far. These are matters of great confidence.'

'You're as bad as Carlo,' she grumbled: 'making a mystery of everything.'

'I think you will find *my* mysteries more exciting than those of a painter's son, a gigolo,' he said tantalizingly. 'Tonight I shall tell you some of my mysteries. We'll be dining out, by the way.'

'I'm not sure if I've got the clothes for dining out,' she said. 'What I wore last night is the closest I brought to an evening dress.'

'You're fine as you are,' he assured her. 'This is the holiday season. Chic and casual is what people wear these days. We complement each other rather nicely, don't you think?' It was true: he was wearing a dark-blue long-sleeved shirt – no tie – over white trousers and white moccasins. On him blue-on-white looked dashing and debonair; she worried that white-on-blue made her look like a spinster from Bexhill.

Ignoring her reservations Lillian nodded. 'Is Fausto coming with us?' she asked.

'No, he's going to stay home with a cold supper and go over his notes and man the telephone while we're out.'

She felt guiltily relieved to still have the Prince to herself. 'I'd like a Tom Collins,' she announced, 'please.'

'You shall have one. I'll fix it myself. I've given Alfredo and Maria the night off. They've gone into Naples with Paolo and Federico to have dinner with Luca's family. He's my caretaker, the one with the rabbit-shooting rifle.'

'Poor Maria – all those steps.'

'Paolo and Federico carried her down.'

'Poor them!' said Lillian and he laughed as he went off to fix their drinks, telling her to go outside. The sun was sinking towards a bank of cloud on the horizon. She walked to the terrace wall for a closer inspection of Alfredo's achievements with the lawn. The guard surprised her by saying, 'Please stay near the house, ma'am.' His accent was very American. Obediently she retreated to sit at the table. When Massimo came out with their frosted glasses she whispered what had happened.

'It's all right,' he said. 'They're inclined to be over-cautious when they're not all here.'

'There seem to be a quite lot of them.'

'Six,' he told her, 'including Luca and his cousin who helps him look after the place. Rosella lives here; she has two rooms on the top floor. Federico and Paolo are my most trusted guards; they were with me in Las Vegas. The other two met us in Salerno with the car.'

'Are they all Neapolitans?' He shook his head.

'They are all from my native part of Sicily. Some of them were born in Naples from families who moved here to find work, but a Sicilian is always a Sicilian. I'm related to some of them. Paolo is my second cousin. Luca is his cousin on his mother's side. Federico is a nephew of my wife's, my first wife.'

'I thought he and Paolo –' she struggled with the vowels – 'were brothers.'

'They are alike. It's a Sicilian look.' He hesitated. 'Giancarlo there –' he gestured to the young guard who had spoken to her, his back to them now as he watched the steps and the driveway and the road above which still bustled with hooting cars and coaches – 'is my grandson.' He smiled at her startled expression. 'Yes, Lillian. I am already a grandparent.'

'The children of your first wife didn't all die.'

He shook his head. 'Yes, they did. Giancarlo is from the other side of the blanket, like Adriana. His father, who died in a motorcycle crash, was the result of one of the youthful "indiscretions" I mentioned earlier. His mother is Rosella.'

'Goodness me,' said Lillian mildly. 'Does he know you're his grandfather?'

'Of course, but like all Sicilians he knows the importance of legitimacy. He knows that he could never inherit my title, my wealth. But he is a loyal protector both of me and my legitimate heirs. As I told you yesterday, blood ties are immensely powerful among us Sicilians.' He took a sip of his cocktail.

Lillian played with her glass. She gave voice to a thought that had come to her in the bath. 'All these men with guns, are they – are you – something to do with the *Mafia*?' she asked and was treated to another of his indulgent smiles.

'How much do you know about the Mafia?'

'Only what I've read in books or seen at the cinema.'

'And what's that?' he probed. The guard – his grandson – was clearly listening although he continued to watch the road from the end of the terrace.

'Well, I mostly read autobiographies and mysteries, but I have read a few crime novels set in America and I seem to remember that the Mafia started in Sicily.' She began to wish she hadn't asked what was now a patently absurd question. The sun slid imperiously behind the bank of cloud. The sea was briefly purple, then indigo.

Massimo continued to smile. 'You are right: the Mafia had its origins in Sicily, but not all Sicilians belong to this criminal organisation and not all men who carry guns are gangsters. And no, Lillian, I have nothing to do with the Mafia.'

He stood up. 'Let's go to dinner,' he said. Lillian took a sip of her cocktail and left the rest on the table as she too rose.

'Was your first wife murdered?' she asked, embarking on a line of questioning that had begun to seem as important as that which touched on her son. This time he did not smile.

'Yes,' he said.

'And your children too?' Even as she asked this, it seemed impossible, unbelievable. The waiter returned with their wine.

The restaurant, on a headland overlooking Amalfi, was in a hotel that had once been a convent. Nothing about the décor – glittering chandeliers, gilt-embossed ceiling, gold-painted walls – suggested vows of abstinence and poverty. The huge room was more than half full and newcomers continued to arrive. Lillian and Massimo sat at a table by the open windows which gave onto a terrace, also crowded with diners at lamp-lit tables. Luigi, the other night-shift guard, sat alone at a small outside table that afforded him a view of the Mercedes parked on the ramp facing the hotel lobby one floor below, both entrances to the restaurant and the swinging kitchen doors that were in a constant state of motion as the large team of waiters bustled in and out.

When she baulked at another helping of pasta, Massimo had ordered avocados and grilled plaice. Now he raised his glass to her before tasting it, something Andrew had done hundreds of times in that other comfortable, unadventurous, safe world which he – and now she – had left far behind. Massimo nodded his approval and the wine waiter half filled their glasses before withdrawing on large flat feet in large black shoes. Lillian sipped a wine that was cool, white and piercingly dry and waited for the answer to her second question.

'My children were with their mother,' he said. 'They were all killed together.'

'But you escaped?'

'I was at a meeting on the night when it happened. If I'd been with them, I could have saved them.'

'Who would do such a thing, murder a woman and children?'

He sighed. 'Mine is not the only family in Sicily to whom this sort of thing happened.'

'Did they find the person who killed your family?'

'It was not just a person who killed my family, Lillian, it was a tradition.' He lowered his voice. 'The person who killed my wife and my children is dead. I didn't kill him myself, but I gave the order to have him killed. But this person had sons, a brother, an uncle, cousins. I could have had them all killed, as they had with my family, but I decided to stop the killing after this one man.'

This casually summarised saga of murder and revenge set him further from her husband than any man she had ever met. Hastings had its dramas, even its share of murders – town-centre knifings, girls raped and strangled on the Downs – and Jack Pemberton's rumoured adultery or Nigel Sadler's imprisonment for assault were not the only scandals that had touched the lives of people she knew; but she'd never expected that she would one day enjoy the hospitality of a man who had cold-bloodedly (or more likely, in his case, hot-bloodedly) ordered another man's death, albeit one who'd massacred his wife and children. In less than twenty-four hours the Prince had confirmed her initial impression of being in the company of a dangerous man. Her mother and George would be turning in their graves, Lillian thought, but there was no denying that she *was* enjoying both the hospitality and the storytelling that went with it.

'This man's family killed your brothers and your father?' she asked, wanting to know more.

'And my grandfather and my uncles and my cousins.'

'This is the reason for all these guards that go everywhere with you?'

'This is part of the reason for that.'

'These are the "enemies" you mentioned yesterday?'

He smiled grimly. 'These are some of them.'

'But why are they your enemies?' she persisted.

'They are my enemies now,' he said. 'But before me they were my grandfather's enemies, and before him his grandfather's enemies. These things go on for generations. *"Vendettas"*, they are called.'

'But why?'

He shrugged. 'Perhaps, in the beginning, there was a reason, some wrong done by one of my ancestors, but after a time there is only the endless hatred and more killings. Historians blame it on the Arab blood that runs in the veins of all Sicilians.'

It was like something out of the Old Testament, Lillian thought: *thy children and thy children's children*. 'Do you still have a home in Sicily?' she asked.

'I have land there, vineyards, and a house, partly ruined, but

I rarely visit. And my sons, although I have taken them to see it, their heritage, will never live there.'

'Why not?'

He was visibly stiff with rage – or tension. 'Because it is not safe for them to live in Sicily.'

'They wouldn't be safe from these people?' Her heart began to pound. Andrew was with one of these boys.

'Away from Sicily they should be safe,' Massimo said as two waiters arrived bearing avocados and thickly buttered bread: 'at least from this vendetta.'

A large party was noisily settling into chairs at the centre table on the terrace outside. Luigi was forking a quantity of spaghetti to his mouth from an overflowing plate; his eyes checked every one of the new arrivals. The moon spread a pale shimmering band across the sea beyond the headland, but the bank of dark cloud was climbing slowly higher on the horizon, swallowing stars in its path, and the evening air still held the heavy electric charge that Lillian had felt on rising from her siesta.

'Death,' Massimo pronounced, 'is not a subject for the dinner table.' While they ate, he spoke about the happier side of his early life in Sicily's Cammarata mountains with no further references to the cycle of violence nor, thankfully, to his juvenile sexual exploits. The village was Monfalcone, which his great-great-grandfather had adopted as the family name when his estate of farms and vineyards and olive groves became the largest and most prosperous. Substitute England's gloomy weather for Sicily's sultry heat and his childhood sounded not too different from Lillian's among the marshes and hop-fields of the Rother Levels. Church had figured prominently in both their lives, as had fresh air and simple country pursuits. Where she'd had a bicycle he'd had a horse, but they had both spent a lot of time on foot in the land around their homes. His family had lived a rustic, peasant life in what sounded like a manor house, whereas Lillian had been raised with middle-class aspirations in a working-class cottage in Rye.

Death was, apparently, a suitable topic for the coffee stage, for now he returned to the feud which had haunted his family's history and culminated in the slaughter of his first wife and their children.

The Monfalcones' bitterest enemies came from the small town of Villalba, fifteen kilometres away; no one now remembered the origins of the rivalry between the two clans, but it culminated in a twenty-year vendetta that only ended when, in 1856, the local Mafia chieftain ('Yes, Lillian,' he smiled, 'the Mafia does have a part in my family's story') imposed a truce by arranging a marriage between a thirteen-year-old Villalba girl whose male relatives had all been wiped out and a seventeen-year-old Monfalcone halfwit who had been spared assassination by virtue of his harmlessness. A tenuous peace existed for decades as the rivals slowly rebuilt their numbers through intermarriage and the importation of cousins from other parts of Sicily.

Lillian stirred sugar into the tiny cup in front of her. His chilling tale was making her shiver, or perhaps she shivered because the encroaching black clouds over the sea, in which distant flashes of lightning were intermittently visible, were pushing cooler air towards the land and the open windows of the restaurant.

In 1916, he went on, the feud was abruptly resumed. Don

Massimo Monfalcone was shot in the heart in broad daylight in Monfalcone's tiny piazza by a distant cousin-by-marriage from Villalba. A group of farmworkers who'd been waiting to present petitions to the Don hacked the assassin to pieces. The Don's eldest son, Faustino, Massimo's father, ordered reprisals against the enemy clan but within weeks he and his two brothers were killed in clandestine counterattacks.

The mantle of head of the family and the responsibility to continue the vendetta now passed to the eldest of the old Don's brothers. But after three months he too was dead, felled by a sniper's bullet whilst out on his horse. During the next year the remaining brothers and many nephews and cousins were also murdered, even some who were still infants, together with some of the widows and daughters of the dynasty. Massimo, studying for the priesthood at the age of sixteen, was spared ('There's some squeamishness about murdering priests,' he told Lillian, 'although it's been overcome often enough'). By the end of 1917 he and an older sister who was a nun were the only survivors from the heart of the Monfalcone clan, and the enemy tribe had been equally decimated.

The task of ending the bloodbath fell on Don Vito Cascio Ferro in Palermo, revered as the greatest Mafia chieftain of all time, the first of the fraternity's 'modernizers'.

'This is part of the traditional role of the Mafia which you won't have read in any of your books or seen in movies,' Massimo said. 'It's not only about extortion and gambling rackets and liquor smuggling. Life in Sicily, even in the towns and cities but especially in the villages, is still very feudal, even today, so the Mafia chief is like the medieval 'Lord of the Manor' in rural England. Sometimes these vendettas are battles for supremacy between rival Mafia groups, but the *capo*, as the chief is called, is just as likely to act as an arbiter in disputes between clans, a sort of cross between the parish priest and a magistrate.'

At the end of 1917 Don Vito Cascio Ferro summoned Massimo and invited him to leave the seminary and rebuild the family. A similar offer was made to one of the survivors in Villalba and the two men swore a ceremonial truce in front of Don Vito and witnesses from the two communities. The seminarian became a producer of wine and olive oil. As a farmer and landowner, he was able to avoid being drafted into the terrible war still raging in the north. Sicilian farms produced a vital proportion of the food on which Victor Emmanuel's armies marched and the Monfalcone estate was the biggest in the region. During 1918, as the war slowly ground towards surrender and peace, Massimo sowed a few wild oats and then married Liliana, a distant cousin from Palermo who was the prettiest of such cousins trotted out for his benefit.

Lillian thought again of Arthur Sadler who'd jilted her and died at Montecassino after helping to liberate Massimo's precious Sicily from the Fascists. George had fought, miraculously unscathed, with Monty's Eighth Army in the deserts of Egypt and Libya. Childhood tuberculosis had left Wilfred with weak lungs which secured him exemption, but Robert had been evacuated from Dunkirk and returned to France on D-Day. She guessed that Massimo had also evaded military service during World War Two. To Lillian this was despicable. But his story enthralled her, and she had to hear its terrible climax.

'Then the enemy clan killed your new family,' she guessed.

'Yes,' he said. His dark eyes narrowed as he frowned. 'Then

they killed my Liliana and our babies.'

Lillian did not prompt him again, realising that this was still a painful episode which he now planned to tell her in any case. But before he could begin there was another interruption, this one on a spectacular scale. An intense flash illuminated the terrace outside and almost simultaneously there came a tremendous roar of sound that shook the open windows and set glasses rattling all over the room. Lillian gasped with surprise. Screams and shouts rose both inside the restaurant and on the terrace where many diners jumped to their feet, including Luigi whose hand scrabbled inside his jacket. Behind him a chair fell with a crash, and he wheeled round. From the kitchen came another crash.

Massimo smiled at Lillian as he calmly lifted his cup. 'I hope you're not nervous of thunder,' he said. 'This is going to be quite a storm.'

'We get some heavy storms in Sussex,' she told him. 'The updraught from the Downs traps the thunderclouds and they clatter around for hours.' With hands that only slightly trembled she picked up her cup and drained it.

Another flash of lightning was accompanied by an audible crack before another huge rumble of thunder reverberated down the mountainside, again rattling windows and glasses. There was more laughter than screaming this time. The group at the terrace's centre table cheered. Luigi resumed his seat, his hand no longer inside his jacket. A few diners were calling for the waiters, two waving money to indicate that they wished to pay and leave.

With no preamble of pattering drops the rain came down in a sudden torrent as if a waterfall had been diverted onto the roof of the hotel. Massimo quickly closed the window beside their table. Outside there was pandemonium: women screamed, men shouted, chairs fell, tables rocked, glasses broke. In the few seconds it took people to reach the shelter of the restaurant their clothes were drenched, revealing that some of the women wore very little under their light frocks. Only a handful of the terrace diners could be reseated inside; the waiters could barely move for the crush of those waiting for tables.

'Let's get out of here,' said Massimo. He signalled not to a waiter but to Luigi who was standing beside the door to the terrace, hair plastered to his scalp, the gun holster clearly outlined beneath his wet cotton jacket. He inched his way to their table and opened a path through the throng as Massimo escorted Lillian out to the now crowded bar and down the marble staircase to the foyer. Some of the sodden diners had been seated at coffee tables; a harassed waiter was attempting to establish which course of their meal had been abandoned in the downpour.

'Don't we have to pay for our dinner?' Lillian asked.

He smiled and shook his head. 'No, we don't. This is one of the hotels I own. We can't possibly go back to the house in this. I'll see if they have a room we can use. Wait here with Luigi, please.' One of the receptionists abandoned her client as the Prince approached the desk. After the briefest exchange of words he returned with a key. 'We'd better not take the elevator,' he said, 'in case there's a power cut.'

'Are we staying the night?' enquired Lillian, apprehensive at the thought that she might have to share a room with him and possibly with the bodyguard as well.

'Hopefully not. These summer storms are usually short and

sharp, but we'll have some privacy until it's over.'

With Luigi now guarding their rear they climbed to the third floor and entered a large room furnished with two double beds and a brocade suite. A corner chiffonier concealed a bar. Lillian declined anything else to drink. She looked out the window while Massimo took a Coca-Cola to Luigi who had stayed in the corridor outside.

They were two floors above the restaurant from which rose a babble of voices. The terrace resembled the scene of a terrorist attack: chairs and even a table overturned, food-plates and wineglasses overflowing with water. The rain continued to fall in a thick grey sheet. A river flowed down the steep driveway from the front of the hotel to the main road, thick with debris from the cliff and soil and plants from the flower borders. Amazingly traffic continued to inch its way along the road, although two stalled cars added to the hazard as other drivers negotiated this obstruction as well as the flood of water and debris that streamed across the road and cascaded along the wall of an old house before tumbling down a flight of steps which appeared to lead to its basement entrance. Lightning flashed every few moments but the accompanying rumbles of thunder indicated that the storm was already moving away.

Massimo poured himself a brandy and lit a cheroot before sitting down in one of the brocade chairs. Lillian seated herself in the other armchair and looked at him expectantly. He smiled and went on with his appalling story as if there had not been this twenty-minute hiatus.

'By 1924,' he said, 'Liliana had given me three sons and a daughter. A cousin from Palermo had volunteered to return and help me; he married a local girl and started a family. My mother was still alive, she had two rooms in my house, but she'd gone white-haired and literally mad from grief while I was in the seminary. She spoke to nobody: not to me, the last of her sons, not even to the old woman who looked after her.'

He drew on his cigar.

'Alfredo and Maria looked after us. Maria was already our cook and housekeeper. She'd had many miscarriages and was now barren, but she helped my wife with our children. I made Alfredo my bodyguard: he travelled with me any time I was away from Monfalcone. His father and grandfather had worked for my father and grandfather. I'd grown up with him – he's a few years older than me: he'd taught me to fish and hunt rabbits. In the twenty months of the feud in 1916 and -17 Alfredo killed three of my family's enemies. He still has a scar from a bullet-wound in one leg and a knife-scar on his right arm from a man he killed with his bare hands.'

This time Lillian not so much shivered as shuddered. This wasn't the plot of a film or an opera, this – for Massimo and his sons and his servants – was the real world. But it wasn't her world. She felt, again, a frighteningly long way from Hastings, from her garden and golf and walks on the Downs and bridge evenings with the Sadlers.

Massimo ignored – or failed to notice – her shudder. He went on:

'I made my cousin manager of my estates while I concentrated on investing in the "other end" of farming: slaughterhouses and cold-stores and canneries. Because the wine in Villalba was superior to the Monfalcone wine, I even opened a wine-bottling plant in the heartland of my enemies.'

'Wasn't that dangerous?' she asked. He nodded.

'Yes it was, but by bringing employment and extra prosperity to their town I was hoping to generate goodwill toward myself and my family. The enemy clan didn't accept my offer to share ownership of the new factory, but they sent their wine to be bottled there. There was every indication that peace, if not brotherhood, would prevail between us. Like me, the survivors were breeding new sons from cousins who had previously fled the vendetta.

'So –' he sighed heavily – 'now we come to the summer of 1924 when my poor mad mother hanged herself in a wardrobe after her old maidservant died of a heart attack, which seemed to be one death too many for her to take. But as always, there is death and there is new life. I had four children and Liliana was pregnant again. We decided that our youngest son – I'd been a third son – would become a priest and our daughter would become a nun. When I left the seminary, I promised the monsignore that I would give one of my sons and one of my daughters to God.'

Lillian almost smirked at this. Parcelling off two of his infant children to the church: really it was as ridiculous as George's doomed resolve to make a builder of Andrew!

'And then –' he paused and took another deep puff at his cigar – 'then we come to a night in September of that year and a man who came across the mountains from Villalba. He knew the mountains as well as I did. He came alone and on foot, avoiding horse tracks and even the paths used by shepherds and goatherds.

'He had been a boy of fifteen when his father made the same journey in 1916 and killed my grandfather and restarted the vendetta. He was in a TB sanatorium in the Piedmontese Alps all though that savage time.'

'He was the one you made the oath with in front of the Head of the Mafia,' Lillian guessed. Massimo rewarded her with a thin-lipped smile but his eyes remained cold.

'Yes he was. And on this night he had come to renege on that oath, to cauterise the wound to his family's honour when blood from his hand mingled with mine.' This sounded like a line translated directly from opera, Lillian thought.

'It was *you* he came to kill,' she said breathlessly.

This time he did not smile as he nodded again. 'But why didn't he try to kill you in – his own town?' She lacked the confidence to attempt 'Villalba'.

'Because any time I went to Villalba I took a dozen armed men with me, not just Alfredo. He'd have needed a small army to try anything in Villalba. In Monfalcone he thought to catch me off guard and unprotected.'

'But you weren't there that night,' she remembered.

Another nod. 'By blind chance – some would say by Divine Grace – I was at the priest's house on the other side of the village.' He took a sip of his brandy.

'Normally, any time I was away from Monfalcone my cousin and two of the most trusted workers would move into my house to look after my family. But this night, because I was only going to the village and would stay no longer than it took to drink a glass of wine with the priest, I made no special provision for my family's protection. It was late summer, harvest time, the estate workers had had an exhausting day in the fields: I hadn't the heart to ask any of them to stay up and keep watch on the house when I would be gone for less than an hour. My cousin promised to keep an eye on the house, but he too had spent the day harvesting and his young wife was pregnant again, like my Liliana. He fell asleep in his own cottage on the estate, and so did Alfredo in his.

'The only person in my house, apart from Liliana and the children, was Maria, in the kitchen at the rear of the central part of the house. This was the original house. Two wings had been added in the nineteenth century, with timber and plaster rendering that imitated the English Tudor style. In summer we lived mainly in the west wing, which was exposed to any cooling breezes; in winter we favoured the east wing, which was sheltered by a stand of pine trees and some outbuildings that were used for stabling and storage.

'Liliana was in the nursery with all the children on the first floor of the west wing as the man from Villalba approached the house, no doubt using the outbuildings for cover. The sun had just set. The ground floor was in darkness, and he would have assumed that I was upstairs with my family. He removed a bale of hay from under the eaves of the stables, dragged it past the kitchen without Maria seeing him and scattered it along the lower walls of the west wing. It was a humid evening, the windows had been left open for ventilation. He pulled the heavy curtains through and torched the hay in several places. Presumably he then just crept off the same way he'd come; he wouldn't have wanted to risk being in the vicinity when the estate workers came running.'

Lillian became aware that she was holding her breath, as if witnessing this horrifying event herself. A growing harshness in Massimo's voice betrayed the fact that retelling this story had brought back all the raw emotion that accompanied it forty-two years ago. The brandy swirled unnoticed in the glass he held, his cigar had gone out on an ashtray at his elbow. The rain continued to lash at the windows, but the lightning flashes were fainter now and the rumbles of thunder came from deeper in the mountains.

'Maria was warming a bottle of milk for the baby. She heard a crackling sound and rushed to the window in time to see the living-room next to the kitchen explode into an inferno – its walls were hung with old tapestries, dry as parchment. The staircase up to the first floor was already on fire, but there was a corridor connecting the attics of both wings to the central part of the house, along which the family could escape. Maria ran to the front of the house where we had a gong for calling the workers to communal meals. She banged on the gong and then ran back into the main house and up the central staircase and along the landing to where a narrower staircase led up to the second floor, to the attics. But there was so much smoke and heat that she couldn't get along the corridor to the west wing, she could see my family wouldn't be able to escape that way. So she retreated downstairs and outside, thinking that my wife might throw the children down to her from a window before jumping out herself. But every room on the first floor was now glowing like a furnace, some of the windows had burst with the heat, flames were coming out of the attic windows and even through the roof where the tiles had begun to explode like fireworks.

'Less than five minutes after the fire started my cousin and Alfredo and some of the estate workers arrived and organised a relay with buckets of water from the stables, but they were too late. The roof of the west wing collapsed.

'By now I had left the priest's house. As I came round the hill that separates the village from the estate I saw the glow beside the pine trees and smoke rising into the night sky. I knew instantly what had happened. Somehow I even knew that this was not an accident but the work of my enemies. I whipped my horse into a gallop and I called on God to spare my children. I promised Him my daughter and *two* of my sons if He would let them live. But if he took them I swore to renounce Him, give no future child of mine to His service. "No more bargains but this one," I told Him.'

Recollected anger had turned Massimo's face as red as it must have been that night as he flogged his horse and screamed out the terms of this final pact with his Maker. There were tears in his dark eyes as he took a deep breath and went on:

'The thick stone walls of the original house prevented the fire from spreading, but the west wing was totally gutted. It was many hours before the estate workers and villagers had dampened the wreckage enough to start looking for my precious family.

'We found them under some charred rafters that had fallen from the roof through to the living-room floor, taking all but one wall of the nursery with them. Liliana and the older children were unrecognisable – two of the children were so fused together by the heat that I had to bury them in the same coffin – but apart from some scorching of the shawl he was wrapped in, the baby was unmarked. His mother had curled him so tightly within the protection of her own body that he looked as if he had only slipped into unconsciousness in his sleep.'

He drained his cognac in a single gulp.

'God didn't seem to want any deals with me.'

***

The rain was now only hitting the windows in sporadic gusts, and the distant thunder had ceased to rumble: the storm was moving further away. The sound of a car horn on the road below the hotel was a startling intrusion.

'How completely terrible,' Lillian said, aware that no words were adequate. She found herself visualising George as she had last seen him in the hospital, three hours after his death, not yet cold but somehow shrunken, a shadow of the lumberjack she had married.

Massimo was reading her thoughts. 'But you have lost your husband,' he said. They were silent for some moments, each lost in remembered grief. He rose to refill his brandy glass. Lillian nodded when he waved the bottle at her and accepted a small measure in a balloon glass, from which she took a tentative sip: she hadn't drunk neat spirits since her days in London with Andrew. Thus fortified, she broke the silence:

'His name was George. He had a mild stroke in 1959 and a more serious one in 1962 which took him a year to recover from. Then, last year – last July – he had a very severe one that knocked him too far down. In the end he died of a heart attack.'

She could go on to describe the hours – days, weeks – she had spent at George's bedside. She could also tell him about the child she had lost, her first son who'd died in the last month of her pregnancy, died inside her, pitching her into a deeper darker grief than any other death she had known. But these were not stories that she was ready to tell to a stranger on a stormy night. As she shifted uncomfortably on the hard brocaded upholstery, she was also uncomfortable with the fact that the story of her loss had taken less than twenty seconds to tell, whereas his had occupied them through dinner and beyond. His eyes, watching her, were still filmed with tears, but that was as likely to be the residue of his own revisited tragedy as sympathy for hers. Forcing herself to reciprocate his honesty, she added:

'I didn't feel the need to curse God for it. I'm not sure what I felt when he finally – got his release. A sort of numbness is what I mostly remember.' She drank some more of her brandy. Not even to the Sadlers had she attempted to articulate the precise quality of her suffering; nor had she and George made a habit of expressing their personal feelings with this 'Continental' candour. It felt strange, disturbing.

'You English are always so phlegmatic in the face of tragedy,' he said, his voice still harsh. 'In Italy we're hot-blooded and completely irrational. I wanted to kill God for what He'd done to me. But the Sicilian code of honour required me to avenge the murder of my family, and I settled for that.'

Lillian enjoyed another delicious shudder. It was hard to believe she was not reading – or dreaming – this conversation. 'But you only had "this one man" killed?' She recalled his exact words while they were waiting for their avocados.

Massimo nodded. 'He had a wife the same age as my Liliana and children as young as mine. I was entitled to take all their lives for the lives he'd taken. Alfredo and my cousin asked to be the ones to carry out my revenge because they blamed themselves for failing to protect my family. But I told them to do nothing against this man's wife and children, only against him.'

'But weren't his children –' she was beginning to see the relentless logic of this barbaric code of so-called 'honour' which was like no set of principles she had ever believed in – 'obliged to revenge themselves on you later?'

'Yes, but I decided to take that chance in order to prevent

another bloodbath. I hoped his children would grow up to understand that their father had been punished for what he'd done to my family, that I regarded the episode as closed and that they should too.'

'And they did?' Another shudder as she pictured an assassin overpowering Luigi in the hall and then bursting into the room to cut the Prince down in a hail of bullets.

'Our vendetta became pointless once I left Sicily for Rome. There were no more Monfalcones in Monfalcone.'

'Your cousin didn't stay on?'

He shook his head. 'Without me there it was just a matter of time before our enemies picked on him, so I moved him to Turin in 1925 and set him up with a grocery store. He's retired now but he owns a small chain of supermarkets, all managed by his sons and sons-in-law.'

'But your enemies are still in Sicily?'

'Two sons of the man who murdered my family are still alive. One emigrated to America after the war; he teaches at a high-school in Chicago. The other son stayed in Villalba and still produces some of the best wine in the region. I've never met him, but my lawyers sold him my bottling plant in 1947.' He picked up his cigar and then put it down again unlit.

'There's probably no real threat to my boys any more, but I wouldn't want them to live in Monfalcone all the same. This year I let Fabio take Andrew to the islands off Sicily's north coast in the yacht, but I gave him identity papers in a false name and made him promise not to set foot on the mainland.'

His words provided a jolting reminder that while she sat here relishing this melodramatic saga, her son was in some still unidentified location with the youngest member of this dangerous and ill-starred family. Anxiety added to her discomfort, she shifted again on the lumpy upholstery.

Massimo rose to his feet. 'It's late. We'd better get back to the house. The rain's stopped.'

Lillian looked at her watch. It was after eleven. Thanks to the coffee and the brandy and the tale he'd told she didn't feel the least bit sleepy. Rising, she followed him to the door. In the corridor Luigi was fully alert in spite of his long vigil.

They took the lift to the ground floor. There was noise from the dining room, but the lobby was deserted apart from a solitary receptionist to whom Massimo returned the room-key. Outside Luigi gave some money to a porter who'd been watching the Mercedes. Like the other cars parked on the slope, its wheels were muddied and clogged with debris. Overhead the sky was clear again, as moonlit and starry as yesterday's.

The short ride back to the castle was an obstacle course, so many rocks had fallen from the cliff; Luigi bumped over the rubble and drove slowly round the larger obstructions. The driveway down to the gatehouse had already been swept clean. The man with the rifle came out of the garage with a lantern and opened the gates. Massimo relieved him of the lamp to augment the moonlight as they started up the now slippery steps. The Prince led with Luigi close behind Lillian in case she lost her footing. There was a strong smell of rain-freshened gorse.

They paused for breath on the second bend. Massimo set the lantern down at their feet. On the terrace above them a shadow detached itself from the wall of the house. In the moonlight Lillian recognized Rosella's son, the Prince's grandson, still on guard duty. He called out softly in Italian. Massimo replied and then spoke to Luigi who left them and went ahead up the steps. Massimo's teeth gleamed as he smiled at Lillian:

'Any more questions?'

She laughed. 'Of course!'

'Go on then,' he prompted.

'Was it Alfredo or your cousin that killed the man who set fire to your house?'

'Guess,' he teased her.

He'd already told her that the aged gardener/chauffeur had killed three of the Monfalcones' enemies in the clan war; Lillian opted for 'Alfredo' and was oddly gratified when Massimo smiled and nodded.

'How did he do it?'

He gave a loud laugh. 'Lillian, really! Your curiosity is positively morbid.'

'Tell me,' she demanded.

'Well – in New York we could have dropped him in the Hudson River with his feet in a bucket of cement.' His expression was serious but she was sure this was another tease.

'The gangsters don't really do that, do they?'

'They do,' he assured her. 'In Las Vegas they bury people in the desert, not always killing them first.'

Lillian shuddered again. 'What did Alfredo do to the man who killed your family?'

He smiled grimly. 'A bullet is just as effective as a bucket of cement. He shot him outside a café in Villalba.'

'But – weren't there any people around?'

'Of course. This was not a random killing: this was an execution – a public execution. Upwards of twenty people witnessed it.'

'And nobody tried to prevent it?'

'Alfredo knew the man came regularly to the same café. He just came round a corner and shot him. The witnesses would have recognised Alfredo and accepted why he was there.'

'Did he go to prison?'

He shook his head. 'No.'

'But – all those witnesses –'

'All said they weren't there or they saw nothing, it happened too fast, the killer came from nowhere, nobody knew who he was.' He smiled at her look of puzzlement.

'This is Sicily, Lillian. There is a code of secrecy and silence – the Sicilian word is *omertà* – over these matters, over anything involving blood and vengeance. I could be sentenced to death for breaking this code tonight to tell you the history of my family.'

Lillian was sure this was an exaggeration. She shivered in the night air.

'You're cold,' said Massimo. 'Let's get you inside.' And, as he had at Ravello, he took her arm again and side-by-side they climbed the last and steepest flight of steps, which only yesterday she had climbed arm-in-arm with the older of his sons. To her amazement it now seemed quite agreeable to be in physical contact with this man, the father of Andrew's teenage paramour, who was by his own admission a lothario and, if only by proxy, a murderer.

Keyed up by the storm and the coffee and brandy and by the violent story he had told her, she spent a restless night.

All this Sicilian hatred and thirst for revenge was unfathomable. Did English emotions run shallower? She thought not. She had loved George for thirty-one years. And look where love for her son had brought her.

The Prince had gone on from the loss of his first wife to other passions: Adriana's mother, the boys' mother who would die by her own hand, and he'd hinted at more mistresses and even whores. Lillian would never love another man, nor could George have ever loved another woman. So perhaps English love was, after all, deeper and truer; Italian love was all mixed up with melodrama and honour and that Catholic veneration of the dead which to an English Protestant, even to one who had 'lapsed', seemed sinister and unnatural.

Massimo was still so deeply affected by something that had happened in 1924, when Lillian was at primary school with the Sadler boys and a ruffian called George Rutherford. Today she had not stopped grieving for her dead husband – it was grief that had launched her on this journey – but once she had seen Andrew she would go back to her humdrum life in Sussex and be at peace with the world, with herself.

Her quest had led her to unexpected places and to some extraordinary people: and it wasn't over yet!

In Hastings a storm such as yesterday's would have moderated temperatures by several degrees; in Amalfi Monday dawned hot and bright again.

There had been no news from the Prince's agents last night, and over breakfast on the terrace he reported only that his 'man in Marseille' was now in Corsica trying to make contact with the Pasquale family.

'Why can't he just phone them?'

'There are houses in the mountains – even whole villages – which don't have a telephone,' Massimo explained.

'It's taking such a long time to find them,' she grumbled.

For today's distraction he proposed a visit to Capri. Fausto would stay in with his homework and the telephone. They would make the crossing in the yacht in which 'our two truants' had been cruising: after sailing it to the mainland from Giglio at first light on Saturday, Fausto had paid the two sons of the Porto Santo Stefano harbourmaster to crew it down to Amalfi; they'd arrived this morning after laying up at Ischia during the storm.

Lillian decided that golfing slacks and a blouse would be appropriate for messing about on boats and she changed into walking shoes. Inevitably the two bodyguards accompanied them down to the platform of rock at sea level, both in jeans and tee-shirts with their shoulder holsters openly displayed. Federico – or Paolo: Lillian had forgotten which was which – carried a basket in which bottles clinked. The Prince was sporting a Las Vegas tee-shirt and garish Bermuda shorts that exposed gnarled legs as hairy as a goat's. Lillian was not looking forward to being seen with him in those shorts in Capri.

Two darkly-tanned teenagers in swimming trunks were scrubbing the boat's deck. It was a cabin-cruiser rather than a sailing vessel, some thirty feet long, sleek and powerful-looking with an array of up-to-date instruments in front of the wheel. Behind the canopied wheelhouse was a sitting and dining area; below decks, a tiny galley, two cabins and a minuscule toilet and shower. Jack Pemberton had a longer if more ungainly boat moored on the river at Rye, which George and Lillian had been invited onto a few times during the years of their business association. Massimo gave the two boys what looked like a generous tip and they scampered up the steps to the gatehouse in their trunks, carrying nothing more than bundled-up shirts and jeans. One of the guards took the wheel and started the engine while the other cast off.

The sea was not much choppier than the Venice lagoon. Half-an-hour out they stopped and drifted while the three men fished, Massimo off the stern, the two guards off the bow. Recollecting similar days on the beach or in a hired boat off the Sussex coast with George and the Sadlers, Lillian stretched out on a padded banquette behind the Prince. A light breeze deflected the heat, and a reflection of the sunlight on the sea danced on the canvas canopy over her head. She fell deeply asleep, waking an hour or more later to find they were under way again, the broken-backed hump of Capri looming ahead of them. Massimo was at the wheel. Nobody had caught anything, he told her. He passed her a thermos and she poured a lemon-coloured drink into two plastic cups. One sip told her it was Tom Collins; she toasted him with a laugh. The two guards were sprawled at the bow, their feet up on the rails, swigging beer from bottles.

The sea became busier as they approached the island, with ships of many sizes from steamers to sailing-boats and dinghies, a few energetic swimmers, a man on water-skis behind a skimming motorboat. Federico and Paolo wolf-whistled two bikini-clad girls in a pedalo and were ignored.

A weather-beaten fisherman in sagging shorts hailed them as they approached the quayside. One of the guards threw him a rope which he tied to a rusty iron ring. Leaving him to look after the boat, the two guards, now wearing windcheaters over their gun holsters, followed Massimo and Lillian along the jetty to the bustling waterfront. Behind a row of houses and hotels, pink and white, the ground rose in steep green terraces, dotted with villas, to a pink-and-white town that hugged the hilltop.

They joined the queue for the funicular railway, a facility, she told him, that her hometown boasted; but Hastings' two short steep cliff ascents were feeble in comparison to Capri's longer gentler climb through vineyards and gardens blazing with bougainvillea. Across the glittering bay Vesuvius with its two peaks loomed over the dense skyline of Naples; the storm had blown away the haze she had seen from the train on Saturday.

The station at the top of the funicular gave into a small pretty square teeming with day-trippers. Massimo's were not the most appalling shorts on display. Hordes of idling pedestrians slowed their progress past shops, restaurants and houses down a narrow lane that followed the contours of the hill, rising and falling.

They stopped at a modest restaurant where an overgrown wisteria shaded the outside tables. The guards sat at a separate table. The wisteria had a trunk as thick as a tree's and vivid green leaves; a few clusters of faded blossom drooped from the trellis over their heads. Again declining pasta Lillian ordered a ham salad. After the cocktail on the boat she also said no to wine. While they waited for their food he talked about Capri. He'd been coming here since the 1920s, most regularly when he and Lidia were living in Amalfi; he had also brought Clara, Adriana's mother. He'd met many celebrities on the island, including Noël Coward and Sophia Loren who had both stayed at Massimo's hotel in Anacapri. Surprisingly he hadn't made the acquaintance of Capri's currently most famous resident, Gracie Fields from Lancashire whom George and Lillian had seen years ago at the De La Warr Pavilion in Bexhill.

'Has the Pope stayed at your hotel?' Lillian asked.

'Not this one, but two of his predecessors did. I've served under four Popes.' The waiter brought beer for Massimo and mineral water for Lillian.

'Am I allowed to ask how you went from making wine in Sicily to being a banker at the Vatican?' She knew this was a more sensitive area than his private tragedies. He smiled amiably and took a swig of his beer before answering; apparently she hadn't overstepped the mark.

'It just sort of happened. I came to Rome in 1924 after the loss of my family and got lucky with my first few investments. At the seminary they discovered I had a head for figures. The old monsignore who was my tutor predicted that I would end up bookkeeping for His Holiness the Pope.'

'And you did!' Lillian laughed.

'Well –' he smiled – 'only in a manner of speaking.'

'I kept the books for George,' she told him, 'until he was successful enough to employ a proper one.'

'Perhaps I should let you look at mine,' he teased. 'I'm not quite as sharp as I was.' They exchanged smiles.

'You were telling me about Rome,' she prompted.

'Yes: well, a man with money to invest, a Sicilian – that gave me a whiff of excitement – and a young widower, which made me a target for mothers with eligible daughters, not to mention a few bored married women. Inevitably I got taken up by Roman "Society", the nobility at Court and all their hangers-on.'

'Is that when you met Adriana's mother?'

'No, I didn't meet her till 1939. I lived like a monk for my first six years in Rome, still grieving for my family. I took my first mistress in 1930, a woman whose husband managed a petrol refinery at Venice and didn't seem to mind what his wife got up to in Rome.'

Italians truly were a different race, Lillian thought. George would not have been complaisant if she'd taken a lover.

'I suppose my anger at God faded along with my grief,' Massimo said. 'I also came to enjoy the company of priests from the Holy See, which was Rome's other social focus.'

'Is that where you met the one who collected me at Rome station – Father Angelo?'

He nodded. 'Actually he's a monsignore.' Lillian wasn't sure where a monsignore fitted into the hierarchy of priesthood, but chose not to reveal her ignorance.

'So that's how you came to work for the Vatican?'

'Partly through Monsignor Angelo and partly through Cardinal Pacelli, who became Pius the Twelfth.'

'The Pope who signed the agreement with Mussolini?'

'No, that was Pius Eleven. Pacelli only became Pope in 1939. The "agreement" with the Fascists was in 1929, the Lateran Treaty.'

'And wasn't there a treaty with Hitler as well?'

'That was also Pius Eleven – in 1933 – although Pacelli *was* his Secretary of State by then and did negotiate the *concordats* with Austria and Nazi Germany. You certainly know your history, Lillian,' he added with one of his indulgent smiles which in this context she found patronizing.

'I know wartime history,' she informed him coldly. 'My husband fought in North Africa. The first young man I ever walked out with died at Montecassino.'

Massimo's expression became contrite. 'You must think me a coward, not fighting in either of the great wars.'

Unable to deny this but also unwilling to damn him with an affirmative answer, Lillian looked down at her glass in which the mineral water still faintly bubbled.

He sighed. 'I feel no shame about the First War,' he said. 'I was more use as a farmer than I would have been as a soldier. But the Second War presented many Romans with a dilemma, not just those in the Vatican.' He lowered his voice as a young couple in tennis clothes entered the restaurant and were seated two tables away.

'Like most rich Italians I initially welcomed Mussolini because he was so strongly opposed to the Communists whom we saw – still see – as a real threat. But even before Pacelli got me into the Special Administration, which is what the Vatican Bank was called in those days, my business activities involved frequent trips to England and the USA, so my sympathies were more with the Allies than with the Axis. I was lucky that my secondment to the Vatican exempted me again.'

Lillian's curiosity had once again overcome her hostility. 'Did you meet Mussolini?'

'I saw him at a few Court functions. He spoke to me once. He made a clumsy joke about "Honourable" Sicilians. "Men of Honour" is what the *mafiosi* call themselves, the men of the Mafia. To *il Duce* all Sicilians were automatically gangsters. After clearing out the Communists he declared war on the Mafia. He appointed a new Prefect called Mori who did his job with a brutality Italy hadn't seen since the Borgias. People were arrested, tortured, executed. Even Don Vito, who'd tried to end my feud with our enemies in Villalba, was imprisoned on a charge of smuggling: this was probably the least of his misdeeds, but it was the only one they could make stick. A bit like Al Capone in America going to jail for tax evasion. You must remember him from movies.'

'I thought he was jailed for being a gangster,' said Lillian.

'No, the tax thing was what they got him for.' He drank some more beer. 'I used to visit Don Vito in prison in Palermo several times a year until he died in 1943.'

'Didn't you risk being – tarred with the same brush?'

He smiled at her metaphor. 'I suppose so, but I owed him a duty of respect as the godfather of my dead sons and I think I enjoyed – "cocking a snoop" – at Prefect Mori. Is that the right expression?' He grinned again as she nodded.

'So – in 1927 Mussolini raised the Prefect's arm in front of the parliamentary assembly and told them the war against the Mafia had been won. This wasn't true, of course. Like the Communists, the *mafiosi* just went underground for a few years.' A band of unruly schoolchildren went past, accompanied by a plump and flustered female teacher. Massimo devoured the children with his eyes. Lillian knew that he was thinking of his first family, perished in the fire.

'Here's a bit of wartime history you may not know. The Mafia helped the Allies during the invasion of Sicily.' Lillian registered a duly surprised expression. 'I played a small part in this,' he went on, 'because my Vatican passport allowed me to travel freely to the US. I acted as a "courier" between the two men who co-ordinated Sicily's compliance with the Allied invasion: an American gangster called Lucky Luciano whom you may also have heard of –' Lillian nodded –'and Don Calogero Vizzini, the Mafia boss in Villalba.

'Don Calò wasn't a member of the family I'd feuded with, although he would have been on their side – village ties are almost as close as blood ties. And Lucky Luciano was from a small town not far from Villalba. He came back to Sicily after the war: the FBI had got him on prostitution charges and he was serving a thirty-year sentence which they commuted to deportation as a reward for his help in the invasion.

'The Allies took the Cammarata region without a shell being fired. Don Calò rode back into Villalba in an American tank. His reward was to be made mayor of his village by the American Officer for Civilian Affairs.'

As well as murder mysteries Lillian enjoyed stories and films about the war; this tale had both elements. 'And did these two gangsters become respectable citizens?' she asked.

Massimo smiled wryly. '"Respected" rather than respectable. I'm afraid they both went back to being crooks! Don Calò's death in 1954 has become part of Sicilian folklore. He had a heart attack in his car. His men lifted him out onto the roadside and just before he died he said, "Life is so beautiful".'

He leaned back as the waiter returned with their food but went on with the conclusion of this episode:

'Lucky Luciano's luck ran out in 1962. He drank a cup of coffee at Naples airport which had been poisoned by one of his partners. They were afraid he was going to "sing", as the Americans say, to the latest government investigation into racketeering.'

While they ate he talked some more about his early years in Rome. As well as Mussolini he had met the King, Victor Emmanuel, and – Nazis visiting Fascists – Goering and Goebbels; he had seen Adolf Hitler at a state reception but had not been presented.

He said nothing more about his work, investing funds for himself and the four Popes he'd served. He described his apartment in Rome; the former residence of a cardinal, it was close to St Peter's Square and had been offered to Massimo in 1940 by the new Pope, Pius XII, 'Papa Pacelli'. The following year Adriana was born, although when she and her mother visited Rome he put them in a discreet apartment by the sea at Ostia. He made no mention of other mistresses – or the whores he'd spoken of yesterday – between the Venetian industrialist's wife and Clara.

In 1946, the year he met and married Lidia, Pius XII made him a prince. The Pope also gave the newlyweds a private blessing when they returned to Rome after their wedding in Naples and honeymoon in Paris. In July 1949, ten weeks after the birth of their second son, the son who was now somewhere in the mountains of Corsica with Andrew, Lidia took an overdose of barbiturates in her bedroom in the shadow of St Peter's while her husband was spending a weekend with his mistress and daughter not twenty miles away at Ostia Mare. Massimo repeated what he had told Lillian yesterday:

'I broke off seeing Clara. God forgive me, I didn't see Adriana again till her mother's funeral in 1959. And I never took another mistress. My work – and my sons – are all I need to sustain me now.'

Lillian wasn't sure she believed this. She'd worked out that he must be sixty-four or sixty-five, and he was very much a man of the flesh, a sensualist. As with his business affairs, she had the feeling that more was being withheld than divulged, something she'd also felt when Carlo began telling her about his and Andrew's life in Venice. Perhaps there were other ugly and sordid details which the Prince felt it necessary to hide from her but, even incomplete, his autobiography was as fascinating as any she had ever read. Against all her upbringing and her best instincts she was enjoying his company more than that of anyone she could think of in Hastings. Whatever Andrew's reaction when he and Massimo's son were brought back to Amalfi, Lillian no longer had any regrets about setting out on this journey – her quest.

'I know only mad dogs and Englishmen go out in the noonday sun,' he said with a smile at the end of the meal, 'but do you fancy living up to your reputation and going for a walk? You'll see some nice views, and there won't be too many people about at this time.'

'I often walk or garden after lunch,' she told him. 'Exercise after meals stops you putting weight on.'

He patted the bulge of his stomach under the tee-shirt. 'Then we'll go for my sake more than yours!'

'My husband was more overweight than you are,' said Lillian, surprising herself with her candour.

'I want to hear all about your husband.'

'You do?' she said, even more surprised.

Disconcertingly, he asked for the loan of her handbag which he passed discreetly to one of the guards, who went to the men's room with it under his coat. It did not feel significantly heavier when Lillian received it back, although she had guessed the reason for the sleight-of-hand.

'I hope you don't mind carrying a concealed weapon,' Massimo said, dismissing the guards as they left the restaurant and set out along the upward-sloping path. 'A gun would rather spoil my "disguise".' He gestured at the Bermuda shorts.

'Oh, so it's a disguise,' she said.

'Well –' he laughed – 'I wouldn't normally be seen dead in an outfit like this.'

The thought of the gun in her handbag generated more a feeling of excitement than reassurance. Lillian had convinced herself that the Prince was no longer seriously in danger of being attacked by a hired assassin. It was an effort not to open her bag and see what a gun looked like at close quarters, but she didn't want to appear gauche.

'This is the first time I've been anywhere near a gun,' she told him.

'Your husband didn't hunt?'

'No. He was a keen fisherman, but that's all.'

'And your son?'

'One of his schoolfriends had an air-gun but Andrew didn't ask for one.'

Noël Coward was right: there were very few other people out in the middle of the day beneath a scorching sun. This was a residential area; since leaving the restaurant they had passed only one small supermarket with no customers and an ice-cream stall whose proprietor was asleep under a nearby tree. On either side of the narrow path were guesthouse-sized hotels and flat-roofed villas with ornate chimneys that resembled miniature minarets. Beyond the houses and their gardens there were flashes of the bright blue sea far below.

'Both my boys have won prizes for marksmanship,' Massimo told her. 'I was shooting in Sicily before I was ten years old. Birds, rabbits, that sort of thing.'

'If you'd stayed in Sicily would you have ended up having

to shoot people?' she dared to ask.

He stopped in his tracks. 'Do you think you could kill for Andrew, for your daughter, for your grandchildren?' he countered.

Lillian, a few paces ahead, also stopped. She turned and met his challenging gaze. 'I can't imagine any circumstances in which I'd have to make such a decision,' she said, conscious that she was begging the issue.

'You English,' he said with an expression that was almost a sneer. Lillian realized that she had finally asked one question too many. He smiled coldly and went on:

'I've never personally killed anyone. And the man who set fire to my house in Sicily was the only man I've ever ordered killed on my account. But if I had to kill to protect my sons today, I would do it without compunction.'

He caught up with her, and they walked on in silence. Lillian felt she had been chastised, put in her place.

The path narrowed and began to climb more steeply. Now she followed him instead of walking beside him. After another level stretch the path became a set of shallow descending steps. Overhanging fir trees shaded them from the sun. The steps levelled out as they approached an open-air café where a handful of people were lunching. Beyond the café more steps led to narrow terraces on several levels, all overlooking a jagged wind-eroded hole in an outcrop of rock. This was called the 'Arco Naturale', he told her: the Natural Arch. Through the hole the sea was visible at the bottom of a long rugged slope, blue turning to emerald close to the rocky shore; a large yacht rode at anchor with swimmers around it.

Straggly pine trees abounded, even on the top of the thin

outcropping where the arch met the cliff. There were a few picnickers on benches in the terraces. Massimo led her to an empty bench that was no more than some tiles cemented onto a shelf of rock. A puppy belonging to the café scampered from group to group, begging for titbits.

'Here's our mad dog!' said Lillian as it bounded over to them; she picked it up and lay it on its back in her lap, where he squirmed with delight as she rubbed his chest and fondled his big floppy ears.

'You were going to tell me about your husband,' the Prince reminded her.

'Was I?' She released the puppy and after a curious sniff at her handbag in which the gun was secreted he loped back to a more promising pair of picnickers. 'I'm afraid my life-story is rather prosaic after yours.'

'Let me be the judge of that,' he said.

And, sitting there in the shade of a conifer, with the scent of pine and the sound of crickets and seagulls, she told him the story – not in the least operatic and with only a little drama – of her Great Romance with George. She told it fragmentarily, jumping here and there in time much as the floppy-eared puppy continued to scamper to and fro the walkers who came to sit and eat their sandwiches or merely to pause and admire the view.

'I was working for a firm of solicitors when I met George,' she began. 'He came into the office one day when I was covering for the receptionist during her lunch-break. This was in November 1934, when you were in Rome meeting cardinals and politicians. I was a secretary, typing out wills and conveyancing agreements and sometimes divorce papers. I knew all about divorce before I knew anything about marriage.' She smiled.

'George came to your firm to get a divorce?'

'No!' She laughed at the idea. 'He was going to take over his brother's bricklaying business and he wanted to register the name of the company. He'd been working in Canada for six-and-a-half years. His father had died in the First War and now that George was back to help support their mother, his brother wanted a turn in Canada. He's still there, my brother-in-law; he and his wife came over for the funeral last year. I asked George what he wanted to call the company, and he said just *George Rutherford, Builder*. So I said, "Why don't you call it *George Rutherford & Son*?" and he said, "I haven't got a son. I'm not married yet." And I said, "No but you will be".' And I remember that I was thinking to myself, *You're going to marry me*.

'Which was a bit naughty, since I was already engaged to somebody else.' She almost blushed: thirty-two years later this was still the most scandalous act of her life. 'He hadn't given me a ring, but we had – an "understanding" it was called in those days. My parents were expecting it – my mother especially wanted it, she wasn't keen on George at first – and Mrs Sadler was expecting it, but –' She tailed off.

'Was this the man who died at Montecassino?'

'No, he threw me over to go out with a girl from the Co-op where my father worked. That was Arthur. This was his brother, Robert – Bob. He's a bank manager now. Back then he was just a clerk. He and his wife are probably my closest friends in spite of me throwing him over. Once he met Amy he got over it. He and George used to go fishing together. He's the one who

160

gave me Andrew's address in Venice. And he got me an extra allowance on my holiday money. You know we have Exchange Control Regulations in England, a limit on how much you can take out of the country?'

'Fifty pounds a year, isn't it?'

'That's what goes in your passport for traveller's cheques and foreign currency. Plus, you're allowed fifteen pounds each time you go abroad.'

'If you need any money –'

Now Lillian coloured. 'No, I'm all right, thank you. I'm not spending anything anyway. You've been more than kind.'

Massimo smiled and made another expansive gesture with his hands. 'So why did you throw over this – Robert?'

'Bob really only caught me on the rebound from Arthur. And he had "prospects", which was what mattered to Mother. She was even happier with Arthur till he turned out to be a bad lot: he was a professional soldier. I'll never forget her face the first time he came to call in his Indian Army uniform, feathers on his helmet. Mother was just dazzled by him! I suppose I was too, to begin with, but there wasn't much under all the dazzle.' Picturing Arthur Sadler in his finery and feathers, she smiled. It felt good, suddenly, to be talking like this about herself, her life. It must be like this when you went to a psychiatrist – not that Lillian had ever felt that need.

'There were actually three brothers,' she told him. 'Arthur was the oldest, then there was Wilfrid, and Bob the youngest. I was a sort of honorary sister when we were growing up in Rye. In games and charades I'd be Maid Marian or Lady Guinevere. I remember once, after a secret visit to the first cinema in Hastings – the Baptists thought films were an invention of the

161

Devil! – they tied me to the railway in a siding at Romney so that my gallant knights Sir Wilfred and Sir Robert could rescue me from wicked Lord Arthur…

'Well, wicked Lord Arthur took the girl from the Co-op to India instead of me, and then there was a scandal with a maharajah's wife and he had to come home and join an English regiment, so perhaps it was just as well I was making do with Bob. He was handsome in a different way from Arthur, not quite so dashing, but –' she floundered – 'there wasn't much to him, you somehow knew he'd never amount to anything. I don't mean money, I didn't want to marry for money, but I wanted a rock to cling to in what the hymn calls "life's tempestuous sea". Arthur was like a cork bobbing at the end of a fishing line. Bob was a bit more solid, but he wasn't a rock: he was only a pebble.'

'George was a rock,' said Massimo. Lillian beamed.

'Oh yes, George was my rock. He was nothing special to look at, but the minute I set eyes on him I knew he'd make something of himself. He already had. He went to Canada to try gold-mining but he ended up being a lumberjack. He looked like a lumberjack, big and brawny with a workman's rough hands. He'd have expanded the bricklaying business even if he hadn't made a bit of money in Canada. George had such energy, whereas Bob was like my father: a decent man, a good man, but he was somehow a bit – slow. George knew you have to get out and make things happen, not sit around and wait.'

She stopped, conscious that she was running on like a steam-train down a steep hill. How different from his story, so measured and well thought-out. But he didn't seem to mind.

He watched her with a faint smile, never taking his dark eyes off her.

'George sounds like my kind of man,' he said.

'You'd have probably got on with each other,' she agreed. 'He was what my mother-in-law called "a man's man", more comfortable around men than around women. Apart from her and me.' Her mind made another connection. 'Does this have anything to do with – the way Andrew is?'

If he thought this theory preposterous, he didn't show it. He shook his head. 'The Vatican's full of men who are uncomfortable around women and I'm sure it's nothing to do with sex or temptation.' He nudged her back on course:

'Your George could have taught me to fish.'

'And you could have taught him to shoot!' She laughed and added: 'Only rabbits, of course!'

'You mean – not people?' he teased. 'He could have helped me eliminate my enemies.'

'We never had any enemies,' she said, serious again. 'We barely had rivals in the building trade. Obviously there's competition for the bigger jobs, but builders often put work each other's way during lean times. George did anyway. And he subcontracted a lot when he went into partnership with a local factory-owner.'

'Your mother got over the disappointment of you not marrying the bank clerk?' He pronounced it the American way: 'clurk'.

'Oh yes – even before I provided her with a grandson. George's mother claimed there was blue blood way back in her father's family – not that George and his brother set much store by this. But my mother liked the thought of me practically marrying into the aristocracy.' She smiled, remembering Carlo telling her that Andrew was still trying to make something out of his grandmother's supposed connections. 'And George did all sorts of things to their house my dad had never got round to. A builder proved to be more use as a son-in-law than a soldier or a bank clerk. And our firm getting bigger and better known, she enjoyed that. It's a pity she didn't live to see him become an alderman in 1955. Though that's hardly the same as being made a prince by the Pope,' she added.

Massimo smiled, acknowledging a tease at his expense. 'Pardon me saying this, but your mother sounds like a bit of a snob.'

Lillian laughed. 'She was! And my dad was only a baker, a milkman's son. Her father had been a Baptist Minister, but he died before he was forty and my grandmother became house-keeper to the new minister who was a widower. My mother worked as a maid at one of Rye's grander houses, and having failed to raise her own station in life, she set her heart on raising mine. I was their only child. She took in washing and mend-ing and did extra cleaning jobs, all so that after I left ordinary school I could go on to Finishing School. When the Depression came, she saw it as the world conspiring against her plans for me. But in 1930, in spite of the Depression, I started at Miss Foster's in Winchelsea.'

She paused. More than being jilted by debonair Arthur Sadler, this was the most painful recollection from her early life.

'I never told my mother how much I hated that school which she'd been saving for, in pennies and shillings, since I was little. Talk about snobbery. The other girls were the daughters of army officers and merchants and doctors. Two were from houses where my mother cleaned. I was from one of Rye's poorest streets. My father was an infantryman and a baker, my mother a housemaid. They were all Anglicans; we were "Chapel". My mother made all my clothes, my shoes came from jumble sales.' She smiled sourly at these bitter memories of thirty-six years ago.

'The shoes were the worst thing. When I started work I blew most of my first week's wages on some new shoes. Amy's always co-opting me into helping her with jumble sales for the Methodist Church or the Women's Institute. I'm happy to help and to give, but I never buy anything second-hand.

'Anyway, I don't know if the grooming and etiquette did me any good, and my mother had already taught me to cook and sew, but I suppose without Miss Foster's I wouldn't have got the job at the solicitors' when I was eighteen and then I might not have met George. I'd have gone ahead and married Bob Sadler, which would have rescued me from being a shop-girl like his sister-in-law or a housemaid like my mother. Life with him would have been – well, safe and dull.' She had sometimes teased George with speculation along these lines.

'Bob might have made a more understanding father to Andrew,' she said, confessing a private thought which she had not shared with her husband, 'although he and Amy have had little but grief from their children. But Bob wouldn't have minded Andrew becoming a window-dresser, whereas George's heart was set on making a builder of him. Thank God he never knew about this – other business.'

'You don't think he suspected?'

'He never said anything to me. If anyone suspected, it should have been me, and I just didn't. Once he moved to London there were always women in his life – girlfriends – he sometimes had more than one on the go at the same time.'

'Many homosexuals seem to enjoy the company of women,' Massimo said. 'Some even marry and father children.'

Lillian stared down through the arch of rock as the swimmers scrambled aboard their yacht; one of them cranked the anchor up, the engine purred into life and they glided out of sight.

She had managed, unintentionally, to skip a vast chunk of her life, jumping from Miss Foster's and the Sadler boys and George coming into her office – everything lumped and muddled together – to Andrew in London, the life he had paraded and the life he had kept secret. What she had left out was the thirty years of her marriage, with all its joys: watching her children grow and develop; family holidays and outings; the comforts that came with prosperity and the fulfilment of George's ambitions; her visits to Andrew in London; Sylvia's wedding and the birth of twin granddaughters; and towering over everything, the truly rocklike presence that George had been through all these years. She had also omitted the occasional sorrows of four decades: her miscarriage; the deaths of her parents and George's mother; the awful rows when Andrew insisted on taking his own road in life, that road which she thought she had shared but which, she now felt, she had really only been permitted to cross intermittently.

The death of his second wife had left Prince Massimo with a jet-setting career, friends in high places, two sons to raise, a mistress – and a daughter – to discard. Without George all Lillian had was gardening and golf and bridge and jumble sales at the Women's Institute. But it would be self-pitying to say this now, however keenly she felt it.

'We can either go back the way we came,' he said when she showed no sign of resuming, 'or we can go down a bit lower and take a different way back. Either way there's a lot more steps.'

'I'm getting used to steps,' she said with a grim little laugh. 'Let's go on. Lately I've been spending too much time going over the same ground.' Her tone was bitter, she couldn't help it, but he did not immediately make any comment.

Walking back to the café they descended a long series of steps and level stretches that wound between fir trees and brambles and thorny cactuses. On both sides the undergrowth was close, confining and humid. Eventually, still not at sea level, they reached a large cavern, called the 'Matrimonial Grotto', he said, the site of sacrificial rites in pagan times. They sat on a rock, enjoying the cool of the cave and the relief of resting their aching calves and ankles.

'You miss your son more than your husband or Sylvia, don't you?' he said.

'Yes,' she confessed. 'If anything happened to Andrew –' She did not finish this sentence.

'Nothing has,' he assured her. 'And nothing will,' he promised. He was silent for a moment, then he said:

'I think we miss people for different reasons, just as we love them for different reasons. If by a miracle I could have either of my wives back now, I would choose Liliana rather than Lidia. Lidia was beautiful, but like so many beautiful women she was vain and empty-headed. Even Clara was a more stimulating companion, which is why I kept on seeing her, I guess, apart from the physical side of it. But Liliana was Sicilian, she knew what made me tick, she was *simpatica*, as we say - it's untranslatable, it goes beyond "sympathy" into a kind of binding of the soul. Lidia had to be always doing things, going places, making decorating plans from magazines and catalogues, she could never be still. Liliana liked to walk or to just sit as we are now. We didn't always have to talk, just being together was enough. There must be a better word than "good company"–'

'Companionable,' Lillian supplied.

'Yes,' he said. 'That's what I miss. I never had it after her. I had company when I needed it, but not in that special sense. And maybe I never knew what I was missing until recently. *You're* very companionable,' he told her.

Lillian blushed. 'I've had years of practice,' she said. 'George and I always enjoyed a very comfortable relationship. He wasn't an exciting man, ours was not a passionate marriage in that sense –' her blush deepened: these were confidences she had never exchanged with any of her women friends, yet alone with another man – 'and he wasn't even very talkative, but I always felt comfortable in his company, very safe and secure. I suppose Andrew, especially as he got older, provided all the excitement. Andrew's more like your second wife, always talking, always on the go. I don't know why I miss that more than my grandchildren or my husband's quiet companionship, but I do.' A lump came to her throat and she cursed him inwardly for reminding her of the misery that had brought her in search of her prodigal son.

Two schoolteachers with a noisy group of children entered the grotto from the opposite side. The children began whooping and catcalling to test the cave's acoustics. Massimo rose and Lillian followed him out into the sunlight. Now their route led upwards through more pine trees. After a while, both panting from the climb, they stopped and leaned on a fence. He pointed out the massive Fariglioni rocks offshore which reminded Lillian of the Isle of Wight Needles. A water-skier was showing his paces close to the shore where a concrete platform provided the only level surface for sunbathers on mattresses and reclining chairs.

'You're an attractive woman, Lillian,' he said. 'There are surely going to be men wanting to give you a – what do they say – "a second bite of the cherry"?

The question lightened her mood and she laughed. 'There have been a few discreet hints already,' she admitted. 'But they're all men who are very set in their ways. I think I'd rather stick to the life I know than try to fit into somebody else's.' Was this true? It was the exact opposite of how she'd felt since Christmas.

'If you change your mind about trying a different life you could marry me,' he said. His expression was serious, but she was sure he was teasing her. She responded as if he really meant his proposal.

'I don't think I'm cut out to be a princess,' she said.

'Why not?'

She began to feel embarrassed again but made an effort not to blush. 'Isn't it obvious? I'm just a country girl, a baker's daughter – a bricklayer's wife.' She almost smiled to think how much she sounded like her mother.

'I think you do George a disservice,' he said. It was disconcerting to hear her dead husband defended by a man who had never met him. 'And my Liliana was also "just a country girl" – born to a peasant family, she'd be the first to admit – who would have become a princess if she had lived.'

'And maybe the idea of your Jet-Set life would have appalled her just as it appals me,' Lillian said frankly.

He gave a long sigh that was almost a groan. 'What you call

169

the "Jet-Set life" is stealing my Fabio away from me just as it's stolen Andrew from you. What I do for a living is nothing to do with the Jet Set, and if you only knew how bored I am with flying here, there and everywhere. I'm tired of the dirty dealing that goes on in the banking world, even in St Peter's. I'd so much like to be able to just sit in a garden instead of an airplane, to read a book instead of a balance sheet, to plan a dinner-party instead of a million-dollar development –' He stopped and laughed at himself. 'Don't tell me – Fausto does: I'd be bored inside a week.'

'I must say I can't picture you reading a book in my garden in Hastings,' she said, smiling at the idea.

'It needn't be Hastings,' he said. His dark eyes stared levelly into hers. Lillian decided to put an end to his teasing. She said:

'May I ask you something?'

'Of course.'

'Can we stop somewhere for a cup of tea? Somewhere with a bathroom.'

He laughed and said, 'You too! I was about to make my excuses and go behind the bushes.' Lillian managed not to blush again. 'There's another café along here,' he said. 'You shall have your tea and I may even be very gallant and let you have first use of their WC.'

Lillian laughed and allowed him to take her arm as the path widened enough for them to walk side-by-side again, the widow from Hastings and her dark-eyed prince who had been touched by the sun or perhaps by the spirits of the Matrimonial Grotto.

After tea and a pastry – 'So much for the benefits of exercise!' said Massimo with another laugh – they walked back through the crowded lanes to the little piazza and took the funicular down to Marina Grande. Aboard the yacht Federico and Paolo were playing a card game she could not recognise on the floor below the canopy at the stern. There was no sign of the weather-beaten old man. After the guards had helped her on-board and cast off the line, Massimo sent them below-decks to continue their game. Lillian sat on the stern banquette, enjoying the rush of cool air and the occasional splash of sea-water. The Prince turned and smiled at her from time to time but made no attempt at conversation, which would have meant shouting to be heard over the engine at full throttle. Lillian wished he would change out of the hideous Bermuda shorts, his 'disguise'.

Listening to the hissing of the sea beneath the hull, the thought came idly to her that only last Monday at this time she had been on the train between Calais and Paris. What a week it had been! A week of revelations: revelations about Andrew, about Carlo and Adriana, about the Prince and his women and his sons; even revelations about Italy, its people, its Church. Her head reeled with all that she had learned.

As the yacht neared the promontory, Paolo and Federico came back on deck. Reversing the engine, Massimo manoeuvred the boat gently into its narrow berth at the base of the cliff.

The long haul up to the fortress house was an ordeal after all the steps in Capri. They made several rest stops on the way up, finally sitting side-by-side on the low border wall on one of the level stretches. Red-faced and sweating, Massimo waved the guards ahead. Inside the house at last they collapsed into pews at the refectory table. Maria brought glasses and a jug of chilled lime juice. She also brought the news that there had been a telephone call from Corsica. Massimo went upstairs to find Fausto. He told Lillian to go ahead with her bath, which Rosella was already running, and promised to send a message if there were any important developments.

Exhausted by the day's exercise and excitements, Lillian fell asleep in the bath. She woke after five or ten minutes sufficiently disoriented to wonder if she'd dreamt that a prince had teased her with a marriage proposal, but the ache in her limbs, dulling into a comfortable lethargy in the warm lemon-scented water, was a reminder that she had spent the day climbing the alleys and byways of Capri, and if she hadn't dreamt the day in Capri with Max – she no longer thought of him as just 'the father of the boy Andrew was with' – then presumably his proposal tease was a matter of fact, not of fantasy. There was no need to pinch herself.

Alice Pemberton, her friend on the Pevensey Levels whose husband had put some very lucrative business George's way, had tried to plant the notion of remarriage in Lillian, but the seed fell on unfertile ground. As she'd told Massimo on their walk back from the Matrimonial Grotto, she expected that sooner or later one of the widowers or divorcees in her social circle would suggest they share the looming drift towards old age, but what was on offer would be only an antidote to loneliness. The Prince had picked up on her use of the word 'companionable' and planted the notion that she might find someone to partner her at more than golf and bridge. Companionship, in that greater, deeper sense, had left her life last September.

That morning, after the ward sister telephoned to tell her that George's heart had finally failed during the night, Lillian went to the hospital and kissed her husband goodbye, kissing his already cool forehead. Even then she could not recall the last time she'd kissed him on the mouth.

Her bed did not seem especially empty; they'd stopped sharing a bed after his first stroke in 1959, when he began to require more layers of bedding than Lillian could comfortably sleep under. Theirs, as she'd told Massimo, had not been a passionate marriage. Was this a matter for regret? Sometimes she'd thought that it was; most of the time it hadn't seemed to matter. Perhaps it mattered now. Despite his claim to have lived monastically since his second wife's suicide, Lillian didn't expect that the Prince would offer any other woman a – what was the word? – 'platonic' marriage. She imagined, for a moment – and then, just as quickly, tried not to – him making love to her. Neither during her marriage nor since becoming a widow had she indulged in sexual fantasies.

Out of the blue, the first nights of her married life came flooding into her mind, every detail as intact as if they had happened last weekend rather than thirty-one years ago.

FRANCE/VENICE: 1935

Despite a year-and-a-half of typing up histories of infidelity, domestic violence and denial of conjugal rights, Lillian had only a sketchy idea of what was supposed to happen on her wedding night. Sex education had not been on the curriculum at Miss Foster's.

Mother had set out to spoil physical love for Lillian. Much preached against by her own dry stick of a mother, the Baptist parson's wife, she had spoken at great length about the vileness of men and the horrors of a woman's marital duties, duties which Father had long since ceased to press. However, she did not, could not, bring herself to go into details.

Lillian suspected that her husband was as much a virgin as she was. Men could, she had learned at work, obtain experience with prostitutes and other types of loose women, but she doubted that George had enjoyed any such liaisons, and it wasn't something she could have brought herself to ask.

As it turned out, nothing happened on their wedding night. It was after midnight when they boarded the Pullman train in Calais. The beds, bunks, were stacked one over the other like racks in an oven. Lillian didn't fancy being introduced to the alleged horrors of conjugal life on something not much wider than a stove. George was a big man: the thought of his great weight on top of her was one of the more intimidating aspects of this enterprise (common sense suggested that sexual intercourse required husbands and wives to be horizontally stacked, also like baking racks).

George seemed similarly disinclined to hurry things along. Back to back in the narrow space between the berths and the wall to the next compartment, they changed into sleeping attire without any unfortunate moments of partial nudity. George's Calvinistic striped flannel pyjamas, reminiscent of Father's, would have to be replaced with something more stylish, she decided as he climbed into the top bunk. She stretched up to kiss him.

'Goodnight, old girl,' he responded. Arthur Sadler, describing the life which the floozy from the bakery must now be enjoying in India, had called Lillian 'old girl'. She shook George – and perhaps mentally shook Arthur.

'Don't ever call me that.'

'Er – oh, sorry then,' he stammered and with that subtle shift in his ruddy colouring which she had come to identify as blushing, he added: 'Goodnight, my dear.'

She gave him another kiss to show that her moment of crossness had passed.

The next night, with the sound of water lapping the lower walls of their hotel and the echoing calls of gondoliers passing each other on the canal, Lillian was inducted into the great mystery.

George modestly kept the trousers of his dreadful pyjamas on as he joined her under the covers. His hairy chest and belly were an intimidating sight. Lillian shivered with apprehension. In silence, keeping carefully apart beneath the covers, she removed her nightdress and George his pyjama bottoms. Fighting her apprehension, she rolled against him. The feel of his hairy body against her skin was like Arthur's tickling moustache but on an overwhelming scale. They still did not speak. Lillian kissed him with what she hoped felt like ardour. Her heart was beating so loudly she was sure he must be able to hear it.

He used his elbows and knees to keep his weight off her as moved on top of her, but he seemed unsure of how to open her up to this hard and unfamiliar part of him that prodded her with an insistent will of its own. Overcoming embarrassment, fear, even some revulsion, Lillian took hold of the intruding column and guided it to its obvious destination. She bit back a gasp of pain as it slowly invaded her.

After only a few strenuous thrusts he gave a quiet groan and immediately withdrew, rolling over onto his back. Lillian was not sure whether what she now felt was relief or disappointment.

'I hope that was all right,' he said, his voice filled with uncertainty.

'I think so, George,' Lillian said. 'It was very nice,' she added to reassure him. The experience had turned out to be neither particularly unpleasant nor particularly pleasant. She wasn't sure whether she would come to enjoy it – how often was it supposed to happen anyway? – but she was confident that she would learn not to mind.

George broke the silence: 'Is it all right if I go to sleep now?'

'Of course it is, George. We've had a long day. Two long days. Two lovely days. George –'

'Yes, dear?'

'You can call me "old girl" if you want to.'

'Are you sure you don't mind?'

'No. I shall be an old girl in the end, shan't I?'

'You'll be *my* old girl,' he said. From George this was the equivalent of a film actor's most ardent and earnest declaration. Everything would be all right, she was sure. Her heart overflowed with love for him, her rock.

AMALFI

The bath water was beginning to cool. Savouring both the wallow in the bath after the day's exertions and also the wallow in the very few sensual memories from her entire life, Lillian ran some hot water and lay back again.

Contrary to all the music-hall jokes, it was her mother-in-law who came to Lillian's rescue.

'I hope you won't mind livin' with my old ma for a bit,' George had said on the day he proposed. 'Only my savin's won't run to keep the business goin' and buy us a house of our own. Not right away, leastwise.' Thanks to a contract his brother had obtained from the District Council George had so far managed to survive the Slump without laying off any of his men.

'We could rent a house for the time being,' Lillian had suggested.

'I don't hold with payin' rent. Waste of good money.'

'I can pay the rent out of my wages at Hayes & Browne.'

'You're not goin' to work after we're married. I'm not havin' people say George Rutherford can't afford to keep his own wife.'

Lillian had been torn between delight at the prospect of a masterful husband to keep house for and anxiety at giving up her independent interesting work at the law firm. She certainly didn't relish the thought of keeping somebody else's house, but did not admit this.

'You concentrate on the business, George. We'll have a home of our own soon enough. I'm sure your mother and I will get on.'

And, surprisingly, they did.

Hazel Rutherford was a large, ebullient woman who went about her housework and gardening singing popular songs from the wireless and Sankey hymns from the Congregational Church. What made her claims to a noble lineage doubly hard to believe was the fact that she went shopping with her hair in curlers under a garish headscarf (this was 'common' in Mother's book) and spoke with a Sussex accent even broader than Father's on the odd occasion when he came out with a 'bain't' or a 'cowwww'. Despite losing her husband and her father on consecutive days in 1916 (just two of the 95,000 British and Commonwealth deaths in the Battle of the Somme), Hazel hadn't stood in the way of George's emigration to Canada in 1929; nor, he said, had her resolutely cheerful letters played a part in his decision to come home.

'Where's this baby, then?' Hazel demanded as she placed potatoes around the half-cooked joint of beef after Sunday chapel in January 1936. Lillian, to her mother's displeasure, now alternated attendance at the Baptist and Congregational services.

'What baby's that?' asked Lillian, peeling parsnips, playing for time: she knew exactly which baby her mother-in-law was referring to.

'My grandchild. Your baby.'

'You'll have to be patient a while longer,' Lillian said, hoping to close the subject. Hazel persisted:

'It's nine months since your weddin'. You could be havin' a baby right now. You *are* tryin'?'

Lillian blushed. 'Of course we are.' This was broadly true, although she would not have needed all her fingers and toes to count the number of times she and George had 'tried' in nine months. She still didn't know whether this represented abstemiousness or wanton excess. Neither of them had developed any great enthusiasm for the act, although they often spoke fondly of the time to come, 'after the baby'.

'I think you ought to see a doctor,' Hazel pronounced.

'Oh, I don't think that's necessary, is it?' In fact this very thought had occurred to Lillian more than once, but the notion of discussing the delay in conception with aged Dr Birkenshaw was even more embarrassing than the present conversation.

'You are doin' it right?'

Lillian went from pink to crimson. 'Hazel!' For once she wasn't uncomfortable using her mother-in-law's first name. 'There's really only one way to skin this cat,' she said with a nervous laugh. 'More than one way to skin a cat' was a favourite expression of Hazel's.

'It's more a question of *when* than how,' said Hazel.

Lillian could get no redder. 'I'm sure I don't know what you're talking about,' she said faintly.

Hazel clanged the oven door shut. 'That's what I was afraid of,' she announced in the stern tone of the Baptist minister preaching of sin and damnation.

And, at the age of twenty, nine months married, Lillian finally learned the Facts Of Life. She'd just started at Miss Foster's when she experienced her alarming first period. Instinct had directed her to the Science mistress, Miss Dawson, who explained the rudiments of menstruation and supplied her with her first sanitary towels; these Lillian washed herself and dried in her wardrobe where, if Mother saw them, they went unremarked. But although Miss Dawson's botany classes had touched on pollination, human – or even animal – fertilization was not a feature of her biology lessons; nor did she include the finer points of ovulation in her extra-curricular talk with Lillian. These and other gaps in her knowledge Hazel now filled, while the roast sputtered in the oven. Lillian's blush slowly faded. By the time George came clumping in through the back door to take off his wellingtons in the scullery, Lillian knew all she needed to know.

'George,' she said a few nights later, 'if we want to make a baby, it has to be tonight and tomorrow and the day after.' Her boldness, even in the privacy of the conjugal bed, surprised her. It certainly surprised George.

'Three nights on the trot? I'll be unfit for work at that rate!' Like Lillian in the kitchen with Hazel, he laughed to cover up his confusion.

'I've had a talk with your mother and she says this is the best time.'

'You discussed – this side of – things – with Ma?' He looked apprehensively at the wall between their room and Hazel's, as if she might at any moment materialize like some ghastly admonishing apparition.

Lillian, to her own further amazement, did not so much as blush as she shared with George her newly gained wisdom. Then they proceeded, scientifically, almost mechanically, to put the theory to the test. Giving themselves a margin of error, they performed on four nights rather than the three Hazel had counselled. It was Lillian who took the initiative each night. The procedure began to seem like a tasteless joke on the part of the Almighty. Any pleasure she gained from it was not erotic but rather the grim satisfaction of completing an assigned task, like helping her mother-in-law conquer a new corner of the garden. It was plain that George regarded it as an onerous duty.

But she missed two periods, and then told Hazel. When she missed another she went to the doctor, not old Dr Birkenshaw but a new younger doctor that the greengrocer's wife had recommended to Hazel. And now she told George.

She had a miraculously easy pregnancy, with just a single week of morning sickness and some midterm discomfort that owed more to the July heat than to the baby. She continued to help Hazel in the house and the garden, avoiding only the heavier chores. And it was in the garden that her pregnancy terminated.

At the end of October, her final month, there was a mild frost one morning. Hazel decided to move her dahlias to the greenhouse. Walking ponderously with a trug full of tubers Lillian missed her footing on the shallow paved steps George had built from the lawn up to the greenhouse. She dropped the basket and then fell heavily onto it on the steps. The handle collapsed under the impact and she felt the baby shudder within her.

There was wetness between her legs. For a moment she thought she'd brought on the baby's birth as it continued to shudder and convulse, but when she looked down, the wetness was blood.

'Hazel!' she screamed. Her mother-in-law heard the scream from the front garden and came running through the house, banging doors open. She saw the bloodstains and said, 'Oh Lillian, what have we done?'

'Get the doctor,' said Lillian.

The bleeding was only a trickle. A neighbour ran for Doctor Birkenshaw, who lived nearer than the new doctor; the old man arrived puffing within minutes, by which time the bleeding had stopped. But the baby was no longer moving.

'He's dead,' she told the doctor. 'My son is dead.' Somehow – and only at this moment – she was certain that her child was a boy and equally certain that the fall had killed him.

'Let's get you to hospital,' the doctor said. At the hospital they performed a Caesarean, the only hope, they told her, of saving the baby. But, as Lillian had known, the boy – it was a boy – was dead.

There was argument over the matter of a funeral. Not having existed outside the womb, the baby was legally still a foetus, the operation amounting to a late-term abortion, her son now just so much surgical waste. But George was adamant that his unbaptised child should enjoy a Christian burial. 'You should have seen him,' Mother told Lillian later, her judgement of George newly revised: 'he was like a raging beast.'

'His men say he's a Tartar to work for,' Lillian replied proudly. George, now more than ever, was the only rock she had to cling to in the great ocean of her misery.

Hazel took her remorse out on the dahlias, consigning the tubers to a bonfire. Neither she nor Lillian ever grew dahlias again.

Lillian was too weak to join the debate about the disposal of her stillborn son, which then became a milder tussle between his Baptist and Congregationalist grandmothers. The Baptist prevailed. Lillian was not allowed to leave her bed for the funeral. Not until a month after her discharge, with Rye in the grip of winter, did she feel strong enough to go with her husband to the tiny grave.

George had carved the headstone himself. The inscription read: '*Alfred Rutherford, beloved son of George and Lillian, born and died 29 October 1936*'.

'I named him after my Dad and my brother,' George said. 'I hope that's all right.' George had exhausted most of his grief in his hour of wrath at the hospital. He knew that Lillian's would be slower to fade.

'Yes, George.' She clung to him, shivering with cold and with dread. The mist-shrouded cemetery was a fearful place.

'We can have another baby, can't we? When you're better.'

'Yes, George. I'll try to be better soon.'

AMALFI

Lillian climbed out of the bath, shuddering from this unanticipated peering into the well of despondency her miscarriage had occasioned. The well, she recalled with anguish, had seemed bottomless.

RYE/HASTINGS: 1937–45

'It's time you pulled yourself together,' her mother said at the end of January. 'You can't go on like this.'

'I can't go on any other way,' Lillian said helplessly.

But as snowdrops and crocuses gave way to daffodils and tulips, the seasonal cycle of regeneration slowly lifted her mood from despair to acceptance, from acceptance to a faint, fragile hope. The garden which had robbed her of her son seemed to summon her, like the bulbs, out of hibernation. Hazel came back from shopping one morning to find her daughter-in-law forking compost into the soil around her shrubs and rose-bushes. After lunch they went together to the greenhouse to pot out some seedlings.

'She's coming up,' Hazel told George at dinner time; perhaps she too had seen Lillian's sorrow as a well.

Lillian found herself, a day or two later, humming as she gardened; soon enough she was singing along with her mother-in-law.

The doctors had said to wait a year before trying to start another baby. George seemed to assume that this meant total absti-nence: he made no sexual overtures in the bed they shared until Lillian, as before, took the initiative a year and a day after the death of their son. Spain's civil war was getting bloodier by the day; newspapers and the radio were full of grim predictions that Adolf Hitler would soon try to annexe Austria, Czecho-slovakia and even Poland. Lillian did not this time instigate a four-night 'spree' but chose a night when she was theoretically at her most fertile. By Christmas, on the strength of only two such conjugal bouts, another pregnancy was confirmed.

'No more gardenin' this time,' said George, a warning Hazel would repeat many times. 'Not till after the baby.'

'Don't be silly, George,' she protested. 'I just have to be careful, that's all.'

But he was insistent and, come the spring of 1938, she gave in, confining her activity to pulling a few weeds and pruning fruit bushes when he and Hazel weren't watching. At the end of a trouble-free pregnancy she went into labour two weeks prematurely – a painful but mercifully not protracted expe-rience – and duly produced a six-and-a-half-pound son with his father's red face and a few wisps of blond hair which Hazel said were a throwback to her mother's family.

Mother wanted her grandson to be named after Father, Jeremiah, which was out of the question so far as Lillian was concerned, although in a partial concession she gave him Jeremy as a second name. His first name was Andrew: an apostle sounded a bit more modern than a prophet.

The red complexion soon faded, which was a relief, and by the time he was four the blond hair had also faded to his father's dark brown, which was a secret disappointment. He had his father's mouth and eyes, but the overall resemblance was to his maternal great-grandfather, the Reverend Obadiah Tyler.

From the first moment of his existence Lillian was besotted with this son who replaced the child she had lost. She loved him more than she'd ever loved George or Arthur or Mother or even God. She understood how animals would kill and sometimes die to protect their young. Twenty-eight years before meeting Massimo Monfalcone Lillian knew she was capable of killing or dying for Andrew.

'I think it's time Andrew had a brother or sister,' George announced at the beginning of 1940. 'You know, just in case –'

'Don't even think that,' Lillian cut him off. In fact both his mother and hers had expressed the same morbid thought.

Depression – and now war – had bitten hard in rural Sussex as everywhere else. When even the District Council fell into arrears with his settlements, George had to pay the men out of his own pocket. Lillian kept the books of *George Rutherford & Son* and knew just how tight their money situation was. A second child was a luxury they could ill afford with George expecting to be called up this year.

'Shall we then?' he pressed her from his side of the bed.

'Shall we what, George?' she teased.

With a heroic effort he managed not to look uncomfortable. 'Shall we give Andrew a brother or sister?'

She smiled indulgently. 'Well, we can try.'

He rolled nearer. 'Is tonight a good time?'

'Next week will be the best time.'

'I'll leave it up to you.'

'We don't have to wait till next week,' she said. 'If you want to – you know – tonight.'

'Next week'll do fine.' He rolled away again.

In March 1941 Lillian's parents died within a week of each other, Mother of a heart attack and Father of a stroke perhaps brought on by the shock of his loss. At the other end of the year Hazel slipped on icy cobbles in Mermaid Street, breaking both hips and one arm; pneumonia set in and she died eight days later.

But in the midst of all these deaths there was new life: Lillian gave birth to a daughter, Sylvia Anne, in the middle of May; she had been conceived last summer when George had a few days' leave at the end of his basic training. Lillian was busy with the baby, with the house, the garden, shopping, cooking; Andrew, approaching his third birthday, was always bursting with ideas and energy: there wasn't much time to mourn the passing of the older generation.

'We're going to be the older generation soon,' she said in a pensive moment by the fire. The children were in bed. George was home on another short leave. During his wife's third pregnancy he'd been building airfields in Kent and East Anglia.

Next week he was to sail to Egypt. Despite all the dangers ahead Lillian knew he was looking forward to what he called 'proper soldiering'.

He looked up from his paper now. 'Are we? I suppose we are. I don't feel old, though, do you?'

'Not really,' she said. She couldn't articulate her feeling that in producing two children she had fulfilled the sum total of her destiny.

George did not join the invasion of Italy in 1943 at the end of the North African campaign. He stayed on in Egypt, guarding Axis prisoners-of-war, and came home days before VJ Day.

In peacetime the physical side of their marriage began to peter out. They decided (was it a joint decision, or just his?) that two children would be enough. It was clear that George had more work drive than 'sex drive', and Lillian's boldness was limited to the needs of procreation: it did not extend to the pursuit of pleasure.

On the day of their twelfth wedding anniversary in 1948 George took her to see a newly built house on the outskirts of Hastings, ten miles from Rye. Most of the firm's work now came from Hastings and its environs. Several of his men lived here.

'I can get a good deal on the sale of Ma's house,' he told her when they had completed their tour of the upstairs rooms and were back in the living room. 'Enough to pay off what I borrowed and start off free of debt here.'

'I don't like the sloping garden,' she said. 'The rain will wash all the goodness out of the topsoil.'

'I can terrace the garden for you.'

'It's a nice big garden,' she acknowledged.

'What d'you think, then?' he asked. She could almost feel his pent-up tension. She turned from the view across Brede Level and the Weald of Kent to the North Downs, an even finer view than she'd had across Romney Marsh from the house she'd been raised in. This now was the view she and George would enjoy for the rest of their life together.

'It's lovely, dear. How soon can we move?'

They did not make love in the Hastings house more than a half dozen times. George was her partner, her companion, her 'soulmate', but he was not – perhaps had never been – her lover in the silly, soppy, romantic way of the heroes in books and in dreams. When Andrew later introduced her to some of the more candid works of twentieth-century fiction Lillian realized that an experience which many considered transcendental had somehow passed her by. She had loved George as much as she could love any mortal being (except perhaps her son), but nothing that had taken place in any bed they'd ever slept in had caused the earth to move.

AMALFI

'I want to hear all about your husband,' he'd said to her on Capri. She hadn't told him – hadn't told anyone – the half of it. It wasn't because she was a prude (though she was afraid that she might be): these moments of intimacy were too few and too precious to share, even with a man who, if only in a tease, had invited himself to add to this precious store.

***

'I'm afraid there isn't any real news,' he told her when she joined him downstairs. 'My people in Corsica are trying to contact the Pasquales through an intermediary.'

'They can't just go to their village and knock on their door?'

'No, they can't.' He poured a measure from a cocktail shaker into a glass and handed it to her. She guessed before tasting it that it was another Tom Collins. 'Corsicans are a lot like Sicilians, a proud race who resent being part of France much as Sicilians resent being governed from Rome. And there's an element of rivalry between the two islands, over wine, agriculture, fishing, tourism – everything really. Dealing with them has to done very – diplomatically.'

'But you're a diplomat,' she said. 'You work with bishops and –' she couldn't remember the title of the priest who'd met her in Rome – 'the Pope,' she added instead.

Massimo smiled indulgently. 'Yes, that makes me seem important, but I don't want to throw my weight around just because my boy and your son seem to have taken up with these people.'

'These people aren't enemies of yours, like the ones in Sicily who killed your family?'

'No,' he said firmly. 'I have no previous knowledge of them. I've never had much to do with Corsica. Their main business is fishing, which is not an area I've ever been involved in, apart from the kind of fishing I did with Paolo and Federico today.' His smile broadened. 'Be patient, Lillian. I'm sure our boys are having a fine time holidaying with them. Corsica is famous for its food, which many people say is superior even to the cuisine of mainland France. Now, come and sit down. I'll put some music on.'

A few of the songs he played on a smart-looking gramophone he'd brought from America were familiar to Lillian from radio shows she had listened to with George over the years, songs recorded by Mario Lanza and other tenors and made famous before all of them by the legendary Enrico Caruso whom Mario Lanza had portrayed in the film biography in the 1950s (Lillian and George went to Brighton to see it on one of Sussex's bigger cinema screens). Massimo's recordings were by people she'd not heard before, local singers, he told her, singing songs from Naples and from Sicily. There were women singers as well as men; they brought a raw intensity to these songs of love and loss and landscape that touched a deeper chord than the polished studio performances by international stars. The Prince translated some of the lyrics for her. As was so often the case with opera, the words sounded trite in English; they were more heartbreaking when you couldn't understand them.

Dinner was what the Americans called a 'cook-out' or 'barbecue', Massimo told her: grilled hamburgers and chicken legs and sausages, with lemon-and-rosemary-scented sauté potatoes and a green salad with sliced tomatoes served separately. The servants and the guards joined them at the outside table. Fausto had not come home; he was staying the night at the seminary in Naples whose archive he was investigating.

After dinner the music continued – now 'live entertainment' with Luca, the rabbit-shooting guard from the gatehouse alternately playing guitar and mandolin and almost everybody else contributing vocals. They were the same or similar songs to the earlier recordings, songs that these people had grown up with, much as Lillian had grown up in Rye with music-hall songs and hymns from the Baptist hymnbook. Rosella had a resonating soprano voice and Giancarlo, her son, was a fine tenor. Alfredo and Maria, both with voices that quavered, sang an aria from comic opera which Massimo told Lillian was 'a little bit vulgar' but was well-received by the other staff around the garden table. The Prince apologised that he could not hold a tune. 'Neither can I,' Lillian replied quickly, embarrassed at the thought of performing in front of these strangers, however warmly they had accepted her into their midst. For some reason Max Bygraves's 'You're a Pink Toothbrush' came into her head. It had played constantly on the radio in 1959, the year of George's first stroke; Lillian had sung it to him as part of his speech therapy. Perhaps if she sang it here, it would sound as lyrical to these Italians as 'O Sole Mio', almost equally mundane, sounded to an English ear. She did not sing it.

Sitting on the terrace, listening to Italian folk songs from Massimo's staff with the Prince smiling across the table at her, she felt a contentment that had been missing from her life for a decade and more, since Andrew – and then Sylvia – left home, Andrew to National Service, Sylvia to her stockbroker husband. She hoped that Richard and Sylvia felt as contented as this tonight; and perhaps Andrew and Fausto's brother were enjoying similar company, around a similar garden table, in Corsica.

'I have to fly to Rome,' he told her at breakfast. 'There's a business meeting I simply must attend. I can offer you a choice of menu. Stay here and read a book or go for a swim in the sea. Or Rosella could take you into Positano, though it's disagreeably crowded with tourists right now. Or you can come to Rome with me and I'll arrange for a guide to take you sightseeing.

Also very crowded, I'm afraid, but a bit more majestic than Positano.'

'Rome,' she chose instantly.

And two and a half hours later they were there. Federico drove them to a military airfield outside Salerno where Massimo's plane was hangared alongside other private and business aircraft. At the cinema and in magazines Lillian had seen the personal jets of heads of state and movie moguls, fitted out like luxury hotel suites, even with bathrooms. The Prince's plane – it was propeller-driven, 'turbo-assisted', he told her, whatever that meant – was a scaled-down airliner, small and narrow, seating six on each side with only the leather front seats wider with padded armrests. Federico did not accompany them. The co-pilot acted as steward, dispensing glasses of water from a tiny galley at the rear, where there was also a small toilet cabin.

They were in the air for less than an hour before landing at another military airfield near Rome to be met on the tarmac by two limousines with chauffeurs and escorts. Father Angelo, tall and crow-like in his priestly garb, greeted Lillian again by bowing over her hand and not quite kissing it. 'Signora Ruthairford, such a pleasure to see you.'

'For me too, monsignor,' she said, hoping she got his title right.

'This is my assistant, Sister Veronica,' he introduced the woman beside him. 'She will take care of you today.' Sister Veronica was an inch or two shorter than Lillian and did not look like a nun. Lillian guessed her to be in her early twenties. She was an even more beautiful version of Adriana Marini's friend Silvia, the mother of Carlo's illegitimate son Marcello, with fine pale-skinned features that had been captured by many Renaissance artists; a few curls of rich titian hair escaped from a fashion-house headscarf that presumably was doing service as a not-quite-monastic wimple. She wore low-heeled shoes and a knee-length dark-grey dress that bore little resemblance to a habit. Lillian was glad she had put on a plain primrose-coloured dress. They shook hands.

'It's OK to just call me Veronica, Mrs Rutherford.' Her accent was more American than the Prince's.

'Only if you call me Lillian.'

Sister Veronica smiled and the nun became a movie-star. 'I'll call you *Liliana*. You'll be Italian today.' Lillian laughed.

Massimo kissed her hand goodbye. He was wearing a black business suit. 'We will all dine together this evening,' he promised. Monsignor Angelo bowed again. Prince and priest climbed into the rear of a black Mercedes and were gone.

The other limousine was a British Bentley, charcoal grey. Was it Massimo's or the Pope's? The chauffeur's livery was also grey.

'Is there anywhere you'd especially like to see?' Sister Veronica enquired as they drove out of the airfield.

'I'm happy for you to surprise me,' Lillian said.

Traffic was surprisingly light for a capital city in midsummer, although trams looked to be full and the pavements thronged with tourists. Most Romans retreated to their beach apartments and country villas in the month of August, Sister Veronica told her. The tourist invasion did not match the size of the exodus. She pointed out the Roman Forum and the Colosseum as they passed them, but she recommended against stopping because of the sightseeing hordes.

The reason Veronica sounded American was because she

was American – from New York. 'My parents migrated when they were small, my father from Sicily, my mother from Naples. They lived a few blocks from each other in an area of Manhattan called Little Italy. My dad followed my grandpa into being a barber and my mom became a ladies' hair-stylist. So it was a match made in heaven!' Lillian smiled. 'They moved to Brooklyn after the war, which is where I was born. They had a salon for ladies on the second floor over a barbershop for men. My mom said it made a change for women to be above men, which wasn't the normal hierarchy in Italian society!' She laughed and Lillian joined in. The limousine was held up at traffic lights as a rackety-sounding tram crossed the intersection.

Lillian wanted to ask how or why a Brooklyn barber's daughter became a nun in Rome, but she didn't wish to appear nosy. The car crossed a bridge over the Tiber and, suddenly, there was St Peter's Basilica ahead of them. A policeman waved them through into the piazza in front of the cathedral. There was a long queue in the colonnade that fringed the vast amphitheatre. Priests and uniformed officials were allowing people into the church in controlled numbers, but no one stopped Veronica as she guided Lillian up the steps and into the great church.

It was a great church, almost too great. Lillian found it overwhelming. She was used to the bland simplicity of Baptist and Congregational chapels and, more recently, crematoriums. The dome was magnificent (although she still preferred St Paul's in London), but the murals of saints and martyrdoms, like those on the walls – interrupted by vast canvases – were almost garish and, for Lillian, too far removed from the hills and villages beside the Jordan river where Jesus had preached his gospel.

194

The huge bronze canopy over the high altar – Veronica told her it was a '*baldacchino*', designed by Bernini in the 1620s – and the same artist's 'starburst' golden window celebrating the Holy Spirit seemed totally disconnected from the crucifixion and resurrection of Christ the Saviour. Knowing how important, how sacred, these treasures must be to the nun from Brooklyn, she did not share her reservations. A priest was chanting a prayer to a congregation of tourists in one of the side-chapels, some kneeling, some standing – a moving reminder that, however grand, this was a place for worship, for services. And she was sincerely touched by Michelangelo's marble *Pietà*, Jesus held in his mother's arms after being taken down from the cross. The sculptor had captured the grief any mother would feel holding a son dead from any torture or sickness. Lillian could not – would not – imagine holding Andrew's corpse, or Sylvia's.

'This is the most beautiful thing here,' she said. Sister Veronica smiled.

'There are so many superb works by Michelangelo. We have another one here in Rome. But first I will show you the face of God.'

Lillian tried to look awed by the prospect. The nun guided her to a door marked *Privato* and boldly opened it. A series of corridors hung with paintings led them into the Sistine Chapel, even more crammed with tourists than the cathedral. Lillian had seen it in a television documentary and also in a slide show at the Women's Institute in Hastings. The fresco of God's finger touching life into his newly created Adam was, of course, the most famous part of the chapel's ceiling. Adam had a somewhat effeminate face and the beginnings of a paunch, and God looked more like Lillian's idea of Noah or the pirate Bluebeard. She kept these heretical thoughts to herself.

'Awesome, isn't it?' Sister Veronica said. Lillian was not feeling awe, but she nodded agreement.

The chauffeur was still with the car in the blazing heat of the amphitheatre. The engine was running to keep the interior comfortably cool. A short drive took them back past the Colosseum to another church, smaller than St Peter's and with a more austere interior. What she had been brought here to see was Michelangelo's Moses, a mysteriously horned Moses holding the tablets with the Ten Commandments. Sister Veronica told her the horns were referenced in the book of Exodus and might be due to a mistranslation.

'Michelangelo is showing us the face of a man who has looked into the face of God,' she said.

'Yes, I can see that,' Lillian said, although in truth she could not. It was the face of a Biblical prophet who but for the horns might as well have been an emperor or one of the gods of the Romans. But the statue had an imposing presence and the eyes seemed to follow you as you moved (she remembered Andrew telling her that the Mona Lisa in Paris had eyes that did that, as did the eyes in many paintings by artists great and minor). Lillian admonished herself for philistine thoughts, but she hoped they might pursue a more secular itinerary for the rest of the afternoon.

Which they did. The chauffeur dropped them in Via Condotti, the city's most elegant shopping street. They had coffee and pastries in the *Caffè Greco*, which dated from the eighteenth century – the customers today were inelegant sightseers in shorts and slacks clutching guidebooks which had brought them here to blow their $5- or $10-a-day budget on a snack. Lillian ventured to ask Sister Veronica how a girl from New York came to be a nun in the Vatican.

'My brother got polio when he was five. I was only a few months old. It was touch-and-go for more than a year. My mom promised the local priest that she would give me to the church if Marco got better. And he did. It was practically a miracle. My mom had been praying to St Anthony and to the Blessed Virgin several times a day.'

'And you had to make good on her promise?' Lillian remembered the Prince's vow that he would give three of his children to the church if they were spared in the fire at his house in Sicily. She tried to imagine having committed her infant daughter to a convent or Andrew to the priesthood. It was inconceivable, and Sylvia would have made as unlikely a nun as Andrew a minister.

'I was sent to convent schools. And luckily for her, I felt a calling from an early age.'

'But what if you hadn't?'

Veronica wetted her finger to pick up pastry crumbs. 'When I was a teenager, there was a girl in my class who reneged on her parents' promise that she would become a nun. Her dad completely rejected her and her mom still can only see her in secret.'

'What happened to her?'

'She became a teacher. A very good one, from what I've heard.'

'But you became a nun?'

'I haven't taken my final vows, but yes, I became a nun.'

'Working for the Vatican Bank.'

Veronica laughed. 'Yes, who'd have thought! I always had a great head for figures. Top of my class in math. The convent sent me to university to study economics. After graduation I worked in the finance offices of the diocese of New York. Then Don Massimo found me and sort of "head-hunted" me to Rome to work with Monsignor Angelo.' Lillian had noted before that she referred to the Prince by his Sicilian honorific rather than his papal title.

'I was top of my class in arithmetic,' she told Veronica. 'And I kept the books for my husband when he went into property development.'

'Maybe Don Massimo will find a job for you here!'

'He's already offered to!' Lillian told her and they shared another laugh.

They spent an hour window-shopping with the tourists. There were shops Lillian knew from London's Bond Street and fashion magazines – Tiffany, Cartier, Louis Vuitton, Bulgari – and others, just as swanky, she had not heard of. None of the shoes in the window of Salvatore Ferragamo were priced.

'If you need to ask the price, you can't afford them.' Veronica said with another merry laugh. Lillian told her about buying shoes with her first week's wages in 1933.

'What was your work?'

'Shorthand-typist for a solicitor.'

'Solicitor? Ah yes, a law-firm. Well, a stenographer would need at least a month's salary to buy shoes from Ferragamo today.'

At the bottom of Via Condotti Veronica pointed out the Spanish Steps and the house where John Keats had lived and died. More tourists sat on the steps and on the rim of the piazza's pretty fountain. The limousine was waiting in a nearby street – Veronica must have told the chauffeur their itinerary. He drove them barely half a mile to a slightly smaller piazza with a much bigger water feature: the famous Trevi Fountain.

'I remember the film,' Lillian said as they walked nearer and watched the tourists tossing coins over their shoulders into the water. 'Ten or eleven years ago. One of my closest friends in Hastings, a bank manager's wife, had a bit of a crush on Rossano Brazzi.'

'So did my mom – a major crush! Did you see the picture he made in Venice with Katharine Hepburn? When she fell in the canal.'

'*Summertime*. I saw it with my son and daughter.' Andrew had been seventeen, Sylvia fourteen. Had Andrew first fallen in love with Venice that year? The film had reminded Lillian of her honeymoon. She couldn't remember why George hadn't gone with them; he must have been too busy on one of his projects.

'It's a much better movie than *Three Coins in the Fountain*. Romance rather than sentimentality.' An interesting observation from a nun, Lillian thought. 'But the slushier they are, the more my mom loves them!' Lillian smiled.

They returned to the car and were taken back across the river to the broad avenue leading to St Peter's Square. In a narrower side-street they stopped outside a four-storey building that in London might have been mock-Georgian offices but here was an understated eighteenth-century palace, now converted into flats. Massimo's was one of two on the top floor. There was a handsome marble staircase but no lift. The landings were hung with Renaissance paintings, religious and classical scenes; they were by insignificant artists, Sister Veronica said.

Massimo had described his Rome apartment over their lunch in Capri. It felt monastic rather than palatial: a small salon with panelled walls, two armchairs and a coffee table, a kitchen in an alcove, a bedroom with a bathroom off it. Veronica invited Lillian to use the bathroom first; she washed her face and reapplied her lipstick. On the bedside table was a photograph of the Prince with his sons on board the yacht with the castle on its promontory behind them; the boys were younger, Fausto perhaps thirteen or fourteen, the younger son not yet a teenager; Massimo's hair was a little less grey. While Veronica used the bathroom, Lillian inspected a shelf of photographs in the salon: Massimo with various clerics, including one with Pope Paul. She wondered how much time the boys' mother had spent here. There were no feminine touches anywhere in the apartment. It was the home of a priest, not of a parent. Perhaps he'd had a bigger flat when Lidia was alive and the children were smaller. If the boys came here they would have to sleep on the floor; there wasn't even a sofa. Had he mentioned owning a hotel in the capital?

A tiny balcony at the rear offered a view of the dome of St Peter's beyond neighbouring rooftops. Veronica made a pot of tea which they drank outside sitting on hard metal chairs. Lillian spoke about the quest for her son that had brought her to Venice and now to Rome. She included the Marinis in her story but omitted Carlo's former career as a gigolo and the revelation about Andrew's homosexuality; these were not subjects to be mentioned to a nun, however modern she might seem.

A telephone call summoned them back to the car. Lillian worried about the driver: did he just sit and wait to be needed, with no food or toilet breaks? Without re-crossing the river, he drove them to an area called Trastevere, with cobbled streets and pretty squares. Massimo and Monsignor Angelo were waiting for them in a restaurant that, like the apartment, had the air of a monastery: panelled walls and a beamed ceiling over refectory tables set in booths with high-backed pews, cushioned to make them comfortable. It was early and the restaurant was not yet busy. At least half the new arrivals were from the church, priests and bishops and – for all Lillian knew – cardinals; some stopped to greet Massimo and the monsignor. The waiters wore white shirts over dark trousers and were presumably not monks. Lillian ordered a salad with anchovies while the others started with pasta. Massimo enquired about Lillian's day and she told him about the Michelangelo's and the shops she had seen.

At Father Angelo's suggestion they had a Moroccan lamb dish which was one of the house specialities and came with rice and couscous. They drank a Chianti which was too dry and too heady for Lillian's taste. Father Angelo led the conversation, talking about shopping in Knightsbridge and on Fifth Avenue. For a priest he was very worldly. Massimo smiled at Lillian constantly and raised his glass to her several times.

The Bentley driver had been dismissed. They returned to the airfield in the black Mercedes. Sister Veronica embraced Lillian and kissed her on both cheeks. 'We had a good day together, Liliana, didn't we?' It was the first time she had fulfilled her promise to call her Liliana. Lillian hugged her.

'Yes, we did. Bless you, Veronica.' Was it permitted for a lapsed Baptist to offer a Catholic nun a blessing? 'I hope we meet again.'

'I'm sure we will.'

Monsignor Angelo once more bowed over Lillian's hand.

The priest and the nun waved them up the short flight of steps into the plane.

'I'm sorry to say, there's still no news from Corsica,' Massimo said as they taxied to the runway. 'They may be out on these Pasquale people's yacht or they could have taken them hunting.'

'Hunting?'

'It's a big sport on the island. Game birds, wild boar, foxes.'

Lillian could not imagine her son shooting anything. He had been squeamish about catching fish with his father.

'Oh well, I hope they're having a nice time,' she said. 'I am. Thanks to you and Sister Veronica.'

He took her hand, lifted it his mouth across the narrow aisle and kissed her knuckles lightly. 'I'm glad to hear it,' he said as the pilot began revving the engines for take-off.

Lillian slept for most of the flight to Salerno, and Massimo fell asleep in the car, driven now by Paolo, on the road back to Amalfi. The climb from the garage up to the house was once again a challenge.

'Straight to bed, I think,' he said. 'Would you like Rosella to make you a drink?'

'No, thank you.' Lillian felt ready to sleep on the floor of the living room. Massimo escorted her up the stairs and kissed her hand again outside her bedroom door.

'Goodnight, Lillian.'

She smiled. 'Goodnight, Max.'

It was the first time she had said his name.

'A quieter day today,' he proposed at breakfast. 'I've got some phone calls to make and paperwork I need to catch up on. Will you be OK on the terrace? You can sunbathe or sit in the shade, as you prefer. If you want something to read, there's a shelf outside my bedroom with books I brought back from the States, or Rosella probably has some magazines.'

'I brought a murder mystery to read on the train,' Lillian told him. 'A Miss Marple.'

'Is she famous?'

'She's Agatha Christie's amateur detective. Margaret Rutherford has played her in three or four film versions.'

'I don't think I've seen those. I've seen quite a few American murder movies. James Cagney?'

'And Edward G. Robinson! He's one of my Hollywood favourites.'

'He stayed in my hotel in Las Vegas three years ago. I shall have to take you to Vegas and we'll hunt down some gangster actors!'

Lillian laughed and thrilled at the prospect. Would it happen? Sunshades had been attached to two of the loungers on the terrace. Alternating between sun and shade, Lillian rejoined Miss Marple in a beach hotel in the Caribbean. The island sounded less exotic than the headland on which she was reading, with an armed guard fifteen feet away; and the murder of a retired major with a glass eye was not as grim as the arson attack on Massimo's house in Sicily. A maid was the next murder victim in the paperback; maids were apt to be killed in Mrs Christie's books. Lillian, who preferred Poirot to Miss Marple, guessed that the holidaying English canon might turn out to be the murderer, on the principle that it was often the least likely suspect who was unmasked. She occasionally heard Massimo's voice raised on the telephone. The indoor dining table was strewn with papers.

Lunch, buffet style, was a selection of salamis served with a salad and cold potato chopped with egg, onion and mayonnaise much as Lillian might have made for herself and George in their garden at home, with ham rather than salami. Despite his grumpiness on the phone the Prince was his usual affable self at lunch. He talked about Las Vegas and Florida, both of which he had visited several times in the last twelve months, looking at hotels and theme parks as potential investments. He described a shopping mall in Florida that sounded as if it had more shops than Hastings town centre.

Fausto arrived in the middle of lunch, back from his researches in Naples. He ate greedily, having perhaps been underfed by his hosts in the seminary where he'd stayed. He proposed a swim after lunch, which his father enthusiastically endorsed. Lillian demurred on the grounds of not having a costume but Rosella produced a choice of two which she was sure would fit Lillian. Lillian tried them on in her bedroom and opted for one with butterflies in the pattern which was a more comfortable fit. She wore a bathrobe down the steps although Rosella and Fausto and Giancarlo, Massimo's grandson who accompanied them to the waterside jetty, walked down in their costumes. Rosella, who was probably a year or two younger than Lillian, had a figure on the verge of middle-aged spread, as Lillian feared hers would be if she didn't go back to playing more golf and swimming in Hastings. Fausto had the pasty skin and slight puffiness of a boy who spent too much time inside, which he clearly did. In contrast Giancarlo, the guard, was tanned with the physique of an athlete. Massimo had gone back to his paperwork, promising to join them later.

They deposited towels on the jetty. Fausto, notwithstanding

his scholarly appearance, dived neatly into the sea. Rosella jumped in with a scream. Giancarlo helped Lillian down a flight of concrete steps that had been scraped clean of slippery seaweed. The sea felt chilly at first, though nowhere near as cold as the English Channel even in midsummer, but once she was in it was a very comfortable temperature.

'Are you OK to swim, ma'am?'

'I prefer not to be out of my depth,' she admitted. 'Please don't call me ma'am. It makes me feel like the Queen. My name is Lillian. Or you can call me Lily.'

'Don Massimo wouldn't like me to call you by your name.' How odd that he used his grandfather's Sicilian title. 'And while you're here you *are* the queen!' She laughed. He kept pace with her as she swam alongside the headland. He warned her not to touch the rocks at the base of the cliff which were festooned with spiny sea-urchins. Fausto was heading towards a wooden platform anchored to the seabed fifty yards offshore. Lillian did not feel confident to swim that far out of her depth and turned back to the jetty where Rosella was already lying on one of the towels. Giancarlo helped her up the steps and then dived back into the water and headed at a champion swimmer's pace to join Fausto on the platform. Rosella pointed Lillian to an inflated Lilo and she resumed Miss Marple's hunt for a murderer in a more distant sea.

Massimo came down after an hour, a formidable sight in bulging swimming trunks. He had what George had called a 'corporation' and Amy Sadler – speaking of her husband – 'a spare tyre', but Lillian thought Massimo could diet himself back into shape, a goal which had always defeated both George and Bob. He produced a pair of flippers which gave her added buoyancy and the courage to swim with him out to the platform. Fausto and Rosella had returned to the house. Giancarlo was talking to two of the men by the guardhouse.

'Did your wife like to swim?' Lillian asked after she got her breath back. They lay side by side on their backs.

'Lidia wasn't keen on the sea. She sunbathed by the pool at the hotel I took you to the other night. She wore a different bikini every time she went. She enjoyed being admired by the men and envied by the women. I didn't want to risk a pool up there –' he gestured toward the headland – 'while the children were small, but the boys took to the sea from a very early age.'

'Fausto's like a fish!'

He smiled. 'Fabio even more so. As you'll see when he and Andrew get back here. Hopefully in the next day or two.'

Lillian found herself remembering beach days in Sussex after the war. Camber Sands, once the mines and barbed wire were cleared, was a family favourite, a vast stretch of golden sand, though you had to beware of the tide which came in at speed. Would Andrew invite Fabio to Hastings? Would Max and Fausto come? An entourage of bodyguards would certainly raise eyebrows at the golf club or any restaurant they might go to. Of course, this was based on many assumptions: that Andrew would come back to England; that his friendship with Fabio continued; that she and Massimo would accept this liaison as they would have if their sons had turned up with prospective daughters-in-law. There was a nice girl in the Baptist Church (her father sold electrical goods in the town centre) when Andrew was in his early teens whom Lillian and George had discussed as a potential girlfriend for their son, but he had spent most of his free time with his schoolfriend David, the doctor's son. None of the society girls he had introduced his mother to in London had the demureness of the girl from church. Demureness was not what Andrew looked for in a girl, and thanks to Carlo it was more than ever clear that her son was not 'the marrying kind'. Were she and Max destined to have a future relationship as not-quite in-laws?

Massimo rolled onto his side facing her. He ran a finger down her forearm which tingled to his touch. She wondered if he might kiss her and was not sure if she wanted him to. She tried not to notice a stirring within his swimming trunks and tried even more strenuously than last night not to imagine him making love to her.

'They will be here, Lillian,' he said. 'Soon. Stop worrying.' He seemed not to be intending to kiss her. Was this a relief? Yes and no.

'I was wondering about what happens after they get back. Where do we all go from here?'

'Who can say? Do you know the song "*Que Serà, Serà*"?'

Lillian smiled. 'Doris Day sang it in that Alfred Hitchcock movie. I've got the record at home. "What will be, will be".' She almost sang the words.

'Well, it's one of the great simple truths of life.'

'I suppose it is.' She smiled again at the thought of a pop song providing a philosophy to live by. Massimo rolled onto his back and appeared to doze. Lillian found the Doris Day lyric reverberating in her head. She knew all the words. Noël Coward had been right to accentuate the potency of 'cheap music'.

After a brief snooze Massimo helped her put the flippers on again and they swam back to the jetty. It was strange how the flippers increased her confidence. Giancarlo had promised to introduce her to snorkelling, although he said the sea urchins were the most prolific and least colourful inhabitants of the water round the headland.

They dried themselves before beginning the ascent. Massimo wrapped a towel round his waist. Lillian wore the bathrobe and carried her book and sunglasses.

'Let's just shower before we go out,' he said.

'Where are we going?'

'Another nice restaurant. We can make it a late lunch or an early dinner.'

'Do I dress up?'

He smiled. 'Dress down. It's not what you would call a posh place.' She smiled at his use of that most English of words.

She changed into a mid-calf skirt, beige with a floral hem, and a peach-coloured blouse. Massimo was wearing American jeans with prominent stitching and a check-patterned blue shirt – he might be taking her to gamble in a Las Vegas casino.

For the first time they left the house unaccompanied. Massimo drove the Mercedes with Lillian beside him. Fausto would dine with the staff. They drove up the steep road to Ravello again and then further into the mountains. There were lemon-groves and vineyards on small plots hacked out of the hillside, and vegetable patches that reminded Lillian of the council-owned allotments in Hastings, for which there was a waiting list. Father had had an allotment outside Rye and entered his onions and runner beans into competitions at village fêtes.

Massimo turned off the narrow road onto a yet narrower track that was not signposted. Shrubs and branches scraped the side of the car. After fifty yards they came to a small plateau on which stood a modest-sized bungalow surrounded by lemon trees. A few tables under a trellis roof, reminiscent of Torcello's *Cipriani*, suggested that this was a restaurant although it was a restaurant without customers. As they got out of the car a woman, older than Maria, came out of the house and greeted Massimo with a squeal of delight. He embraced her and introduced her to Lillian. 'This is Rosaria. She's originally from Monfalcone. I think of her as my honorary grandma, although we're not related. Her daughter was a friend of my Liliana. She works for the local government in Naples.'

'Signora.' The old woman curtsied to Lillian who assumed she was not expected to curtsy back. She offered her hand and the old woman kissed it, as Massimo sometimes did. Lillian thought it would take her a long time to get used to this strange hierarchical society in Italy. She could not imagine the golf club staff or her cleaning lady, who'd come to Hastings from London as a wartime evacuee, kissing her hand.

They sat at the outermost table under the trellis, with a view up the mountains, which were higher and deeper than they seemed from the coast. There were a few more isolated cottages, but the landscape was mostly trees, wild and cultivated. Rosaria brought them a chilled white wine, which Massimo said was their own brew: it had a hint of lemon in its bouquet.

There was no menu. 'Except on weekends you get whatever she's making for her husband,' Massimo said. The starter, inevitably, was pasta, a shell-shaped version Lillian had not encountered before, flavoured with cream and a herb mix that included pine-nuts, basil and garlic, also not served in any Italian restaurant Lillian had been to at home. 'Pesto sauce,' he told her. 'Originally from Genoa. We sometimes have it with chopped ham or salami.' It was delicious. Lillian wondered if pesto could be found in Hastings – or pine nuts if she was to make her own version.

The main course was a thin veal steak under a tomato sauce. Veal Milanese was a dish she had encountered before, but Rosaria's sauce, obviously homemade, was richer and more garlicky than an English restaurant version. They drank second glasses of the lemony white wine. Dessert was a lemon mousse, thick and sharp, and with it came glasses of a sweet lemon liqueur – called *limoncello* or *limoncino*, he told her, particularly popular in the Neapolitan region. Lillian promised herself to look for a cookery book with lemon recipes when she returned home.

She remembered to ask him a question that had come into her mind yesterday. 'Do the boys stay with you in Rome? Did Lidia? Your flat is like a bachelor's mess in the army and even more like a monastery.'

'So it should. The other residents are all priests, including a cardinal from Africa. If we had stayed the night yesterday I'd have put you in a hotel. My Lidia had relatives in Rome that she stayed with. If the boys come now I put them in a hostel for visitors in the grounds of the Vatican. Or they sleep on airbeds on the floor, which is what some of the other residents do, although we're encouraged not to do this.'

He talked some more about his life in Rome and the circles in which he moved, a mixture of financiers and top Vatican clergy. Lillian was embarrassed that she knew nothing more recent about Italian politics than Mussolini's execution by partisans in 1945; they'd hung his body in a petrol station alongside that of his mistress whose name Lillian couldn't remember. The current prime minister's name, Aldo Moro, was unfamiliar. He led a coalition between his party, the Christian Democrats – 'more or less the equivalent of your Conservative Party,' Massimo said, 'but with very close ties to the church' – and the Socialist Party. Despite being excommunicated by the Holy See, the Communists controlled some municipal councils, as impossible in England as rule by Fascists like Oswald Mosley, who had been discredited and imprisoned during the war.

'You had a coalition government in the Depression,' he reminded her.

'And in the war,' she said. Wartime history was safer ground. 'A National Government, it was called. It's hard to imagine a coalition between Labour and the Tories today. The unions would never stand for it.'

'We have a lot of trouble with the unions in Italy. They are big supporters of the Communist Party. Does Hastings vote Conservative or Labour?'

'It's been solidly Tory since 1945. The same MP. I usually vote for him, but two years ago I voted Liberal after going to a talk by Lady Violet Bonham Carter.' She smiled to excuse her naivety. Massimo smiled back.

'And George?' It was still odd to hear him say her husband's name.

'Oh, George was a diehard Tory, but he missed that election because of his stroke. He was horrified when Labour won. So was I. Sir Alec Douglas-Home is like a country squire, you know you can trust him. Harold Wilson looks more like a rent-collector or a door-to-door salesman. I wouldn't trust him with the loan of my lawnmower.'

Massimo laughed. 'I may quote you on that! My friends in Rome are wondering what kind of man they may be dealing with if Britain has another go at joining the Common Market. Next time I take you to Rome we'll have to dine with an Australian banker I know. He's much given to re-allocating politicians into more ordinary careers.'

Lillian smiled again, intrigued by his assumption that he would be taking her to Rome again: was this imminent or on some anticipated future visit? She was relieved when he switched to talking about the film stars he and Lidia had occasionally met, although Sophia Loren and Gina Lollobrigida were the only ones whose names were familiar. Lillian did not know that Lollobrigida was an accomplished painter and sculptress as well as a film star. From an article in *Woman's Journal* she already knew that Sophia Loren and Carlo Ponti had married in France this spring after the Vatican refused to recognise the divorce from his first wife. She was shocked when Massimo told her that Loren's sister was married to Benito Mussolini's youngest son.

'Gina Lollobrigida's very pretty,' Lillian said, 'but Sophia Loren is truly beautiful. I loved her in that film she did with Cary Grant.'

'*The Pride and the Passion*,' he said. 'What my American friends call "a popcorn movie." Did you see *Two Women*, the picture she made for Vittorio De Sica a few years back?'

'No.' Lillian didn't recognise the name. 'We rarely get foreign movies in Hastings.'

'I think this had a general release. She won an Oscar and some other awards for it.'

As with Sister Veronica yesterday, Lillian had another

moment of feeling provincial and unsophisticated; she had lost touch with contemporary culture since Andrew abandoned the London life he had so often shared with her. Massimo went in search of their hostess, who came back with him to say goodbye to Lillian. The return drive down the mountain in the dusk was nerve-wracking; Lillian hoped he hadn't had too much to drink. Outside the guardhouse the men were watching a football match on a small television which they had moved into the doorway. Inside the house Fausto was on his own – Rosella and Alfredo and Maria presumably had a TV of their own in their top-floor quarters. Bent over photocopied ecclesiastical documents on the kitchen table, the studious youth was incongruously jiggling to music on the radio; Italian pop music sounded as tinny and trite as its British equivalent. The Doris Day song came back into Lillian's head, along with '*Volare*', which had been repeatedly sung on variety shows in the late 1950s. Massimo ordered Fausto to turn the music off, which he did without argument, shuffling his papers together to take upstairs where he perhaps had another radio in his room.

Massimo ruffled the boy's hair when he came to kiss his father goodnight. Lillian was surprised when Fausto then kissed her solemnly on both cheeks. '*Buona notte, Signora Liliana.*' This sounded a lot more affectionate than 'Mrs Ruthairford' and made her feel that she had been elevated from merely being the mother of the man who had seduced his younger brother.

Massimo produced a bottle of Limoncello and they drank some more of the sweet sharp liqueur listening to scratchy recordings of Beniamino Gigli singing operatic arias. Following his son's example, Massimo kissed her on both cheeks when she stood up to go to bed.

'*Buona notte, Signora Liliana.*' She smiled and risked saying: '*Buona notte, Signore Max.*'

'*Signor Max,*' he corrected her. They shared a small laugh. Lillian went upstairs thinking it was more exciting to have her cheek kissed by Massimo than by Bob Sadler, the only other man to kiss her since she was widowed.

'I've got another meeting today,' he told her on the terrace at breakfast. 'Hopefully it won't be too long. You can come along for the ride. Bring your book.'

The 'ride' was another journey on the yacht. Paolo and Federico again accompanied them. Paolo took the wheel; Federico sat beside him. Massimo ushered Lillian into the rear of the cockpit. He was not dressed for a boat ride; he wore the black business suit he'd worn in Rome yesterday. Lillian was wearing the pleated skirt and yellow blouse she'd worn on her first day in Venice when she began the search for her son.

It was a shorter trip than the crossing to Capri. Rounding the next headland, there was a view of Positano: villas and low-rise apartments and hotels in a colourful sprawl from the elevated coast road down to a beach packed with sun-loungers and umbrellas up to a small jetty at one end. Heading out beyond two more promontories with castles like the Prince's, they approached a cluster of three islands, rising from the water in rugged cliffs, all topped with thick trees that appeared to grow out of solid rock. They were called *Le Sirenuse*, he told her, named by the ancient Greeks for the sirens they believed to live there. The largest island was in the shape of a dolphin, he said, and one end of it did indeed resemble a fish's tail. Just below the summit was a square fortress-like building of similar size to Massimo's.

'The house was rebuilt in the 1920s on the ruins of a four-teenth-century watchtower like mine,' he said. 'The owner was a Russian ballet dancer called Massine. The architect was Corbusier.'

'I'm sure Andrew would recognise those names,' Lillian said, 'but I'm afraid I don't.'

He smiled. 'Well, they meant nothing to me till I bought the islands five years ago.'

'You're the owner?'

He nodded. 'I have a tenant here, a retired bishop from Calabria.'

'Do bishops retire? I thought they stayed bishops all their lives, like kings and queens.'

Another smile. 'Well, in Italy we sent our king into exile in 1946 after the people voted him out in a referendum. Priests and bishops do retire, although many continue to preach and hold masses into old age. Cardinals usually retire at seven-ty-five, but they are allowed to vote for a new pope up to the age of eighty. Only the Pope has to stay in office till he dies. Anyway, Bishop Domenico lives here in retirement. He runs it as a retreat for priests with health problems. Sometimes they just need to take a break. Or they may be having a spiritual crisis. There are three here at the moment. You won't see them today – the bishop's taking them to a special mass in Naples for Saint Clare of Assisi. Today is her Feast Day.'

'Did she know Saint Francis?'

'Yes, she became a nun under his influence. There are those who say she was his girlfriend, but believers regard that idea as a heresy. Sister Veronica's convent is dedicated to Saint Clare.'

'She's nice. I liked her.'

'I could see that she liked you.'

Paolo manoeuvred the yacht alongside a narrow jetty. Two other yachts were moored offshore, one of them three times the size of Massimo's with several crewmen bustling on board.

'That looks more like a film star's boat. It's not the Pope's, is it?'

He smiled. 'No, just a businessman from Sicily. We've yet to be honoured with a visit from Papa Paolo. The smaller yacht has come from Sardinia. These are the people I'm here to meet with.'

He helped her onto the jetty and held her arm as they climbed a stony track up the wooded hillside. Paolo followed them; Federico stayed with the yacht. Halfway up the hill there was a fork in the path; Massimo escorted her a few yards to a small cottage with a veranda facing the sea beyond the island's harbour..

'There should be coffee and some biscuits in the kitchen,' he said. 'It's best if you stay here. It would be easy to fall off one of the cliffs. There's a telephone connected to the main house if you need anything. I must ask you not to come up to the house. Our meeting is very confidential – not that any of it will be in English.'

He kissed her hand before heading back towards the fork in the path, where he rejoined Paolo and they continued up to the fortress. Lillian went into the cottage, which contained just one whitewashed room with a single bed and an armchair and a kitchenette in an alcove. She was reminded of a bedsit Andrew had rented in London before he moved into his first self-contained flat in South Kensington. The cottage had a modern bathroom with a bath and a separate shower stall; there was a wardrobe and a chest-of-drawers – she didn't open them – but no personal items to suggest that there was anyone in residence.

The rear of the cottage was built into the hill. A herb garden on one side offered a series of scents as she bent over plants that were familiar from her own garden. Geraniums and marigolds beneath a gorse-like shrub on the other side looked dry and she watered them with a jug from beneath the kitchen sink. The veranda had a pair of striped deckchairs similar to those in her shed at home and she settled into one of these with Miss Marple. Within half an hour she had finished the novel; its resolution – belladonna poison and the major's glass eye were crucial elements – seemed far-fetched even by Agatha Christie's always elaborate criteria. Lillian went to the kitchen and was about to risk pouring a glass of tap water when Paolo knocked and entered with a flask of lemonade and a plate of sandwiches.

'From Don Massimo,' he said. Unlike Giancarlo, Paolo only spoke English in short phrases. Lillian had yet to hear a word in English from Federico.

'Please thank the Prince,' she said.

'*Sì*, signora.' He bowed and left her. The lemonade was as flavoursome as Maria's. The sandwiches were tuna mixed with herbs and mayonnaise on crusty bread. Lillian found herself remembering wartime fish paste, which had tasted of something that might or might not have been fish. Today's sandwiches were delicious, although Lillian would have preferred brown bread.

A dusty shelf at one end of the veranda held some dusty American paperback books. She selected *The Snake* by Mickey

Spillane, a writer Bob Sadler regularly read. Lillian had seen the film of one of the Mike Hammer novels, *Kiss Me, Deadly*, although the only thing she remembered now was the title. She smacked the book against the wall to shake out the dust before settling back into her chair. Mike Hammer's secretary, Velda, who was also his girlfriend, was sheltering a young runaway. Spillane was a more lurid writer than Agatha Christie: the plot involved assassins and spies and millions missing from a bank robbery. After three chapters Lillian put the book down and dozed in the deckchair, much as she might be doing in her garden in Hastings today if the search for her son had not brought her to this dolphin-shaped island in the Mediterranean. A touch on her arm wakened her to find the Prince standing over her. She remembered waking in the house in Burano to find Carlo – she had momentarily thought it was Andrew – bending over her on the blue denim sofa. Massimo smiled, and she found herself again thinking how handsome he was. His was a more solid handsomeness than Carlo's or her son's or Giancarlo's who was the best-looking of Massimo's guards, his grandson.

'Bishop Domenico and his guests are back, so I'll have to leave showing you the house till next time.'

Next time, again. Lillian had another vision of a future life in a wider horizon than her bridge circle and golf club in Hastings. Behind Massimo at the junction of the two paths a portly man in a black business suit like Massimo's stopped, looked towards them and bowed his head: was he bowing at Max or at them both? Lillian smiled in his direction as Massimo nodded an acknowledgment. The fat man continued down the path, followed by two rough-looking guards.

'Is he the one from Sardinia or the Sicilian?' she asked.

'He's from Sicily.'

'His bodyguards look very fierce.'

'Sicilians *are* very fierce. Haven't you noticed?' He grinned. Lillian laughed. The three men were now out of sight. Massimo pointed to the novel on her lap. 'I see you're reading one of the books I brought from America. The bishop has a weakness for US crime fiction. He leaves them here in case his guests want a more secular read than the Holy Bible. Bring that one if you want to finish it at home.'

She left the Christie novel on the dusty shelf. The bishop would find it a more sedate read than a Mike Hammer story, although there were plenty of murders. They set off down the path to the jetty, Massimo again taking her arm. The large Sicilian yacht was heading out to sea; the smaller Sardinian-owned boat had already gone. The bishop's motorboat – similar to Carlo's in Burano – was moored behind the Prince's.

Paolo and Federico were smoking and playing cards on deck. Massimo shunted them down into the cabin and sat behind the wheel, removing his suit jacket. Lillian took her usual seat in the rear of the cockpit. The motor opened with a roar and they surged back towards the coast. Lillian drank in the view and once more felt as far from the cliffs of Hastings as if she were in the Caribbean with Miss Marple and her misfit companions.

As Massimo turned the wheel to bring them parallel to the Amalfi coastline, the sun fell fully on the stern. Lillian moved into the shade of the canopy beside him on the bench behind the wheel. He slowed the engine, reducing its noise as well as their speed, and smiled at her again. He took hold of her hand. The eyes that were so nearly black seemed to engulf her. Lillian felt herself drowning in those dark unblinking eyes. She realized that the spell of this country, this sunlit sea, this surging yacht, this man, was unlocking a part of her that she thought she had shut away forever when George died, or perhaps years earlier when George's illness started and Andrew began the uncoupling of his life from his mother's.

Tears rose in Lillian's eyes and rolled down her cheeks. Massimo had not released her hand. He used his hand to move hers and wiped her knuckles across her tear-stained cheeks, then brought her moistened knuckles to his lips. Now her eyes were so blurred with tears that she could barely see, but she could still see those dark, dark eyes – eyes that had sentenced a man to death and a woman to banishment – as he lowered his face towards her and softly, lingeringly, kissed her on the mouth. Lillian's other hand, which she must have raised as if to fend him off, was trapped against his chest as he drew her closer to him and through his shirt she could feel the powerful beat of his heart against her palm. She could also feel – she thought she could even hear – the accelerated pounding of her own heart.

He was only the fifth man to kiss Lillian's mouth in all her fifty years. Apart from George and the two Sadler boys, Arthur and Bob (their brother Wilfred, her childhood favourite, had never so much as kissed her cheek), there had once been a bold black-haired Gypsy who'd lifted her to her feet and kissed her as she arrived, flushed with excitement, at the bottom of the helter-skelter of a travelling fairground outside Rye at the age of fifteen, just before she started at Miss Foster's School For Young Ladies. The kiss of the Gypsy, brief and gentle and deliciously moist, had been Lillian's first kiss and the one by which all the others were measured. Arthur Sadler's kisses, modelled on those of cinema stars, had been technical exercises, like practising scales on the piano, rather than demonstrations of passion. Shy and hesitant, his brother's kisses barely seemed to touch her and certainly left no permanent impression; he still kissed her at social functions, though now only on the cheek and always in front of his wife. From the first George's kisses had always seemed clumsy, rudimentary even, a perfunctory show of proprietorship and duty as much as of affection – though not for a moment had she ever doubted his love and fidelity. Not since the fairground Gypsy (who'd haunted her dreams long years after her ride on the helter-skelter) had Lillian experienced such a thrill from a simple, almost chaste kiss as she felt now with the boat rocking in the wake of a freighter half a mile from them.

She was lost.

Massimo released her mouth but he did not release his hold on her and neither did he release the magnetic hold of those eyes which threatened to wash her overboard. Then he said, whispered, 'I'm not sure if you're ready for this yet, Lillian, but will you try to think about – giving *love* another chance?'

Lillian could not think, yet alone formulate a reply to this impetuous, impossible question. She said:

'Oh, Max.'

The climb up to the house was less of a trial today; she was getting used to it, like going up to the compost heap or the tool-shed at the top of her steeply terraced garden at home. Nevertheless, as she flopped onto one of the outdoor dining chairs, she was giddy and breathless, less perhaps from the climb than from his kiss on the boat. He smiled down at her.

'Tea or Tom Collins?'

'It's a bit early for gin!' she said. 'A cup of tea would be nice.'

'Your wish is my command.' He gave a mock salute and went into the house. Lillian was feeling – as when he first appeared on the landing five days ago – like a schoolgirl.

The telephone rang. Massimo's tone was peremptory, then subdued. He was still smiling when he came back with her tea on a small tray, but she sensed a tension in him.

'I need to make some more calls. Rosella's running you a bath. Come down when you're ready. We'll have an early dinner. Eating in tonight.' He escorted her indoors and crossed to the telephone on an antique desk a few feet from the portrait of his doomed second wife. Lillian took her tea upstairs and undressed for her bath.

'I'm not sure if you're ready for this yet,' he'd said on the boat less than half an hour ago, 'but will you try to think about – giving love another chance?'

He was right. She wasn't ready. Lying in the bath she replayed his kiss. She also recalled her goodbye kiss – on the cheek – from Bob Sadler when he and Amy dropped her at the Dover cross-Channel terminal ten days ago. She remembered kissing George's forehead on the morning of his death last September. Arthur Sadler's kisses – 'Lord Arthur', dashing and faithless and also doomed – could only be recollected dimly although the memory of the fairground Gypsy's kiss when she was fifteen was still almost as vivid as today's kiss on the boat. She reflected on these men who had all loved her (perhaps not the importunate Gypsy!) and whom she had loved, to varying degrees and for different periods of time. That part of her life had died, she'd thought, last September, with George. Only now, less than a year later, a man she'd known for only five days – a *prince!* – was asking her to think not just about remarriage (his remark on Capri apparently had not been a tease) but about *love*.

She was not looking for – what had he called it? – 'a second bite of the cherry'. She had come to Italy only to search for her libertine son who was still off God knows where with his – what had Carlo called him? – 'flavour of the month' plaything. But Fate it seemed had other plans for her.

The bath was cooling. Rather than run more hot water, she stood up and reached for a towel. Returning to the bedroom, she found a folded sheet of crested notepaper propped against the dressing-table mirror. His handwriting was like George's, short wide strokes with low heads and tails:

'*There is progress. Come down when you are ready. M.*'

Lillian fought the inclination to rush downstairs in her bathrobe. What 'progress'? When would Andrew and the boy be here? Were they finally on their way?

What did one wear for an early 'at home' dinner? Not the burgundy again. She was dressing for a man who wanted her to think about love and remarriage. She settled on the pale green cotton dress she'd worn for her excursion to Burano which had ended in dinner with Carlo on Torcello – motorboat rides and revelations. Sandals were a bit too casual, but she didn't want to tower over Max if he kissed her again. Other than lipstick she wore no make-up.

He was engaged in a heated discussion around the kitchen table with Fausto and Alfredo and four of the guards when Lillian came downstairs. Rosella stood behind her son with her arms folded and a severe expression on her face, while

Maria, looking equally solemn, was stirring a huge pan on the stove. Massimo had changed into his jeans and another check shirt that was predominately red. When he saw her through the archway he said '*Basta*' loudly, and the men fell silent. He murmured something to Fausto and then came through the archway. The dark eyes sparkled as he raised her hand to his lips. He said:

'My dear Lillian, you look so cool, so elegant, so English. Roman women spend millions of lire trying to get that look. They would kill to have your complexion.'

Lillian blushed and told herself in her mother's voice that she was becoming more schoolgirlish with every minute that passed in this man's company. He ushered her out onto the terrace and – 'D'you think we can manage a few more steps?' he asked with a theatrical groan – down to the lower lawn which Alfredo had patched and drenchingly watered. There was a flagstone path and he led her along this, avoiding the wet grass, until they reached a weathered wooden bench close to the edge of the cliff. The sun was still high in the west but its heat had lessened. The sea shimmered in bands of green and blue; waves broke soundlessly against the rocks at the bottom of the hundred-foot cliff. Massimo pulled a handkerchief from his jeans pocket and dusted the bench before they sat down. Lillian looked at him expectantly. He took one of her hands and held it between his. Then he sighed, a long deep sigh.

'Lillian, my dear,' he began, 'this is very difficult. I – I have not been entirely honest with you. I have not been telling you the truth about our two sons.'

Lillian's hand clenched inside his. 'Oh God,' she said. 'Something's happened.'

He squeezed her hand. 'It's not as bad as it sounds. It could have been bad but it – won't be.'

'What do you mean?' she demanded. 'Your note said there was progress.'

'And there is. We now know what these people want.'

'Why should they want anything?'

He continued to squeeze her hand, not enough to hurt but enough to keep her under control, in his power. 'They are holding our boys as – hostages.'

Lillian thought she might pass out. She took a deep breath before speaking:

'Hostages for what?'

'This is what my meetings and calls the last three days have been about. My man from Marseille has met with a – representative of the Pasquale family. They want money, of course.'

'How much money?'

'Two million dollars.'

Lillian had stopped keeping George's books in 1950, when the post-war reconstruction boom made his business big enough to hire office staff, but she still had a head for figures. She quickly converted two million dollars into pounds sterling. She also had a fairly accurate idea of her present net worth, the sum of her deposit accounts plus the rough value of the share and property portfolio a broker friend of Bob Sadler's had bought with the proceeds from the sale of the assets of *George Rutherford & Son*. 'I might have to sell the house,' she announced calmly, 'and it will clean me out financially, but I can raise my half.'

Massimo dared to laugh. Lillian wanted to hit him. 'My dear Lillian, I hadn't realized you were such a rich woman. It's lucky for you I'm not a gigolo like Carlo Marini. But from these people's point of view your son isn't worth any fraction of the two million dollars. It was his misfortune to be with Fabio when this happened. We'll get Andrew back when we meet their terms for Fabio. It's *me* they want to bargain with. They know my son is worth more to me than any amount of money –'

'Have you been to the police?' she interrupted, this thought only now occurring to her.

'The police are useless in a case like this.'

'But surely the French police could find them? You know they're in Corsica, you know who they are.'

This time he squeezed her hand so hard that it did hurt. 'Lillian, Corsica is a big wild island like Sicily, with caves and mountains and secretive villagers. There are hundreds of places these people could hide them.'

'Who are these people?'

'They're part of something called the *Union Corse*, the Corsican Union. They are – gangsters – the French equivalent of Italy's Mafia.'

She freed her hand from his. 'And they dare to ask a ransom for the son of a man who works for the Vatican?'

'Unfortunately, my younger son has rather undermined the Monfalcone image of honour and integrity. According to what my Marseille agent was told two days ago, Fabio assaulted this Pasquale man's daughter on board our boat in the harbour at Giglio last week. Luckily he didn't succeed in raping her.'

'And Andrew was a party to this – assault?' she asked incredulously.

'We won't know the truth of what happened until we get

them back. From what Fausto learned in Giglio we know they had dinner with this girl two nights running while her mother was engaged in some sort of sex party with the crew of her own yacht. I imagine the girl led Fabio on and then pretended he'd attacked her.'

'No,' said Lillian. 'If the girl was – like her mother – she would have kept quiet about it. My God, I know Andrew's been mixing with some immoral people since he left England but I can't believe he's capable of something like this. He's more of a stranger than I was expecting.' She fought back tears. 'Why didn't you tell me what was going on?' she demanded, feeling a surge of anger towards him. 'You've been telling me a pack of lies, you and your son.'

'There was no sense in getting you worried until we knew where this situation was headed,' he said with a calm that only fuelled her anger. 'Up to now we've been relying on guesswork. When Fausto went to Giglio last Friday he saw the bodies of two men brought in by a fishing-boat.' Lillian's hands clenched again involuntarily. 'They were the captain and a deckhand from the Corsicans' yacht, presumably the two who'd been fooling around with the boss's wife instead of protecting his daughter. And the crew of another boat reported seeing Fabio and Andrew on the deck of the Corsican yacht when it rendez-voused with a motorboat which took the mother and daughter on board.'

Driven by the lightest of sea breezes a small yacht glided past the headland, its sunlit sail a luminous yellow. 'Why didn't you get the police onto it while they were still at sea?' Lillian asked. Anxiety was taking the place of anger. It seemed inconceivable not to notify the authorities of a kidnapping.

'It was too late. They'd had time to make landfall. And anyway, these people had just shot two of their own men. If they received a radio message that the police were watching the ports, they might have killed our two boys and dumped them overboard.'

Astonishingly, Lillian found she could accept the logic of this reasoning in an otherwise unfathomable situation. He took hold of her hand again before continuing:

'Even though we'd begun to suspect that these Corsicans were considering holding Fabio for ransom, we hoped they would have second thoughts in the light of who I am, whom I represent. The idea was for my man in Marseille to offer a token sum in order to settle things quickly and quietly. But this business of assaulting the girl moves it into a whole new ballpark, as the Americans say. My position is weakened by my son having violated their daughter's honour, the honour of their clan. The Corsicans are as fanatical about this as we Sicilians.'

Medieval nonsense, Lillian thought: this man's wife has been sleeping with the crew of his yacht, his daughter goes off with men she's only just met, and he worries about the honour of his tribe! 'You haven't mentioned how old this girl is.'

'Nineteen,' he told her. 'Nineteen-year-old virgins are thin on the ground in France, so this is all about the virtue of a girl who probably gave it away four or five years ago to some schoolboy or deckhand.' He laughed grimly.

'What happens now?'

'If this was America, we might play for time, try to bargain with them, but we can't risk that here. They're liable to cut off one of Fabio's fingers or an ear and send it to me to show they mean business.' Lillian shuddered. 'If they knew you were here to identify it, they might start by cutting the finger from Andrew.'

Lillian gasped, still shuddering. She tried to free her hand, but he held onto it.

'I don't like to alarm you, but this is what we're up against. There are bandits in Sicily still who do this sort of thing and even gangs on the mainland who make a living out of kidnapping the children of rich parents.'

'So what are you going to do?'

'I'm going to offer an exchange of hostages.'

'But who have you got to exchange?'

'*Me*. I shall offer myself in exchange for our two sons.'

'But – won't they be afraid to hold you hostage?'

'It puts them in an awkward situation. It shows I have respect for the honour of their daughter, their family. But – yes, it will burden them with a more embarrassing hostage.'

'But if they can demand two million dollars for your son, what kind of price will they put on you?'

'They're more likely to want me to help them with a *service* rather than with money. This is what I have been discussing with my colleagues in Rome and the men who came to the island today.'

'What service could you do for a gang of thugs?'

'As I told you the other evening, there are areas where their business activities clash with those of the Sicilians and the Sardinians. I am seen as a "negotiator" in some powerful circles. And people like these cannot put their money in ordinary banks like the one your friend Robert manages. They need a special kind of bank that offers more than the usual services without asking any of the usual questions.'

'And the Vatican Bank would let you take on people like these as clients?'

He released her hand. 'The line between what is rendered to God and what to Caesar isn't quite as clear as it was in first-century Palestine,' he said. Lillian wasn't prepared to settle for a cryptic answer.

'You'd be willing to take in money that came from kidnappings and robberies – and drugs and prostitution?'

'My dear Lillian –' under the circumstances she wished he would stop using these endearments – 'these are matters which you must know that I can't talk about. In any case, the important thing is not what I can or cannot do, so much as what these people think I might be willing to do.'

'And what will happen if you tell them you can't give them what they want?'

'Fausto will pay them the two million dollars. They will have to settle for that and let me go or – kill me and risk the consequences.' The calmness with which he spoke of his own murder took Lillian's breath away. She said:

'And what would be the consequences?'

'They would be exposed not only to the vengeance of my sons – I've given you some idea of Sicilian vengeance – but also the anger of the Roman bank and its many clients from all sorts of unusual quarters.' Another cryptic reply.

Lillian was silent for what seemed to be a long time. She stared out at the sea and the distant green hump that was Capri. Her mind, far from teeming, was almost numbed. 'You must realize that I can't possibly think about – my future – *our* future – when you're willing to make deals with people like these,' she said finally. It was painful to say this, but it needed to be said.

He responded by rising to his feet. 'Let's go up to the terrace. I told Alfredo to fix us some cocktails up there. The ice will be melting.'

Lillian followed him across the flagstones. 'When will this – exchange – take place?' she asked, addressing the broad back of his red check shirt. He stopped and turned. She almost bumped into him. He took hold of her forearms. She hoped he was not intending to kiss her again.

'Tomorrow,' he said. 'I'll fly back to Rome this evening. Father Angelo's arranged a meeting with a French cardinal who may be able to apply some pressure before I go on to Marseille in the morning.'

'You're going tonight?' she said, aghast at the speed with which events were now moving after several days during which nothing had seemed to be happening.

'Yes,' he said. 'This time tomorrow you'll be out here having cocktails with Andrew and my naughty Fabio.'

'And where will you be?'

'In Corsica, I suppose. Or Marseille. I don't know where they'll keep me. It won't be for long.' He stared deep into her eyes. She thought for a moment that she wouldn't mind too much if he kissed her. 'You mustn't worry about me, Lillian. My position makes me very nearly "untouchable". They aren't going to put bits of me in the post.' He gave another cheerful laugh.

'Don't joke about it,' she begged. His expression became serious. His eyes were locked on hers.

'Lillian – *Liliana* – please don't make any decision about the future until you've had time to think it through. I realize it shocks you that I'm willing to reach accommodations with criminals, but my work has always involved some of the world's harsher realities, things you've been spared.'

Not knowing what to say, Lillian said nothing. He did not kiss her. He released her arms and turned to start up the steps to the terrace. Lillian followed. The late afternoon sun streaked the grey stone fortress with a cheerful tinge of pink.

Giancarlo, Massimo's grandson who had taken her swimming yesterday, was back on duty at the end of the terrace overlooking the steps to the gatehouse. A cocktail shaker and two glasses were embedded in a bowl of ice on the wrought-iron table. A small platter held olives and small cubes of hard Italian cheese. Lillian speared squares of cheddar and pineapple on cocktail sticks for her friends when they came for bridge in the afternoon. Massimo poured their drinks and left Lillian with hers while he went indoors to make more calls. Rosella was laying three places at one end of the dining table. The sunlight pouring into the living room illuminated the white beaded dress in the portrait of Lidia, the second wife – Princess Lidia.

Lillian sat on the terrace in one of the cushioned chairs, sipping her Tom Collins. Eschewing the hard cheese, she ate an olive; Rosella had left an empty dish for the stones. The air was warm, oppressively humid; there was no breeze that she could feel. The sun, lower now, cast a golden sheen across the sea between the cliff and the fading smudge of Capri where Lillian had begun to lose her heart and, it seemed, her senses.

It was challenging to accept all he had told her. While she had supposed Andrew to be elusively engaged on some holiday escapade with Max's irresponsible son, he'd been a prisoner, his

232

life – or his limbs – hostage to this Corsican thug whose daughter the Prince's son had all but raped. She hoped the boy would come home to a thrashing, even if it had to be administered by Alfredo or one of the guards if Max was too squeamish to beat his precious son.

She could not begin to find the words for what she would want to say to Andrew. The life she'd enjoyed with him in London, playing what her mother would have called 'fast and loose', seemed to mock her now. Carlo had prepared her to face the fact that her son had even less moral scruple than she'd imagined, but nothing had prepared her for the discovery that he had become totally debauched.

Did she still wish she hadn't come, had stayed in Hastings, grieving, lonely and loveless, but ignorant of this intrigue that Andrew was caught up in? If she had not come to Italy she would have known nothing of this peril to which he had been briefly exposed. It would have been another of his sordid secrets.

But if she hadn't come to Italy, she wouldn't have met the Prince – Max. For five days he had set out to distract her from her quest, which she now knew had taken a dangerous turn, but in those five days he had lifted her out of despondency up to a place where anything – everything – seemed possible.

Massimo came out onto the terrace. His cocktail had gone warm; he emptied it into the ice bucket, poured himself another and topped up Lillian's glass. He toasted her and they clinked glasses.

Lillian did not drink. 'I've been thinking about Andrew,' she said.

'About me too, I hope,' he said with a smile.

Lillian mustered a smile but went on with what she wanted, needed, to say. 'When Bob Sadler was trying to put me off coming to Italy, he said Andrew was "lost" to me, and everything I've heard from Carlo and now from you seems to prove the point. For years I resented George's view of our son as a "bad lot", but he was right and so was Bob: I should have washed my hands of Andrew years ago.'

She stopped, feeling more wretched than she had on the clifftop. There was no comfort in confiding these bleak thoughts to a sympathetic stranger, not even to a sympathetic stranger who wanted to rescue her son and plan a whole new future for her.

Massimo was still standing. He set his glass down and, from behind, put both his hands on her shoulders. 'Disappointing sons,' he said. 'This is what we talked about five nights ago, our first conversation in this house.'

Lillian nodded, fighting the urge to shed tears. 'I'm sorry,' she said; 'you're risking your life to get him back for me and here I am talking as if he's not worth saving.'

He squeezed her shoulders. 'Don't forget I too have a son who is a "lost cause" at seventeen,' he said. 'I wish my Fabio was a bit like his brother, not so much a playboy, and I wish Fausto had just a little of Fabio in him, wasn't quite so serious all the time.'

'It's no good wishing,' Lillian said miserably. His hands pressed her shoulders again. Inside the house Alfredo was standing in a similar position behind Fausto's chair at the dining table, his hands on the boy's shoulders. Fausto was back in the dark suit he'd worn when he collected Lillian at Naples station five days ago.

'Before we go in to dinner,' Max spoke again from above her, 'there's something important I have to tell you. About your grandchild.'

'My grandchildren are in Hong Kong,' she said. 'What have they got to do with any of this?'

'This grandchild hasn't quite been born yet,' he told her.

'Adriana,' she guessed instantly. 'You hinted at this when you said that some homosexuals get married and have children. Adriana's having Andrew's baby?'

'Yes, she is.'

Lillian's head reeled. 'Why didn't she tell me, or why didn't Carlo?'

He took his hands from her shoulders and moved to sit facing her across the table. 'She was ashamed to tell you and she forbade Carlo to say anything. It's my decision to tell you. Clearly you have a right to know.'

'My God,' Lillian said bitterly, 'what a mess he's run away from. He knows it's his child?'

'Oh yes.'

'Was there never any question of his marrying her?'

'I think not.'

'But Carlo married her to give the baby a respectable name? How noble he is.'

'They're not married,' he said. 'They just pretend to be for the sake of appearances in Burano. He offered to marry her but she refused. After the baby's born they plan to go their separate ways. Carlo's going to marry some widow on whom he's already fathered a child.'

A happy ending for Silvia and little Marcello, thought

Lillian. But not for Adriana and her unborn child. 'What a mess,' she said again. Massimo reached across the table to touch her hand but she waved him off crossly. 'More lies you and your children have been telling me,' she added.

'Lillian, I'm sorry. But it's not such a mess as it looks.'

'How can you say that, with Adriana pregnant and Andrew off God-knows-where with her brother?' She forced herself to stay calm. 'How did this come to happen, anyway?'

He sighed. 'My daughter met Andrew in Milan last year when he and Carlo were doing up the apartment next to where she was living with her aunt, Clara's sister.' Lillian nodded: this much she'd already heard from Adriana. 'She was attracted to Andrew. And he to her, although perhaps not to the same extent.'

'Carlo told me Andrew's a homosexual; now you tell me he's made your daughter pregnant. I don't understand: can't he make his mind up between women and men? It seems so – perverse.'

'Some men are like that: bisexual. It's very common in Italy and not unknown in England and America, I assure you.'

Lillian was not assured. Like George she'd always dealt in black and white, not in shades of grey. Her son's life seemed to be a cesspit of every form of depravity. 'Did Adriana know about – the other side of his life?'

'Not at first. But even before she introduced him to my sons, he was flaunting a young barman he was involved with. This was before Adriana got pregnant.'

'And that didn't deter her? Or did she get pregnant –' Lillian blushed – 'by accident?'

'Oh no. She admits she hoped it would pressure him into

marrying her. Some women think they're the one person who can rescue a man from homosexuality or other so-called vices. Women think love changes everything. Maybe sometimes it does.'

'But not with Andrew?'

'I don't think he was ever in love with Adriana. It was just a passing attraction.'

'Will he take an interest in this child – *his* child – do you think?'

Massimo spread his hands. 'That's a question you'll have to ask him tomorrow. But whether he does or doesn't, Adriana and the baby will be well provided for. I shall pay Carlo Marini to make this child legitimate, give it his name –'

'You will do no such thing,' Lillian interrupted him quietly. 'This is my son's child, it will take my son's name or I'll know the reason why.'

Massimo looked at the firm set of her expression and said: 'As you wish, Lillian. This child shall be a Rutherford –' he hesitated – 'although just for you I could make it a Monfalcone.'

Recognizing the considerable implication of this offer from a man with his curious code of principles, she unbent sufficiently to say: 'That's very kind of you, but I will settle for my son accepting the paternity.'

'You're not going to insist that he marries her, are you?'

'Don't you think he ought to? For your daughter's sake – and the baby's?'

'It would be most unwise. Homosexuals should not marry.'

'But you said –'

'I know what I said, but it rarely works out. A bisexual man will ruin a woman's life and her child's too. This child will not lose much if they don't marry. I know that you will love it, and I shall love it too, for your sake as much as for my daughter's.'

Lillian gave a small nod to acknowledge this elaborate and – to her – rather false-sounding attempt at gallantry.

Massimo rose to his feet. 'Dinner is ready,' he said. 'We want to try and get to Rome by ten for our meeting with the cardinal.'

'Is Fausto going with you?'

'Yes. He will bring Fabio and Andrew back here tomorrow.'

'Will he be safe? Will you all be safe?'

'Quite safe. Paolo and Federico will be with us and my man in Marseille is organizing other – precautions. Don't worry, Lillian. There is a procedure for exchanges like this. It will go like clockwork.'

She stood up and followed him indoors. He closed the terrace doors on his grandson and the other night-shift guard; with the high temperature and the lack of breeze there was the threat of mosquitoes, he said. A bowl of lemons and oranges at the centre of the dining table only partially masked the pungent aroma of insect-repellent coils smouldering in saucers on the floor. Federico and Paolo were eating their dinner in the kitchen, served by Rosella. Maria and Alfredo waited on Massimo and Lillian and Fausto.

Dinner was Maria's Sicilian rabbit stew which Fausto had promised Lillian on her arrival five days ago. It tasted unusual and delicious – Massimo told her what herbs went into the flavouring of this favourite dish – but Lillian had no appetite and made only a small inroad in one helping while he and his son waded through several. Struggling to make conversation, Lillian asked Fausto about his studies and was treated to a long discourse on medieval law, which was a small part of his legal studies in Siena and a large part of his life's passion. His English became almost as fluent as his father's as he spoke of examining old wills and title deeds in church crypts and museum basements. Straining to maintain a show of interest, Lillian remembered some of the obsessions Andrew had developed in his teenage years – from train-spotting to the *Saint* stories and (around the time he left home for university) film-stars such as Humphrey Bogart and Bette Davis. Perhaps Fausto too would gravitate to a more congenial hobby.

The boy was speaking about the vast archives beneath the National Library in Florence where he'd spent the first few weeks of his summer vacation. He broke off in mid-sentence as if aware that her attention was wandering. 'I think maybe this is not very interesting for you,' he said.

'No, it's fascinating,' she assured him guiltily. 'But I'm afraid I don't have Andrew's knowledge of Italy's art and history.'

'I think our cultural heritage is only a small part of my country's fascination for your son,' Fausto observed, the sarcasm making him once again sound older than his eighteen years. Despite her reservations Lillian suspected that, like Andrew, like Max, she would find the other Monfalcone boy more appealing.

She declined a dessert. Massimo ate some cheese and an apple. Fausto excused himself and went upstairs. The servants withdrew to the kitchen.

'If only he wasn't so serious,' Massimo said, abruptly resuming their conversation on the terrace. 'I hope that wasn't too boring for you?'

'Medieval law is rather over my head,' she conceded. 'And isn't it all rather a waste of time if he's going to end up working in hotels?'

'Hotels and real estate won't be enough to satisfy Fausto, but he'll need them to underwrite his real career. These old documents he studies aren't just about the ownership of property and titles, they're about the transfer of power down the generations, between church and state. Since my son's inheritance bars him from the church he will have to go into politics. Families like ours have a sacred trust to protect this country from the creeping advance of Communism and Socialism. Fausto feels this already. I expect great things of him.'

From would-be priest to prime minister-designate! It seemed unbelievable that they were talking about an eighteen-year-old student. But the boy was 'deep', as Hazel would have said, and with a father like Massimo who could say what he might become?

'What about his brother?' she asked.

He smiled again. 'I'm not sure my Fabrizio will ever amount to more than he is now: a playboy, pretty but useless.' He sighed. 'I can even tell you how he will die: at the controls of a fast car, a boat, a private plane.'

Lillian shivered. 'And Andrew?' she ventured to ask. 'What does your crystal ball see in his future?'

Massimo pushed his chair back and walked round to her side of the table. She stood up, he pulled her chair away and led her into the living room alcove, whose lemon-yellow walls glowed from the setting sun as if lit from within. They sat on the settee beneath the portrait. Once again he held one of her hands between both of his.

'My dearest Lillian,' he began, and Lillian now welcomed the endearment, 'I only met your son for half-an-hour last spring,

240

but I don't think you should let anyone talk you into – writing him off. He's clearly worked hard to make himself a success in interior design. His personal life must seem shocking to you, his mother, but I've seen homosexuals in America – and bisexual men in Italy – who are much more promiscuous than he seems to be.'

Almost absently he lifted her hand to his lips, kissed it. Lillian's mind was once again in turmoil. She became aware that there was no longer a murmur of voices from the kitchen; the staff had crept quietly upstairs.

'I don't expect the relationship between our sons will last beyond the end of this vacation,' he went on, echoing Carlo's words on her last evening in Venice. 'Fabio doesn't know what he wants out of life, whereas I think – most of the time – Andrew probably does. I wouldn't want to get your hopes up with the idea that he'll go back to Hastings, open an antique shop and marry a farmer's daughter, but I think when he sees the trouble you've put yourself through to find him again, he'll be more considerate in the future, perhaps come home for a few holidays and invite you out to wherever he's working.

'God only *lends* us our children, Lillian. We have to let them make their own way in life, however unhappy we may be with the paths they take. The best we can hope for is that when they cease to need us as parents, they still need us as friends. You had that with Andrew in London, and perhaps you can have it again after this.'

Unable now to help herself, Lillian was weeping again. He drew her head onto his shoulder. Tears ran down her face and dripped onto his lapel. 'You've suffered terrible losses, my darling,' he went on again, inexorably. 'We both have.

Tomorrow you'll get Andrew back, but it won't be forever. You can't expect that. You must make a life of your own, Lillian – find your way forward.'

Lillian's mouth trembled and she closed her eyes to staunch the flow of tears. Wordlessly she lifted her head and, taking the initiative with a man for the first time since her courtship with George more than thirty years ago, pressed her trembling lips to his mouth. Massimo moved his left arm from her shoulder and placed his hand lightly on her right breast, not pressing, just resting it there gently like the head of a drowsing baby. No man other than her husband had ever touched Lillian's breasts, and George's touch had never seemed so poignantly tender, had never sent such exquisite currents of electricity coursing through her.

Massimo freed his mouth but he did not remove his hand from her breast. He spoke, his face so close to hers that he seemed to breathe the words into her mouth:

'If all goes well in France, I shall come back and invite you to let me find a way forward for the two of us.' He took a deep breath before adding, 'If things go badly, I know that my last thought will be of you.'

Lillian opened her eyes. Inches from hers his eyes, huge and black in the pale sunlight reflecting off the walls, engulfed her again, swept her away.

'Come back,' she said. 'Send our sons here and then come back for me.' She reached up with one arm to draw his head down again, and her lips, no longer trembling, found his mouth.

In less than an hour he was gone.

Lillian stood beside Rosella in the doorway of the stone vestibule and watched as, flanked by Federico and Paolo in dark suits, Massimo and his son descended the steps to the gatehouse. Twilight bathed the path and the surrounding rocks in dark shades of pink; the gorse bushes almost flamed with luminosity.

Massimo had changed into the dove-grey suit in which he'd arrived on Saturday evening. This elegant, titled businessman was going to put himself in jeopardy to save his reckless son and the boy's dissolute companion, her son. Before leaving he had said farewells to the men on the terrace and to the servants. Alfredo stood in the archway from the kitchen with his arm around Maria, who like Rosella was openly weeping. Fausto had already left the house after bowing over Lillian's hand. Finally crossing to Lillian in the living room archway Massimo kissed her gravely on both cheeks.

'One last thing, my dearest,' he said. 'I shall tell Fausto that you are aware of what is happening in Corsica, but you must not let him know how much I've told you about my past and the work I do. Italian men keep many secrets from their women, and he would not approve of my taking you so far into my confidence.' He seemed in awe of his own eighteen-year-old son, an odd emotion for a parent.

Lillian nodded, unable to speak. Tears filled her eyes but she managed not to shed them. The dark eyes gazed deep into hers as he lifted her hand to his lips. Then he turned to enter the vestibule and disappeared after the two guards. Lillian followed Rosella into the doorway. At the bottom of the steps Massimo looked up and gave a gesture that was half wave, half salute, before joining Fausto in the rear of the Mercedes. The two men standing on either side of the open gates bowed as the car passed between them. Through brimming eyes Lillian watched it climb the narrow curving driveway, turn left onto the main road and accelerate out of sight round the first bend. One of the men trudged up the drive to close the top gates.

Rosella was still sobbing as she shut and locked the metal grille and the oak front door. Lillian went up to her room where the urge to weep passed, leaving a disorienting mix of anxiety and euphoria. She undressed and cleaned her teeth, climbed into bed and turned out the lamp. Wrinkling her nose at the smell from the mosquito-repellent, she lay back on the pillow and, at seven forty-five, went instantly to sleep.

ROME

The meeting with the French cardinal was a waste of Massimo's time, like those he and Monsignor Angelo had had on Tuesday with the Vatican Bank's security chief and two financiers whose families had experienced kidnappings. Surrendering himself to Pasquale was the only way to save his son and Andrew. The exchange was to take place tomorrow afternoon at a private airfield outside Marseille.

Massimo took Fausto and the two bodyguards for a nightcap to a bar in Trastevere opposite the restaurant where he had dined with Lillian and Monsignor Angelo and Sister Veronica. It was after midnight when they went to the apartment close to Vatican City. Federico insisted on staying in the car outside the building. Paolo and Fausto slept on airbeds on the floor of the living room. Lying on his back in the austere bedroom, alone for the first time since leaving Amalfi, Massimo found his thoughts turning to Lillian.

How amazing that seventeen years after Lidia's death and the ending of his liaison with Clara he should find himself falling in love again, inside less than a week, with a foreigner, a woman more than twice the age of his first two wives, with soft yielding breasts that reminded him more of his mother than of any of the women he'd taken to his bed!

Until this week no woman had succeeded in penetrating the protective shell he'd built around himself since Lidia killed herself after learning about Clara. From time to time he availed himself of professional women of the 'high-class' kind who frequented certain bars in Rome and major hotels in Las Vegas and other US cities. Some of them, particularly the Americans, possessed skills that fulfilled a man's most pornographic fantasies.

As he'd told Lillian, his life centred on his sons. Fausto, always precocious and more serious than other children, provided mental stimulus and Fabio, an affectionate child, provided a kind of romantic focus. With whores to take care of his sexual needs, Massimo had long felt that his life was complete without a wife.

At sixty-four he was beginning to plan for retirement. He would retain two or three homes, sail with his sons, travel to far-flung places, help Alfredo with maintenance chores and gardening, maybe attend auctions of paintings and fine furniture and lend his name to a few good causes.

And perhaps in the back of his mind had lurked the thought that he might, finally, marry again. But any third wife would surely be another Lidia, young, with that fragile luminous beauty that a man felt compelled to own, to possess, to display.

Or maybe a woman in her thirties with tastes and interests of her own, a woman (not, of course, an ex-mistress) like Clara, who'd been thirty (to his thirty-eight) when their affair began and forty-one when he ended it in the guilty aftermath of his wife's suicide. Neither before nor since had he made love to a woman over forty, but only hours ago he had all but proposed to a woman of fifty! Was he growing senile or merely sentimental?

Something in him had felt drawn to Lillian at their first meeting. She was a handsome woman in an essentially English way: tall, with strong features, nice hair, good skin. As they spoke over cocktails he found himself admiring her courage in overcoming her grief for her husband and setting out to find her undeserving son. He liked her candour and her lack of artifice as they shared their thoughts of death and duty and sons who disappointed their fathers.

Giving her an edited version of his life story the next day had started out as a way of postponing the need to tell her what Fausto had seen and heard in Giglio, which boded ill for Fabio and Andrew. Even with some of his most heinous sins glossed over it had been for him a kind of catharsis, better than the Confessional with all its rules and rituals, its rubber-stamped pardons.

And then a day later, on Capri, listening to the account of her life, a humdrum life with a few pallid echoes of the dramas in his own, the one thing he had envied was the long years of companionship she'd had with George. What he needed to fill his life – the years that remained – was not another child bride like Lidia or a prima donna like Clara, but another simple, honest, companionable countrywoman like Liliana... or like

Lillian.

Liliana, thirteen when he married her (a detail he'd spared Lillian), nineteen when she died in the fire, would have been sixty now, ten years older than Lillian, whose name she shared. Had she lived, there might have been different tragedies – perhaps, like Lillian, the loss of a child; and there would have been other women – not Lidia, but certainly Clara; and they would have had a life together, a long one like Lillian and George's with its shared history, its continuity.

Thinking about the life he might have had with Liliana and the life he might yet have with Lillian, he turned onto his side and tried to sleep in his monastic bedroom on the Vatican border. He could hear Paolo snoring in the next room and hoped it would not keep Fausto awake.

AMALFI

By morning the haze had returned; the day was as humid and oppressive as the night. Despite the absence of the Prince and his son security remained high: two men on the terrace, two at the gatehouse, plus Alfredo, the aged chauffeur/butler/gardener who had killed three – no, four – of his master's enemies.

Solemn and still tearful, Rosella served Lillian breakfast on the terrace, then washed and set her hair which was dry and salty from swimming two days ago. Lillian remained indoors, alternating between her room and the living room. Last night's anxiety and euphoria had given way to numbness. She resumed the Mickey Spillane novel she had brought back from the island, but the real-life drama of Massimo's imminent exchange of himself for the two hostages in Corsica constantly intruded into the novel's multi-stranded storyline.

She could not stop reviewing their kisses, the hand-holding, all his endearments. He wanted her to think about the 'way forward' when he came back from this confrontation. She was sure he intended to formally propose to her. Princess Lillian! She smirked at the mere idea of this. Even Andrew would have to feel trumped! I shall need a whole new wardrobe, she thought. Will I have to learn Italian? How will I cope with all these bodyguards and servants everywhere? Am I completely mad even to contemplate marrying a man I hardly know, a prince, a 'financier' – a man whose son Andrew has run off with?

She gave up on the crime story and went out to the terrace. Alfredo was trimming the edge of the lawn with shears; he greeted her with a salute. Lillian smiled at him and descended to the lower terrace to sit on the bench at the cliff edge where Massimo had told her about their hostage sons last night. Listlessly she watched the yachts and ferry-boats out beyond the headland. Her mind teemed.

After a solitary lunch of soup and a salad on the terrace she wrote postcards – views of Capri she had bought while they queued for the funicular back to the harbour on Monday – to send to Sylvia and the children, to the Sadlers and Alice Pemberton, to her cleaning woman. Not yet ready to tell anyone about Andrew's predicament or her unexpected romantic entanglement, she wrote only that Andrew was in Corsica with the son of a Sicilian prince and that she was waiting for him at the Prince's castle in Amalfi. How grandiose it sounded! She gave the cards to Alfredo; his English was very limited but he promised to send them to '*la posta*' with one of the men. Lillian returned inattentively to her paperback.

At seven o'clock she came down from a failed siesta and a shower to sit once more across from the painting of her grandmother's namesake. Alfredo brought her a Tom Collins. 'No message, signora,' he said. 'The *telefono*, it is not ringing.'

Lillian thanked him. She sipped her cocktail, picked up a fashion magazine and promptly discarded it, then did the same with the paperback. After her languid day she was finally beginning to feel nervous and restless. She wondered if she should go for a walk, though the steps were a daunting constraint and Alfredo would surely insist on one of the guards accompanying her. She sighed and dismissed the thought of a walk.

She looked up at the portrait of Lidia. The painter had captured the arrogance of a self-centred young woman confident of her beauty and position, unaware that she was doomed to die by her own hand. Lillian's daughter wasn't as beautiful as Massimo's princess, but she'd always possessed a smugness about her looks and what she saw as her husband's standing in the community; Lillian saw an echo of Sylvia in the sulky immature face of Lidia Monfalcone.

Early-evening sunlight, soft, mellow and golden, poured into the central room through the open French window onto the terrace. A movement caught Lillian's eye and she turned from her contemplation of the portrait to find its subject standing – re-framed – in the doorway, haloed by dazzling rays of sunshine like the Redeemer in a medieval canvas. Her heart stopped and she gasped.

But it was not Lidia Monfalcone who moved clear of the halo of light and into the room: it was the younger of her sons, Fabrizio – Fabio. Like the woman in the painting he was dressed all in white: white trousers and short-sleeved shirt, white canvas shoes. The resemblance to his mother was startling: the same delicate build and elfin features, the same fair hair – blond with a hint of auburn; he even had the same sulkiness in his expression as he advanced across the room towards Lillian who had risen to stand in the archway from the lounge area.

Behind him, still in his clerical black suit, came his brother, Fausto, unsmiling, the 'cold fish'. Behind Fausto – Lillian felt her heart restart and hammer in her chest – Paolo and Federico.

And behind the two guards: nobody else. No Andrew.

Some instinct told her that he was not about to make a belated appearance within the halo of light in the doorway or pound dramatically on the front door. Somehow she knew, before anybody spoke, that he was not with them.

He wasn't dead. Even at the depths of unhappiness in Hastings she had always, obscurely, known that if anything terrible happened to her son she would feel it by some primordial maternal telepathy, no matter how great the physical distance between them. There would be a shift in the shape or the substance of the void his absence created. He wasn't dead. But he wasn't here, of that she was certain. The blood pounded in her veins.

'Where *is* he?' she demanded, not waiting for Fabio to introduce himself or be introduced by his brother. 'Where is *Andrew?*'

Before he could answer, Rosella came running in from the kitchen with a cry that was almost a scream and flung herself at Fabrizio, engulfing him in her arms and covering his face with kisses. Massimo was plainly not the only one who favoured the younger of his sons. The other servants followed a few seconds behind Rosella; Alfredo bowed deeply to the older boy, then seized one of Fabrizio's hands and kissed it fervently. Meanwhile Maria fell on her knees before Fausto, wrapped her arms around his thighs and clung to him, murmuring endearments; evidently Fausto had mastery in Maria's affections. He tolerated her display for some moments before freeing himself from her embrace. She struggled to her feet and as Rosella released Fabrizio and belatedly curtsied to his brother, the old cook pulled the younger boy against her great bosom and kissed his cheeks. Tears were once again streaming down the faces of both women; Alfredo's eyes were moist.

Lillian was partly touched and partly appalled by this emotional extravagance. The colour rose in Fabrizio's cheeks at being the centre of so much attention, but his brother remained calm and controlled, almost aloof, amid all the excitement. He finally dismissed the servants with a curt word and, as Alfredo shooed the reluctant women back to the kitchen, turned to Lillian with an apologetic smile.

'You must pardon this fuss, Mrs Ruthairford. We came in this way to make a surprise for everybody.' He lifted her hand and kissed it in a style that emulated his father's gallantry. 'May I present my brother Fabrizio.'

Still flushed from the servants' overwhelming welcome, the other boy bowed formally. '*Madame*.'

Lillian acknowledged his bow with a perfunctory nod before returning her attention to the older boy.

'I'm sorry – please – excuse me – you must tell me why Andrew's not with you.'

'I will,' he said. 'Please, let us all sit down, Mrs Ruthairford.' He waved her back into the lounge area, where Lillian impatiently plonked herself back in her place facing the portrait. The guards had also retreated to the kitchen at a gesture from Fausto, who seated himself at the opposite end of Lillian's settee with careful attention to the creases in his black trousers. His brother crossed to sit beneath the painting of their mother. Frantic with worry as she was, Lillian found herself again aware of the extraordinary resemblance between the Princess and her younger son. It was easy to understand why Massimo, besotted with his lost wife, should favour this son, the wayward son, the one destined – like Andrew – to break a parent's heart.

By no stretch of the imagination did he look like a rapist. He didn't look old enough to be a rapist. At seventeen he was still a boy, although his voice when he'd greeted her in French had a hint of his brother's and his father's resonance; it was not the adolescent voice his appearance promised. But, unlike his brother, Fabrizio was 'unformed', giving only a few clues to the kind of man he might grow into.

She turned her gaze to the boy on her right who had remained silent during her brief appraisal of his brother. He gave her another of his narrow smiles before starting to speak.

'Your son is in France, Mrs Ruthairford. He did not wish to come back to Italy. Of course, if he knew you are here, I expect he would come, but he does not know this.'

'You didn't tell him I'm here waiting for him?'

'I did not see him to tell him anything.'

'Is he safe?' Her intuition that Andrew was unharmed might not be as reliable as she'd supposed.

'Yes, he is safe.'

'I don't understand why he doesn't know I'm here.'

'If you will permit me to explain the arrangements we made. I think my father told you that we did not inform these people that you were here because we did not want them to try and make another ransom for Andrew?' Lillian nodded.

'My father and I met these people this afternoon,' he went on. 'Not these people – two of their men – at a small flying club outside of Marseille. I stood with them while my father had a few moments with Fabrizio inside our aeroplane, then my father came out and got into their car and I went into the plane with Fabrizio and our pilot took off for Rome. We went to collect some fresh clothes for Fabrizio and then we came on to Salerno.'

Lillian pictured the scene as he spoke, not in cinematic terms of continuous motion but as a series of snapshots, like flicking through a photograph album. Fausto at the Corsicans' car – one of those big black Citroëns with rising suspension – beside two swarthy French versions of Paolo and Federico. Massimo, tears in his eyes, embracing his favourite son inside the cabin of their small aircraft. Massimo at the car shaking hands – no, embracing also his other son, the future politician. Fausto returning to the plane, not looking back, his brother's frightened face at one of the porthole windows. The plane's wheels leaving the ground as it took off. The Citroën passing through the airfield gates in a convoy of similar vehicles, all with darkened glass.

And Andrew was nowhere in these pictures.

The boy had not stopped speaking:

'As soon as I came to the car I could see that Andrew was not with them. They told me he has gone to a hotel in Marseille. After this – business – in Corsica, I think he did not wish to have a meeting with my father and me.'

Lillian felt sick with disappointment and frustration that yet another hurdle had been put in the path of her reunion with Andrew.

'How can you say he is safe?' she challenged. 'What's to stop these criminals from taking him back to Corsica or wherever they have taken your father?'

'We have a guarantee from them that no harm will come to your son while my father is with them.'

'And you can trust them?' she scoffed.

'Yes, Mrs Ruthairford, we can trust them. You might not believe this, but there is honour among thieves.' He smiled another brief humourless smile.

'But your father will have asked them to get word to Andrew that I am here waiting for him?'

He shook his head. 'No, Mrs Ruthairford, we cannot ask any favour from these people while they are holding my father. And there is no reason for us to show any interest in Andrew since he has gone away by himself. If they think he has some value to us, this makes a danger for him and increases the danger to my father.'

'So what do I do now?' Lillian asked, disappointment bringing her to the verge of tears. 'Give up and go home?'

'Mrs Ruthairford, do you think we will abandon you after all the trouble my brother has made?' He spoke as if Fabrizio was not sitting there with them, a sullen expression on his face much like his mother's in the portrait. 'My father promised to bring you to your son,' Fausto continued, 'and it is now for me to keep my father's promise. But instead of Andrew to come here I think you must go to France and he can come to you there.'

'But how do I find him?' she cried. 'You said it's dangerous for him and your father if we show any interest in him.'

'We will use a man who has no connection to my father, a private detective maybe. He will be employed in your name. He can tell the truth: your husband has died and you have come to look for your son. Nobody will interfere with this, Mrs Ruthairford. Even gangsters have mothers.'

'So where do I go now?' asked Lillian dispiritedly.

'You go to Marseille,' he said. 'Tomorrow you go to Marseille.'

Alfredo came through the arch with drinks on a tray: lemonade for the two boys, another Tom Collins for Lillian. Fausto solemnly toasted Lillian, and Fabrizio raised his glass to her with a sudden smile that seemed to illuminate the room. Lillian was startled to discover that she could see what must have attracted her son to this sulky teenager: smiling, he was like one of those lovingly, even jealously, sculpted Greek or Roman statues – perfect in form and feature, the very epitome of gilded, heedless youth. For the first time Lillian saw that a boy could be beautiful in the same way that a girl was, and could similarly drive an older man into wantonness and folly.

Fausto told her that he planned to fly to Rome in the morning, to be more readily available for the next turn of events in France or Corsica – and also, Lillian guessed, to be able to access funds if a ransom was demanded for the Prince. From Rome Lillian could take a commercial flight on to Marseille.

'Do not worry about the expense, Signora Ruthairford. My father's money will pay for your ticket.'

'That's very kind of you,' she said, feeling uncomfortable and wondering how much of her limited sterling the air fare would have taken and how much she would have to pay for a hotel in Marseille. She was already dreading resuming her search in France, which was only necessary because Andrew had lacked the courage to come to Amalfi and face the consequences of his reckless behaviour with Max's son.

Dinner – another hearty stew – was served indoors by all three servants with much fussing over the new arrivals. Lillian again had little appetite. Conversation was as stilted as during Lillian's two dinners with Fausto and his father. They did not talk any further about Massimo or Andrew or the next day's arrangements or what she might find in France. The younger boy made no contribution to the conversation and only gave one- or two-word answers when directly addressed by his brother. His physical beauty notwithstanding, Lillian wondered how Andrew had put up with such moody company in the close confines of the yacht for the last three months – or was he only sulking now as a result of being abandoned by Andrew at the end of their week as hostages? Lillian would have liked to ask about their time in Corsica, to know what they had had to endure, what Massimo was even now enduring, but since neither of the boys broached this subject, she felt unable to bring it up.

Another topic she could not raise was their father's not-quite-proposal. From their silence on the subject she could infer that he had not told them or, if he had, that they did not approve. It was hard to envision a future as stepmother to the serious older son, the future prime minister, or to his petulant brother, the novice playboy.

As at previous meals in Fausto's company, it was a relief

when it ended. After her long day of tensely doing nothing but wait for what had proved to be another disheartening setback, Lillian felt emotionally more than physically drained. She excused herself to go to bed early.

'I will take you to your room,' Fabrizio surprisingly offered, this short sentence the longest she had heard from him so far. 'I also will go to my bed.' Like Fausto's his English was careful, over-grammatical, slightly accented, not as natural sounding as their half-sister's or Carlo's.

Fausto rose and bowed across the table. 'Goodnight, Mrs Ruthairford. I think Rosella must wake you a little bit early in the morning. We will go to the airport in Salerno no later than nine o'clock.' Lillian nodded and said goodnight.

Fabio scampered ahead of her up the stairs. He waited on the landing and then, as Lillian smiled at him a little uncertainly, he stepped forward, gave her another of his dazzling smiles and kissed her on both cheeks.

'Goodnight, *madame mère*,' he said and turned to scamper up the next flight of stairs.

Lillian's schoolgirl French was – just – adequate to understanding how she had been addressed by this discarded plaything of her spineless son.

MARSEILLE

Paolo and Federico had stood beside the Monfalcone plane on the airfield outside Marseille with handguns on show as a deterrent to any double-cross by the Corsicans; Gustave, Massimo's agent in Marseille, had two Sardinian mercenaries in the back of his van, armed with sub-machineguns. No doubt Pasquale had men hidden among the hangars and randomly parked cars in case the Sicilians attempted a rescue. Neither side had breached the stand-off, and after an emotional few moments with Fabrizio (who told him that Andrew had gone to a hotel in Marseille and intended to make his own way back to Italy) Massimo was driven out of the airfield by two of Pasquale's 'goons'. One of them had blindfolded him as they left the airport, apologizing profusely for the inconvenience to '*votre excellence*'.

Marseille was not a city he knew well, apart from the harbour which he'd sailed into twice. The many turns and back-doubles the car took were probably intended more to shake off any pursuit than to confuse him, but he had no idea where he was when they finally stopped and let him out of the car inside what sounded from the acoustics like a warehouse or factory building. The blindfold was removed, with more obsequious apologies, in a small bare office.

There had been no pursuit for his captors to shake off. Attempts to retrieve hostages by stealth never succeeded; armed rescue usually ended with dead hostages. As he had told Lillian, Massimo would rely on his negotiating skills and his standing.

The office in which he waited was windowless but brightly lit; it boasted a small washroom. After half an hour his captors brought him sandwiches – tuna and mayonnaise – and a bottle of wine; and within an hour he met their employer.

The goons, still grovelling, blindfolded him again. He heard the clatter of other chairs being dragged into the room and then he was addressed in accented French by a man who introduced himself as the father of the girl Fabrizio had '*déshonorée*'. He too called Massimo 'Your Excellency'. French was not a language in which Massimo had any fluency; nevertheless, he stumbled through an apology for his son's misbehaviour, thanked M. Pasquale for the boy's release and casually enquired what had become of his English friend. Pasquale said that his men had assured Fausto (*'l'autre fils de votre excellence'*) that *'le monsieur anglais'* had been taken to a hotel *'dans le Vieux Port'* and was in no danger from Pasquale's organization. Massimo guessed that Andrew had chosen to avoid an uncomfortable confrontation with the family. Lillian was in for another setback, but not an insurmountable one. It would be easy enough to locate Andrew and reunite him with his mother. Not dwelling on the subject of his son's former companion, he came, abruptly, to the point:

'*Parlons de ce que vous voulez de moi.*' Let's talk about what you want from me.

'*Votre excellence est trop gentille,*' Pasquale gushed.

He did not ask for two million dollars – or any other sum. He didn't want to open a bank account in the Vatican. He wanted a small favour, which Massimo could almost certainly deliver, and a large one, which he almost certainly could not.

The smaller issue concerned fishing rights in the Ligurian Sea between Corsica and mainland Italy. This could have been arbitrated without recourse to kidnapping, although Massimo did not say so. It would entail speaking to politicians and union officials, two areas in which Massimo had valuable contacts. It would also involve the Sardinian Mafia, who had sent one of their senior *consiglieri* to the meeting on the island yesterday, as had the Russo clan from Sicily. These were the two men Massimo had described as 'businessmen' to Lillian, the men with whom he had discussed the likely terms for the release of

Fabrizio and Andrew.

The big issue concerned improved access to the US drug market. Narcotics was today the underworld's single biggest area of criminal activity. The Corsican Union's attempts to infiltrate this market had resulted in some spectacular failures. Only last December, a hundred kilograms of heroin, worth some sixty million dollars, had been uncovered by narcotics agents in Columbus, Georgia, acting on a tip-off, inside an imported French refrigerator.

Massimo had foreseen the request for access to the US drugs market. This, rather than a bank account at the Vatican, was what he'd had in mind when he told Lillian that the Corsicans might be more interested in a 'service' than in money.

On his visits to the US Massimo had met many of the country's Mafia chieftains who, like their Sicilian progenitors, liked to be called 'Dons' and 'Godfathers'. He'd told Lillian that he had just bought the Pope a casino in Las Vegas; he hadn't told her that the vendor was the head of a New York Mafia 'Family'.

The prospect of pleading the Corsicans' cause to the US drug barons was not one he relished. He deplored this lethal traffic that preyed on the weak and destroyed young lives. In any case, the American Dons would be deaf to such pleas. Already some of the black and Latin American distributors were trying to muscle in on the more lucrative import side of the business. None of the Families would be willing to cut the Corsicans in on a slice of the action. The narcotics trade had spawned brutal 'wars' between Mafia clans in Sicily and those on the mainland. The Sicilian *consigliere* yesterday had not offered any support from his Don and expressed incredulity that Massimo imagined that he might. Other Dons Massimo had spoken to in calls from Amalfi had been similarly unforthcoming.

This was not what Pasquale – and whoever was occupying the other chairs – wanted to hear. Massimo assured them that he could prevail on the Sardinian Mafia which controlled the Ligurian fishermen and offered to take 'soundings' with the American Families on the possibility of the Corsican Union accessing the US narcotics traffic.

Still polite but audibly less gushing, Pasquale thanked him and promised to get back to him later. He and his companions left the room, there was the clatter of chairs being dragged out, Massimo's blindfold was again removed and he was alone with his thoughts which, now that both his sons were safe, immediately returned to the wives he had lost and the woman he would try to make his wife when this drama was played out. Sitting in the hard chair with one arm on a plain wooden desk he drifted off to sleep for several hours, only waking when one of the goons brought him a pot of coffee and some bread and cheese. French cheeses were always excellent but their bread was only edible in the morning when it was fresh.

It was close to midnight when the two men blindfolded him once more and led him back to the car. A few turns and back-doubles preceded a long straight stretch on a fast road which felt and sounded like a motorway. After leaving the motorway a handful of turns brought them to a temporary halt while heavy gates were noisily opened; then they were on a gravel drive for two or three minutes. When they let him out, there was the smell of country air, a garden, and the sound, nearby, of large growling guard dogs, German Shepherds or

Dobermans.

He was now in the hands of a different set of goons who helped him up a flight of stone steps into a large echoing stone-floored entrance hall. Here he sat for half-an-hour in a pew-like hard wooden seat while footsteps and snatches of whispered conversation echoed round him. No refreshment was offered, and there was noticeably less deference from his guards when they finally prodded him to his feet and led him to another sizeable room, a library he guessed from the smell of polished wood and leather and cigars and a musty odour which probably came from old books in deteriorating bindings.

He was pushed into a comfortable leather chair. The blindfold was not removed, although he could have removed it himself at any time if he'd chosen to.

'*Prince Monfalcon*,' said a quavering voice, rendering his name into heavily accented French.

'*Monsieur*,' acknowledged Massimo, nodding his head. At no time in the next three-quarters of an hour did his interlocutor introduce himself, although he must have known that Massimo knew who he was: the aged head of the *Union Corse*, revered and feared in his native Corsica for his munificence and the ruthlessness of his justice, a figure as legendary as any of the great Mafia Dons although he was more reclusive than Don Vito or Don Calò and lacked the flamboyance of American Dons like Capone or Luciano. His French was impenetrably overlaid with Corsican; one of the guards had to translate most of his remarks. So far as Massimo could tell there was no one else in the room other than the old man and the two guards.

The conversation was a repeat of the one Massimo had had with Pasquale. The ancient Corsican re-emphasized the disgrace and dishonour that Massimo's son had brought to Pasquale's daughter (whom he referred to as '*la fille de mon lieutenant*', never naming Pasquale), and Massimo renewed his apology for Fabrizio's delinquency for which, he stressed, the boy would be punished. Then the old man reiterated his organization's demands and Massimo restated his position, trying to give the impression that the five percent he was offering was closer to fifty percent. The Corsican was not fooled.

'Did you come here only to waste my time and yours?' the guard translated.

'*Je suis venu pour mon enfant*,' said Massimo simply: I came for my child. The old man was silent for a moment. Then he said:

'Aah, *les enfants*.' And he sighed a deep rattling sigh. Massimo responded with a sigh of his own. There was a longer silence as two fathers quietly contemplated the pains of parenthood. For those few moments Massimo felt a bond, almost a kinship, with this terrible old man who could order him to be set free in an instant or, just as casually, order his execution.

The moment passed. The Corsican coughed, cleared his throat and returned to talking about drugs and the problems the French had experienced in recent years, in New York and in Georgia. Massimo made an effort to show concern for these difficulties and confidence that they could be surmounted. No threats were made by either side: Massimo knew the risks both to his reputation and to his family if he promised something he could not deliver; and the Corsicans knew the risks they would run if they did not free their 'Very Important Hostage'.

At the end of forty or forty-five minutes Massimo was dismissed with a courtesy almost equal to that shown at the

Pasquale warehouse. The two guards took him out into the hall and up a stone staircase to a small bedroom. As soon as he heard the door lock, he removed the blindfold.

The room's one window was a barred recess with wire-meshed glass. There was no washroom or any kind of plumbing. The only furniture was a single divan bed, made up with clean linen and neat blankets; its base rested on uncarpeted floorboards. The guards had left the recessed ceiling light on. Despite the final show of civility in the library he was more plainly now a prisoner. He took off his jacket and lay on the bed, staring at the ceiling.

He recalled the things he had revealed to Lillian – and the things he had not. No sooner had the veil of her son's duplicitous life been lifted than Massimo had imposed on her another tissue of deception. He had told her some of the truth about himself, a few half-truths and at least one enormous lie.

'All these men with guns,' she had asked him five nights ago on the terrace: 'are they – are you – something to do with the *Mafia*?'

'Not all Sicilians belong to this criminal organization,' he had replied – this was true – 'and no, I have nothing to do with the Mafia.' This was a lie.

As it was, he'd gone on to tell her more than he had intended to, more than he'd revealed to any woman since Liliana who came to him out of that world of blood-bonding and revenge – and was destroyed by it.

'Are you something to do with the Mafia?' He was *everything* to do with the Mafia! The Mafia was at the core of his life, his existence. The Mafia was the reason for the century-long feud that had taken Liliana and their children, his father and all his uncles, his grandfather and other men – and women – of the Monfalcone clan back through the generations. Massimo's great-great-grandfather had been the *capo di capi*, the Chief of Chiefs of the Sicilian Mafia; his path to that 'pinnacle' was strewn with the corpses of rival clan-leaders, notably the leader of the clan from Villalba. Many had expected Massimo to scale the same peak.

He joined the Society of the Men of Honour at the end of 1917 when he made the transition from kneeling below the great altar in the monastery to kneeling at the feet of Don Vito Cascio Ferro in Palermo.

Five years later the *capo di capi* sent for him again.

Massimo could still, vividly, remember the day in August 1922, when he was put in a position not too different from the one his aged Corsican 'host' was in today.

PALERMO, 1922

He was seated, alone, at the foot of a big oak table in an oak-panelled room in Don Vito's palazzo. At the head of the table sat the ageing *capo di capi*, dapper in an American seersucker suit, flanked by the *consiglieri*, his counsellors. Don Vito began by inviting Massimo to outline his plans for a new wine-bottling plant at Villalba.

'Do you think to disarm your enemies with employment in this establishment?' Don Vito enquired.

'I have no enemies in Villalba,' Massimo replied disingenuously. 'I have sworn an oath.' There were nods of approval at this demonstration of integrity – or guile.

'You have an old head on those young shoulders, my son,' said Don Vito. It was a signal honour to be addressed as 'my son' by the *capo di capi*. 'But why do you not build a bottling plant in Monfalcone,' he went on, 'so that it may benefit your own community?'

'Because – forgive me, Don Vito – the wine of Monfalcone is like the piss of goats, suitable only for sending in barrels to the cousins in *Cosa Nostra* –' the whole table laughed at this reference to 'Our Thing', as the Mafia in the USA was known – 'whereas the wine of Villalba is fit to be served to the nobility of Palermo and their illustrious guests.' There was more laughter at this allusion to Don Vito's frequent appearances at the city's finest tables.

'Let us drink a glass of Marsala,' Don Vito proposed, 'and turn to the matter of the cement factory at Agrigento.' He nodded at the pair of bodyguards who sat beside the doors at the far end of the room.

A decanter of the dark sweet wine was circulated while a short fat balding man was brought in and seated next to Massimo at the bottom of the table. Dressed in a beige cotton suit with sweat marks under the arms, he mopped his perspiring brow with a garish red-spotted handkerchief. Like Massimo, he knew that he was on trial today.

'Good day, Your Excellency, gentlemen,' he said. 'I hope Your Excellency's health is sublime.'

Don Vito ignored this fawning salutation and did not deign to look at the newcomer. 'What is your report on Signor Bertoni's accounts?' he enquired curtly of Massimo, who had a small pile of ledgers in front of him.

The cement factory's accounts had been sent to Massimo seven days ago, with the summons to this meeting. He too avoided looking at the trembling fat man beside him, who was related by marriage to Massimo's wife.

'Signor Bertoni increased his profit on the new road to Catania by ten percent over the estimate through the addition of more sand to the concrete mixture. He has hidden this in his accounts by claiming a twenty percent increase in the cost of the foundations which he did not incur. I have confirmed this with the quarry manager, one of whose bookkeepers furnished Signor Bertoni with a second falsified set of receipts. The total amount involved is –'

The *capo di capi* held up a hand to silence him. This was not a matter of lire, not even of thousands of lire: this was a matter of principle. Don Vito now cast his gaze bleakly on Signor Bertoni, squirming and sweating in his chair. 'What do you say in answer to this accusation?'

The cement factory manager gulped. 'But these are the books for the tax inspectors from Rome, Your Excellency,' he stammered. 'I have other books, other figures… in another place…' He tailed off miserably under Don Vito's unremitting gaze.

'Then why did you not produce those books for Don Massimo?' Another honour: at the age of twenty-one, to be called Don by the Mafia 'supremo'. Don Vito answered his own question: 'There are no other books.' He raised his voice. 'You have tried to cheat me and now you dare to lie to me.'

Signor Bertoni was visibly trembling from head to foot. His hands made gestures that pleaded. 'Have mercy, Don Vito,' he cried.

'There is mercy only where there is probity,' Don Vito

pronounced. It was a sentence of death. Massimo had known from the moment he found the discrepancy in the cement factory accounts that Liliana's uncle-in-law was doomed. At a nod from the *capo di capi* the guards pulled the shuddering sweating man from his chair and dragged him out of the room. The *consiglieri* now fell to debating how the sentence should be carried out. Don Vito was fastidious in these matters. A lesson must be taught.

Signor Bertoni's fate was decided within minutes. He would be concreted, alive, into the next section of the new road to Catania. An example must also be made of the dishonest book-keeper at the sand quarry. Let him be shot and his body left in the mountains for the wild animals.

Massimo went home to Monfalcone, to Liliana. Her fertile body had so far given him a daughter and two sons, and she was pregnant again. In fulfilment of his promise to the monsignore, his daughter, now three, would go to a convent in due course, but neither of his sons. There would be more sons and, no doubt, more daughters. God's second turn would come. There was plenty of time.

PROVENCE

Lying on the bed in a locked room somewhere beyond Marseille, Massimo guessed that Signor Bertoni, as he waited to be brought into the presence of Don Vito, must have felt much as he did now. How the man felt after his brief 'trial' was an emotion Massimo hoped he would not have to share, now or ever.

There had been other Signor Bertonis in the course of the next two years: men – on one occasion, a woman – called before the summary justice of the *capo di capi* and his counsellors for acts of dishonesty or treachery against the Honoured Society.

On the strength of his accounting and investment skills, Massimo was promoted to the rank of *consigliere*. It was clear that Don Vito was grooming him for the succession, but Massimo was conscious that he lacked both the ambition and, even more vital, the ruthlessness the position called for.

This squeamishness played a part in his response to the murder of his family which ended the pact with the enemy clan. Massimo had had enough of killing, the endless thirst for vengeance, the endless obsession with honour. He'd broken with God, he wished he could break with the Mafia, although he knew this was impossible. Only dead men left the Honoured Society.

PALERMO, 1924

Don Vito wept for a few symbolic moments on Massimo's shoulder. Massimo had shed no tears for the children a sadistic God had taken from him; he did not weep now.

'There will be another woman, my son,' Don Vito said, 'and more children. Believe me.'

Massimo nodded bleakly. 'I know it. I pity the poor woman whom fate blights with loving me, but I know that this woman will cross my path one day.'

'But not in Sicily, I think,' Don Vito said. 'I think you are done with Sicily.'

Massimo marvelled at the old man's perspicacity. Born a

peasant and still barely literate, he had an uncanny ability to see into the minds of his 'lieutenants'. Massimo knew better than to dissimulate to the *capo di capi.*

'If I stay in Sicily and my enemies do not come to kill me, I think my anger will destroy me,' he confessed.

'Your enemies will not come. This I can guarantee. What you have done to this animal who slaughtered your family, this rationing of your vengeance, is unusual, to some it is shocking, but already it brings you respect. Suppose I send you to America to work for *Cosa Nostra*?'

Massimo's jaw dropped open. 'Shall I keep the books for one of the *capi* in New York or Chicago?'

Don Vito smiled benignly. 'My son, you have come a little distance past bookkeeping!'

Massimo spread his hands. 'Whatever.'

'But I ask myself if it must be America,' the old man mused. Massimo was now bewildered.

'I only know that I must leave this accursed island,' he replied honestly.

Don Vito clapped his hands. 'That's good, then. You will not go to the United States. You will go to *Rome.*'

'Rome, Don Vito? But I am no longer a priest and was never a politician. What can a poor farmer do in Rome?'

'You have skills beyond tilling the land, Massimo. Already you have turned the heads of some of the great ladies of Palermo and impressed their husbands also. I want you to do this again in Rome.'

Massimo pretended not to have guessed what the wily old *capo* was leading up to. 'I am to be a *putana* then, a gigolo? You want me to squeeze the tits of some fine Roman ladies?'

Don Vito's decayed teeth showed as he laughed at this vulgarity. 'I want you to squeeze the balls of their husbands! I am sending you to do a little shopping for me, Massimo. I want you to buy me a minister or two, a pair of senators, and perhaps one of His Majesty's *consiglieri*.'

'And what about that "other" city in Rome?' Massimo smiled. 'Shall I shop for you in the grand "bazaar" of Saint Peter?'

Don Vito leaned forward. He did not smile. 'Can we do it, my son? Can you buy me one of the Holy Father's bishops?'

Massimo could not erase the smile from his own face. 'Don Vito, if you send me to shop in the Vatican, I shall come back with nothing less than a cardinal!'

PROVENCE

What he'd told Lillian about his forty-two years in Rome was half the truth – less than half. Yes, he'd ended up as one of the Pope's bankers, but Massimo was serving both God and Mammon. There had long been areas where the Mafia's activities trespassed onto territory owned by the Holy See, from the slums of suburban Rome to the shopping galleries of Italy's most elegant city centres.

Before Massimo became a banker – and after – much of what he did was the same as he had been doing in Sicily, the activities that were the core of the Mafia: blackmail and extortion. Only the scale was grander and more intricate in Rome.

Massimo had been pushed rather than 'called' into the priesthood. He'd taken up agriculture in the Cammarata because, like loyalty to the Men of Honour or the urge to reproduce, it was in his blood. But in the subtle and devious world of State and Church politics he found his true vocation, as an 'ambassador' for the third great force in Italian affairs.

In Sicily Massimo had learned that he lacked the Borgia taste for blood. In Rome he discovered that he had a Machiavellian instinct for intrigue. He had an ear for the hint, the little jest, sometimes just a single word dropped into a conversation that indicated which fruit were ready for plucking. This senator yearned to live like a nobleman; this adviser to the King had gambling debts; this general drank to excess; this minister's wife had an appetite for young men; this bishop shared that taste. Some, as Don Vito had known, could be bought; some could be frightened: all, to varying degrees, could be controlled. If all else failed, Massimo would step aside and the kidnappers and the hit-men moved in.

One vote on a particular committee might determine which company received the contract to build offices, a hospital, a highway, a dam. A word from a suitably placed official could ensure that an overzealous magistrate or an obstinate police prefect was banished to some alpine outpost and replaced with someone more amenable. Doors could be induced to open or to stay permanently closed. Even Fascist doors.

When Mussolini declared war on the Mafia, Massimo began moving the underworld's funds from Sicily to safe havens in Switzerland and the USA. Monsignor Angelo, his closest friend at the Vatican, was performing a similar duty with 'Peter's Pence'.

So, yes, it was true, as he had told Lillian, that he had become one of the Pope's investment advisers. But first and foremost he had been Don Vito's man in Rome, and after Don Vito was imprisoned, Don Calogero Vizzini's.

In contrast to the dandyish Don Vito, the Villalba *capo* had not cast off his peasant origins; he remained slovenly in his dress, rough in his speech, coarse in his ways. The Chief Justice's funeral was the first time Massimo had seen Don Calò close-shaven and wearing a suit. With two of his bodyguards he drew Massimo into a side-chapel of the packed cathedral. Massimo waved Alfredo back into the nave.

'You will have nothing to fear from me, Don Massimo, or from anyone in Villalba,' said Don Calò, lowering his loud voice to a rasp.

Massimo nodded his head, the farthest he was willing to go in showing respect to the 'caretaker' *capo di capi* while Don Vito languished in his Ucciardone prison cell less than three kilometres away.

'I am at your service, Don Calò,' he said, 'as I am still at Don Vito's. You must tell me what you require of me.'

'Don Vito and I want you to continue this service of yours, Don Massimo. This fire will not stop burning. We are scorched, but they will not burn us out. Don Vito has entrusted you with our money and with our lives.' His eyes narrowed and he held Massimo in a direct gaze. '*I* trust you. Stay in Rome. Stay close to the shadow of the Holy Father. Make friends, if you can, with these whoreson Fascists. Do not come to Sicily again. Send me messages only by men you can trust.' He offered a weather-beaten hand, which Massimo lifted to his mouth and briefly kissed.

Don Calò nodded to his guards and they flanked him back

to the echoing nave.

A few months later Don Calò was arrested by *il Duce*'s anti-Mafia prefect on the new charge of 'criminal association'. Convincing proof of Massimo's value to the *capo* from the stronghold of his enemies came when a Fascist deputy he'd recently befriended secured Don Calò's release from a five-year sentence after a mere five days in the cell next to Don Vito's.

Massimo remained in contact with Don Calò through Alfredo, who on regular visits to his mother Lucrezia in Monfalcone always stopped in Villalba to pay his master's respects to the man who, on Don Vito's death in 1943, assumed the full mantle of *capo di capi*. But Massimo would never feel as protective of – or as protected by – Don Calò or any *capo* after him as he felt with Don Vito.

In the late 1950s he had guided the creation of a 'Sicilian Mafia Commission' or '*Cupola*' to arbitrate disputes between the clans, which increasingly centred on the heroin trade. The Commission failed to prevent an all-out war between two of the clans in 1962, in which civilians and military policemen were caught in the crossfire of shootings and bombings. Almost 2,000 *mafiosi* were arrested in a new government crackdown. Massimo's influence prevented no more than a handful of senior figures from being jailed. Its ineffectualness laid bare, the Sicilian Commission was dissolved. Massimo made enemies of those he had failed to help. No one clan head was today seen as the *capo di capi* although more than one clan leader 'pretended' to the title.

In both Italy and America there was no let-up in the war between the various regional Mafias. And in Sicily, factional feuding and age-old family vendettas never ceased. Disputes continued to be settled with guns, knives or, growing in popularity, car bombs.

PROVENCE

The Mafia had outlived Mussolini's Blackshirts and it would outlive today's red-shirted Socialists and Communists. Like popes, *capos* died and were succeeded, although sometimes the succession was a bloody and medieval process. Massimo had told Lillian he'd served four popes: in the same period he'd served a higher number of *capos*. There were always politicians and judges, policemen and prosecutors, bankers and bishops, union leaders and journalists to be suborned with bribes or threats. And there were vast sums to be 'legitimized' through investment in industry, intensive farming, real estate and leisure activities.

But his importance as an 'envoy' between the Vatican and the Mafia had diminished in recent years. Today's was becoming more a modern Mafia than even the far-sighted Don Vito had dreamed of. In Sicily, as in the US, some of the Families were no longer headed by geriatrics in peasant dress or pre-war suits, but by younger men who wore today's sharper styles, men whose most valued lieutenants were as likely to be accountants as hit-men. Professional bankers from North and South America now masterminded the 'laundering' of Mafia funds in Caribbean tax havens and other countries with accommodating fiscal regulations. The legitimate investments Massimo had overseen in hotels and casinos and amusement parks were self-perpetuating, controlled by management teams with no formal links to *Cosa Nostra*.

Massimo, like the ancient Corsican whose prisoner he now was, was one of the last of an ancient breed, one of the dinosaurs. The time was plainly coming, whatever happened now in Marseille, for him to step down. But – here he'd told Lillian another half-truth containing another huge lie – like Don Vito he was grooming his own successor: his eldest son. Not to enter politics, although that was always a possibility, but to enter the Society of the Men of Honour. Fausto's cold nature and calculating intellect would make him unstoppable. Massimo fully expected his son to re-take for the Monfalcones the ultimate prize. He would become the most formidable *capo di capi* since Don Vito, perhaps the greatest of all time.

And then there was Fabio. Had Massimo's obsessive love for this younger son, the very mirror of his mother, caused him to grow up with a sense of himself as the object of men's passion rather than women's? This unfortunate business with the Corsican girl seemed to indicate that Fabio was at least developing into a bisexual. Please God, he would sire some children. It was hard to picture the ascetic Fausto as paterfamilias of a great new clan, so it would fall on Fabio, plainly already a sensualist like his father, to safeguard the Monfalcone name while Fausto took care of its inheritance.

At sixty-four Massimo considered himself a happy man: rich beyond his needs, not as powerful as ten years ago but still a force in the intricate web of Mafia politics, wifeless but blessed with two promising if complex sons.

And now there was Lillian.

The sound of the key in the door interrupted his reverie. Massimo levered himself off the bed as the door opened. A young man entered, dressed in a wide-lapelled dark-striped suit; he had black slicked-back hair and the flashy good looks Massimo always associated with gigolos like Carlo Marini. The young man bowed deeply.

'*Venez, s'il vous plaît, votre excellence*,' he said. Massimo recognised the voice that had interpreted the old man's Corsican French. He put on his jacket and held out the blindfold. The guard shook his head.

Out on the landing Massimo asked to use the bathroom and was shown to a closet-sized toilet with no hand-basin. The young guard allowed him to close the door, which had no lock. A tiny barred window gave a view of roof-tiles.

They saw nobody as they walked along the landing and descended a winding wooden staircase. A narrow stone-floored passageway at the foot of the stairs passed the kitchen, from which even at this hour cooking smells and the sound of voices issued. A doorway at the end of the passage brought them into a large integral garage. Three vehicles were parked under neon strip-lights: a long black Cadillac limousine with curtained rear windows, a blue Renault Floride convertible and an ageing white Renault van with muddy tyres and scratched paintwork. Beyond the long open front of the garage the lights illuminated gravel, a stretch of perfect lawn which Alfredo would have envied, a small round rose-bed, a well-trimmed hedge. Somewhere outside a dog barked and others joined in.

Massimo's guard opened the rear of the van, which was incongruously furnished with two deckchairs and an ill-fitting oblong of patterned carpet. A length of crudely shortened velvet curtain on bare wire screened the rear from the driver and passenger seat. The young guard warned Massimo to watch his head as they climbed in and sat in the deckchairs. The driver got out to close the rear door; when he returned he spoke in dialect through the curtain to Massimo's escort who grunted a reply. They set off, gravel rattling in the wheel arches.

The last time Massimo had ridden in a 'furnished' vehicle had been in the 1930s, in a converted hearse fitted out like a miniature living room with French Empire chairs, a small inlaid table and chandelier-style wall lamps; it belonged to Al Capone, the colourful and profane Chicago crime-lord. He hoped that the Renault van was not tonight serving the purpose of a hearse. Were they taking him back to Pasquale's ware-house; to the harbour for transportation to Corsica and further 'negotiations'; or to the airport to await a reunion with his sons? His escort, barely outlined in the glow of a cigarette, made no attempt at conversation, and dignity forbade Massimo to ask questions of a minion, a goon. He would know soon enough.

They drove for half an hour on deserted roads; it was approaching two a.m. – well into the 'graveyard shift', Massimo thought grimly. For a few minutes a glimmer of street lighting penetrated the gap above the curtain, then they were in the country again, not on a motorway this time but on a side-road that twisted and climbed and fell. Raindrops pattered on the roof, the tyres hissed, there was a distant rumble of thunder. Massimo remembered Sunday's storm in Amalfi when he and Lillian had taken refuge in a room of his hotel while he told the story of the fire that consumed Liliana and his infant family.

The van stopped. The driver got out; Massimo heard clicks as his joints stretched in the silent night air. When the rear door opened there was again a rural smell, rain-freshened although it was no longer raining. Massimo and his escort climbed out.

There was not much to see: a single mountain silhouetted against a lighter patch in the dark-clouded, threatening sky; nearby, a chain-link fence; beyond it, a long low modern building without lights.

The driver, an older man than the goon with the gigolo looks, banged on the side of the van. The passenger door opened. Massimo had not known there was a fourth person in the vehicle. He did not expect to see the ancient head of the *Union Corse*; probably it would be Pasquale.

Then the man came into sight, and Massimo knew why they had come to whatever godforsaken place this was. It was a man he had briefly described in answer to one of Lillian's questions, a man he had never met but whom he recognised instantly, so strong was the family resemblance.

When Massimo left his estate at Monfalcone in 1924 after the fire and the burial of his family, this man had been a boy of six or seven; now he was close to fifty, bald, fat, with a jowled face, dressed in the kind of heavy black suit Sicilian men wore to weddings and funerals. Tonight he was dressed for a funeral of sorts.

His name was Federico, the same as Massimo's trusted lieutenant, but he was known as Rico. He was the owner of vast vineyards around Villalba. His only brother was a high-school teacher in Chicago. In December 1917 his father and Massimo Monfalcone, both sixteen, had knelt side by side in front of the mighty Don Vito Cascio Ferro. Each of them cut his right palm with an antique but newly sharpened knife that had been used many times in this ceremony that was almost a sacrament. Don Vito took a handkerchief and tied their bleeding hands together and the two boys, men as of that moment, swore an end to the vendetta between their clans.

In September 1924 Rico's father crossed the mountains from Villalba to Monfalcone alone and on foot to abjure his oath and block the rise to fearful eminence of the new leader of the accursed Monfalcones. He piled hay around the lower walls of the west wing of Massimo's house and then torched it and stole away into the humid darkness. Three days later, in the main piazza in Villalba, Alfredo jammed a shotgun into the mouth of Rico's father, shattering some of his front teeth, and fired both barrels, blowing off most of his head.

'I know you, Rico,' Massimo said now, the Sicilian greeting of recognition sounding strange in his ears after so many years.

'I know you, Don Massimo,' the other replied. His voice quavered. This was a man unaccustomed to violence. He had paid the *pizzù*, the 'tribute', to Don Calò and his successors, but he had turned his back on the Mafia to dedicate himself and his family to viticulture, producing wines that were said to rival Tuscany's finest. But today, summoned by the Corsicans, he had come to fulfil his duty, to honour an oath sworn on his father's coffin forty-two years ago.

Surely there had not been time to fetch him from Sicily, even by private plane, since Massimo's meeting in the warehouse with Pasquale? No, he had been in France already. Someone – one of the Dons Massimo had telephoned, or perhaps the fat *consigliere* who'd scoffed at his request for help yesterday and bowed to him and Lillian on the footpath – had identified Rico as a man with a historical motive to avenge a father murdered decades ago. Guessing that Massimo would not be able to meet their terms, the Corsicans had invited Rico here to do their dirty work for them. Obviously they hoped to deflect any reprisals from France to Sicily, from Marseille to Villalba.

From the hierarchy of the Mafia there might not be reprisals. The Dons would weigh up the risk of a 'war' with the Corsicans, its toll in terms of 'soldiers' and expenditure and the interruption to normal business. Was it possible that some of them felt, as Massimo himself did, that their Vatican envoy had outlived his usefulness and were tonight using the *Union Corse* and an old Sicilian vendetta to expedite his retirement?

The younger of the goons offered Massimo a cigarette, which he declined. The driver produced a key to open the padlocked gate of the nearby fence. With the driver leading the way and the man from Villalba bringing up the rear, they processed down a wet path between flowerbeds. There was the scent of flowers and a herbal background aroma that might have been basil or just pine. In front of them a lake appeared, its surface a patchwork of grey beneath the dark night sky; it terminated in a massive new-looking dam. Rico gasped. Massimo's heart turned over, but he did not so much as miss a step.

A narrow road crossed the top of the dam between thigh-height parapets. The reservoir seemed low; there was a drop of twenty-five or thirty metres to the lake. On its open side Massimo could not see the height of the dam; there was the faint sound of water in a sluice or run-off.

They walked in procession to the middle of the dam. Here the driver stopped and turned. He gestured Massimo towards the edge on the dam's open side. Looking down, Massimo saw a gleam of water some ninety or a hundred metres below, a smaller lake in a narrowing ravine that ended in a second smaller dam. He turned to face the semicircle of men. The young interpreter was the closest to him, the man from Villalba the farthest.

Rico pulled a gun from his pocket, an old heavy pistol that had perhaps belonged to his father. He took two steps towards Massimo and extended the gun in a hand that shook.

'Please forgive me, Don Massimo,' he begged.

'I do not forgive you, Rico,' Massimo said coldly. 'My sons will kill you for this.' Fausto's retribution would be swift, surgically precise and as judiciously measured as that of Don Vito or Don Calò.

'And my sons will kill your sons,' Rico said, anger overcoming his fear.

'If God wishes,' Massimo said. But it was not his sons who were foremost in his mind at this moment, but Lillian. He wished that he had made love to her on Wednesday after their swim out to the platform or that night when they came back from the restaurant in the hills, but he had known that she was not yet ready for this. Lillian was not a woman you would take to your bed before you had taken her to the altar. Yesterday when he kissed her on the boat and then, on the sofa below Lidia's portrait, when she had kissed him, he felt confident that he could love this woman – and that she could love him. He had put his hand on her breast; she had allowed this. When the time came – the time would not come – she would let him make love to her.

He couldn't remember the last woman he'd made love to – not made love to, merely fucked in a commercial transaction – some nameless whore in Las Vegas, as expert and as unmemorable as any other. He thought that Lillian would not be accomplished in this area, would be awkward and embarrassed; but he thought that she would be a 'comfortable' partner and, in her way, unforgettable; and he wished he had that memory to take with him as Rico slowly squeezed the trigger.

From the top of the mountain there came a vivid flash of lightning and an almost instantaneous rumble of thunder. Rain poured onto the mountainside and advanced across the lake in a sheet that hissed on the grey flat surface.

Rico, from a distance of two metres, fired at Massimo's chest. The sound reverberated across the lake like another clap of thunder. Clutching his chest, not dead but mortally wounded, Massimo stumbled and might have crumpled into the roadway, but the young guard with the gigolo looks took a step forward and pushed him so that he landed on his back with a groan across the top of the parapet. Then, as the torrent of rain reached the dam, his momentum carried him over and down. He fell without a sound, his last thought – as he had promised her – of Lillian.

PART THREE

PROVENCE

A foolish son is the heaviness of his mother.

PROVERBS 10.1

'Fancy meeting you here, Mrs Rutherford,' said a familiar voice from behind her, rising out of the hubbub as she paused to get her bearings in the Arrivals hall.

Lillian found herself speechless with pleasure. She hugged him as he leaned forward to kiss her cheek. He laughed and said, 'That was worth a hard day's driving.'

Handsome and debonair in a cream-coloured shirt and the dark-green slacks he'd worn to Cipriani's, he didn't look as if he had driven across Italy and half of France. Swallowing, Lillian found her voice:

'I'm so happy to see you, Carlo. How very good of you to come. And what a lovely surprise! I was expecting to be met by some mysterious Frenchman.'

'Well, don't forget I *was* a mysterious Frenchman until last week!' Lillian felt as delighted as if the Prince – or Andrew himself – had come to meet her.

Carlo took control of her baggage trolley and led her out

of the terminal to the far end of the taxi rank where he had left his car, a white Lincoln convertible, illegally parked. After loading her cases he ushered her into the passenger seat and sat behind the wheel. He smiled at her again.

'You certainly get around, Mrs Rutherford.'

'So do you!' she said, relieved and exhilarated to find herself in his company at the end of her zigzagging journey by air from Salerno to Marseille via Rome and Nice. 'To what do I owe the honour?' she enquired mockingly.

'Purely to your good fortune!' he replied in the same tone as he started the engine. 'I phoned last night after you'd gone to bed, and Fausto told me about you coming here today, so I volunteered to drive down and meet you. He promised not to say anything, so it could be a surprise.'

'It's certainly that!' she said.

'Fausto said he would get somebody checking the hotels to find where Andrew's staying, and I can help with that. I've known Marseille since I was a boy. My mother came here to paint, and then after she died I did all sorts of odd jobs in and around here, on yachts in the port and in bars and restaurants. I know a lot of people here – including some in the criminal underworld, which I hope won't be needed.' He pulled out of the car park into a gap in the stream of cars and taxis leaving the airport.

'You know about – these Corsicans?' she asked, unsure how much the secretive Fausto would have told him. 'And this girl the Prince's son assaulted?'

He nodded. 'I honestly think it can only have been some fooling around that got out of hand. Fabrizio trying to score a point against Andrew. According to what Fausto told me, her family aren't actually accusing him of raping her.' He honked the horn at a French driver who overtook in a burst of acceleration as a traffic light turned red.

'I'm still shocked that Andrew was a party to something like this.'

'They'd probably been drinking. And remember, Fabrizio's only seventeen. This is what he is – an oversexed Italian teenager.'

'That hardly justifies what he's done with this girl. And there's no excuse for Andrew.' The lights changed, they moved forward again in slow traffic.

'I must say, it's a bit feeble of him to cut and run rather than stay and face the music with Fabrizio's family.' Lillian had forgotten how much he could sound like her son, making this kind of disparaging remark.

'Is there any news about Max?'

'Max?'

'Prince Massimo. You know he's handed himself over to these gangsters?'

Carlo nodded again. 'Fausto told me. But I haven't spoken to him today. I'll give him a call when we get to where we're staying. What was the situation when you left this morning?'

'We were up frightfully early to get to the airport. Fausto said there wasn't any news about his father. Is he going to be all right? He told me these kidnappers sometimes – cut bits off their victims and post them to their families.'

'I honestly don't think they'd dare do anything like that to him,' Carlo said. 'I told you he's a pretty big wheel in Rome.' He gunned the engine as they ascended a ramp onto an elevated section of road. Beyond the usual warehouses and factories on the outskirts of any major city, Marseille looked to be more Italian than French in appearance, with a predominance of red-tiled roofs. A gilded statue above the tower of a hilltop church, perhaps the cathedral, dominated the skyline. Lillian rummaged in her handbag for a headscarf. Carlo's hair began to blow in the slipstream as the traffic speeded up. Smiling at her again, he said:

'Actually I do have some news for you.'

'About Andrew?'

He shook his head. 'About Adriana.'

'She's had the baby!' Lillian guessed excitedly.

'Yes. This is why I phoned Amalfi last night, but we decided the news would keep one more day. They did a Caesarean yesterday morning. It's a girl. We're going to call her Clara, after Adriana's mother.'

Incongruously Lillian found herself thinking of Clara Bow, the 'It Girl' who'd been in some of the first movies she saw as a teenager. 'Is Adriana all right?' she asked.

He shook his head again. 'No, she's very weak. Which is why they decided to bring the baby out a couple of weeks prematurely. They say it's gone way beyond anaemia. It's going to be touch-and-go whether she pulls through. But she has a lot of willpower – it must come from her father – so please God she'll make it. She knows I've come here – and why. She sends you her love.'

As they began to clear the suburbs the terrain, beneath a clouded sky, was rugged, not unlike the region between Amalfi and Naples. The air was cool but not cold.

'So I've lost a son and gained a granddaughter,' Lillian said. He looked at her in amazement.

'You know?'

'Max told me. I wish *you* had, whether she wanted you to or not.'

'I did want to,' he said earnestly. 'Did the Prince also tell you we're not really married?'

'Yes. It's very noble of you to protect her from scandal.'

'I would have married her for real – we have enough in common to probably make it work – but she says that we don't have enough *passion* for each other, which I guess is true.'

Lillian thought that Adriana's need for 'passion' might come from her father. 'What does she plan to do if – when she gets better?'

'Start a new life on her own. Prince Massimo will help set her up somewhere. Not in Venice.' He smiled at Lillian. 'She could move to England! Since her mother died she has no real ties to Italy, apart from her aunt in Milan who's not easy to live with.'

Lillian contemplated with pleasure the prospect of having a grandchild in England again, then remembered that Max probably had other plans for the two of them, centred more on Italy than on Sussex. She decided not to spoil Carlo's surprise with one of her own.

'If she doesn't recover,' he said, 'Silvia and I plan to offer to adopt Clara. Hopefully the Prince will give us his approval.'

'You'll have some explaining to do in Burano!' Lillian said. He grinned in reply to this. 'As far as the baby's concerned,' she went on, 'I'm going to insist that Andrew takes some responsibility for his own child – and if he doesn't, then I will – with Max's help. I can't believe how outrageously Andrew has treated this poor girl – and her baby.'

Anger surged in her as she reminded herself that Massimo

– with his history, his revelations, his flirtation with her and now the danger he'd put himself in – had deflected her from the central purpose of her journey: her son and the chaos his self-centred, degenerate lifestyle had wrought upon everyone who came into contact with him.

'I don't suppose you can explain any more than Max could why he should be like this,' she said, aware that she had asked him almost the same question on the telephone the night before she left Venice: 'not able to choose between men and women?'

He shook his head. 'No, I can't. Some men are just like that.'

'Are you?' she asked. He glanced at her again before replying: 'Not now, but I have been.'

Was this how she would feel when she found Andrew? For a moment she thought she would be sick. The feeling passed and she said:

'Can you tell me something about it? Without any unpleasant details, of course.'

'It's probably commoner in Italy and France than in England,' he said, decelerating in order to concentrate on his answer. 'The difference between us, I think, is that I always go back to women, whereas Andrew ultimately prefers his own sex.' His expression became uneasy. 'Am I shocking you?'

'This whole business shocks me,' she admitted. 'But I'd rather know the full story than go on – not knowing.' It suddenly occurred to her to ask: 'Was Laurence Dickinson's friendship with Andrew – more than just a friendship – do you know?'

'Yes it was. Laurence told me that Andrew was the second great love of his life.'

Lillian was now blushing. 'And – you and Laurence? Forgive me for asking.'

'Please.' He lifted his hands briefly off the wheel and spread them in an accommodating gesture. 'I went to England four years ago principally to be Laurence's – "gigolo", let's not beat about the bush. Obviously things worked out rather differently from what was expected.'

Lillian was silent for a few moments. 'I suppose I should have had some doubts when Andrew and Laurence became friends,' she said finally. 'Laurence is more my generation than Andrew's. But he'd been married and he had a daughter, although she wasn't living with him then. I thought he perhaps saw Andrew as the son he'd missed having when he was married.' She hesitated again. 'Forgive me for asking this, but was your relationship with my son that of a – gigolo?'

'Lillian – excuse me, I do beg your pardon – Mrs Rutherford – I'd hate you to think that for a moment. Oh, I'd been kept by men as well as by women long before I met Laurence and I obviously couldn't put as much into our partnership as Andrew, but if I'd simply wanted to be kept again I assure you there were plenty of better opportunities, particularly among the people I was telling you about in Venice. I'm not asking you to accept that Andrew and I had some lofty spiritual relationship, but if I've ever been capable of loving a man, then your son was that man, believe me.'

His earnestness made an appeal of this declaration and although she was embarrassed by it, Lillian mustered a reassuring smile. 'Richard – my daughter's husband – calls me "mother-in-law", which I've always hated. Please do call me Lillian.'

'I guess I'm the ex-son-in-law you didn't know you had,' Carlo said, also smiling as he lit a cigarette one-handed.

'Well, that's Andrew's loss even more than mine,' she said, surprised at how quickly her anger and disgust seemed to be fading and even more surprised to find herself able to accept that this sometime gigolo had loved her son. 'Why didn't – things – work out between you?' she ventured.

He exhaled smoke. 'It really only worked out for the first few months while we were doing up the Cannaregio flat and finding our feet. But the high society circles he was working his way into didn't interest me, I'd done enough of that before in Venice and in France, and the friends I made while I was working at the Europa – waiters and gondoliers – weren't grand enough for Andrew, so we began to go our separate ways. We became just flatmates and then, when the business started to expand, we were workmates as well. We're still the best of friends, but –' he tailed off with another shrug.

'Did Andrew take other – companions?'

'He likes to refer to them as "adventures". None of them meant very much or lasted very long. He had an affair with the American sculptress he took to the Volpi Ball and before her there was the young wife of an elderly count with a palace on the Grand Canal.' Carlo didn't volunteer any details of affairs with men, although Lillian recalled Max mentioning a young barman Andrew had 'flaunted' during his relationship with Adriana. Lillian realized with some surprise that, including Max's son and Laurence Dickinson, she had met three of her son's male lovers.

'I'm sorry he's left you in the lurch,' she said.

He laughed cheerfully. 'Oh, I've done all right. I've never gone short of girlfriends – or mistresses, to use a more old-fashioned word.'

Lillian smiled to cover her embarrassment. 'And now you've found Silvia again,' she said. 'That's something you must tell me about, but that's not what I had in mind. Adriana told me your interior design business can't continue without Andrew.'

'She's right, but I do have another iron in the fire. Last April I leased a bar at Lido di Jesolo, which is –' he grinned again – 'the Veneto's answer to Hastings, the most popular beach resort in the region. It's barely paying its way this first summer because I had to have a manager to run it while I carried on with other things, but if I run it myself and convert the basement into a discotheque I ought to make a decent living from it.'

'Have you got the capital for the conversion?'

He shook his head. 'No, but I can raise a mortgage on my house in Burano. Unfortunately Silvia's house belongs to her mother-in-law, but she's going to stay on at the lace factory until we get back on our feet. We'll be alright.'

Clearly Andrew had left him in the lurch. Lillian sighed to herself. Despite the birth of her new grandchild and the near-proposal from Max, her journey had run into more tragedy than blessings: Adriana dangerously ill, the Prince a hostage, Carlo impoverished, Andrew at loose in Marseille looking for – what was he looking for now?

'What you said just now,' Carlo began – he might have been reading her thoughts. 'You haven't *lost* Andrew. He's only – "mislaid". You still have your son.'

'Do I?'

'As much as you ever have.'

'And how much is that?'

Carlo did not reply to this. His expression offered little comfort. They both fell silent.

***

293

The Saturday evening traffic was light. Within twenty minutes of leaving the suburbs of Marseille they entered the outskirts of another large town. This, he told her, was Aix-en-Provence, where he'd gone to school and where his mother was buried. After a few miles on a bypass they turned onto a narrower road bordered by hills and woods. There were farmhouses, large villas in landscaped gardens and smaller houses clustered into roadside hamlets. The sky was increasingly cloudy, but in the distance Lillian saw the looming outline of a mountain with a sharp triangular peak.

Just beyond one of the hamlets Carlo turned the car into the muddy yard of a farmhouse. In the twilight the farm was already in darkness except for a lighted window in a small two-storey outbuilding that adjoined it at one end. Parking the Lincoln next to a battered van, Carlo guided Lillian over a flagstone path that kept their feet clear of the mud.

The interior was like a crude version of his house in Burano or the guest cottage on Massimo's island: a single room, square rather than oblong, with a rudimentary kitchen in one corner. An earthenware vase filled with wild flowers stood in a stone fireplace. The fireplace wall was bare brick; the others had been whitewashed. The furnishings were simple and rustic: flowered curtains, three unmatched armchairs, a pinewood table with an assortment of dining chairs, a pair of pine chests, a battered mahogany sideboard. The unglazed red floor tiles were partially covered by patterned rugs. A rickety wooden staircase led up the wall adjoining the farmhouse.

'This is a kind of homecoming for me,' Carlo said. 'I lived here with my mother until she died.'

'You told me about living in France with your artist mother

when we went to dinner in Rye four years ago,' she reminded him. 'The night before you and Andrew left to drive to Venice. I never expected that I would come and stay in your house.'

'I hope it's not too much of a comedown for you after a prince's castle, but I thought we'd be comfier here than in a hotel.'

Lillian smiled at his use of 'comfier'. 'It's cosy,' she said. 'It reminds me of my parents' house in Rye.'

'The French call it a *gîte*,' he told her. 'A cottage tacked on to a farm to house employees or for storage. Nowadays the Dufours – the farmers – rent it to holiday-makers in the season. We're lucky it's not let at the moment: they were keeping it free for a family visit this week and one of the grandchildren got sick.'

Lillian gestured at two watercolours on either side of the fireplace and asked: 'Did your mother paint those?'

He shook his head. 'They're from the flea-market in Marseille. I sold the last of Mum's paintings to pay for her funeral. I'd love to buy one back, to take to Burano to remember her by, but I've never tracked any down.'

He took her upstairs. Overriding her protestations, he gave her the master bedroom, a large whitewashed room with a brass-framed double bed. While Carlo returned to the car to fetch their luggage Lillian stepped out of her shoes and lay full-length on a deliciously soft eiderdown, flexing her toes. She heard his feet on the wooden stairs, the creak of the front door, a click as he opened the boot of the Lincoln. Somewhere nearby an animal snorted, a horse or a cow. She heard nothing else. By the time Carlo had climbed the stairs again, unconsciously humming under his breath, so pleased was he to be back in his adolescent home, Lillian was fast asleep in the middle of the bed. He gently rolled the eiderdown over her and crept out of the room, switching off the light.

Lillian slept for eleven hours, exhausted by yesterday's long day in planes and airports and perhaps also by the stress of the last forty-eight hours: Massimo's hostage exchange and the disappointment of Andrew not returning with Fabrizio. She awoke at six-thirty, feeling refreshed, invigorated and starving hungry: she hadn't eaten since the stewardess served First-Class passengers smoked-salmon and cucumber sandwiches during the ninety-minute transit stop at Nice yesterday afternoon. She had awoken after midnight to use the bathroom, tiptoeing along the creaking landing by the light of her bedside lamp. On the wall above the antiquated bath hung an antiquated gas water-heater; this too was reminiscent of the house she had grown up in. Before returning to bed Lillian removed her crumpled skirt and blouse and located her nightdress in the suitcase Carlo had deposited on top of a pinewood chest of drawers. Now she quietly unpacked a change of clothes and her walking shoes and slowly descended the rickety stairs, trying to minimize the noise she made although sounds outside indicated that the farmers were up and about their duties.

An elderly fridge in the kitchenette contained milk, butter and some bread rolls that were stale and tough. Lillian found a packet of tea, but no teapot; she boiled a blackened kettle on the gas-cooker and improvised an infusion using a strainer. A dented tin yielded three fig biscuits.

She was just settling into an armchair when the stable door rattled and opened. Carlo entered, carrying a brown bag from which protruded a long *baguette*. His tee-shirt had large sweat patches, his white moccasins and the trouser-leg bottoms of his jeans were splashed with mud, his hair was tousled, he needed a shave, but he still looked as if he'd stepped off a film set. He greeted her with a smile: 'You're up early.'

'I've been creeping around like a church mouse so as not to disturb you,' said Lillian.

'I went to bed straight after you did – though not with my clothes on! – and woke up half-an-hour ago feeling energetic, so I ran down to the bakery. Fresh bread, even on Sunday! And *madame* gave me some new-laid eggs. Are you hungry?'

'Ravenous,' she confessed. 'I'll make breakfast.'

'Okay. I'll get cleaned up.' He went upstairs.

Over coffee and scrambled eggs and warm bread she asked him to tell her about his earlier life in this cottage with his mother.

'I was born in 1939,' he said, 'in March, in the house in Burano, but my mum had to take me home to Scotland when the war started. We went back in 1945, and then a year later my dad died from a head-wound he'd got in the battle at Montecassino.' Lillian shuddered at another mention of the place where Arthur Sadler had been killed.

'He left us a bit of money which my mum said would go further in France, so we came here where she'd always wanted to paint. When the money ran out we had a hand-to-mouth existence, living on her painting until I was old enough to do a few odd jobs after school and in the holidays. I was sixteen when she died – she had ovarian cancer, it was a terrible death.' Tears filled his eyes. Lillian put her hand on top of his. He smiled at her and went on:

'I buried her in Aix and then went to Nice, where a married woman whose yacht I'd crewed on the previous summer kept me for a couple of months. When she became bored with me she passed me on to one of her friends, and that set the pattern for the next few years: sometimes working in bars and restaurants or on boats, sometimes being kept by rich married women and divorcees or, if I was really desperate, by men.'

Lillian made an effort not to look shocked by what her mother – and George and the Sadlers – would have considered a chronicle of vice, a catalogue of sin. She took her hand away from his to refill their coffee cups.

'When Laurence found me in 1962,' Carlo said, 'I was singing in a restaurant on the Costa Brava.'

'You sing too?' She thought of the impromptu 'concert' on the terrace in Amalfi.

'Yes –' he grinned – 'mostly for my supper! Anyway, Laurence invited me to Bexhill to be his chauffeur, although I didn't imagine that was all he had in mind. And in Bexhill, as you know, I met Andrew and he talked me into going back to Venice.'

'Where you already had a son by a married woman,' she said. An image of cherubic Marcello climbing onto the lap of the hideous statue on Torcello came into her mind.

Carlo put his cup down. 'Actually she was only engaged when I came along and – "swept her off her feet", so to speak. That was in 1960, the first time I'd been back to Burano since school holidays with my mother.' He paused to light a cigarette.

'I'd had a very bad few months when I came to Venice that year. I'd been mixed up with a crowd of movie people in Paris who were the most decadent people I've ever met. I'll spare you the details, but I came home to Burano to find a refuge – even though everything in my dad's house was ruined by damp and neglect.'

A tractor started up in the yard outside.

'I'd known Silvia since we were kids,' he went on, 'and Renzo, her fiancé, was my second cousin. But when I came back in 1960 Silvia wasn't a child anymore, but a woman of eighteen.' He inhaled deeply on his cigarette.

'In the state I was in she was like a radiant angel, so pure, so beautiful, and so patient with Renzo. He'd been a rough sort of boy with a nasty temper and now he was a violent man, drinking heavily and picking fights with the other fishermen. But their families were close and they stupidly imagined that marrying her would calm him down.

'There was a part of me that saw her as a kind of salvation and another part of me, after Paris, that wanted to spoil her. She was a virgin, of course – most Italian girls still are – so I really did spoil her for Renzo.'

'Did he find out?'

'Yes. A fisherman friend of his saw us running around naked on one of the deserted islands in the lagoon. Renzo was waiting with a knife when I got home that evening. Luckily for me, somebody pulled him off before he could do much damage. He would have got away with killing me – a "crime of passion".'

Lillian recalled Massimo's tale of his adultery and the wife who'd committed suicide. Carlo's story was like the plot of another opera: a ravished girl, an avenging lover with a knife. 'And yet he still married her?' she said. He nodded.

'Even after he found out I'd made her pregnant. I was gone by then. Silvia refused to come away with me, so I went off to Spain on my own. I didn't know what happened until the next time I came to Burano, which was three years later, with Andrew. Renzo's mother had wanted him to break off the engagement and let Silvia live in disgrace, but he insisted on going through with the marriage.'

'And she went along with this?'

'Being pregnant, there wasn't much of an alternative.'

'Does Marcello know you're his father?'

'In his mind I'm more a sort of uncle. With all his faults Renzo was good to the boy, and Marcello still thinks of him as his father. But even before Andrew and I moved into my house I went to find Renzo and offered to support Marcello. It wasn't easy – his pride was injured – but the money I gave them was a big help. Funnily enough, he and I became friends again. I used to join him and his pals in bars and brag about the women I'd had when I was a gigolo and about a ladyfriend I had in Padua, who was the wife of one of our clients. I didn't want Renzo to think I represented any kind of threat to his marriage.'

'Did you?'

'Yes,' he admitted. 'As soon as I saw Silvia again, I knew it wasn't over between us and never would be.'

'Did she feel the same way?'

'You wouldn't think so, the way she acted towards me. It wasn't until Adriana came to live with me that she even started speaking to me, but I told her my marriage was a sham, just a way of making Adriana's pregnancy look "respectable", and I finally told Silvia that I still loved her. And she confessed that she loved me.'

'Was this after her husband died?'

'Before.' He stubbed out his cigarette. 'So his drowning was very – obliging,' he added callously.

'And did you and she…?'

He smiled at her reticence. 'No, we didn't. Not then and not since. She only comes to my house to look after Adriana. I know what you're thinking: Carlo the big lover-boy –' he broke off with a self-deprecating laugh.

'I wasn't thinking any such thing,' Lillian protested, not entirely truthfully.

He smiled again. 'This time we're doing everything by the book. When Adriana goes off with her baby and Silvia and I announce our engagement, the local people will see it as a happy ending and not another scandal.'

'And you'll carry on living in Burano?'

'Yes. I can commute to Jesolo by boat. My roving days seem to be coming to an end. I have Andrew to thank for that. Watching him get more and more restless has made me keener to settle down.'

Running a beach-bar seemed a mundane future for Carlo the ex-gigolo and restorer of palaces and grand apartments, Lillian thought. Perhaps he would go on to greater things – buy a smart restaurant in Venice or in Rome. But he would have his Silvia and little Marcello – and perhaps there would be more children.

While Lillian cleared the breakfast table, Carlo went to the farmhouse and telephoned Rome. Fausto and Fabio were still sleeping; Paolo told him there was no news of the Prince. Yes, he knew that *la signora inglese* was with Carlo; she would be informed when 'Don Massimo' returned to Rome. Paolo made a note of the farmhouse number and gave Carlo the number of the Monfalcone agent in Marseille. Carlo rang the agent who told him he'd failed to find *le monsieur anglais* registered in any of the major hotels last night. Carlo arranged to meet him in the city and join the hunt.

He relayed the lack of news to Lillian before setting out for Marseille in the mud-splashed Lincoln, still in jeans but now wearing a striped red shirt. Lillian reluctantly agreed to remain at the farm: trawling the smaller hotels and bars would be easier for the two men without her in tow.

Carlo described the route to the village, half-a-mile away, and recommended a restaurant where she would obtain a decent lunch. He gave her some francs to keep her going until he could take her to a bank tomorrow.

After he left she sat down at the pine table and wrote a letter to Bob Sadler on a sheet of notepaper which she found in a drawer of the sideboard. She told Bob that she was now in France, still trying to catch up with Andrew.

'*A young woman in Venice has just had a baby by him,*' she wrote after a moment's hesitation, '*so I have another grand-daughter! Her name is Clara – ask Amy if she remembers Clara Bow at the pictures! I shall have to change my Will when I come home to provide for them. There's no chance of him marrying her.*'

After further hesitation she wrote: '*Andrew also has a business partner in Venice whom he's treated very badly. I want to give him £10,000 to help him start a new venture. Can we get round Exchange Control regulations to do this?*' She decided against telling him that Andrew's partner had turned out to be Laurence Dickinson's intended chauffeur from four years ago.

What she had written so far would seem to confirm Bob's – even George's – lowest opinion of Andrew, she realized. She did not mention Massimo or the hostage situation.

'*I may go back to Italy after I find Andrew, so I don't know when I shall be back in Hastings. But I shall have lots to tell you!*'

Smiling at this understatement she ended the letter by sending love to Amy. Folding the letter inside an envelope, she left it on the sideboard to post on Monday when Carlo took her to the bank. Feeling the need for some activity, she set out for the village, wearing a cardigan which she removed before she reached the main road. Provence was not as stifling as Italy but it was hot nevertheless, even at eight-thirty. There was no sign of last night's clouds; ahead of her as she walked along the edge of the road the triangular mountain peak stood out against a clear blue sky, rising starkly from its forested lower slopes and the wooded hills that led towards it.

The mountain was Mont Sainte Victoire, Carlo had told her, much painted by his mother as well as, famously, by Cézanne. The landscape had barely changed since the Post-Impressionists' time, except that the valley beyond Ste Victoire had been dammed and flooded to form a reservoir; Carlo, as a boy, had climbed the mountain many times, alone or with schoolfriends, and had watched the building of the dam.

The road hugged one side of a shallow valley. Vauvenargues, the village, was not much bigger than the hamlets they'd passed last night: a collection of houses, cottages and farms, mostly built of stone. On a small rise in the centre of the valley stood a *château*, four square storeys of rendered stone with a low roof but no turrets or ornamentation. According to Carlo it was owned by Pablo Picasso, although he no longer lived there.

The *boulangerie* had a small gloomy bar where Lillian ordered a *café au lait*, pleased that her schoolgirl French was adequate to the transaction. The baker and bar-owner was as dour as his emporium. Her French faced a sterner test on her return when, as she was picking her way across the flagstones, the farmer's wife emerged from the house, greeted Lillian with great cordiality and invited her into her kitchen for an early aperitif (a clock in the hall was just striking ten). If Lillian understood correctly, Madame Dufour distilled the herbal-tasting concoction herself.

Whilst Lillian was struggling to make conversation on the topic of '*nos enfants*', the telephone rang. It was Carlo, calling from a bar in Marseille with the startling news that Andrew was – improbably for him – camped in a 'refuge' on top of Mont Ste Victoire with a French guide, less than five miles from Lillian. 'I'll explain when I get back,' said Carlo.

Lillian felt her heart begin to beat faster. 'I'll start out straight away.'

He laughed, not unkindly. 'Lillian, it's more than a thousand metres high. Three thousand feet. You won't make it.'

'Don't be ridiculous,' she said. 'George and I have been to the top of Scafell, and I once climbed Snowdon with Andrew. They're both over three thousand feet, I'm sure.'

'With all respect, you're not as young as you were when you did that sort of climbing.'

'You should see the climbing I did with Max – in Capri and up and down the steps to his castle in Amalfi. After a good night's sleep I feel fit for anything. Remember I garden all day in Hastings and play golf twice a week,' she added, exaggerating her golf and gardening schedule.

'Lillian, I know this mountain. It's a long steep climb, very rough towards the top. I truly think it would be too much for you.'

Lillian's eyes abruptly filled with tears. 'Carlo, this is what I left England for. It's taken me two weeks to get this close. I can't hold back now. I'll do anything to find him.' Her voice broke. 'Anything.'

He had heard the catch in her voice. 'Dear Lillian,' he said gently, suddenly sounding more like Massimo than Andrew. 'I surrender… But wait till I get there. Don't try it on your own. We'll do it together. It'll take me an hour to get back to you. Okay?'

'Okay,' said Lillian. 'But – hurry.' She put the phone down and wiped her eyes. On her way back from the hall to the kitchen she worked out what she needed to say:

'*Mon fils –*' she hesitated – '*est sur la montagne. Carlo – Sharlz – va retourner et aller avec moi sur la montagne.*' She didn't understand Madame Dufour's reply, but her tone sounded sympathetic and she hoped her hostess did not take her abrupt exit amiss.

It seemed a slow hour before the Lincoln churned back across the yard. Lillian changed into her golfing slacks and a long-sleeved shirt that would protect her arms from the sun and any wind on top of the mountain; she tucked a scarf into her waistband in case she needed to shield her head or her hair. Inspecting her face in the bathroom mirror, she decided against putting on any make-up before what was sure to be a sweaty climb but rubbed in some face cream in the hope that it might help against the sun.

For the last fifteen minutes before Carlo's arrival she alternated between sitting at the table and standing in the open doorway, rising at least half-a-dozen times at the sound of a car on the main road. Finally, she ran recklessly across the paving stones as he was getting out of the car and hugged him fiercely, unable to contain her excitement.

Carlo smiled. 'I told *Madame* you were my auntie from England, but she must be wondering if you're one of my "patronesses"!'

Lillian giggled nervously in spite of her anxiety and impatience. 'Does she know about your other – career?'

'She must have suspicions. I did bring one or two of my married ladies here. Shall we get going straight away? I'm sure you're bursting to be off.'

'Change your shoes,' Lillian instructed him. 'You can't climb a mountain in slip-ons.'

'Slip-ons is all I have. I didn't come prepared for mountaineering. I'll manage.'

They set off on foot, Lillian in her sturdy Church's brogues, Carlo in soft leather moccasins from Ferragamo in Venice. The ascent to Mont Ste Victoire began with a gentle descent to the floor of the valley on a farm track only a few hundred yards down the main road. Rainfall had left puddles and mud-piles raised by the wheels of farm vehicles. Pine-trees towered on either side, and yellow-flowered gorse and a holly-like shrub with small prickly leaves lined the path. Poppies grew in profusion beside clumps of lilac and lavender. A tractor rumbled down behind them; they pressed against the bushes as it passed them before turning down a narrower track towards a smallholding. At the bottom of the valley a shallow stream rustled beneath the path in a culvert. The track rose, then dipped to where a second stream trickled across it. Now the path began to rise more steeply.

As they climbed, Carlo related what had happened in Marseille. The Monfalcone agent had told him that the talk in the harbourside bars was of the Vatican 'bigwig' who'd surrendered himself to the *Union Corse* in exchange for his teenage son who had assaulted the daughter of a middle-ranking 'lieutenant' in the Union. Prince Massimo had been taken to the house, outside Marseille, of the revered Head of the Union – 'presumably that's where he still is,' Carlo said as they paused to get their breath back, sitting on rocks below the pine trees at the side of the track.

'They haven't taken him to Corsica?' Lillian panted.

'We think not.'

'How did you find out about Andrew being on this mountain?'

'I was coming to that.' The waterfront gossip did not include mention of an Englishman being involved in the exchange of hostages, but checking local bars after he and the agent divided their search Carlo found someone he knew drinking coffee after morning Mass: a stonemason who made his living repairing ecclesiastical buildings. Years ago Jean-Luc had done some restoration to the chapel at the top of Ste Victoire, part of an abandoned priory that was still the site of pilgrimages. In exchange for pocket money Carlo had helped him lead mules laden with building materials up to the summit. Jean-Luc had a younger brother, Thierry – 'He's very good-looking, but I remember him as a bit of a teenage hooligan,' said Carlo. It was Thierry, now twenty, who'd taken up with Andrew. 'It looks like he hasn't wasted any time finding a replacement for Fabrizio.'

Andrew's sexual tastes and a thirst for excitement were leading him into ever more treacherous waters. The revulsion Lillian had briefly felt in the Lincoln yesterday returned. Or perhaps her queasiness was just the aftertaste of Mme Dufour's aperitif, or the exertion of the climb or even the effect of the odour of pine that pervaded the mountainside, cloyingly strong.

Carlo looked uncomfortable at having touched – again – on a distasteful subject. 'Trust Andrew to pull a stunt like this,' he said. 'First the son of a papal prince, now a delinquent from the slums of Marseille.'

They were staying in one of the harbourside hotels mainly used by prostitutes and sailors. Jean-Luc had lunched with them in the port yesterday and learned that they planned to spend a night on Ste Victoire; part of the priory had been converted to a refuge for pilgrims and hill-walkers.

Fighting to overcome her sense of nausea, Lillian laughed grimly. 'I can't imagine Andrew sleeping on top of a mountain,' she said; 'and George must be turning in his grave at the thought of him staying in a – brothel.'

Carlo grinned. 'I admit it doesn't sound like his style, but he'll enjoy slumming for a few days. Now that you're here, he'll change to a hotel *de grand luxe*.'

'What about this young man he's with?'

'He'd be part of the slumming. Not the first, I'm afraid, and unlikely to be the last.' Carlo's tone was harsh. Lillian realized that he felt more bitter towards her son than he had admitted last night.

They stood up and moved on. The mule-track or pilgrim trail remained wide and increasingly steep. Lillian's calves ached more than they had in Amalfi or Capri and she was soon panting harder than before, but determination kept her going. Carlo was also puffing, and his inappropriately shod feet slithered on the stony path. Neither of them spoke, saving their breath for the climb.

Twenty minutes later they paused again, sitting side-by-side on a large slab of rock. 'Stupid of me not to bring a bottle of water,' Carlo said. 'Hopefully we'll get something at the top.' Lillian nodded. Her chest had begun to ache.

'I've been meaning to ask you,' he said after a moment: 'what do you think of Fausto and Fabio?'

'I only met the younger one for an hour or two on my last night. He's rather sweet, but far too young for Andrew I'd have thought, though obviously I don't understand much about – that sort of thing. I had a bit more time with his brother. I think he's more reserved than cold, very serious about everything, but I quite took to him.' Almost without meaning to, she found herself blurting:

'I think their father's going to ask me to marry him when he gets away from these people. I haven't said yes – well, not really – but I think I will.'

Carlo looked at her in amazement. 'How long were you together – five days?'

She blushed and nodded. 'I suppose he has rather swept me off my feet. He's – not like anyone I've ever met. He told me a lot about his family history and what he does for the Vatican.'

'I'd be more interested in what he hasn't told you.'

'He is a bit secretive about some things,' she admitted.

'I bet he is! Well, I guess you've a good idea of what you'll be getting into.' He grinned again. 'You're a bit of a "dark horse", Mrs Rutherford!' She laughed. 'And I hope you and your prince will be very happy,' he added.

Lillian patted his arm. 'Thank you,' she said and rose, with an effort, to her feet.

After an hour's climbing they were past the halfway point, although the summit didn't seem appreciably nearer. A huge metal cross crowned the peak, seventeen metres high, Carlo said, dating back several centuries. The angle of ascent became ever steeper. Lillian too had to watch her footing on the stones in the track. They stopped again, both panting for breath. Carlo sat on the exposed root of a pine tree and looked at her with concern.

'This is too much for you.'

Lillian leaned against the trunk of another tree. She felt sick with exhaustion. 'No,' she gasped; then, miserably: 'Yes, it is. I'm not as fit as I thought I was. Neither are you! But we can't give up now.'

'We're not giving up,' he said. 'If Andrew can climb this fucking mountain – *pardon mon anglais*! – then so can I.' He laughed. Lillian was more amused than shocked by his expletive. 'But you don't have to come any higher,' he said. 'You can wait here while I go on and find them and then we'll pick you up on the way down.'

'They may not be ready to come down.'

'Ready or not, they'll come down,' he said sternly.

'But this boy, this – hooligan – might get nasty.'

Carlo gave another grim laugh. 'By the time I get to the top, I shall be in a nasty enough mood to cope with any twenty-year-old tearaway,' he predicted. 'I may wring both their necks before I bring them down.' Lillian forced a weary smile.

He looked at his watch: five past midday. 'I'll be as quick as I can, but it'll take me half-an-hour to the top, a bit less coming down. Hopefully we can all get back to the village in time for a late lunch.'

He stood up and took a few steps away from her, then turned back and kissed her cheek.

'Relax, Lillian. We've found him. It's all over.'

'If you say so,' said Lillian. Her anxiety and nausea were from more than the climb. Now that the long-delayed reunion with her son was finally so close, she felt apprehensive. Would Andrew be angry? Would he scorn her in front of his young companion? She felt angry herself, that he had brought her to this ludicrous location, halfway up a French mountain.

Mustering another smile, she touched the side of Carlo's face with one hand. 'You've done so much for me,' she said. 'Not just today. You're everything I wish Andrew could be.' She surprised herself with this last thought even as she gave voice to it.

He took the hand with which she'd stroked his face and kissed it gently, reminding her of Massimo. His eyes glistened. 'Now there's a notion to send me off with a spring in my step,' he said. And he set off again with a pantomimed bouncing stride.

Lillian smiled. Her feeling for Carlo was, at this moment as strong as her feeling for her truant son a mere – unreachable – half-mile away.

Out of the blue she pictured herself walking into the bar of her golf club with one of them on each arm – surely there would be one or two people even in prosaic Hastings who would guess that this debonair duo were more than mere business associates? Dismissing this as a rose-tinted fantasy, she contented herself with the more realistic thought that Carlo would be back with Andrew and this wretched Frenchman within the next hour.

Just before a bend in the track he turned, no longer bouncing, and waved. Lillian waved and then he passed out of sight.

She sat down on the tree root that he had rested on. As well as the pervading aroma of pine there was a faint perfume of lavender. She plucked a stem from another nearby shrub; it had a purple flower, leaves like catmint and a scent redolent of tobacco. Her throat felt dry. Leaning against the tree trunk, bone-achingly weary, she closed her eyes and dozed off, only waking fifteen minutes later at the sound of voices. A young couple came up the track, puffing and shiny with perspiration. They were dressed in shorts, tee-shirts and hiking boots and carried bulging rucksacks. With beaming smiles and '*Bonjours*' they puffed past her. It seemed that Italian gigolos and the mothers of fugitive Englishmen were not alone in venturing out in the midday sun. In case any more hikers or pilgrims passed, she retreated a few yards into the trees before squatting to relieve herself.

A flash of turquoise caught her eye and she walked further into the wood. The trees thinned as the slope fell away and suddenly there was a panorama of forest and fields all the way to Aix, the town no more than a hazy blur. Below her a tree-lined lake, vividly blue, ended against a wall of concrete. Imagining the drop from the other side of the dam in the steep valley, Lillian shuddered.

She became aware of a sound not far above her, a clattering noise which, as it came nearer, she identified as the engine of some ancient motor vehicle. No ordinary car could negotiate the steep slippery track which at this height still seemed more suited to mule transport. Pilgrims would be roughly thrown about in the back of a truck. Perhaps a tractor was used for logging or for re-supplying the refuge. She hurried back through the trees.

She was no more than ten or twelve feet from the path, separated from it by the last few trees, when the vehicle passed, wheezing and clanking and emitting clouds of dirty exhaust smoke. It was a battered army jeep that looked as if it might date back to the war, with open sides and a tattered canvas top. Nearest to her, clenching the wheel with white-knuckled hands, was a swarthy young man with greasy hair plastered almost flat to his head. Beyond him, talking to him, laughing as he spoke, looking towards Lillian but not seeing her, seeing no further than his companion at the wheel, was Carlo.

Not Carlo. A plain white shirt, not one with red stripes. White teeth in a darkly tanned face. Long dark hair flying in the bouncing jeep. Fifteen feet away.

Andrew.

Lillian tried to call out but no sound emerged from her parched throat.

The jeep bounced and rattled down the track as she ran through the trees. A branch whipped the scarf from her waistband. She ran down the track as the jeep clattered round a bend. She ran on, sliding and slithering but somehow not losing her footing. Her heart pounded in her chest and a sour taste filled her nose and throat. By the time she reached the bend the jeep was out of sight. Lillian opened her mouth and screamed hoarsely:

'*Andrewwwww.*'

The clattering sound of the engine faded, and only birdsong

and her own harsh breathing disturbed the silence on the pine-clad mountainside.

'*Tu as vu cette femme?*' Thierry interrupted another Venice story.

'In English.'

'Did you saw that woman?'

'Did you see. What woman?'

'A woman was run in the road.'

'Running. I didn't see her. *J'ai les yeux seulement pour toi.* Maybe she wanted a lift.'

'*Quoi?*'

'*Peut-être elle faisait l'autostop.*' He made a hitch-hiking gesture.

Thierry grinned and concentrated on controlling the jolting jeep, tuning out the resumed anecdote which, like most of the Venice stories, involved name-dropping contessas and princesses he'd never heard of and had no interest in.

The Englishman was beginning to bore him. Sex never held Thierry's interest for long unless there was some extra 'ingredient' to add spice to the encounter. It had been better in Corsica: amusements *à trois* with the Italian kid whose father Thierry had pushed off the Bimont Dam on Tuesday night.

Looking down at the dam from the top of the mountain last night and this morning had given Thierry a kick. He wished *le grand chef* had let him kill the Sicilian m*afioso* himself. Letting the man from Sicily fire the fatal shot was '*pour la politique*', the ancient Corsican had said. Thierry cared nothing for *la politique*, he just liked killing people. He'd been killing people for the old Corsican since he was seventeen. Killing was better than sex.

He yawned as they rattled down the mountainside. If the Englishman thought his story was boring Thierry, *tant pis.* He'd slept badly in the refuge, the wooden platform becoming harder beneath the sleeping bag as the night wore on. They'd had sex three times, twice in front of the fire and once running out naked in the rain and wind and doing it against a rock below the great crucifix, the idea of blasphemy heightening the excitement for Thierry.

This morning, early, a group of hikers had arrived, young Parisians, noisy and antisocial to the two outsiders. After them came a priest with a party of pilgrims who'd been *too* sociable, inviting the campers to join them in a service in the chapel; Thierry laughed as the pilgrims later knelt below the great iron cross where the Englishman, too, had knelt last night.

After the pilgrims came a trickle of hikers. By midday Thierry had had enough. They rolled up the sleeping bags and packed the food in a rucksack and headed back down to the jeep, taking a shortcut down a steep rocky gully.

Le grand chef had instructed Thierry to protect *le monsieur anglais* whose security was guaranteed under the arrangements with the Sicilians. Thierry hoped the old man would change his mind and order him to kill the Englishman. Perhaps at last he would get the chance to combine a 'hit' with a sexual experience: he imagined cutting the Englishman's throat while he was kneeling to administer one of the *pompiers* at which he excelled. The thought was exciting, exquisite. Thierry squirmed uncomfortably on the lumpy seat of the clapped-out borrowed jeep. One of the front wheels hit a rock in the track and the jeep rose violently into the air. He clung grimly to the steering wheel as they thumped back onto the ground.

'*Merde*!' yelled Andrew as his head banged against a metal bar supporting the tattered canvas roof.

'English, please,' said Thierry. And he laughed, pleased with his joke, pleased with their breakneck ride, pleased to have a raging hard-on at the fantasy of cutting the throat of this pretentious foreign *tapette*.

Passing the parked jeep a few minutes after he left Lillian, Carlo had guessed that it might belong to Thierry and Andrew, too lazy to climb all the way on foot. But when he reached the priory below the towering iron cross, they were not there. A hiker described two men who appeared to have spent the night in the refuge and had left barely ten minutes earlier; the older of the two was perhaps an Englishman although he spoke fluent French.

From below them came the sound of an engine which sputtered before it fired. Carlo ran to where he could see down the mountain slope. He briefly glimpsed the jeep as it rounded a bend before disappearing into the first of the pine trees.

'*Andrewwww!*' he yelled at the top of his voice, even though there was no chance of them hearing him above the rattling noise of the engine. For a moment he thought he heard a faint echo of his cry, which seemed improbable on the open mountainside.

Apart from the hikers at the summit, nothing else moved on the mountain now that the clanking jeep had passed out of earshot. Or had it stopped where Lillian was waiting? Perhaps the longed-for reunion was taking place at this very moment.

Carlo hurried down the mountain. A near-vertical descent was possible through gullies where movement would be out of sight of anyone on the pilgrim path that wound more gently around Ste Victoire's shoulders. He plunged into one of the gullies, guessing that this was how he'd missed Andrew and Thierry on his way up. The summit which looked so bare from the road supported a dense undergrowth. Loose stones dotted the jagged slippery bedrock that had been thrust to this height by primeval eruptions and earthquakes when the European and African landmasses sundered and the Mediterranean was formed. Carlo had gone no more than fifty metres when a stone turned under his left shoe and he twisted his ankle.

'*Merde,*' he said aloud. Andrew had once remarked that cursing in French was more satisfying than in English or Italian. As he sat nursing his foot he thought he heard the jeep again. Surely they wouldn't go back to the village without him? Had they somehow missed Lillian? He struggled to his feet, wincing as he put weight on the throbbing ankle.

Just above the place where the jeep had been parked, where the mule track shrank to a narrow zigzagging path, Carlo found two more hikers who were picnicking before tackling the final – and steepest – third of the mountain. They were solicitous about his limp.

Yes, they answered his question, they had seen two young men –'*deux jeunes gens*' – loading the jeep with their camping equipment, maybe a quarter of an hour ago just before they stopped here for lunch. And yes, ten minutes before that they'd seen a brown-haired lady in green trousers sitting beside the path: she had been asleep but she woke and smiled at them as they passed.

They also told him they had yesterday visited the *Barrage de Bimont*, where there was some excitement: a man's body had been found in the reservoir above the *Barrage de Zola*, the nineteenth-century dam lower down the valley. The body had apparently travelled down the channel linking the two reservoirs. The dams were a popular recourse for suicides, but there was talk of shooting: a jealous husband perhaps, or a gangland killing.

He resumed his hobbling descent to the top of the track where the jeep had been parked. After a further ten minutes he reached the spot where he'd left Lillian. There was her scarf snagged in the branch of a tree, but no Lillian, and no jeep. He retrieved the scarf and called her name before limping on down the track.

He saw her as soon as he rounded the next bend. Midway between this bend and the next, she was lolling against the trunk of a withered pine tree. The sun was beating down on her unprotected head. Carlo called again:

'Lillian?'

She opened her eyes, which immediately filled with tears.

'Oh, Carlo.'

He sat down beside her and put his arm round her shoulders.

'My dear Lillian,' he said, unaware that this would immediately make her think, again, of Massimo.

Carlo's ankle was now swollen and puffy. Lillian improvised a bandage with her scarf before they set off down the track. With frequent stops it took them almost two hours to make it back to the farmyard. Mme Dufour saw Carlo limping across the mud and came to inspect his ankle. She insisted on her husband driving him to the hospital in Aix where the ankle could be x-rayed and more firmly bandaged or maybe plastered.

Lillian was invited back into the house and served a lunch of spicy sausage and beans in a rich sauce. Once again she laboured to keep up her side of the conversation, her confidence growing in spite of the handicap of her limited French vocabulary. She told the farmer's wife that her father had been a farm-worker in his youth, before the Great War, and that she grew potatoes, carrots and cabbages in her garden in Hastings – alongside berry fruits whose French names she didn't know.

Brie cheese and apples were served as a dessert. Lillian pantomimed sleep in order to escape to the cottage. Worried now about Carlo as well as Andrew, she didn't think she would be able to sleep, but exhaustion overcame her and she passed out within seconds of resting her head back on one of the chairs. A knock at the door woke her after more than two hours. Carlo wouldn't need to knock. It must be Mme Dufour with news from the hospital. Lillian rose sluggishly and went to open the stable door.

And there he stood.

'Hello, Mother,' said her son.

The emergency department in Aix was understaffed on Sunday. It took more than an hour for Carlo to be x-rayed and another thirty minutes for the result to be relayed to the doctor in Emergency. Ligaments were strained but not torn. A nurse bandaged his ankle tightly and, after another long wait, a physiotherapist came and prescribed exercises. He must not use a stick: it was important to keep the weight equally on both ankles. The muddy moccasin was a tight fit on his left foot.

M. Dufour waited patiently throughout the three hours

they were at the hospital, not saying much and content to leaf through fishing and mountaineering magazines. Carlo seethed with impatience and could not concentrate to read anything. It was after six when they got back to the farm. An old pick-up truck Carlo faintly remembered was parked in the yard. The farmhouse door opened and Jean-Luc came out, grinning widely, with Mme Dufour in the doorway behind him. Carlo had forgotten that the stonemason's wife was from Vauvenargues; her parents were old friends of the Dufours.

'*Je l'ai trouvé*,' he announced with pride. I found him. '*Il est là. Avec maman.*' He's there. With Mummy.

Carlo waved an acknowledgment as he carefully picked his way across the flagstones. He knocked on the cottage's stable door, which was opened by Andrew, looking much more tanned than when he'd last seen him in April, on the renovation project in Ravenna. Behind him Carlo could see Lillian in one of the armchairs, a broad smile on her face as she turned towards the door.

'Carlo, *saluti*!' Andrew held out his hand, which Carlo shook, the gesture feeling odd. He found himself recalling the countless times they had kissed – and with what passion – in the early weeks and months of their relationship, in French hotels, in their attic apartment on the Cannaregio. Now, three and a half years later, they were – how had he described it to Lillian? – 'workmates... the best of friends'. What he felt towards Andrew at this moment was far removed from friendship. He freed his hand and crossed to Lillian who rose and hugged him. She looked exhausted, and he sensed that being reunited with Andrew had not fully released her from anxiety.

'Carlo, how's your ankle? You're not in plaster, so it isn't broken?'

As he answered her enquiry, he wondered how she had reacted on seeing Andrew at the end of her long quest. Tears of joy? Tears of relief? Had she castigated him for all the anguish he had caused and the dangerous situation he had helped to bring about for Fabrizio and Prince Massimo? Carlo was not given to violence, but at this moment he felt a powerful urge to slap Andrew or land a punch on him.

There was a tension in the air – was he the only one to feel it? – as he related his treatment at the hospital and Andrew repeated the story he had already told his mother, about Jean-Luc coming to his hotel and driving him here. He told Carlo that he had been released ahead of Prince Massimo's arrival yesterday. 'One of the guys who looked after us in Corsica took me to a hotel after we came over by boat.'

'Thierry?'

'You know him?'

'From when we were kids. I worked for his brother who brought you here. How come you didn't find Lillian when you came down Ste Victoire in his jeep?'

Andrew raised his eyebrows at Carlo's use of his mother's first name. 'I missed her, and Thierry obviously didn't realise it was *maman*.'

A knock at the door heralded the arrival of Mme Dufour with a plate of the sausage stew for Carlo. She took away the plate she'd earlier brought for Andrew which Lillian had washed. Carlo set to the food with relish.

'Will you go back to Hastings with your mother?' He didn't know if this question had already been asked and answered.

'Of course I will. Sorry I took off for so long, but it's not every year you get the chance to cruise around the Mediterranean.'

'I guess not.' The urge to hit Andrew was still strong.

'You've obviously managed well enough without me on the Ravenna job.'

'Yes, it's going OK. A few of the usual hiccups on the plumbing and electrics. You know about the baby?'

'Mother's told me.' He was not showing any reaction to the fulfilment of fatherhood. 'Is Adriana going to be OK?'

Carlo shook his head. 'We'll have to wait and see. We don't know if the pregnancy aggravated her anaemia somehow or if it would have happened anyway.'

There was an uncomfortable silence. Where to begin, with so much to discuss? And how important was he to the discussion? Carlo keenly felt the need to get back to Burano and Silvia. Silvia was spending long hours at the hospital with Adriana and the baby; a neighbour or his Torcello grandmother looked after Marcello. The work in Ravenna had to be completed – and the Jesolo cellar converted into a discotheque, although it would not get fully busy until next year's summer season. Andrew must take his mother home to Sussex and sort out his own life while they waited for the Prince to negotiate his release and resume his plans for himself and Lillian. In spite of his resentment towards Andrew, Carlo smiled at the thought of the Prince sweeping Lillian off her feet. Had she told Andrew about Don Massimo's proposal?

Another knock on the door. Carlo answered it, expecting that Mme Dufour had brought something to follow the stew. But it was the stonemason with a summons to the telephone: a call from Rome.

'Let's hope it's good news about Max,' Lillian said.

'Max?' Andrew raised his eyebrows again.

'The Prince. He told me to call him Max.'

'Did he now? Very Daphne du Maurier!'

Lillian laughed, pleased that Andrew had made the connection that had eluded Massimo.

On their way across the yard Carlo asked Jean-Luc if he was free to drive him to Venice in the next day or two. 'I'll pay you and give you the fare back to Marseille,' he said in French. '*Par le train ou par avion, comme tu prèfères.*'

'OK, buster,' Jean-Luc's English was largely learned in cinemas.

As expected, it was Fausto.

'*Hanno assassinato mio padre.*' They have murdered my father. His voice was cold, emotionless.

'At the *Barrage de Bimont*?' Carlo said.

'You knew already?'

'There is talk in the village.' He stumbled into a commiseration, which Massimo's son cut short:

'My father will be avenged,' he said. When Carlo had spoken to him from Venice he had not detected a Sicilian accent in his Italian; now he did. Carlo shivered, knowing the savage Sicilian code of vengeance, which sometimes extended through successive generations. He had no response to this chilling statement. After a few moments Fausto asked: 'Signora Ruthairford is with you?'

'And Andrew. We found him today.'

'Tell him to forget that he ever knew the sons of Massimo Monfalcone.'

'He is the father of your newborn niece in Venezia.'

'I do not think he will play any part in the life of my sister's child. My brother and I shall provide for her and her child. If she dies, we will arrange for her daughter to be adopted.' How old was Fausto – eighteen? He sounded mature beyond his years.

'My fiancée is looking after Adriana and the baby. We plan to marry as soon as possible. And we would very much like to adopt baby Clara if Adriana dies.'

'I will consider your offer when the time comes. Please extend my thanks to your fiancée for the many kindnesses she has extended to my sister.' There was no audible warmth in his voice as he expressed his gratitude. 'I must go now. We are flying to Marseille to reclaim my father. *Buona sera.*' And he rang off before Carlo could return the courtesy.

'Did you hear about the body in the reservoir?' he asked Jean-Luc, who with the Dufours was in the same room as the telephone.

'They are talking about it in the harbour bars.'

'It is the father of the boy Andrew was with in Corsica. Prince Massimo Monfalcone. From the Vatican Bank.'

'*Mon dieu, quelle tragédie,*' said Mme Dufour. '*Il s'est suicidé?*'

'*Il a été assassiné.*' The word Fausto had used in Italian: assassinated. It was stronger than *tué*: killed.

He walked back across the flagstones to the cottage. Lillian rose expectantly from her chair as he entered. She must have seen something in his face. Her heart stopped for the second time today, and tears filled her eyes.

'Oh God,' she said. 'He's dead, isn't he?'

It was Carlo, not Andrew, who crossed to enfold her in his arms.

'Lillian, I'm more sorry than I can say.'

She wept. 'Oh, my poor Max.'

At a little after midday on Monday Jean-Luc collected Carlo and Lillian from the farm cottage in Vauvenargues. Lillian was quiet and no longer tearful, although she had cried on Carlo's shoulder again after the stonemason drove Andrew back to his hotel. Leaving his pick-up in the yard, Jean-Luc drove Carlo's Lincoln to the Marseille waterfront. On the way he told Carlo that it was not widely known that the man found in the reservoir was a Sicilian prince from the Vatican Bank. Someone from the mortuary in Aix-en-Provence had revealed that the victim had been shot before being thrown off the Bimont Dam. Carlo did not share this detail with Lillian in the rear of the car.

The hotel did not look like a brothel, which was a relief to Lillian. She waited in the car while Carlo limped inside. He found Andrew sitting in the bar on the ground floor, smoking a mentholated cigarette. He wore the same white cotton sports shirt and designer blue jeans that he'd worn yesterday. A denim jacket hung from the empty chair beside him, on which rested a plastic supermarket bag.

'Where's your luggage?'

'This is it. Everything else was on Fabrizio's boat. I suppose it's in the garage at Amalfi, if they haven't thrown it away.'

'Jean-Luc's driving you and your mum to the airport. Where's his brother, your new "*ami particulier*"?' In French 'special friend' sounded sarcastic; he meant it to.

'He stormed out last night after I came back. He wanted me to take him to England, but he's not really the kind of boy you introduce to Mother! I've left him a note in the room. He was going to take me to Corsica for a few days.'

'You didn't get enough of Corsica last week?'

'We weren't sightseeing. We only saw the inside of the villa where they kept us.'

'This "thing" with Thierry started while you were there?'

'He provided some "entertainment" on the island which helped relieve the boredom of our captivity. You know what they say: "Two's company, three's a party." *Une partouze.*' Carlo was astounded that Andrew could be so sanguine about being a hostage of the thugs who had murdered Prince Massimo. 'There's an edge to sex with him,' Andrew said. 'He's the best since you, *caro mio.*'

'I'm not your *caro mio* any more.'

'Yes you are.' He met Carlo's gaze levelly. 'You always will be, *caro mio.*'

As he had last night when they shook hands in the doorway, Carlo recalled the intensity of their first months together. Tongues in each other's mouths as they kissed. Other images filled his mind: Andrew's tongue exploring, worshipping his body; Andrew threshing beneath him, moaning with excitement. Had there been an 'edge' to their love-making? Driving Lillian to Vauvenargues on Saturday, he'd told her that Andrew was the closest he had come to loving a man. That might have been true three years ago; it was not true now. Tonight – or by early tomorrow – he would be back in Burano with Silvia and all that she promised: a love that went to passion and beyond. He chose not to respond to Andrew's repetition of the endearment.

'You know the Prince was part of the Sicilian Mafia? A big part, I'd guess. You've been playing with fire.'

'Fabrizio never said. I assumed his dad just paid his dues,

like other businessmen in Italy.'

'Last night I told Fausto that Silvia and I are keen to adopt Clara if Adriana doesn't make it.'

'Clara?'

'Your daughter.'

Andrew, for a moment, looked shamefaced. 'It would be very good of you and Silvia to take her. And I'm sure it's the best option for – Clara. Obviously I shall expect to chip in on the financial side of things. What did Fausto say when you told him?'

'Chipping in' seemed a cavalier response to the situation he had created in Venice. And the Monfalcones' wealth would eliminate any need for Andrew to contribute.

'He made it clear the family will take care of the "financial side", for Adriana's sake. And he said to tell you to forget you ever knew the sons of Prince Massimo.'

Andrew stubbed his cigarette into an overflowing ashtray. 'He's never liked me. Of course he doesn't attract admirers the way Fabrizio does.' Typical of Andrew to see envy where others would see disapproval, disgust.

'Let's get going. You and Lillian have got a plane to catch.'

Andrew raised his eyebrows. '"Lillian". You seem to have formed quite a bond with my mother.'

'I've told her everything. The whole story. You and me. Over dinner at the *Cipriani* a fortnight ago.'

'The *Cipriani*, eh? You spoiled her!' Andrew laughed. 'Or did she pay?'

Carlo was once more fighting the urge to hit him. 'Of course I paid.'

'But why tell her after I'd kept it all from her for so long?'

'She came that far – this far – to find you. She had a right to know, Andy.'

'How did she take it? "The whole story"? You and me? The Great Romance.'

'She cried when I first told her. But by the time I picked her up at the airport on Saturday she seemed to have accepted it. I'm guessing she discussed it with Prince Massimo and he helped her come to terms with things.'

'She and the Prince know Fabrizio was – "*mon ami particulier*"?' He raised his eyebrows as he borrowed Carlo's euphemism.

'Didn't you realize that last night?'

'I assumed she saw him as just someone I went sailing with. Like the boy I was at school with. David.' Andrew was again looking uncomfortable.

'She thought Fabio was "sweet" but a bit young for you. I don't know how the Prince felt about the situation.'

'And Thierry?'

'Your mother knows he's this week's "playmate". I didn't tell her he's part of the gang that held you to ransom. Has she told you the Prince sort of asked her to marry him?'

'She did! I'm finding it hard to take seriously. I can't see Mother as a princess – living in a castle! Probably he was just having a flirtation.'

'Or maybe Prince Massimo saw more to her than you ever have. I certainly did. She's quite a woman. I wish you appreciated how lucky you are to have her as your mother.'

'Oh, but I do. I always have.' He stood up and picked up the plastic bag.

Carlo's ankle throbbed as he rose and put his weight on it.

***

Fausto Monfalcone, at this moment, a few miles away in the mortuary of the hospital in Aix-en-Provence, was looking down at the body of his father on a gurney. On opposite sides of the Prince stood Paolo and Federico, his loyal lieutenants, now his son's lieutenants. They both had tears streaming down their faces. Fausto was rigid and implacable, as he had been in the harbour at Porto Giglio when he saw the bodies on the deck of the fishing boat, the bodies of two crewmen from the Corsican yacht.

'Yes,' he told the brigadier of police who stood at the foot of the gurney beside the senior pathologist, 'that is my father, Prince Massimo Monfalcone, from Vatican City.'

'Please accept the condolences of the Marseille Police Commissariat,' the brigadier said. 'We shall employ all our resources to find the perpetrators of this grave offence.'

Fausto nodded. He knew that the police were unlikely to find his father's assassins. There were many gangland killings in Marseille, only a few of which led to a judicial prosecution. The Monfalcone agent had learned within a day that the Corsican Union had ordered Massimo's killing, and that an old enemy of the Monfalcones was flown from Palermo to Marseille to carry out the execution. Monsignor Angelo in Rome had already received a call from a *consigliere* in Sicily, telling him to urge Massimo's sons to restrain their desire for retribution: there must not be a war with the Corsicans.

'Blood calls out for blood, *monsignore*,' Fausto had said to Father Angelo in Massimo's apartment last night, speaking in Sicilian, a language he had learned as much from Alfredo and Maria as from his father. Monsignor Angelo had been raised in the slums of Palermo. The priesthood had taken him to Rome, but he was Sicilian to the core of his being.

'Exercise caution, my son,' he said. 'Your father understood the benefits of making peace with his enemies. This you too must learn.'

'My father's enemies broke the peace. They must pay.'

Father Angelo sighed a deep sigh. 'I have prayed for your father's soul. I will pray for you also, Fausto.'

'*Cóme vuole.*' As you wish. He hoped this would not sound impudent or insincere.

The Prince had not been in the water long enough to be bloated, although his face was greyish. His crossed hands were visible above the drawn-down sheet that covered his body; they hid the wound in his chest from the bullet of the wine-grower from Villalba. Someone had brushed his hair ahead of the identification by the older of his sons. Lillian would have still seen him as the handsome man who greeted her on the landing of his castle in Amalfi and teased her with a marriage proposal two days later, looking down on Capri's Fariglioni rocks.

Paolo fell to his knees and kissed Massimo's right hand. Federico knelt on the other side of the gurney. Fausto did not kneel. He addressed his father's body and repeated the oath he had sworn to Father Angelo: 'Blood calls out for blood.' As last night, he spoke in Sicilian, which the two officials from Marseille would not understand.

His vow reverberated in the high-ceilinged mortuary, not unlike the echo of Massimo's voice in the Matrimonial Grotto in Capri when he introduced Lillian to the Italian word '*simpatica*' and they discovered that each of them valued the notion of 'companionability'.

'Don't wait,' Lillian said as they joined the queue to collect tickets at the Air France counter. 'You and Jean-Luc have got a long drive ahead of you.'

There were tears in her eyes as she hugged him. 'Bless you, Carlo, for everything you've done for me, and for Andrew. I hope we meet again at a happier time.'

'We will,' he promised her. 'You must come to Venice when we baptise Clara.'

He offered Andrew his hand, which was ignored as Andrew too hugged him. Carlo was not sure he wanted to be hugged by Andrew.

'Bless you, *caro mio*, for looking after Mother. Sorry to have put you to all this trouble.'

Carlo freed himself from the embrace. 'I'm not going to say it's OK, but I guess it will have to be. Call me when you're back in Venice. You will be back?'

'Of course. There's all my stuff in the apartment in Sottomarina. It will need to be stored till I decide whether to carry on in Venice or not.' His personal effects, not Adriana and the baby, would bring him back. Would there be more renovation projects if he returned? Did Carlo want this? The house in Ravenna had kept him busy during Andrew's absence, but his life had re-centred on the bar in Jesolo and on Adriana and Silvia. It was too much to expect that Andrew would be a father to Clara, but perhaps from now on he might be a better son to Lillian. She would, in time, Carlo hoped, become a grandmother to young Marcello as well as to her new grand-daughter. In two short weeks she had become as important to Carlo as his own mother would be if she were still alive in Provence or Burano.

Her lips trembled as she smiled at him before turning as the queue moved forward. She was perhaps having similar thoughts. Carlo limped back to Jean-Luc in the car in the drop-off zone. They headed towards Menton and the border and the motorway to Genoa, Verona and Venice. To Silvia and Marcello. To Adriana and baby Clara.

Barrage de Bimont

Some thirty-six hours later, approaching midnight on Tuesday, Fausto stood with his two lieutenants on the roadway atop the Bimont Dam. It was a calm clear night. The moon shone down on the small group of men. On the ground in front of them lay the stonemason's brother, Thierry, whom they had picked up walking from a bar to his parked jeep in the Marseille docks. Paolo had approached him from behind with a chloroformed pad which he held over Thierry's mouth for the few moments it took him to become unconscious. Paolo then bundled him into the hired van in which Fausto sat beside Federico at the wheel. Now Thierry squirmed on the ground, blindfolded, his hands and feet bound with electrical cable. At a nod from Fausto Federico removed the blindfold.

'I am the son of Massimo Monfalcone,' Fausto said. His French, like his English, was over-precise. Before the identification of his father in the mortuary at Aix he had last spoken French in the archive of Notre Dame Cathedral in Paris during a research visit two years ago. 'You killed my father here on Friday.' He pronounced this as a fact, not as a question. He said '*tué*' – killed – not '*assassiné*'.

'I did not shoot him,' Thierry said. His tone was insolent. He did not seem intimidated by being back at the scene of Massimo's execution. 'The man from Sicily shot him.'

'A man who works for me has spoken with your driver. You pushed my father over the dam.'

'Yes, I did that. It was the command of my master. *Vous connaissez mon chef?*'

'Yes,' Fausto confirmed, 'I know your master.'

'He will have you killed for this.'

'You overestimate your value. Your master will do nothing.'

Thierry looked up at the young man standing over him who was close to him in age and came from a similar culture. Thierry had administered Corsican justice. Now he was to receive Sicilian retribution. There were rules and customs in the criminal underworld, much as in the world of civilised men and women where justice was rarely as swift but often equally harsh. At this dam, in deserted coves, in forest clearings, Thierry had watched men die – traitors, enemies of *le grand chef*. Some begged for mercy; some died silently, philosophically. Thierry opted to die philosophically. He said nothing more.

There was no gun tonight, although a gun could easily have been obtained by the Monfalcone agent, Gustave, who had supplied the chloroform. Gustave had spoken yesterday with the Corsicans' driver who'd been overheard bragging in a bar about his role in the execution of the man from Rome. On a pledge of clemency the driver had named Thierry as the gang member who had thrown Massimo off the dam and pointed Gustave towards another waterfront bar, where fifty francs secured a promise from the barman that he would be telephoned the next time Thierry visited.

Fausto nodded to his two lieutenants. He did not pronounce a sentence of execution. Their presence here was a death sentence. Paolo and Federico bent down, lifted the young Frenchman by his bound hands and feet and threw him over the dam on its steepest side. He fell without a cry. The only sound was the splash as he went into the water of the reservoir.

The two lieutenants looked over the parapet. Fausto did not.

'*Andiamo,*' he said. '*È fatto.*' Let's go. It's done. The English expression '*Revenge is sweet*' came into his head as they walked back to the rented van: where had he heard it or read it? It wasn't true. He felt no sweetness now, thinking of his papa lying in the mortuary ten or twelve kilometres from here.

BURANO

In Burano at this time, Carlo Marini was listening to music in the lounge of his father's canal-side cottage which he and Andrew had rescued from dereliction two and a half years ago. On the record player Edith Piaf was singing about love and abandonment. Carlo preferred French love-songs to those from Italy; Italians tended to find joy even in the depths of tragedy; the French wallowed in desolation.

Despite the music, Carlo's mood was not one of desolation. Silvia had brought him dinner this evening after his day of resting the damaged ankle. Marcello was with her. Silvia had spent the afternoon at the hospital: Adriana was not expected to live to the end of the month; she might not last till the end of this week. Silvia would sit with her and the baby again tomorrow while Carlo minded Marcello; he would visit on Thursday.

'Let's get married,' he had begged Silvia after Marcello fell asleep in front of a cartoon on the television. 'Marry me.'

'Later,' she said. 'Soon.'

She meant after Adriana died. But there would have to be an appropriate interval between Adriana's death and the 'widowed' Carlo marrying the widow Silvia. Proprieties had to be observed. It would not be soon. It might not be till next year, after the anniversary of her husband's death, Renzo the fisherman. But it would be.

Carlo hummed along to Edith Piaf singing '*Je ne regrette rien.*'

HASTINGS

In Hastings, an hour earlier than Burano and the Bimont Dam, Lillian was putting on her nightdress. Two days after climbing the mountain in Provence she still felt exhausted. She had done nothing more strenuous today than watering and some weeding in the garden that George had terraced in the spring and summer of 1948. She and Andrew had dined with Laurence Dickinson in his hotel on the seafront. Andrew called Laurence '*Lorenzo*', as if he were an Italian.

Lillian, in the dining room, had smiled at the thought of how embarrassed Laurence would be if she told him she knew that her son had been his lover – 'the second great love of his life,' Carlo had said. She wondered who had been the first. Andrew must know, but he might not like to be questioned about it. She sensed he was unhappy with how much Carlo had told her.

'Let's not tell Laurence about Max wanting to marry me,'

she'd said in the car driving him to the hotel.

Andrew grinned. The novelty of 'Max' still amused him. 'Why not? It isn't something that happens every day. Especially not in Hastings!'

'I'm not ready to share it with anybody except you. And maybe your sister.'

'Don't tell Sylvia. She'll see it as you cheating on Dad.'

Lillian laughed at this, but thinking about it over dinner, as Andrew regaled Laurence with tales of Venetian high society, she realised that Massimo had been the second great love of *her* life – maybe the third if she included her girlhood infatuation with Arthur Sadler, lying now in the cemetery at Montecassino, no more than a hundred miles from the Monfalcone castle in Amalfi.

Thinking about it again as she got ready for bed, she chastised herself for forgetting that the children had been the greatest love of her life. After Italy and Provence, she was no longer entirely sure if this was true of Andrew, her more-than-prodigal son. And, in addition to Wendy and Jane in Hong Kong, she now had a granddaughter in Venice – and Marcello, Carlo and Silvia's son whom she was already taking to her heart.

Andrew, she knew with a painful bitterness, would not take his daughter to his heart. Did he have a heart? She recalled their conversation in the farm cottage on Sunday.

'I don't know how you could leave such a mess and go off with that boy as if nothing had happened,' she'd said. 'Abandoning Adriana.'

'It was an *affair*, Mother. Affairs end. People move on. I know this isn't the way you and Dad lived, but it's how people live today. It's how I live.'

'But you left her expecting a baby.'

'Well, yes, that was a bit careless of us.'

'"*Careless?*" Totally irresponsible.'

'I would have given her the money if she decided not to keep it.'

'You mean if she put the baby up for adoption? You would pay the agency fees?'

'No, I meant if she wanted to go for a termination.'

'An abortion?' Lillian felt sick at the suggestion of this, immediately thinking of Alfred, the stillborn son she had lost thirty years ago. 'Do they do them in Italy?'

'They do them anywhere, if you're willing to pay. A woman I knew in Rome had one, though not on my account. She had it done by a gynaecologist in a very respectable clinic. Adriana's a devout Catholic of course, which rather rules it out as an option.'

'But not for you, apparently.' Lillian still felt nauseated. Did Fabrizio, the Prince's playboy son, hold life as cheaply as this? Max had given his life for this boy – and for Andrew. 'Have you paid for an abortion before?' she asked. 'One of your London girls?'

'No, Mother, I haven't.' Was this true, she wondered. 'Adriana's the first to be – in this situation.'

Lillian had never discussed abortion with her mother; it would never have been possible. Andrew's world with its shabby values was far removed from the world she had grown up in and remained in through the thirty years of her married life.

'It's lucky for you that Carlo stepped in to save the day.'

'Yes, he's a better man than I am.'

You can say that again, she thought. The nausea began to subside. 'We must thank God for Carlo,' she said. 'And his Silvia.'

'Talking of Silvias, how's *our* Sylvia getting on in Hong Kong?' he asked and, uncomfortable with the present conversation, Lillian had allowed them to move onto less contentious ground.

A noise above her ceiling as she got into bed reminded her that her prodigal – feckless – son was now, finally, back home with her. When she climbed the stairs to say goodnight, she'd found him going through a trunk in his attic bedroom, a trunk filled with sports kit and old homework books from his schooldays.

As his mother drifted off to sleep on the floor below, Andrew unfolded a loose-leaf page that fell out of one of the books. It was an English essay, written at fourteen: '*Where I hope to be ten years from now.*'

Andrew's essay – how neat his handwriting was! – began: '*I hope to be an artist, not of renown but of recognition, living beside the Adriatic or in the mountains of Provence.*'

ROME

On Wednesday Massimo's body was released by the authorities. An undertaker supplied a hearse to take the Prince from the mortuary in Aix to Marseille airport, where Fausto was waiting with his lieutenants and Gustave, the Monfalcone agent. Gustave kissed Fausto's hand after the coffin was carried into the Prince's aircraft. In Rome a hearse drawn by four black horses took the coffin to a convent chapel in the Vatican gardens, where the nuns washed Massimo and wrapped him in a shroud.

Fabrizio had flown to Rome from Naples. Father Angelo and Sister Veronica brought him to the chapel to pay respects to his father. The boy bent and kissed Massimo's cold grey forehead. Like his brother, he did not weep. Sister Veronica wept prodigiously, as did Maria at noon the following day when she came to say goodbye to the employer she and her husband had served through his two marriages and two widowhoods. Like Paolo and Federico, who had kept a vigil beside the open coffin last night, Alfredo had tears in his eyes as he knelt and kissed the Prince's right hand. Giancarlo, Massimo's grandson, had driven the caretaker and his wife from Amalfi to Rome; he too was coldly expressionless as he kissed his grandfather's hand.

Monsignor Angelo said prayers, some of which required responses. Maria and Sister Veronica responded loudly and crossed themselves with vigour. The men and the sons of Massimo Monfalcone mumbled their responses and crossed themselves perfunctorily. Looking down at his shrouded father, Fausto knew that all of them, except Sister Veronica and perhaps Father Angelo, harboured vengeful thoughts.

HASTINGS

Over lunch on Thursday Lillian returned to the subject of her newborn granddaughter.

'What are you going to do if Adriana dies?'

He met her gaze calmly across the conservatory table. 'It's *when* rather than *if* she dies,' he said. Was he really as callous as he sounded? 'I think Carlo and Silvia will decide what should be done.'

'Andrew! This is *your child*.'

'Mother, we both know I'm not cut out for fatherhood. Adriana told me she'd like Silvia to look after the baby if anything happened to her. And before we left Marseille Carlo said he'd already discussed adoption with Fausto. He'll make a better father than I would.' He seemed to be washing his hands of the child.

'Silvia's lovely,' Lillian said. 'Her little boy will like having a baby sister. Carlo's son.'

Andrew chuckled. 'My word, he really did tell you everything! And he calls you "Lillian".' Was her son a little bit jealous? She hoped so.

'I'm going to give them some money,' she said. 'For my granddaughter'. She had asked Robert Sadler about sending money to Carlo in Venice (the letter she'd written in Vauvenargues was still in her handbag). It would be difficult to bypass Treasury-imposed limits on overseas transfers, but Lillian had thought of a way to circumvent the restriction. She would withdraw the ten thousand pounds in instalments and give it to Carlo in cash – he could come and collect it or she would take it to Venice when she went for the baby's christening. Bob Sadler would not approve, but she wouldn't let him stop her. 'It'll have to be cash because of the exchange control regulations,' she told Andrew now.

'My mother the currency smuggler!' he said. He seemed not to notice – or he didn't mind – that she was compensating Carlo for her son's shortcomings. 'How much are you planning to give them?'

'I thought ten thousand pounds.' Disappointingly, even this didn't lift his eyebrows.

'I can give them that,' he said calmly. 'Or its equivalent in lire. More if they need it. If and when. There are funds in my account in Venice. Property renovation is quite a lucrative business. Look at Dad. He didn't leave you a pauper.'

'Well, at least you're showing some responsibility,' she said, pleased to find that her son had a fraction of his father's sense of doing the right thing, the honourable thing. She still intended to give Carlo the ten thousand pounds.

Andrew laughed. 'Who'd have expected it?' he said.

At six o'clock she was back in the conservatory with a gin and tonic. She planned to ask Andrew to show her how to make a Tom Collins, but this evening he'd gone to have drinks with David Yates and his wife in Bexhill. David had been Andrew's best friend at grammar school.

The telephone rang. It was Carlo, with news that Adriana had died during the afternoon. He seemed calm. Lillian knew from last year that grief was sometimes diluted when death had been anticipated. Carlo yawned as she was offering her condolences.

'Oh dear. Excuse me, Lillian. Silvia brought Clara home with her yesterday. Babies don't let you get much sleep, do they?'

'I remember!' she said with a smile.

'I've spoken with Fausto,' he told her. 'The family agree for me and Silvia to adopt Clara. In fact, we haven't been to register the birth yet. It would make things a lot easier if we put my name as the father. And it's what people here think is the case. It will forestall any gossip in Burano. Will you be okay with that?'

'No, I'm not,' she said, 'but I can see it makes sense. Max told me he wanted you to do this. It means you're letting Andrew off the hook.'

'Andrew always gets off the hook.'

'We have talked about it,' she said. 'He knows you'll make Clara a good father. He's promised to give you some money for her support. And I shall help too.'

'I will take it as an act of kindness from you, dearest Lillian.' The endearment immediately made her think of Massimo. 'Andrew mentioned some financial help before you left France, but his track record on promises isn't exactly encouraging.'

'I shall keep on at him to make sure he does his duty by you and the baby.'

'He won't be within reach of your influence for long, I suspect. Sorry to say this after all you've done to get him back.'

'Some American woman he knows has bought a house on the French Riviera that needs doing up. I suppose that's going to be his next – venture.'

'That must be Abigail,' Carlo said. 'The sculptress. I heard she was talking about moving to Saint-Tropez.'

The sculptress had been Andrew's mistress, Lillian recalled Carlo telling her in the car last weekend. What a quagmire her son's life had been; would it always be so?

'Four years ago,' she said, 'just before you stayed here when Laurence's house burned down during that crisis about Cuba, Andrew told me he felt he was "finished with England". I don't think he's ready to give us another chance. Selfishly, I wish he would stay here or live in London again – that would be near enough, like it was before – but I've never believed in holding him back.'

'I'm sorry, Lillian.' There was a catch in his voice now, which hadn't been there when he spoke of Adriana's death. 'Maybe

I'd have been a disappointment to my mum if she'd lived, but I like to hope I wouldn't have.'

'I'm not sure she'd approve of some of your career choices –' she laughed – 'but you've turned out to be a son any mother would be proud of.'

He chuckled. 'That's twice this week you've managed to put a spring in my step – what's left of it!'

'How *is* your ankle? I should have asked sooner.'

'A bit more comfortable today. I'm hoping I can drive to my bar in Jesolo on Saturday. Tomorrow we'll have to go into Venice and register Adriana's death. And Clara's birth. Birth and death – the life cycle. Excuse me going all existential.' He laughed again.

'Carlo, I must ask you this. Will you tell Clara he's her real father?'

'Of course. When she's old enough to handle the truth.'

'I hope Andrew won't completely walk away from her life.'

'Well – we'll see. You know Andrew.'

'Yes,' Lillian said. 'Better now, thanks to you, than I thought I did.'

ROME

Massimo's sons kept a vigil beside his coffin until midnight on Thursday, with Paolo, Federico, Giancarlo and Alfredo. The funeral mass took place mid-morning on Friday in the Vatican church of Santa Maria Regina, a 'Baroque Revival' building dating from the 1920s. The staff of Massimo's bank turned out in force, from its presiding cardinal to a lowly filing clerk.

The Minister of Finance represented the state. The Pope sent two archbishops and a second cardinal. Four Dons from Sicily and the mainland attended, one of whom liked to be thought of as the current *capo di capi* although the role was disputed by a rival who sent one of his *consiglieri*. Fausto would have preferred the Mafia not to be present, but Monsignor Angelo counselled against excluding them. Father Angelo assisted the Archbishop of Palermo who officiated at the ceremony. Maria sobbed loudly throughout the service. Fabrizio stood beside his brother in the porch and shook the hands of each member of the congregation as they left. Father Angelo kissed the hand of the self-designated *capo di capi*; Fausto did not and a dig of his elbow deterred Fabrizio from doing so.

There was no funeral lunch. Pope Paul proposed a toast to Massimo's memory at dinner with some of his cardinals that evening.

SUSSEX

Carlo had notified Lillian of the time of the funeral in Rome. Her heart ached for Max's sons as much as for herself, but she knew they would have strong support from the devoted servants and the guards, who were as close as family; indeed one of them, Giancarlo, *was* family.

On Friday Andrew took the train to London to visit his former partner in a graphic design business in Mayfair. Alcohol had taken its toll on Algie; the business had floundered and Algie was now living with cirrhosis. After dropping Andrew at the station Lillian drove twenty-five miles west to Seaford Head and walked down the valley towards the cliff at Hope Gap. She had scattered George's ashes in the undergrowth here last year with their daughter. It was a favourite stretch of the South Downs which she and George must have walked a hundred times. On the rocky shore at Hope Gap the children had looked for tiny crabs when they were young.

There was a bench overlooking the steps down to the sea. A couple of hikers were just getting up from their picnic lunch. They smiled at Lillian as she took their place, recalling the hikers who'd smiled at her on the mountain in Provence above the lake and the dam where Max's enemies had murdered him.

At this moment in Rome they would be praying or chanting over his coffin. And Carlo's Silvia was having a mass said in Burano today for Adriana and her father; Adriana's funeral would be on Monday. Lillian was fairly sure that the Baptist church she'd been raised in did not go in for memorial masses. Bob and Amy Sadler had arranged for their Methodist minister to officiate at George's cremation. Lillian had had nothing to do with any church for many years and felt no inclination to commune with the God of Catholics, Baptists or Methodists. Their God had not saved Adriana and Massimo – or George, or Lillian's stillborn child.

Today was the first time she had come to Seaford Head since she and Sylvia had scattered George's ashes. Amy went frequently to the cemetery in Bexhill where she'd interred her parents' ashes three and four years ago; she always cried, she told Lillian, and she spoke to them, mostly to her mother who'd supported her through the many tribulations her children had brought. It was more than ten years since Lillian had visited her parents' grave in Rye or Hazel's, her mother-in-law, who was buried in Hastings. She often thought of George, especially when she was gardening on the terraces he'd made for her, but she wasn't given to talking to him. Today, however, the day of Massimo's funeral, she felt the need to confess to her husband that she had kissed another man in Italy and would have married him if he had returned safely from France. A part of her obscurely needed George to tell her that this would have met with his acceptance, his approval. She shed a few tears, not sure whether they were for George or Max – or for herself.

George had died by degrees over months – years. Massimo had been taken from her in an instant. Her heart ached for both of them. The pain of grief would lessen with time, but it would never leave her. Max had not stopped mourning Liliana and the children of his first marriage. She would not stop mourning for him, nor for George.

Images of Massimo flooded her mind: his handsome face, his dark eyes, his gleaming smile as he toasted her with a cocktail or a glass of wine, on his terrace above the whispering moonlit sea, in his hotel on the night of the storm, in Capri and Rome and in the mountains beyond Ravello. His fingers on her arm as they lay on the raft below his headland. The thrum of his heartbeat against her hand the first time he kissed her on the yacht. The painful squeeze of his hands as he told her the truth about their wayward sons. His hand on her breast as she tearfully kissed him beneath the portrait of his second wife before he left to surrender his life in exchange for Fabrizio's and Andrew's. Tears filled her eyes again as she thought of the memories – the secrets – they had shared with each other and his promise, which she was sure he had fulfilled, that his last thought would be of her.

Where might they be today if his enemies had freed him? In his castle? In Rome again? She smiled as she recalled his promise to take her to Las Vegas – and introduce her to some actors from gangster movies. The joke had turned sour: gangsters had killed him and ended their dreams.

Tomorrow evening she and Andrew were to dine with the Sadlers at the Mermaid Inn in Rye, although Andrew had warned her he might stay in London for a night or two. Bob and Amy would want to know about the mysterious beneficiary of her generosity; she did not intend to tell them Carlo had been a gigolo and her son's lover. Nor would she reveal her feelings for the Prince who'd wanted to marry her. Massimo, she would say, had been 'a charming host'. He had certainly charmed Lillian.

The Sadler children had caused their parents years of worry: Nigel, the same age as Andrew, twenty-eight now, was jailed at twenty-one for assaulting a girlfriend who tried to leave him; his sister Lucy, twenty-five like Sylvia, persistently took up with unsuitable men. After leaving prison Nigel started a new life in Manchester; Amy had told Lillian there was a new girlfriend – was she safe? Lucy, divorced at twenty-four, had a Scottish boyfriend on the go, a department store security guard – was he, finally, the right man for her?

Lillian knew she had been a lot luckier than Bob and Amy. Sylvia never gave her a moment's worry. She'd fallen in love with Richard at senior school, a bright decent boy from a churchgoing family. On the days Lillian went to see Andrew in London, Sylvia had happily cooked for her beloved father, or she and George would dine at the golf club or with Richard's parents who accepted from the start that their son and the

Rutherfords' daughter were destined for each other. Lillian knew that Sylvia had made a good marriage and was happy in her life in Hong Kong.

This, she thought on the bench in the sunshine, was what parenting – being a parent – was all about. Worrying about your children – were they steady, were they settled, were they happy? They brought joy into your life, but they also brought heartache.

Andrew's distancing himself from his father and then from her too had inevitably brought anxiety, but visiting him during his years in London had been the high spot of Lillian's life prior to this year. And her quest to find him had nearly brought her a new husband. It had brought her a new grandchild and the prospect, even without Massimo, of a new chapter in her life.

Her 'rolling stone' son would – soon, in all likelihood – roll out of her life again. She was readier for this now. Next time she hoped he would not cut her off for four long years. Thanks to Carlo, as she'd told him yesterday, she understood Andrew better than she had before she set out for Venice two and a half weeks ago.

Carlo had told her the Prince's sons intended to bury him in the family vault in Monfalcone. Lillian didn't think she would ever go to his grave. Carlo said that men of influence in Sicily could have saved Massimo but for some reason had chosen not to. Sicily had killed his first family; now it had let him die; Lillian wanted nothing to do with Sicily.

What Massimo – Max – had hoped would be for himself and Lillian would now not be. But his abiding gift to her was to have opened her eyes, her heart, to the prospect that there was – there would be – a future. Walking back up the hill to the car park, passing her husband's ashes, she started to hum and was surprised to find that, almost without meaning to, she was humming '*Que Serà, Serà*'.

SICILY

From Rome Massimo's coffin was flown to Palermo where it was met by another hearse and two limousines which took the Prince's sons and their retinue of bodyguards and servants the hundred kilometres to the parish cemetery in Monfalcone. Fausto and Fabrizio watched with solemn faces as their father's coffin was carried into the family mausoleum by his grandson and Paolo and Federico with two men who farmed the Monfalcone estate. Alfredo held his sobbing wife's shoulders.

The crypt contained the tombs of six generations of the Prince's ancestors. His coffin was placed beside his first wife, Liliana, and their slain children. His second wife's family had taken Lidia to their family's vault in Naples. Fausto stood stone-faced but he took hold of his trembling brother's hand and held it firmly as Monsignor Angelo sprinkled holy water on Massimo's coffin before following the two boys and the pall-bearers up the dank stone staircase. Outside he spoke a prayer in Latin and a Sicilian benediction while the cemetery guardian sealed the mausoleum gate. Fausto and Fabrizio waited in the limousine as Maria and Alfredo laid flowers at their parents' graves on the other side of the cemetery. Father Angelo accompanied them and said another prayer. Maria shed more tears.

Leaving Monfalcone, Fausto and Fabrizio drove back to Palermo with Maria and Monsignor Angelo. They stayed in one of the city's top hotels, owned by their father, part of his property 'empire' which would now be theirs. They dined in the hotel. Maria cried again when Father Angelo proposed a toast to the Prince.

Giancarlo, Massimo's grandson, and Paolo, Federico and Alfredo stayed on in Monfalcone. They dined at the house of a nephew of Alfredo's and drank many toasts to the Prince's memory.

Village people were early risers and thus early to bed. It was an hour before midnight when their host drove the four men in his pickup to an extensive vineyard on the outskirts of Villalba, fifteen kilometres from Monfalcone. An unmade road led through the estate towards the house; the entrance gates had been left open for years. The driver remained with the pickup half a kilometre from the house as the others walked the rest of the way in bright moonlight, carrying cans of petrol and two rifles supplied by Alfredo's nephew.

The house was in darkness. A nineteenth-century farmhouse, it had been extended and modernized, much like Massimo's former home in Monfalcone, partly destroyed and unoccupied. Some of the windows on both floors were open, letting in any cooling breeze there might be. So far as they knew, the owner, Rico, would be alone with his wife who was famous for her version of *tiramisu*, the coffee-flavoured dessert which she contributed in prodigious quantities to village feast-day celebrations.

The men walked round the building, pulling out curtains on the ground-floor and dousing them with petrol. Paolo and Federico ignited the rear of the house while Giancarlo and Alfredo lit the petrol-soaked curtains in the front windows.

The flames ran greedily through the inside of the house which became an inferno within minutes. A male figure appeared at one of the open bedroom windows. Giancarlo shot him in the chest and he dropped out of sight. A woman screamed in the room behind the man. As the flames roared higher, the screaming stopped.

Paolo and Federico rejoined the other two. They walked back to the pickup and returned to Monfalcone. Paolo, Federico and Giancarlo, on the flatbed of the truck, had a view of the distant conflagration until their descent from the hilltop finally hid it from sight. The two lieutenants had tears in their eyes. Giancarlo's face, like Alfredo's beside his nephew at the wheel, was implacable.

The vineyard owner, Rico, had two sons and a daughter in Villalba, each with several children. The two sons and the son-in-law assisted in the production and distribution of fine wines. Fausto had instructed Alfredo's nephew to make it known to the family that tonight's fire was the full extent of his retribution for the assassination of his father. Gustave, the agent in Marseille, was to convey a similar message to his contacts in the Corsican Union in respect of the death of Thierry at the Bimont Dam. Fausto understood, from his father and from Alfredo, that vengeance, even when it was rationed, sent a message. There need not be a war or the resumption of an ancient vendetta.

Tomorrow Alfredo and the three lieutenants would set out early in the second of the rented limousines to join the others in Palermo for the flight back to Salerno in the Prince's plane. Monsignor Angelo would fly on to Rome. By mid-afternoon Massimo's two boys and their guardians would be reunited with

Rosella and Luca in the fortress house outside Amalfi where, over Tom Collins cocktails two Saturdays ago, on the night when they met, the Prince and Lillian had sat on the terrace and talked about disappointing sons.

EPILOGUE

THE AEGEAN: 1984

'How come you're not at university?' the grey-haired man asked his guest, pouring from a cocktail-shaker into a new glass and topping up his own. Below the blistering white terrace a tumble of rocks shimmered in the heat. Beyond the low cliff an empty blue sea shifted languidly beneath an empty blue sky.

'I'm taking a year out,' replied the younger man. His bony boyish face was raw with sunburn. He took a sip of his daiquiri and wished it was a pint of English beer or even an insipid local lager. 'It's called a Gap Year.'

'And you've been – island-hopping, you said?' Tall and slim like his guest, the older man had a face leathery from years of tanning. The greying brown hair was lank, worn long over the frayed collar of a faded blue-and-cream-striped satin shirt. On the white plastic table-top between them lay a gold Dunhill lighter monogrammed *A.R.* in thick roman capitals, next to a pack of American mentholated cigarettes.

Jonathan nodded. 'Sort of. I was in Chania and Ayia Napa.' This was a partial truth. He'd been on beach holidays to Crete and Cyprus with schoolfriends last year and the year before.

He had come to this house by way of Venice and, before that, the Sussex coast. But he was not ready to reveal this.

'Ghastly tourist traps,' his host sneered. 'I've stayed on islands you've probably never heard of. Lampedusa. Lipari. Giglio. Montecristo.'

'I didn't know Montecristo is a real place.'

'An ancient volcano off the coast of Tuscany. A nature reserve now, but in centuries past it's been a military garrison, a notorious prison and a monastery.' Andrew Rutherford reminded Jonathan of his dad in London who also liked to show off titbits of cultural history picked up in his travels.

'I thought the prison was imaginary. My grandpa gave me *The Count of Montecristo* to read when I was a kid. One of those Classics Illustrateds.'

His host chuckled. 'I remember them!'

'I've been to Corsica,' Jonathan said. 'My school did an exchange trip when I was fifteen. I stayed with a family in a village near Ajaccio.' This was true. It was also intended as a prompt.

Andrew drew deeply on his cigarette and then extinguished it in an overflowing terracotta ashtray. 'Many years ago I was kidnapped to Corsica by the local Mafia,' he informed his guest after this theatrical pause. The prompt was working.

'Wow,' said Jonathan, who already knew this. 'Sounds like *The Godfather*!'

'That's exactly how it was,' Andrew said in a tone full of self-satisfaction. It was clear he relished having an audience for his stories. He lit another cigarette.

The tale he told over the next twenty minutes added only incidental details to what Jonathan had heard in Venice. Not until he reached the climax of his story – parting from Fabrizio Monfalcone on their return to Marseille – did he mention his mother:

'Had I known that my mother had been looking for me in Italy and was waiting for me in Provence I wouldn't have gone off with – what was his name? – Thierry.'

'Did she catch up with you in France?' Jonathan asked, a question to which he knew the answer.

His host unscrewed the cocktail-shaker and held it out again. Jonathan shook his head. The cheap local rum left an aftertaste like diesel. Andrew poured himself another daiquiri.

'Yes. She was a game old bird – she still is at nearly seventy! That summer she climbed halfway up Mont St Victoire, the mountain Cézanne painted so repetitiously. I'd spent the night up there with Thierry, who was –' he sighed – 'violently beautiful and beautifully violent.'

Fabrizio Monfalcone and a barman at the other end of the Venetian lagoon had also been described as beautiful; Carlo Marini – 'my lover for almost two years and the foreman on my renovation projects' – was 'film-star handsome.' In Venice Lido last week Carlo Marini had described Thierry to Jonathan as 'a cute but dim-witted Marseille street-urchin who dreamed of becoming a *film noir* hoodlum.'

'He took off in a hissy fit when I declined to take him with me to England,' Andrew continued. 'And then, the day after Mother and I flew home, he died an appropriately violent death.'

'How?' This part of the story was new to Jonathan and might be new to Carlo.

'A couple of months later when I was back in Marseille I ran into his brother in a bar and he told me Thierry had been found at the bottom of a dam, the same place where Prince Massimo, Fabrizio's father, had been found a few days earlier.'

'Bit of a grisly coincidence.'

Andrew shook his head. 'There was some kind of feud going on between the Italian Mafia and the French gangsters who kidnapped us. I thought the Prince was just a banker and a hotel magnate, but maybe if you're Sicilian you're automatically part of the Mafia. Thierry may have been involved in the Prince's murder and his death was a revenge killing, though a young thug hardly equated to a millionaire prince. I've often wondered what other reprisals there were and who gave the orders for them.'

'His son?' Jonathan guessed. 'The boy you were with?'

'I didn't think so at the time, but you never know with Italians. His older brother was the cold-blooded one, the one everybody expected to take over their father's business empire, although he became a priest instead. He's a bishop now, attached to the Vatican Bank.'

A mangy-looking dog limped across the arid rock-strewn slope between the terrace and the cliff edge. 'What happened to the younger brother?' Jonathan asked, although Carlo in Venice had given him a digest of the Monfalcone clan history from feudal times to the present day.

'That's even more of a surprise. Back then he was just another pretty but useless rich brat, but today he runs a chain of hotels in Europe and the USA. I've seen his picture in magazines. He's been married twice, has five or six children.'

'Do you see much of your mother?' It would be interesting, Jonathan thought, to compare Andrew's version of this to what he had learned in Venice.

'I try to get back to England every year or two, and she's made a few trips to see me, when I've been living somewhere fit to entertain one's mum. She hasn't been here, although it's not as rudimentary as some of the places I've rented.' He paused before adding what was obviously intended to be a teaser. 'She has a part-time husband.'

'Only part-time?' Jonathan queried, although Carlo had told him about Andrew's stepfather. He'd shown Jonathan photos of Lillian and a burly grey-haired man in the patio garden of Carlo's house in Burano and on the terrace of a famous restaurant on an adjacent island.

'Her husband's Australian, lives in Melbourne. He won't move to England, and Mother doesn't want to leave Sussex. Their marriage is like an ongoing holiday romance. They met in Hong Kong eight years ago. She was visiting my sister who lives there, and Clive was on a cruise ship heading for Malaysia. He'd been widowed after a long first marriage, like Mother. Now she flies to Australia for two months during our winter, and they fly or cruise to somewhere in the Far East. During our summer Clive goes to England, stays with her in Hastings and they do some European holidays, usually by train, visiting palaces and houses with famous gardens. Gardens are their shared passion. And they're both keen golfers.'

'I'm not sure how I'd feel about having a stepdad,' Jonathan said. This wasn't true: he'd grown up with one whom he'd always thought of as his real, his only father. 'Do you get on with yours?' he asked, hoping Andrew might reveal some deeper feeling.

'I don't see much of him. I went to their wedding six years ago, in Hong Kong, but I haven't been invited to Australia and he hasn't come with Mother to visit me. He's a lot like my dad, who I had a difficult relationship with. I get the feeling Clive doesn't approve of me. Maybe there's a touch of "lavender" in his past, there often is with men who're anti-gay.'

Jonathan nodded although he knew this view of homophobia was simplistic. Clive might disapprove of Andrew simply because he was a sorry excuse for a son to Lillian.

'Mother goes to Venice at least twice a year, sometimes with him, sometimes on her own. She goes to see Carlo, my "ex", and his wife. They run a successful restaurant in Venice Lido and a disco-bar in Lido di Jesolo. Their children call Mother "our English grandma" – their other grandparents are dead. They have three children, although their oldest girl is actually my daughter.'

'Really?' Jonathan had been told this in Venice, but he raised his eyebrows to invite further explanation, which Andrew seemed to have no qualms about supplying.

'Her mother was Prince Massimo's illegitimate daughter. We had a brief affair in Venice in – when was it? – Sixty-something. She died just after the baby was born. My daughter's very artistic, which I like to think she gets from me. She's in Florence now, doing a course in art history.'

He seemed to take some pride in his daughter, whom Carlo had promised to introduce to Jonathan if he returned to Venice when she was home.

'Her uncles, the Prince's sons, are helping to pay for her education. And so does my mother. And I contribute a bit, funds permitting.'

'How often do you see her?' This too Jonathan already knew.

'I've never seen her.'

'She doesn't know you're her father?'

'Carlo is the only father she knows. It's up to him if he wants to tell her. My mother waited twenty-eight years to know the truth about me. It won't hurt my daughter if she has to wait that long.'

My mother was right, Jonathan thought: *you are heartless.*

'Your mum really *is* her grandma.'

'Yes, although she hasn't been told this so far. They're very close. She's been to stay with Mother a few times over the years. And Mother and Clive sometimes take her with them when they're travelling.'

'So she's getting a taste of the jet-set life.'

'Hardly. They don't stay anywhere that you'd call posh. Clive's comfortably off, he's a retired property developer like my father, but he's even more conservative than my dad was – small "c" and capital "C". But he and Mother seem to enjoy each other's company – in instalments, as I said. I sometimes think Mother's still carrying a torch for Massimo, the Prince who was murdered. She believes he would have married her if his enemies hadn't killed him. They were together for less than a week in Amalfi, but somehow he made a deeper impression than Clive has in eight years.'

There was a noise from inside the house. Andrew went to investigate. Jonathan walked to the edge of the terrace to stretch his legs. A lone sailor tacked past below the cliff in a yacht with a vivid red sail.

Two weeks ago, at the start of the quest that had brought him here, Jonathan had walked up a hillside farm track on the outskirts of Hastings and looked down on Lillian Rutherford as she sat reading a plastic-sheathed library book beneath an awning on her rear garden terrace. He longed to walk down to the fence, call out to her and introduce himself.

'You must do it,' Carlo Marini had said last week in Venice Lido. 'Go again. You won't have to tell her. She'll guess instantly.'

Carlo had guessed before Jonathan said anything. Sitting with a newspaper at a metal table outside his restaurant, he looked up at the young man walking towards him. He grinned and stood up.

'My God, you don't need to tell me. I know who you are. You've got his eyes, his chin, his hair.'

'Most people think I take after my mum,' Jonathan said.

'I met your mother, didn't I? Twenty-plus years ago.'

'She remembers you. She says you look a lot like him too. Andrew.'

'Yes, I'm an Italian version of your father!'

Your father. It was odd, discomforting, to hear it said. This September he had set out to find him, but now that he'd met the original of the man he and Carlo both resembled, he couldn't imagine actually saying it: *You don't know me, but I'm your son.*

Carlo, 'the Italian version', had worn better than the original. At forty-five he was an elegant man, still 'film-star handsome.' Andrew, one year older, had gone to seed, with his over-tanned skin, his under-groomed hair, his smoker's teeth and his worn-out shirt.

For a moment, as he said his goodbyes in Venice, Jonathan had found himself wishing that Carlo was his absentee father. Silvia, who'd joined her husband and their visitor to eat the dinner she cooked, would be his beautiful stepmother. Marcello, the handsome cheerful barman, would be his stepbrother.

Lucrezia, a pretty teenager who came back from the beach after lunch with her friends, would be his stepsister. And Clara, studying in Florence, what would she be – his half-sister?

'Don't tell him,' was Carlo's farewell advice. 'It won't do you any good. But, please, do tell Lillian. She's going to love you. You're the age Andrew was when he first moved to London and began giving his mother the happiest years of her life.'

Jonathan was sporting a four-day growth of beard. Andrew had not made the connection between the twenty-one-year-old backpacker he'd found peering over his terrace wall less than an hour ago and the face he looked at in the mirror – or that face as it had been in his youth. Jonathan returned to his chair as his host came through the sliding glass door between the living room and the terrace.

'He's back from the village,' he said without identifying who 'he' was. 'Making a bit of lunch. You'll stay and eat with us?'

'Yes, thanks very much.' Jonathan was curious to meet 'him', the Mystery Man. Was he the latest in the long line of lovers, or merely a servant?

'He's brought some beers. Would you like one?'

'Yes, please.'

'We'll have beer with our lunch.'

'How long have you been living here?'

'Nearly five months. My lease is up next month. I have to decide whether to renew for another six months or move on somewhere else.'

'Where would you go?'

'Sometimes I go to where there's a project waiting – a renovation job, a bit of interior decorating. Or I just follow an impulse.'

'You didn't think of staying in England after your mother went looking for you?'

'No, I'd long felt that I was finished with England. I cherish my old ma, but she knew there was no point in asking me to stay for more than a week or two.'

Heartless, Jonathan thought again.

'So where did you go next?' Again Jonathan hoped to add some detail to what Carlo had told him.

'Saint-Tropez on the French Riviera. It became *the* place to live after Brigitte Bardot bought a house there in the late 1950s.'

'Did you meet her?' Jonathan had seen some of Bardot's films – France's 'sex kitten' – in retrospective shows at London's National Film Theatre.

'Yes, she gave legendary parties. She stopped making movies, but she was a better actress than people gave her credit for. I did up a house near hers for an American artist, a sculptress who'd been my mistress for a while in Venice. We sort of picked up where we'd left off for a few weeks until her husband insisted she join him in Paris.'

Jonathan did not want to hear about mistresses. Mistresses struck too close to home. Andrew seemed not to want to dwell on this either.

'I did a couple of other interiors on the Côte d'Azur and had an affair with a beautiful young French actor who'd had a part in one of Brigitte's pictures. He left to go to Los Angeles, although sadly his Hollywood career never came to anything.'

Another 'beautiful' lover: the list was endless.

'Then I gatecrashed a party at Cap Ferrat given by some exiled Romanian nobility and met a Spanish tycoon who'd seen the sculptress's house and invited me to do a revamp on his villa on the Costa Brava. I'd always promised myself a Brett Ashley phase!' He smirked. Jonathan wondered who Brett Ashley was but didn't ask.

Andrew created another dramatic pause, drawing deeply on his cigarette.

'So in the summer of 1967,' he continued, 'I hired a chauffeured car to take me to Spain. The driver was Algerian, young and handsome and playing very hard to get. I had to double the fee for the trip before I could lure him into my bed when we stopped for the night in Narbonne.'

One more conquest, Jonathan thought. He wondered if he himself met the criteria. He wasn't beautiful, he wasn't 'film-star handsome', but he was in good shape and he was young. Youth was the currency homosexuals traded in.

'And Spain is where my past caught up with me again,' Andrew added.

A shout came from inside the house. It wasn't English: was it Greek?

'Lunch is ready,' his father said. 'Let's go in.'

At least there would be beer. And, evidently, a second chapter of the Saga of which Carlo Marini knew only a little. More lovers, for sure. More mistresses? Maybe another melodrama like the hostage-taking and a murder that had to be avenged. And Jonathan would have more time to think about whether to declare himself – or not.

Of the four grandparents he had known as a child, only one was alive – 'Gramps' in deepest Devon, technically a much-loved step-grandfather who had encouraged him to make the journey that had brought him here today. 'He's part of who you are,' he'd said in his rolling West Country voice. 'Maybe not such a big part, but you need to know him.'

'Dad', Jonathan's even-more-beloved stepfather, had been neither for nor against this quest. 'Let your mother be your guide,' he said.

If he did reveal who he was and why he was here, would there be a dramatic reconciliation – or merely embarrassment?

Of one thing he was certain. He would go back to Hastings. He would declare himself to Lillian, the 'part-time wife' of an Australian businessman. The baker's daughter who had nearly become a princess. His grandmother.

ACKNOWLEDGEMENTS

For various reasons, *Lillian and the Italians*, which I began writing in the 1970s, has taken decades to finish and bring to press. A number of Venetian residents, both native and adoptive, regaled me with stories of *la Serenissima* in the 1960s, the era of Andrew and Carlo. Most would prefer to remain anonymous (one I plied with liquor to lubricate an already loose tongue), but there is no reason not to mention Elsie Lee Gozzi, proud owner of the House of Fortuny, a grand and colourful lady who entertained me on several occasions with her hospitality and her reminiscences.

Harry Marinsky and Paul Bernard in Tuscany provided the introduction to Contessa Gozzi and to Sir Harold Acton, who invited me for tea in his glorious *palazzo* outside Florence and fed me some social history.

To these (some of them now dead) and to others I extend heartfelt thanks. Tony G. Aley, formerly resident in Lecce and Turin, provided linguistic assistance. Roderick Brown and Juliet Paris gave invaluable editorial advice.

Carlo Marini's house in Burano and Prince Massimo's castle outside Amalfi are real properties, although I have taken liberties with their interior design as well as with their ownership. The islands called *Le Sirenuse*, off Positano, belonged at the end of his life to Rudolph Nureyev; did he buy them from Fabrizio Monfalcone?

The purge of expatriate 'undesirables' in Venice is a matter of record, though I have 'adjusted' its timing. A woman tourist on the island of Giglio some years ago told me of the existence of a Mafia 'envoy' to the Vatican.

Don Vito Cascio Ferro and Don Calogero Vizzini were real-life Mafia *capi di capi*. My principal sources for the history of the Mafia are listed below; to readers seeking deeper insights Norman Lewis's account of the 'Honoured Society' during and after World War Two is especially commended, together with David Yallop's investigation into the labyrinthine world of Vatican finances. I should also tip my hat to the late great Mario Puzo who kick-started my interest (along with the interest of millions of readers) in the machinations of the Mafia.

D.G.

BIBLIOGRAPHY

Luigi Barzini: *The Italians* (1964) and
                     From Caesar to the Mafia (1971)

Norman Lewis: *The Honoured Society* (1964)

Robin Moore: *The French Connection* (1969)

Peter Nicholls: *Italia, Italia* (1973)

David Yallop: *In God's Name* (1984)